THE ABYSSAL PLAIN:

THE R'LYEH CYCLE

Edited by William Holloway
and Brett J. Talley

JOURNALSTONE
YOUR LINK TO ARTIST TALENT

ISBN: 978-1-950305-32-2 (hc)
ISBN: 978-1-950305-15-5 (ebook)
Library of Congress Control Number: 2019943778

First printing edition: November 29, 2019
Printed by JournalStone Publishing in the United States of America.
Cover Design and Layout: Mikio Murakami
Interior Layout: Lori Michelle
Edited by Sean Leonard
Proofread by Scarlett R. Algee

JournalStone Publishing
3205 Sassafras Trail
Carbondale, Illinois 62901

JournalStone books may be ordered through booksellers or by contacting:
JournalStone | www.journalstone.com

THE ABYSSAL PLAIN:

THE R'LYEH CYCLE

TABLE OF CONTENTS

AMMONIA

by William Holloway

Ammonia is dedicated to the memory of Brian Sheppard and all those taken from us by the disease of alcoholism and addiction.

QUINCY SLEPT, BUT there were no easy dreams on the last night of human peace. He dreamed of water, of a great deluge. Sometimes he was an ant, and the water poured down ant-sized corridors, washing all the citizens of the ant megalopolis down, down, down into the depths of the earth to die together in a writhing drowning pool.

"Millions, millions, millions . . . " he murmured in his sleep, only to fall each time back into the dream cycle, this time as a black cat. He clung to the branches of a cedar tree, the only one he'd managed to catch onto as the water swept his cat-self down the flooded streets to the river.

Was there a river anymore, or just distinctions in elevation? Higher up and you could watch the world go by, spinning in eddies and whorls in this new reality of black rushing water. Too low and you were in the soup, and once there it was simply a matter of time.

So he watched from his perch, fascinated by the sheer magnitude. Everything was uprooted, everything was misplaced, and everything was arrayed around him. A rising tide may lift all boats, but boats are for the lakes and oceans, not for the middle of cities.

"Millions, there's millions of them . . . " he shouted, breaching the surface of his nightmare landscape. He was in his tiny room, dirty threadbare blanket tangled around him, the striations of the uncovered mattress carved over his body. They weren't just sweaty indentations, either; they were scratches and abrasions. He'd really been tossing, his body fighting his brain's efforts to keep him asleep.

As soon as his brain acquired a semblance of focus, the nausea twisted, and he lurched for the warm forty on the floor. He tilted it back, as the taste in his mouth was far worse than warm stale beer. It was a taste he'd become frighteningly familiar with: dried vomit in his nose and mouth, dehydration and alcohol poisoning. So stale, room temperature beer from last night was a step up, as least by Quincy's reckoning.

WILLIAM HOLLOWAY

He lifted his body, but his sweaty blankets had become a lasso to trip him up. He fell, arms too shaky and slow to catch him. He saw the floorboards coming, and greeted them with his face.

He'd managed to stay conscious for minutes, at best.

Things hadn't always been this way for Quincy. He'd been voted most likely to succeed by his graduating class in the 8th grade, but he was in his forties now, and 8th grade was long ago. A life begun on overconfidence led to a life with no obligation to try. Things would just come to him because he was brilliant, so brilliant that he shouldn't have to break a sweat like regular people. And when the regular people sailed past the regular landmarks in life, and he was standing still, overconfidence and entitlement became victimhood and rationalization.

As bad for Quincy as his small natural intellect was the face he saw in the mirror. Quincy was a good-looking boy who grew into a good-looking man. Until recently, he'd gotten by on getting by, but the hard facts of advanced alcoholism at a relatively young age had hit home. His hands shook, he smelled, and his eyes had yellowed.

He was in his forties, but looked at least fifty.

Still, he was a handsome man, and women outside his league still did a double-take. Most, but not all, left it at that. Once they discovered that he was an unemployable drunk, they lost all interest.

There were some, however, that saw his handicap as a bonus. Certainly a man with such limited options couldn't stray far, but they underestimated that there were other women like them. Women with severe self-esteem issues; drunks and druggies. So he bounced from bed to bed on a downward spiral of sick and deranged women. He went from bed to couch to curb. Over and over.

His latest was Suzy, an overweight bleach blonde with leathery tanning-bed skin and a leathery two-pack-a-day voice. She loved him. He screwed her best friend. They broke up. They got back together. Over and over.

So his family helped him get back on his feet, and he got a tiny efficiency in the last affordable part of the East Side. He got a job on a painting crew because his dad sold paint and knew a guy. He lost the job because he got too drunk to work. That was a six-pack job, not a twelve-pack job. So he got really drunk to drink it away. He turned up the Pearl Jam and Soundgarden to ten . . .

And here he was, not even a fucking cigarette butt in the fucking ashtray. He fished through his pockets. Fuck.

AMMONIA

It was gonna be Dorals today.

Time to hoof it to the Habeeb store, then come home and start nagging that fuck who fired him to pay up now because Dorals didn't work with nothing to wash them down.

A *few weeks before* . . .

One of the more valuable pieces of real estate on planet Earth lay between Australia and South America. Tens of thousands of square miles of ocean, uninterrupted by islands and empty of ships. Even the mighty U.S. Navy was largely absent from this sector, all except for boomers.

This bit of the globe was a natural habitat for the enormous ballistic missile submarines that form one leg of the strategic triad of nuclear bombers, Minuteman land-based intercontinental ballistic missiles, and Trident submarine-launched ballistic missiles. The U.S.S. *Georgia* had been on station for two weeks now, silently waiting for the call to unleash an apocalypse of twenty-four Trident missiles, each with eight warheads.

Boomers listen very carefully to the world around them. Although the Cold War had been over for almost thirty years, the principal existential threat to the U.S. lay in the Russian Federation. While the Russians were unlikely to start a war, they still retained the capacity to wage war against the U.S. The Chinese threat existed, but they didn't really have the ability to track something like the *Georgia*, despite its behemoth size. So the *Georgia* was on the lookout for Russian attack subs first, Russian boomers second, and Chinese subs third.

Their understanding was that a Russian Typhoon class sub, accompanied by an Akula class attack sub, was hiding in the sea lane traffic around Indonesia, approximately one thousand miles north of their position. The Chinese weren't scheduled to begin a boomer patrol of this stretch of the South Pacific for two months, and when that happened, they'd be tracked by both American and Japanese attack subs.

While they knew that it was almost impossible for the Russians or the Chinese to sneak up on them—every Russian or Chinese sub that could actually pose a threat would be tailed by an American or Japanese sub and surface warships—they never let their guard down.

They listened, very carefully. So the deck officers of the *Georgia* were the first to hear it.

The first thing was a bizarre spike in background radiation passing through the water. Ordinarily the atmosphere and the ocean absorbed this radiation, but for a split second it was as if the rules had been suspended.

The radiation alarm, silent but terrifying as a banshee's wail, went off. Next to a run-in with an enemy sub, this was the most frightening thing imaginable.

But in a matter of seconds, it was determined that neither their missiles nor their reactor were the source. That left another warship's reactor or missiles as the culprit; but that, too, was quickly ruled out. The radiation spike indeed had a component of gamma radiation, but also contained equal measures of nearly every other kind of invisible radiant energy: alpha, x-ray, everything. It had the textbook fingerprint of cosmic background radiation, just in the wrong place. It didn't come from space; it came from the bottom of the ocean, far to their south.

A flash, as if by an invisible bolt of lightning.

Then came the thunder.

***

When the cataclysmic buffeting had passed, the *Georgia* was forced to surface, forced to send a distress signal of the most dire sort: An American ballistic missile sub was adrift and no longer seaworthy, a national security situation that had not been equaled since the Cuban Missile Crisis.

The entire submarine had been twisted in a wringing torsion. The missile tubes were bent, the missiles themselves cracked and leaking rocket fuel. To preempt the inevitable fires, the tubes had been flooded with water. There was no breach of the reactor or of the warheads, but without the ability to launch, this boat was combat ineffective.

Captain Clark stood atop the conning tower, looking across the devastated horizon through his antique binoculars. He knew it was unlikely that he would see anything they didn't already know, but having eyes on the situation often told what no number of electronic sensors could tell. He bit down on the mouthpiece of the old corncob pipe, wishing the 'no tobacco aboard subs' rule wasn't so zealously enforced by the Navy. His granddaughter had bought him the pipe when she found out his turf was the South Pacific, an homage to MacArthur. He hadn't had the heart to tell the eight-year-old that he was Navy, not Army.

"This is gonna smell really bad, really soon."

His XO, nicknamed Bamboo because his polysyllabic Thai name contained the syllables *Bam* and *Boo*, managed a bitter laugh. "That's not going to be the taxpayer's first concern."

8

AMMONIA

Clark managed his first smile since his world inverted less than a day ago. "Are you telling me this is going to be expensive?"

Bamboo looked up at more than a hundred Navy F-18s swarming through the skies. A Naval exclusion zone had been declared for five hundred miles around, and neither the Russians nor the Chinese would be bold or dumb enough to play chicken. Everyone knew that a boomer surfacing was nothing to trifle with. On occasions when Russian boomers surfaced and American destroyers were present, the Russian sub captains rammed them, no questions asked. And a boomer is two to three times the size of a destroyer.

In a case like this, there would be no ramming, only a hurricane of anti-ship missiles from the orbiting Navy fighters. They would stay on station, refueling in midair until the rest of the Pacific fleet arrived. There was already another fleet steaming around the horn of South America to reinforce, and soon Air Force F-22s would join in, transforming the already formidable presence into a gauntlet of steel.

Bamboo nodded. "Yeah, boss, I'd say so. You talked to the Secretary?"

Clark took the pipe out of his mouth and spat. "SecDef and two admirals so far."

Bamboo continued to stare in disbelief at the surface around them. "So, did they have any good gossip?"

Clark shrugged and put on his Wayfarers, also a grandkid gift. "The Russian Typhoon bounced a satellite message to Vladivostok; our guys knew they'd do that after something like this . . . whatever this is. They said they think the epicenter of the 'event,' as they call it, is under the Ross Ice Shelf."

Bamboo pulled his eyes away from the surface and looked hard at his boss. "They didn't call it an earthquake? You know, some of their acoustics and passive sensors are better than ours. What does McMurdo say?"

Clark shook his head and put a hand on the man's shoulder. "McMurdo is gone."

Bamboo's face went blank. McMurdo had been on his bucket list. His doctoral thesis had been on the fluid dynamics of glaciers. He'd done time studying glaciers in Alaska before the Navy, and had hoped to sign up for McMurdo Station after this tour of duty.

Clark nodded. "The Russians flew an Antonov over from Vostok. They called it in to us. There aren't going to be any survivors. They also say the shelf is fractured and moving."

Bamboo shook his head, trying to clear his mind. "Whaddaya mean, moving? It's always moving, but . . ."

Clark grinned a crazy grin. "Shattered and floating out into the Southern Sea."

Bamboo looked him straight in the eye. "Bullshit."

Clark took the Wayfarers off and looked back out through his old binoculars. "Scout's honor."

The XO turned and looked back out over the horizon. "Boss, this wasn't any kind of earthquake that I've ever heard of. This part of the world is geologically stable."

Clark didn't put the binoculars down; he just motioned to the millions, billions of dead fish covering the surface of the water. "Tell that to these guys, I'm sure they'll agree. Anyways, it's an event, not an earthquake."

Bamboo's face screwed up as he did the math in his head. "The shockwave went from the bottom and bounced off the underside of the ice shelf, and the shape of the bay channeled it outwards. It rolled along the bottom and hit us, but left lucky bastards like these twits in the clear." He motioned to the one ship on the horizon, the NOAA research ship *Sea Lion*.

Sea Lion appeared relatively unscathed. The ship had been thoroughly jostled, but their main issue was that they'd lost power temporarily, and every electronic data-containing device on board had been wiped. They had power back, but wouldn't be permitted to turn on engines until the fleet had arrived.

"The Norwegians say a meteor hit the ice shelf."

Bamboo scoffed. "Any meteor that could do that would be bigger than Tunguska, and they'd have seen a flash, not to mention that there'd have been a blast that people heard in Timbuktu."

"So it was an event."

"Pffft."

"That's 'Pffft, Captain,' please."

"Oops, sorry, Captain."

Clark still peered out over the horizon like an ancient mariner, scanning in little arcs. Suddenly he swung back the way he came, squinted, then handed the binoculars to Bamboo. "I think the stink factor's gonna get worse. What's that?"

Bamboo accepted the binoculars and found what the captain had been looking at. "Yep, it's fixin' to get ripe in this little corner of paradise. That's a dead sperm whale."

AMMONIA

As if on cue, his secure phone buzzed, and he read the message on the screen. "It's Jerry on deck, he says the *Sea Lion* radioed even though they weren't supposed to. They're actually down here to study the sperm whales. They want to get in a speedboat and check out the carcass."

Clark shrugged. No one was supposed to witness a boomer surface, much less ride around in a speedboat within visual range, but they'd seen everything they could conceivably see already.

Bamboo saw his expression and frowned. "Half of these fu—half of them are gonna be Greenpeace hippies."

Clark grinned, and Bamboo immediately didn't like it. Even though Bamboo was every American's stereotype of the uber-brainy Asian man, he was also from Houston, a redneck down to his Ropers. "Tell them they can do it, but only with an escort. You like patchouli, right?"

***

And it crept across the globe, but Natalie had bigger problems, namely her boss. She had a degree from Columbia School of Journalism, but it takes more than a degree to break the scene in Washington, DC.

They'd been having an affair for about three years. She knew he'd never leave his wife, and knew he didn't feel the way she did for him. He didn't love her.

Did she love Erwin? Yes, she did. She knew she shouldn't, but she did.

Was he aware that she loved him? Sure, but he did everything he could to *keep it casual.*

It stung.

She stared into the bathroom mirror, cursing her fortune and fate. Natalie was a *damn fine-looking specimen,* or so the Speaker of the House had explained. Inwardly she smiled, but the face looking back couldn't.

Fuck him.

Yep, she had a make-it-or-break-it dilemma ahead of her. She'd just been propositioned by the Speaker of the House right outside the Oval Office. Right in front of an old blue-haired secretary who'd been at her desk since before Watergate. The secretary had merely raised an eyebrow and gone back to her crossword puzzle. The Marine was a statue who only moved to open the door to the Oval Office.

Just fuck him.

Do it.

Fuck him.

To hell with the fact that his wife had multiple sclerosis and lived in a wheelchair. To hell with the fact that there was a running blog documenting the stupid, racist, sexist things that the man said. And he said them openly and proudly, right in front of a media that gave him carte blanche to get away with it.

He never said the "n-word," but stood in front of black audiences and said, "You people." He even adopted a laughable black accent while doing it. When squarely faced with these gaffes, the media talked about what a "well-meaning" and "big-hearted" man the Speaker was.

When the sex tape of his son and a teenage girl came out, complete with cocaine and bragging about how tight he was with the president, the media swept that under the rug, too. It became nothing more than a rumor bandied about on the political internet.

Fuck him, or at least go in there and suck his cock.

But she couldn't. She'd never been like that. Sure, she was no virgin, but she'd never fucked for any reason other than love, despite the incestuous city she lived in. She'd been raised by her *abuela*, a woman who'd built a single corner store into a chain of corner stores. No education, no high heels, and no getting on her back or knees to make the ladder easier. She'd been a hard, cold, calculating woman who told Natalie she could go to college or start stocking the candy aisle. Natalie picked college.

You're still young enough to be good-looking, and you're worried that your abuela would think poorly of you for getting your knees dirty for the Speaker? You're not gonna look like that forever, bitch, now pucker up!

Her alter ego glared at her in the mirror.

Save your morality for the church picnic. Everybody gets their knees dirty in this town. If you don't have what it takes, go back to Austin and mop out the public bathroom at EZ Mart . . .

She walked back into the waiting area. The secretary glanced, the Marine didn't move a muscle, and the Speaker leered, showing giant fluorescent white teeth. He looked at Natalie like she was a toddler and he was a hyena.

In her absence, a bookish man had entered the waiting room for a few minutes of the president's time. He wore a cheap suit, and his balding head was damp with perspiration. Clearly not a player. His visitor badge said NOAA.

The Speaker extended his arm for her to come over. He was definitely going to put that arm around her, and his hand was definitely going to explore her tit.

AMMONIA

"Natalie! What took you so long, didn't Gloria refill the damn tampon launcher?"

Speaker of the House Rider took his other arm and put it around his NOAA hostage, and nearly took both of them down doubling over laughing at his own joke.

The secretary looked up, thought the better of it, and went back to her crossword.

Natalie winced inwardly and got close enough for Rider to pull her in for way too much body contact, and within seconds his hand wandered over to her boob. She tried to subtly maneuver, but the man was an old hand at this sort of thing. Her boob was going to be his until he was done with it.

"So, Natalie, this is my new friend Chipper from the NLRB! Chip, this is Natalie. She's Erwin Klein's slave. Sorry! I mean assistant."

Rider's gleaming white teeth couldn't get any bigger or whiter.

The man uncomfortably reached over to shake with his left hand, because Rider had his right pinned to his side. "Chester Slayton, NOAA."

Their eyes met in shared misery. "Natalie Castellanos, the *Post*."

Rider blew in. "The *Post*! Damn, girlfriend, I'll bet your folks are shitting themselves over that back in Booger Holler!"

Chester and Natalie smiled like Speaker of the House Rider had just recited the Magna Carta from memory. *That's how it happens. People like Rider get away with it because people like me are too afraid to rock the boat lest we go into the drink, and no one in this whore town is gonna toss you a life preserver.*

She tried to make conversation to avoid feeling her left tit die of disgust. "NOAA? You must be here because of the aurora and the earthquake."

Chester smiled, slightly surprised that a girl who looked like her knew what NOAA even was. "Yeah, we're still not sure if it even was an earthquake, or some other kind of geomagnetic phenomenon, but the Ross Ice Shelf is now an island and has rounded the east coast of South America, and is moving north . . . "

Rider squeezed both of them. *Shut up, the Speaker of the House is about to say something deep and wise.* "Those lights in the sky are proof that we're ruining God's green earth, which is why we're moving forward! Not backwards! With a massive new plan to build the green economy of the 20th century. Progress, people!"

Chester wasn't savvy enough to know when to keep it zipped. "Well, sir, it's complicated. See, the aurora is in the thermosphere and is ordinarily a product of solar wind or the magnetic fields surrounding the earth, but in this case . . . "

Rider nodded like he was being told a Bible story by his grandfather and finished the man's sentence for him. "Amen, brother! If we could only get Congress and the anti-science mob to join us in the 20th century, geez!"

Chester's mouth hung open. He glanced from Rider back to Natalie, stunned. He had no idea that stupidity, balanced by low cunning, could carry a man all the way to these high echelons of power.

***

She glanced at Chester's card, but the black words on the white cardboard weren't registering. Her hands shook, and her breath was a little less breathy than she'd like. Her tongue ran over her teeth.

Erwin's text message had been unambiguous. *This is your big chance. You play this right, and you'll get your own byline.*

And by *her big chance* he really meant *their* big chance.

Her boyfriend, lover, whatever, wanted her to fuck another man in order to advance both of their careers.

She wanted to cry, but no tears came. Only the memory of betrayal.

She'd been a junior in high school, she'd gone to the concert with a dozen other kids. Her *abuela* had been serious about that part. There had to be a bunch of other kids, not just one or two boys, because that's how you get raped, she'd said.

It hadn't been rape, but it had opened her eyes.

The music was deafening and pounding, the crowd heaved and surged, and she was carried weightlessly on the human tide. She'd stopped moving her feet a while back, but the crowd carried her. Every claustrophobe's nightmare, even though Natalie wasn't claustrophobic. This was no fear or anxiety, this was real. She really was being squashed. There was no way out.

No way out but up.

She pulled and she pushed and then she was on top, and then she knew.

She knew that sense of liberation that all the juvenile delinquent boys at the skater table knew. She was crowd surfing. She screamed in joy at this deliverance from terror, this being lifted up. The crowd screamed, she screamed, the band screamed, and the music blew her like a leaf across the face of the crowd, rolling this way and that on a sea of hands.

Hands all over. Hands all over her body.

AMMONIA

And then the first finger went in. She jerked away, her mind immediately calling it an accident. *These things happen in our liberated process.* Then the second went in, then a third. She was on top of a crowd, a sacrifice to its will. She fought, she struggled, she covered herself, but she had another hole they greedily searched as well. And as soon as it began, it was over, and she crashed down to the concrete and was forgotten. When she finally fought her way to the bathroom, she stuffed a wad of toilet paper down the back of her pants.

An older girl looked at her with a kind of hard knowing. "That's why you don't crowd surf, honey."

"I can't even begin to tell you this, but you are *in*." Erwin nodded from behind the wheel of his horrifically expensive Mercedes. He looked ecstatic, and his eyes showed a kind of proud reappraisal. "And once you're in, you've got a *way*. You didn't have a way before, apart from your relationship with me. Now you've got a way, and it's all about the way."

The first and only tear fell down her cheek, leaving a wet trail that Erwin couldn't not see. He nodded his head; he understood.

Okay, I'll slow my roll a little bit.

He gave her a playful slug on the shoulder. "Okay, *partner*, who's the little dweeb that went in the OA after me?" OA was their professional assessment of the Oval Office.

She didn't answer his question; she answered her own question. "My friend Cindy back in Austin is a stripper. She gives blowjobs to her loyal clients. She didn't tell me, but another friend found out and told me."

Erwin nodded, understanding that she was having a tough time processing what she'd just done, what had just happened to her. "You're not Cindy. You're not a whore. You're doing important work, more important than any whore could ever understand."

But she couldn't escape the sinking suspicion that whores might understand quite a bit.

She sniffled. "He works for NOAA. Even though they're saying this is environmental, they know it isn't. The aurora didn't just come out of nowhere, and that ice shelf didn't just off and start floating our way accidentally."

Erwin scrunched up his eyebrows. "The aurora is caused by atoms or some shit in the atmosphere."

She shook her head, her heart not in the conversation at all. "Thermosphere. Has zip to do with CO_2."

His eyebrows went back to their rightful place and he cleared his throat. "Of course it's environmental. Everyone knows it. It's just religious fanatics that think otherwise."

She was done with this part of the conversation. All she wanted was to go home and scrub herself till she was red and raw. "I dunno, boss, my mind is elsewhere at the moment."

He nodded. She still needed a bit of soothing and coaching. "It's okay, and it's all for the greater good. We're here not just for ourselves; we're here for justice, and sometimes you gotta break all the rules."

He held up his fist and looked over at her. "By any means necessary, right?"

Her mouth got ahead of her brain. "Erwin, we're fucking. You're married! Now you think I should fuck *another* man. How the hell do you do it?"

She was surprised that he wasn't mad. Instead he just gave her a wise and sad smile. "Kiddo, this is DC. It's not about loyalty."

She didn't ask, because looking at the glistening oak dashboard and his ten-thousand-dollar suit told her every answer she needed to know about *loyalty*.

***

"My captain, why have you forsaken me!" Bamboo didn't care what these hippies thought. Fucking academics who didn't make tenure and were doing time on a research vessel to pad their resume.

Or something.

Clark, you bastard.

And he was right. They really were wearing patchouli, and actually introduced themselves by listing off their respective academic bona fides. No engineers, no physicists, but a lot of big brass in fields that sounded like they were made up to justify keeping someone on the payroll.

So far, they hadn't told him a single thing he didn't already know, but were overflowing with nuggets of wisdom that he knew to be false at face value.

Yes, they were both in rubber rafts on opposite sides of an enormous and very dead sperm whale. This was a big male, sixty-plus feet long. He hadn't been dead long, time of death probably concurrent with the event.

The one scientist in the raft, a marine biologist named Watkins, nodded and pushed his glasses up the bridge of his nose. "His name was Waldo the Third. Determined to be the son of another big male by the name of Waldo the Second . . ."

AMMONIA

"So we know where Waldo is, at least." It was Mike Jackson, the UDT diver and pilot of their little raft.

Bamboo turned and shook his head. "Was he killed by the shockwave?"

Watkins nodded sadly. "Looks like it actually broke his back." He pointed to the grotesque kink in the whale's figure.

Bamboo squinted at the shredded carcass. Huge sections of skin, giant areas denuded of flesh, the hollowed-out ribcage.

"Doc, I might be a mere physicist, but I don't think shockwaves do that."

Watkins shrugged and pushed his glasses back up his beak. "Well, some of this is consistent with what he'd get from going after a good-sized giant squid. But I'd have to say that the majority of this was done post-mortem."

Jackson took off his atrocious wrap-around sunglasses and squinted at the big floating carcass. "These things fight with giant fucking squid?"

Watkins grinned. "These Antarctic sperm whales? That's their principal food source. These guys are all about the calamari. They dive down to an area called the abyssal plain. It's the home world of the giant squid."

Bamboo rolled his eyes. *Simpletons all.* "So, mystery solved. This guy was diving for a squid when the earthquake . . . "

Jackson held up a finger. "Event."

He tried to continue. "Okay, Waldo the Third was going for takeout when the event happened, and ended getting eaten by his dinner. Is that good enough for you, Doctor?"

Jackson continued to smile the smile of a man pretending not to understand what he'd just been told.

Bamboo cleared his throat. "So, uh, Watkins. What happened to Waldo?"

Watkins looked down, then pushed his glasses up again, trying not to laugh. "It looks like what you said. He died while hunting, then his carcass got scavenged by squid. And from the looks of these marks, probably the kind and size of squid that we'll never see with our eyes."

Jackson dropped the grin and furrowed his brow. "So, doc, riddle me this. Why'd that wave kill Waldo, but not Waldo's dinner?"

***

Quincy balanced on the middle place between sleep and waking consciousness, not wanting to sleep nor wanting for wakefulness. His dreams had become worse than his waking life, where before they were a soft spot of peace and contentment.

WILLIAM HOLLOWAY

He used to find himself in bed with this woman or that woman, or debating his detractors and emerging victorious in the victor's rightful place: in the arms of this woman or that woman. But always women. They were his reward for being who he truly was, his reward for braving a world that could never truly appreciate him.

Oh, they called him a drunk and a loser, but how many of them had seen the ecstasies and delights that he had? How many could really boast of conquests unimaginable to lesser men?

And that was truly the crux of the matter. He was not like them. He was not a lesser man. He was born to greatness, even if this world existed solely to deny him that right.

Suzy had come over last night with a bottle. He remembered her blubbering about their breakup, then the fucking, then nothing else.

The bottle was empty on the floor. No idea when she left.

He would have to open his eyes. He didn't want to. He didn't want to see the yellowing walls or the overflowing ashtray. He didn't want his mind to engage because his life wasn't what he'd wanted. He'd wanted to walk out on stage and rock the house, but he'd been kicked out of every band he'd ever been in.

Yeah, he'd partied like a rock star; he just hadn't ever been a rock star.

Today was going to suck. He'd tried to wake earlier, but his hands shook too bad to lock the door behind him on the way out. He tried to eat some peanut butter, to get something solid in his stomach, but it came back up.

Maybe that was an hour ago, maybe not, but right now he was on the floor next to the toilet.

He knew this humiliation, he knew that he had caused all of this, but he also knew that to look too closely was to invite an anxiety attack and heart palpitations. It had happened before, and he'd ended up in the emergency room.

He took the edge off with Valium for a few days, and got to day four with no alcohol. The next day he was out of pills, and something happened to the world around him. The lights were unbearably bright, every sound the scraping of nails on a chalkboard, every smell a sewer of vomit and shit. His skin didn't fit, at least not until he went to the Habeeb store and got a six of Blue Bull.

Good old Habeeb. Always there when he was broke as a joke, always let him slide until payday.

AMMONIA

He covered his face and ventured a peek between his fingers. Too bright. He hoisted himself up, and flipped the light switch off so he could open his eyes. He slumped against the wall and caught his breath. He got to his feet and saw stars. His eyes acclimated, and he took a deep breath.

He flipped the light on and took a look.

Time to get to the Habeeb store.

Quincy closed the door behind him and held his hand to steady the key into the keyhole.

He looked out at the intersection, then glanced to his watch. Two fucking PM and the intersection was still under water. No wonder there wasn't any traffic. He'd seen a lot of flooding in his life in Austin, but nothing like the last few days.

Down the stairs, nice and slow, hold that handrail. Shaky hands and a slick staircase. Very careful and he was down in the parking lot. The other side was under water, but he didn't have to go that way.

And what the fuck. Suzy's shitty, horrible yellow Camry was sitting right in front of him.

His feet carried him over and he looked inside. Doors unlocked. The keys were in the fucking ignition. Oh shit. Did her car break down? Was he so drunk he didn't even remember it happening?

He turned the key and it started right up. Would it be super fucked up to drive her car to the Habeeb store? Yeah, but who cares. Then it hit him. Fuck. Her car smelled horrible. Like ammonia. He opened the door and got out quick. That kind of smell was going to make him blow chunks.

No, walking a block was much preferable to the smell in that car.

***

He felt bad because Raj was a really nice guy. Obviously lonely and very shy, and Quincy took advantage. Habeeb—Raj—spotted him beer when he was broke, and he knew it was out of his own pocket. And sometimes he hadn't paid him back. Okay, most of the time he didn't pay him back.

But Raj never nagged him about it. He wanted to be liked that bad. He thought Quincy was cool. He always asked him about women and about what music was cool. And the next time he'd walk in the door, Raj would enthusiastically show him that he'd bought that band he'd recommended.

Sometimes he'd awkwardly sing along with the lyrics. That was always super annoying. Sometimes he'd ask when they were gonna hangout "on the scene" and Quincy would try to not laugh. He smiled and pulled open the glass door at the Habeeb store, the bells tinkling to announce his entry.

Pretty damn dark in here. No lights, AC hum or crackly fluorescents, no ululating Habeeb music, or that even worse Habeeb techno music. Just total quiet.

He walked past tampons and motor oil, towards the back office and the freezer. "Raj? Hey, Raj, you back there?"

Nothing.

He knocked on the door. Still nothing.

He turned the knob and peeked inside. This was a risk, because Raj's old man might be back there. He always crinkled up his nose as if Quincy smelled like a cat box.

No one in there. He turned the handle on the door to the freezer. "Hey man . . . Raj? You there, Raj?"

Nothing. What the hell? While this area was gentrified to the point of being as unrecognizable as the East Side, there were still pockets that were gamier, this being one of them. You could still score dope in the laundromat next door, if that was your thing. In other words, not the kind of place where you'd leave the store unattended, not even for a minute.

He stood, tapping his foot, wondering what to do. Sweat began to form on his brow. It was really muggy in the store, and it smelled like nasty floor cleaner. Ordinarily it smelled like a headshop, with all the incense, but they must've really mopped this place out with some kind of disgusting ammonia.

He really, really, really needed a smoke.

The freezers were fogged over, the windows covered with condensation inside and out. He leaned his forehead against the glass, then opened the door to be hit with a blast of cold air.

Ice cold fucking beer.

"Hey, Raj! Hey, man, if you're in here somewhere, you need to come out! No time for a nap, man!"

Still nothing. Quincy walked back to the front door and looked up and down. Totally dead on Cesar Chavez Street. Not a single person. Weird, but this rain and flooding was probably keeping people away. Lake Austin (excuse me, Lady Bird Johnson Lake) had breached its banks several nights, the big ugly statue of Stevie Ray sticking out of the muddy water like . . .

He walked over to the All Night Laundromat and pressed his face up against the window. No Raj in there either. No one in there, not even the old Mexican dude with the walker, perpetually folding old-man slacks, his cover for selling smack.

AMMONIA

Quincy walked back to the store, closed the door behind him, and walked over to the counter. He reached behind the register for a pen, pulled out one of the little brown bags they used for tall boys and wrote, despite his shaking hands:

Raj, I came by but you were gone. Man, you really shouldn't leave the door open like that! Either way, I'm short on funds so I'm going to have to get you back for the smokes and the beer.

He walked out with a pack of American Spirits and a case of Natty Light.

Back next door to his little apartment building, wedged in between the strip with the convenience store and the laundromat and a row of little East Side shacks, still home to some Mexican families. That wouldn't last long, though. He'd seen city workers lately, measuring with survey stakes and transits. That meant that old houses like these were about to be replaced with hyper-expensive lofts.

The march of progress, or so they said.

Usually there were little old Mexican ladies in rocking chairs on the porch of the little shack nearest his apartment building. Not today, though. And the tight little parking lot of his building was completely full on a Tuesday (pretty sure it's Tuesday) at just past noon. But no construction guys drinking beer on the tailgates of the pickups.

The bleat of a truck horn stirred him from his trance, standing and staring at nothing. A full parking lot was hardly a thing to stare at, or to even wonder about.

He turned around to face a chubby Mexican lady laughing behind the wheel of a roach coach: Luz Marie, proud owner of Luz Marie's Tacos. She had this parking lot, and others like it, staked out to feed the army of construction crews building up East Austin into rich-kid paradise, their own efforts pricing themselves out of the neighborhood.

Quincy inwardly cringed at the thought of how many crews he'd been fired from for his drinking, but it didn't last when the humid air budged enough to give him a whiff of meat and beans swimming in lard. In the first instant a wave of nausea passed through him, pushing a shiver of sweat from his pores, and in the second a rumble passed through his guts. He hadn't eaten since yesterday.

"*Que paso*, stinky! Where the fuck my *mojados* at?" Luz smiled broadly. She thought he was cute, but still called him "stinky." He was pretty sure he didn't smell. Well, right now he was pretty damn sure he smelled, but in general he didn't consider himself a smelly guy.

WILLIAM HOLLOWAY

He walked over to the rolled-down window, leaned in and gave his best laid-back guy smile. "Dunno, Luz Marie. Maybe . . . "

He ran out of words. Too hungover. Absolutely no game with a hangover like this.

She pulled her cheap sunglasses down a bit and gave him a skeptical look, up and down, eyes pausing a second too long on his shaking hands. "You all right, man? You look . . . "

"Yeah, rough. My old lady bailed, so . . . "

Her eyes flashed hopeful, but went skeptical again at the case of beer. "No work today? Painting, right?"

He shrugged, then lied. "They called it off because of all the rain and flooding."

She chuckled. "Well, shit. Every single fucking worksite is totally empty, so it ain't just you."

She leaned on the horn of the old pickup, looking for any motion in the doors and windows of his apartment building. Nothing.

She whispered, "What the fuck, man."

She looked back, confused and concerned. "I haven't sold a single taco today. By this time I'm usually calling my *tia* and telling her to hurry the fuck up on the second batch, because these boys get pissed when you drive past them on empty, you know what I'm sayin'?"

He shook his head a bit. "No one?"

She nodded. "I've been up and down this bitch. Nothing on Holly. Not a soul on any of those jobsites! Over at the elementary school there's like a million kids on the playground. Today, like five kids and a teacher. Nothin', man!"

He squinted and pointed south. "What about closer to the river or the old folks' home?"

She shrugged. "That's the weird thing. The closer to the lake, the less people."

He smiled his smart-guy smile. "Well, that lake is actually a river, and it makes sense because of all the flooding. You probably need to head a few blocks north. Less flooding further away from the lake."

She still looked perplexed. "Yeah, I suppose so, but north of here ain't my turf. I'll be stepping on toes, and Mexican bitches in taco trucks ain't no joke."

"You can't let all this go to waste . . . "

"What'll you have?"

AMMONIA

"I'm a bit short today, but if you want to hang out and have a few cold ones . . . "

She smiled real big.

Fat girls always try harder.

***

"Well, at least they're supposed to . . . " Quincy stared back at the mirror, wondering why Luz Marie was such a fucking bitch to take off like that.

Fat girls are supposed to try harder! That's their fucking job!

Didn't she know he was doing her a fucking favor by throwing it in her? A bit of "don't ask, don't tell" with a fat girl. He had the beer, she had the tacos, and he was doing her a favor anyways. Fucking bitch!

They'd sat at the little table in his "dining room" for the first few beers. They'd smoked the half-joint Suzy left in the ashtray, then to the couch, and then she got an attitude.

She wrinkled up her nose when he put his arm around her, even leaning in to take a whiff. She told him that he smelled. Not just bad, but *like shit*. He knew he needed a shower, because it'd been a few days, but nothing some deodorant and clean clothes shouldn't fix.

Then the fucking bitch stood up, walked over to his mattress on the floor, and pulled aside his ratty old blankets to get a look at it. Sure, he didn't have a sheet on it, because the laundromat cost money and he was a bit low on funding, but she didn't need to be a total bitch about it.

She looked at the mattress like it was some kind of war crime, then back at him like he was a war criminal.

"*Pinche baboso*," she muttered, then walked out. Before she closed the door, she looked over her shoulder. "Jesus. Take a fucking shower."

So his mattress was a bit stained. He drank too much. Sometimes he pissed while he slept.

He looked at the face in the mirror again. "Fucking bitch."

The truth of too many things looked back, so he looked away, and turned the knob on the little CD player from the 90's and cranked the Stone Temple Pilots to ten, or at least as loud as the little old thing would go.

Quincy squeezed his eyes shut and tried not to think about it, to not think about failure and isolation, about the life that could have been his. Wife, kids, a house, a new car every few years. A sense that he knew who he was and where he was supposed to be.

He tried not to think about trying to join the Navy after getting kicked out of his millionth band. He tried not to think about the fact that his only peers in the music scene that still talked to him were heroin junkies.

Everyone except junkies looks down on you because you piss yourself every night and can't hold on to anything. Not a girl, not a job, not an apartment, nothing.

And then he heard it. A scream, a man screaming in Spanish out on the street. Not a normal scream, a terrified scream, a haunted scream of loss and existential terror.

Then gunfire. *Bam! Bam! Bam!* Until he lost count. Ten, eleven shots fired. Loud. Close. Right out on the street in front.

He quickly turned down the radio, ducked, and ran to the window, pinching down the blinds to get a look.

Nothing. No one at all.

The place was well-lit, with street lights on both sides and the big fluorescents of the convenience store and laundromat adding to their illumination.

Nothing. And no crowd, either.

No one on the balcony gawking. No looky-loos on the street.

There should have been a lot of people out there, but there was nothing. And this wasn't a big ghetto, where people know not to look out the window when shit goes down. He was one block removed from expensive lofts and townhouses.

Quincy cracked the front door.

Nothing. Not a fucking sound!

He listened a bit longer. Still nothing.

He walked out on the balcony. No neighbors.

A cold sweat trickled down his brow. *It's impossible that I'm the only person who heard that.* He took a deep breath and walked over to his neighbors' door and knocked. No answer.

He tried the next one. He knocked, and the door swung open: totally black inside. He hadn't intended that. "I'm sorry! Excuse me, I was just wondering if you heard that . . . "

Nobody home. He closed the door behind him, but not before he smelled that godawful ammonia again. *Fuck. What the hell? Bitch complains about me stinking while that shit is going on?*

Quincy closed the door behind him and whispered, "I'm sorry."

He heard a muffled thump and the sound of something sliding or dragging. Like there was something big moving stealthily through the space between the ceiling and the roof. Then he heard a metallic clank, then nothing more.

AMMONIA

Something is very, very wrong here. Every hair stood up on his body, and cold sweat pumped from every pore. He took a big slam from his beer and walked cautiously back to his apartment and locked the door behind him.

He put a folding chair beneath the utility door to the attic crawl space. He turned on the lights, then pushed the utility door up and peeked inside, and was hit with a choking wave of the ammonia smell.

He dropped the door back in place and retched, crawled over to the fridge for a cold one, and downed the whole thing in one go.

"What the fucking fuck is going on?"

He grabbed another cold one, steeled himself, and walked back out on the balcony, hearing that strange thumping again, then the sound of something dragging across the fucking roof.

What the fuck? Are there people up on the roof of the apartment building at 9 PM during the week? Quincy trotted down the steps, then to the edge of the parking lot to look back at his little apartment building.

Nothing. And his was the only light on in the whole place. Ordinarily he'd hear Telemundo or some Tejano shit out of every window. But now nothing, not even a single light on, but every parking spot was taken.

He walked backwards onto the empty street to see the roof of his building. More nothing. Wet pavement, wet cars, giant puddles. Streetlights and drizzle.

He kept walking backwards until he stumbled on the pavement. He landed in a shallow puddle, looking at . . .

It's a fucking gun. And there's spent shell casings all around, glittering on the wet street.

And then the sky opened.

***

Quincy listened and drank and he watched the big drops covering the pavement, overflowing the curbs, running as rivers through the streets. After several hours, the scene remained the same.

Streetlamps and rain, but no cops.

Suzy's car still in the parking lot.

The case of beer nearly empty, the pack of smokes as well.

He exhaled, big, through puffed-up cheeks and thought about going back to the Habeeb store. Humiliating, but that's what he needed to do. There would be no sleep tonight, not unless he drank more.

And beer required cigarettes. Two great tastes that taste great together.

And even now, he couldn't get that smell of ammonia out of his head.

He cleared his throat and stepped out onto the balcony. All the exterior lights were on, but not a single neighbor had a light on in their homes.

Did they all go on vacation? Is it a Mexican holiday? Cinco de Mayo? Is that even a real holiday?

Is it possible they've all been deported?

He'd never known anyone who'd actually been deported, and half of his life had been spent on construction crews. And it was August, so no Cinco de Mayo.

Every parking spot was full, and he could swear no car had moved for a few days now. Suzy still hadn't collected her car.

There was a lull in the rain, so he cautiously took the stairs. They were wet, and he was drunk, and he'd fallen more times than he cared to contemplate.

Drunk every single time.

Suzy's car was still there . . .

He walked back to Raj's Habeeb store. The power was back on since he'd been there last. He opened the door and felt the blast of cool air on his damp greasy skin. He glanced to the counter, but no one was there.

He took a deep breath, "Hey, man, anyone . . . "

And nearly gagged on the stink of ammonia.

He put a hand over his face. "What the fucking hell? Raj! Hey, man!"

He stepped back out the front door for some decent air, then yelled inside, "Raj, where the fuck are you, man? You can't stay in there with this shit or you'll die, dude!"

Silence. Just the sound of water dripping from the roof and the whirring of the air conditioner. No cars. No music. He was pretty sure it was Friday night, so this area should be happening right now.

He yelled for Raj again. Nothing. He took a deep breath of outdoor air, then went to the counter. His note from last night was still sitting there.

A chill slid up his spine, and cold sweat poured out of his scalp. *Something is very, very wrong here.* His hands shook too much for another note, so he grabbed a pack of smokes, and then another to be safe. Then to the fridge for another case, and then he was out of there, trying to avoid dropping his cargo from his shaking hands.

This was all wrong, and he was sure he knew why: drinking had fully caught up with him. His body was breaking down, and his mind was going too.

Yep, he was going crazy. This had happened before his last time in rehab. He thought shit and said shit that made no sense, not even to him. He didn't go full drool cup, but it was close. He'd also been hooked on Xanax, but just hadn't figured that part out. When he ran out, he thought he could just drink his way through it. He'd been wrong.

Now here he was, a few years later, in this bad a shape on alcohol alone.

I would kill to just be around another person. I could just listen to them talk about whatever stupid shit they talk about and get lost in their blather. At least enough to escape this isolation, this creeping sensation that I'm the only human around for miles.

Suzy's car. Should I drive it over to her place? Am I too fucked up to drive? Of course, so take the side streets . . .

"Quincy."

His heart stuttered. He dropped the case and fumbled the smokes. A taste of puke filled his mouth and a tiny squirt moistened the back of his already dirty drawers.

He whirled to face the speaker, and recognition filtered through. Dave McMaster. Junkie Dave. Tall, skinny, completely tatted. Wife beater and khaki Dickies. Backpack and cowboy boots.

"Maybe I'd prefer to be alone . . . "

"Nah, brother, we stand amidst splendor and riot, the beginning and the end. The stars are right. And you and me? We're here to serve."

***

The USS *Emory S Land* had steamed at full power from Guam, and most of the crew had disembarked onto her. Only a skeleton crew remained aboard the USS *Georgia* after it was determined that there would be no salvaging her. The boat was a total loss, and the miraculous fact that she hadn't sunk was lost beneath the horror that the human race was just beginning to comprehend.

The Pacific Rim was a wasteland of shattered cities hewn by earthquakes and drowned by tsunamis. The West Coast was in ruins, part of a line of devastation extending from Alaska to Cape Horn.

New Zealand and Hawaii had essentially ceased to exist.

Yes, the human race was only now beginning to comprehend the scale and power of the earthquake under the Ross Ice Shelf.

"Event." Bamboo enunciated the word as he worked the notepad before him, covered in mind-boggling formulae, trying to understand mathematically what he'd survived.

He knew it wasn't an earthquake, the captain knew it wasn't an earthquake, the admirals knew it wasn't an earthquake. Hell, even the president probably understood that the event hadn't been an earthquake.

So . . . what did this?

Bamboo sighed and leaned back, closed his eyes and yawned. He'd been at this for a few days now. The reactor had been deactivated. He'd overseen that, and the removal of the nuclear fuel. Now a crane worked from the deck of the *Emory S Land*, gently removing the missiles from the *Georgia*, but only after divers went into the tubes to get exact radiation measurements.

The warheads were undamaged, but wouldn't remain that way if one of the rockets exploded, which could happen if they did any number of things wrong. This was most certainly a worst-case scenario, and it felt like it too.

But still, Bamboo's mind wouldn't let it go. Not just because he'd wanted to do a year at McMurdo, but because nothing added up. And because of the need for strict radio silence, he'd been cut off from all news and information, except what Captain Clark gave him. And, bless him, Captain Clark was a father figure to him, but he wasn't a physicist.

He felt Clark's hand on his back, giving him a reassuring pat. "I understand, son. You feel like a fifth wheel."

"Yeah, Cap, you could say that again."

"You've been doodling that stuff for days now. Have you solved the riddle of the Sphinx yet?"

Bamboo closed his eyes and allowed himself a bitter little chuckle. "Trying to do a rough calculation of what amount of force could shatter the Ross Ice Shelf."

"A hydrogen bomb could do that, right?"

"Not even close."

"Wow. What about a volcano underneath? That's what the Swedes think happened. A giant cave full of magma collapsed, all the water hit it and it exploded."

Bamboo turned and regarded his boss. "Do they know about that radiation spike that happened before the primary wave?"

Clark gave a very skeptical shrug. "Only you and me and the Joint Chiefs know about that."

"The Russians?"

Clark shrugged again. "I can't say, but they're every bit as smart as we are."

AMMONIA

"Boss, I've never seen anything like that spike before. It was like a very powerful blast of radiation combined with black hole noise." He paused for a moment, neither of them saying anything, and then finished the thought. "Nothing does that. Nothing."

Clark shook his head. He could feel the pent-up frustration of his chief engineer. He nodded sadly. "Every scientist in the world should be on this thing, but the closest thing we got to Stephen Hawking is you . . . and that pothead over on the *Sea Lion*."

Bamboo laughed. "Yeah, that guy. But he's a biologist."

Clark cleared his throat. "Well, I've got good news and I've got bad news."

Bamboo arched an eyebrow. "Bad news first. It can't really get any worse than it already is, can it?"

***

Bamboo found himself in the same raft again, with Chief Petty Officer Smartass, AKA Jackson the UDT diver, crossing a reeking seascape of rotting sea life of every kind. It covered the surface, several inches thick. Dead fish, dead dolphins, dead turtles, dead things he couldn't identify at all.

The *Sea Lion* sat parked on the horizon, left with a skeleton crew, just like the USS *Georgia*.

Apparently Watkins had a hard time understanding radio silence, so Clark had sent Bamboo and Jackson to threaten to add him to the layer of dead things in the ocean.

Watkins had called the *Georgia* and specifically asked for Bamboo. He said he had something extremely important to show him.

While Clark joked that it was probably a very large reefer bong, and Bamboo couldn't rule that out, Watkins claimed that he had made the discovery of the century and needed another scientist to confirm it.

Bamboo knew Clark didn't care one whit about Watkins or his discovery, and this was all ostensibly about going over there to throw the man or his radio overboard. Clark also knew it would help Bamboo to mull their situation over with another scientist, even if it was a dirty hippie.

When they boarded, they were greeted by Watkins alone. He looked even worse than expected for a man stranded on a ship in the most remote corner of the world. He was pale, and his hands shook.

Jackson made officious noises about radio silence and national security, but Watkins was utterly unphased. He told Jackson to go to the bridge and do his worst, then hurried Bamboo down to a laboratory in the bowels of the ship.

Jackson shrugged and followed them.

Before they even opened the door, the smell hit them.

Jackson made a retching noise. "Whoa, doc, I don't care if this is Nobel-worthy. If it smells like that, we should sink this ship right now and call it an accident!"

Watkins opened a panel on the wall and handed out respirators. He didn't put one on himself. With his hand on the door to the lab, he turned to them. "Gentlemen, what you're going to see here . . . "

His mouth stopped moving. He'd run out of words. "I . . . guess all I can do is show you."

***

To Bamboo and Jackson, it was an undifferentiated mound of rot atop a wide aluminum table. But to Watkins, it was as if he'd uncovered King Tut's tomb. There was excitement, colored with a terrified awe.

They just stood and stared into the mound, Jackson trying not to think about what he was seeing, and Bamboo connecting the dots. "So . . . it looks like you guys dragged poor old Waldo back here for an autopsy and pulled this out of his stomach?"

Jackson's lights came on. "Oh, this is a giant squid! You wanted us to come here to, I guess, um . . . document this? Provide corroboration?" He paused for a moment. "This is big deal scientifically, right?"

Watkins nodded ever so slightly. "Ordinarily, yeah. But this goes way beyond that."

Bamboo nodded. "Okay, cool. I wanted off the sub, and if it means helping document a deep-sea find, then I'm good with that. Do you have some rubber gloves?"

Jackson groaned behind his respirator. "Great. Just great. You guys mind if I go somewhere else? I can tell this is gonna be gross."

Watkins didn't say anything, and Bamboo looked carefully at the man's facial expressions. "Yeah, go ahead, Jackson. This ain't your department."

Jackson didn't wait for them to reconsider. He was gone in seconds, the heavy door slamming behind him.

Bamboo didn't take his eyes off Watkins. "What's really on your mind, Doctor? I know that even a civilian, even a really dumb civilian, knows better than to radio us the way you did. So tell me why I'm standing here looking at this pile."

AMMONIA

Watkins' eyes never left the remains in front of him. "Did you know that there's no such thing as a freshwater cephalopod?"

Bamboo shook his head. "I didn't know that."

Watkins nodded. "This guy can go upstream."

Bamboo did a slow clap. "It's the end of the world as we know it, and this is the big deal?"

Watkins finally raised his eyes from the carcass. "That burst of radiation that preceded the shockwave: what did you make of that?"

Bamboo puffed out his cheeks and exhaled hard. "That's exactly what I should be discussing at MIT or Los Alamos, but I'm stuck here. Why are you asking?"

Watkins nodded and looked back to his find. "Your man Jackson, that first time we met on the raft, asked why the shockwave killed the whale, but not the squid. This squid was already dead, chewed up. It was probably other squid that caused most of the damage we saw, post-mortem."

"I'm not sure what you're telling me, boss."

"The shockwave didn't kill the squid."

"All right. I suppose this is important here, so why don't you tell me why?"

Watkins shook his head again. "No idea. Maybe something about the frequency or resonance . . . I'm just speculating. But the radiation, that close to the epicenter, ground zero, whatever it was, should have cooked them too, but it didn't."

Bamboo understood that this man was exhausted and sleep-deprived, but he did have a story to tell, even if it was just some odd rambling speculation.

Bamboo sat down on a metal stool. "Doc, we've got plenty of time. I get that you've got a lot on your mind. Just let me have it."

"We found that Waldo would have died of radiation poisoning, but the shockwave killed him first. The squid weren't harmed by either."

"How would you know that, Watkins? All you've got is a chewed-up pile on a table. There could be *beaucoup* dead squid at the bottom."

Watkins shook his head slightly. He took out a pencil and prodded what looked like an enormous tentacle. "There are metabolic changes and other processes at work, even post-mortem, for this specimen. There's a kind of tissue lividity, a swelling you'd associate with . . . *enormous* internal changes."

"Okay. What kind of changes? Why is this important?"

"This squid has been changed, Doctor."

"I'm not following."

"Something changed this squid. It's as if it's been reprogrammed to be something else. Something new."

Bamboo wondered if Watkins was going stir-crazy, but something about his demeanor said otherwise. He was still a scientist, and that part of his mind was still in control.

"All right. Do you think it might be environmental, some kind of pollution? You know, I read about antibiotics and even steroids making their way into the ocean and causing . . . "

"No."

"No?"

"That blast of radiation. Have you ever seen anything like it?"

Bamboo shook his head. "No, not like that. I'm not sure what does that."

"I think it was a code, a signal that activated something dormant in the genome of this creature."

"I'm lost again, doc."

"I think something or someone has reprogrammed this squid. I think this one, if he was still alive, would be at home in fresh water. I suspect that it can leave the water for brief periods, and I suspect that it can camouflage itself like an octopus."

"I've seen that. It's amazing how they can blend in and . . . " Bamboo stopped speaking, and silence hung for several moments. "Doc, how many of these things are there?"

***

They sat on the stairs leading up to Quincy's apartment and drank. Junkie Dave took it slow; beer fills your bladder up quick, and heroin makes it hard to piss because it relaxes the muscles down there. But that was okay; Quincy took up the slack.

He'd drunk three so far. He was gonna need it if his company was going to be Junkie Dave. He sighed, took another swig. "Okay, so you were telling me about 'The Rapture of the Deep'. What does that even mean?"

Dave sat on the hood of Suzy's car, then stood up and walked over to the door and peered inside. "Does your old lady smoke? Think she's got some butts in the ashtray?"

Quincy squeezed his lids shut so he wouldn't roll his eyes in disgust. This was the thing about Dave he hated the most. They'd been roomies at his second stint in the Austin Recovery Center, and Dave had always fished through his ashtray for butts. He did that shit walking down the sidewalk, everywhere he went.

Fucking disgusting homeless junkie shit.

"You know you can just ask me for one. I got a full pack."

Quincy took the pack out, making sure that Dave didn't see the other pack. It looked like he was supporting Junkie Dave tonight, and didn't want him to get presumptuous.

Dave nodded in total appreciation and lit up. Quincy again had to squeeze his eyelids shut so he wouldn't roll his eyes. He remembered how Dave had actually cried when Quincy blew up at him over it after rehab. He'd been between places and had crashed with Dave for a few days.

They'd slept under a bridge. Quincy didn't like thinking about that.

Dave blew out an exaggerated cloud of smoke. "Can't you feel it? It's in the air that we breathe. Rain for forty days and forty nights. Cities destroyed. Everything upended . . . "

"So God's pissed. So what?"

Dave chuckled. "I think we had it wrong the whole time, brother. I don't think God is God, at least not anymore. There's a new sheriff in town."

"The Devil, you mean? All this shit with the earthquake and the tsunami in the Pacific? It's like the Antichrist or something?"

"No. No, man. We been talking about it, you know, at the camps, and sometimes . . . "

Quincy weighed his options. He didn't want to be alone, but Junkie Dave wasn't always the best company. Even when he wasn't shooting dope, he was a fucking idiot.

He turned around and looked at his apartment on the second floor. His was the only light on, like everyone else in the building had just vanished.

"Go on, Quince, knock on some doors. See what happens."

He turned back to regard Dave. He didn't like that he was transparent to a true moron like Dave. "What have you been talking about at the camps? What does that even mean?" He shook his head in disgust that he was discussing gossip in the homeless camps.

"It's gotten so clear, man, so pure. Everyone knows everything. We're all an open book to one another, and all of the secrets, all of the lies have been laid bare. And you know what? It doesn't fucking matter. It was all an illusion anyways."

"Okay. What was an illusion?" Quincy asked.

"The world. Society, man. You and me? We're fucking failures in that world. Outcasts. Losers. Nobodies and pieces of shit. Problems to be solved—at very best, man."

"Uh . . . thanks. Speak for yourself. I ain't no goddam loser."

Dave gave him a skeptical look that felt presumptuous. Maybe Dave was all of those things, but Quincy was going to show them all one day.

"No. You're not. It's not gonna happen, never was, buddy. But the good news is here, man, and that world is fucking dead, just doesn't know it yet."

That cold chill crept up his spine again, that scared, baffling moment where he really didn't understand what was happening. That moment had happened far too often these last couple days.

"How did . . . " He looked up at Dave. "Did I say . . . "

He sat there like a dipshit with his mouth hanging open.

Dave didn't say anything back. He just let Quincy sit there staring, before asking, "Have you been over to the laundromat?"

Quincy shook his head and muttered. "Yeah. Had to get some beer. It's right next door. Why?"

"You know Old Man Temo?"

Quincy said, "Yeah. The dope man. So what?"

Dave reached into his pocket and pulled out a large plastic bag full of smaller plastic bags, each with a little ball of tarry heroin inside.

"Oh shit. Dude. What the fuck did you do?"

"It was on the floor."

"Seriously, go take it back. You do *not* want to fuck around like that."

"He's dead, man."

Quincy stood up, about to walk upstairs and never talk to Junkie Dave again. There could be a thousand dollars of dope in that bag, way more than enough to get Dave and anyone else involved killed for the transgression.

Dave laughed. "Of course I didn't kill him or steal this shit. He's dead and he's not going to need it anymore."

Quincy looked him dead in the eye. "Is that what the shooting was about?"

Dave looked quizzically. "I heard gunshots earlier, but I was blocks away."

Quincy shook his head in confusion. "So the gunfire wasn't about that dope?"

Dave laughed again. "Might have been, but whoever was shooting learned real quick that it won't help, not when *they* come."

AMMONIA

Quincy pointed to the middle of the street, still wet but not currently underwater. "Happened right in the middle of the street. There's a goddam gun just laying there with a bunch of fucking brass all around it."

He expected Dave to run over there and snatch it. Guns were money at the pawn shop, but he didn't.

"I don't need guns, man. They don't mean shit anymore."

Quincy's mind did pinwheels as he stared Junkie Dave in the eye, picked up the case of beer, walked up the steps. He didn't want to be around anyone anymore, especially Junkie Dave.

Quincy heard Dave sigh behind him, as if he was running out of patience with a small child. "I can hear it, man. I can hear everything, you know."

He whirled around to tell Junkie Dave once and for all what a piece of shit he was, but Dave was gone, as if he'd never even stood there in the first place.

Quincy stopped near the top of the staircase, closed his eyes, then squeezed them shut to dispel the grime in his skull. He'd been insulted, badly, by Luz Marie, and now by Junkie fucking Dave. A fat bitch in a taco truck and a fucking junkie who slept under a bridge.

His breath shuddered and hitched in his chest, and a hard sob wracked his body. A weak little moan escaped his lips.

There's a gun in the middle of the street. Go see if it has any bullets and put it in your fucking mouth, you loser, you fucking emotional cripple, you fucking charity case.

He shook his head back and forth like a dog, covering his eyes and face with his free hand, tears mixing with the constant drizzle. He peered between his fingers, expecting the neighbors to be laughing at the *pinche baboso*, but still no one was there, just the gentle tap of rain and the highway in the distance.

Had he ever been able to hear the highway from here? It had to be more than a mile away . . .

The hairs stood up on his arms and crawled up his back and an icy sweat came again. How many times had that happened today? Something was seriously, catastrophically amiss. But what?

His mind bounced between grief for how poorly life had treated him these last few days, and the alien silence.

Maybe you should yell for Dave to come back, and shoot some dope with him. That will fix you up, right as rain . . .

But he knew all too well that he would hate himself in the morning if he stuck a needle in his arm, he would hate himself far more than he did with his usual hangover.

He looked down at the case of beer. He'd drunk all fucking day, but nothing put a dent in the bullshit in his mind. He needed something stronger, something with a bit more kick.

He listened to the silence once more and knew what to do.

He set the case of beer by his front door and walked over to his neighbor's door. He knocked, the sound echoing through the empty street. He knocked once more to be sure, then turned the knob, went inside, and fumbled for the light switch. It came on and he saw it, exactly where it had been when his neighbor had tried to be sociable with him. It was a bottle of Sotol: Mexican moonshine. He grabbed it and flipped the light off.

***

There was a desert in his mouth, stretching down his throat and up his nose. It burned and burned and burned. Something acrid singed his eyes, and the ugly grey beams through the blinds punched straight into his brain.

Quincy gasped in pain. His nose was full of alcohol vomit. He rolled to the floor, and his heart pounded like he'd run a marathon. He kicked feebly at the sheets tying his legs together and felt the damp of piss soaking him from his chest to his knees.

He let out a whimper of pain and confusion and despair. This was not who he wanted to be, and he'd tried, he'd really tried, to be someone else. But he'd failed.

The screwdriver of pain shot from one temple to another, sending arcs of ugly black stars across his vision. It was a blur, but he could see the bottle on the table surrounded by beer cans. He'd drunk the entire thing.

His ears came online, and he heard the tinny noise of headphones. A genuine fucking Walkman from the 80's playing a genuine fucking cassette tape from the 90's. His dad had found it in a box in the garage, hoping it would cheer him up. All it did was remind him that he was approaching middle age and had nothing to show for it. Nothing material, no accomplishments, no relationships, no record at all that he had lived, apart from six or seven arrests, all of them alcohol-related.

He couldn't live with it, and he couldn't live without it. Every time he'd quit, the lights became too bright, the sounds too loud, the air painful in his lungs. His skin like an ill-fitting suit that he wanted to scratch off his bones. People were ugly, stupid, venial and cruel. He couldn't look anyone in the eye. He fidgeted and paced, tossing and turning while the thoughts became a whirling hall of knives to crucify him. So he'd drink, and sooner or later he'd find himself here.

Over and over and over.

Kill yourself.

Over and over and over.

Kill yourself.

It will never get better, it will never change. Sure, you'll put the plug in the jug, you'll say the words and do the fucking hokey pokey, but in the end you're right here, choking on your vomit.

He struggled over to the fridge, praying there were a few beers left to take the edge off.

The cold air flowed over his skin, enough to provide a sensation, but not to take the pain away. And there was no beer. Quincy sat up on his knees and swayed, his head like a lead weight his neck couldn't support.

He crawled over to the sink and pulled himself up, his face lingering above the filthy dishes. He turned the knob to be rewarded with a blast of lukewarm water.

He drank and he wiped puke from his mouth and nose, his hand feeling back into his hair. Yeah, it was in there too.

Then he slipped.

He was in no condition to catch his fall. His head smacked onto the kitchen floor with his full weight behind it. What had been a splitting hangover headache was now a pain so blinding that he wished he was out cold yet again.

"Quincy."

Even in the half-light of semi-consciousness, he knew it was Junkie Dave.

"That had to hurt, man."

Quincy still hadn't even opened his eyes, but he squeezed them closed even tighter, praying that Dave was just another part of his bad dream. "How the fuck did you get in here, asshole?"

"Oh, come now, Quincy, what kind of talk is that? Especially for a man too afraid to open his eyes."

Tears flowed from between his eyelids. "I'm not kidding, man, it hurts."

"And it's gonna hurt till the day you die, buddy. It's not gonna get any better. I hope you understand that, man."

Quincy felt his throat constrict, and the air whistle in his chest. "Fuck off, please, fuck off, Dave!"

"No. Not leaving. We're gonna hit bottom together, man, and then we're gonna keep digging until we find the center of the pain that is your life, that is this shitbox of a world. How does that sound?"

Quincy was sobbing now, struggling to breathe, in the grips of a full-blown anxiety attack.

Dave lit a cigarette from the pack on Quincy's little table. "Thanks, by the way." He took a big drag and regarded the pathetic man on the floor. "You're too much of a chickenshit to kill yourself quick, but too much of a coward to do anything else but kill yourself slow. Does that sum it up?"

Quincy couldn't stand. He tried but flopped back down, his cheek smacking the floor, leaving a greasy, tearful print. He tried to get his breathing under control. His heart beat too hard and too fast, the pressure in his skull enormous. He knew this was one way alcoholics died, by heart attack or stroke, especially after a fall.

He heard Junkie Dave at the table behind him, the flick of the lighter, the soft rasp of the needle against cotton, scraping across the blackened bowl of the spoon, the hiss of water and dope cooking. He heard him tap and flick the syringe to clear the bubbles.

He heard Dave's cowboy boots across the kitchen floor. He heard him squatting down and felt Dave squeezing his arm above the elbow.

Then the soft sting of needle through skin, and then the absence of pain.

***

Natalie and Erwin only met once in his office, on that first day she'd become his assistant. Since then they'd always met on the go, usually in his relentlessly expensive BMW. Somehow the damned thing maintained its new-car smell even though they both smoked in it.

And fucked in it.

She looked at the cigarette, and maybe for the first time in her life she fully regarded the white cylinder, the brown filter, the glowing orange ember. Such a small thing, such a trivial indulgence . . .

Erwin was rattling on about something. Senators on the Hill. Obstruction of the president's agenda. *Our* president's agenda, always with a heavy emphasis on the word "our."

Her mind came back to the car. Erwin was still talking. "The man was saying something to the effect of, 'We can't move forward with any of these regressive policies,' and that moron from Idaho had the temerity to respond with a completely glib . . . "

"Erwin, I'm pregnant."

Her boss didn't say anything immediately, but he did clear his throat and slip a finger in between his collar and the skin of his neck, easing the tightness a bit.

He didn't look at her, but she could see with her peripheral vision that he was doing the math inside his head, looking for options, looking for angles, looking for a way out or a way even further in.

He cleared his throat again. "We need to think about this."

She took a deep breath and squeezed her eyes shut. "We are not *all in this together*, Erwin. Whatever you do, don't talk that shit, or I might . . . "

He put on his phoniest smile, his pretty blue eyes glittering behind his Prada frames. "Nat, I know that no words are going to fit the bill, no matter what I say. *But*. And you need to think hard about those buts, and think about where you want to be in five years."

She didn't say anything. Her mind had gone blank, focused entirely on the texture of the leather upholstery beneath her fingers.

His voice never faltered; it simply didn't do that, because composure was a political necessity in his world. Still, he sounded like a desperate teenager to her, madly grasping at straws. "Do you have anyone you can speak with? A girlfriend or maybe a gay guy? They can really be the best listeners."

She whispered as she looked out the window at the Capitol Mall by night, lit by glaring white lights. "You're the only person I know here. I say hello to people, and they say hello to me. We're ghosts to each other."

Then she turned fully in her seat. "You. That's it."

He nodded thoughtfully. "What about back home in Dallas?"

She shook her head. "Austin. I'm from Austin."

He smiled. "It's still safe and legal there, you know, if that was your plan."

* * *

The absence of pain is a thing in and of itself. Yes, that sounds like an oxymoron, but to a broken man, a lack of pain is a thing with length and width and height. A giant thing, radiant as the dawn. But as anyone who has lived can tell you, the sun will retreat and darkness will prevail, and when it does, those things in the shadows will come out into the light.

Pain, despair, and loneliness.

Anger, resentment, and futility.

The absence of pain is beauty, a beauty the sufferer knows will fade. But for now, Quincy could breathe again. The massive weight on his chest was taken away by his friend Junkie Dave and his needle.

His eyelids fluttered and his head nodded, his gaze pinned to the fucking wall . . .

He puked, and it felt like . . .

Rain. He and Dave were walking in the rain. Just a light drizzle now, because now it never really stopped. It had been either raining or drizzling ever since the earthquake on the West Coast.

Well, it was more than just the West Coast. It was . . . all the way down the coast into Mexico, Central and South America.

"The Big One. That's what they say."

"Who says that?"

"Them. You know, them. They. It."

"Are we talking or am I just thinking this?" Quincy asked.

"We're talking and we're walking, talking about Them. They and Them and everything they say. They've always been talking, and you always thought that what they said was important. Now you're just figuring out that they've just been talking to fill the silence."

"Why do they care?"

"Because that's all they know how to do, Quince. Talk, and shit, and fuck, and eat, and make up rules for you and me to make it all seem like it matters."

Quincy laughed. A real laugh. "Fuck it."

Dave laughed back. "Fuck them."

Somehow they were at 5ᵗʰ and Pedernales, looking at the back of some trendy new lofts surrounded by a big black iron fence.

Quincy tapped out a smoke and lit up, even though it was immediately damp. He took a big drag, then ducked into a little alcove in the side of a building and leaned against the wall, his head nodding once to his chest.

"What was the topic, Dave?"

"Them. You know, them that make the world go round so that we can ride the train."

Quincy motioned to the fancy buildings around them. "Do you think this is where they reside? Or is it Washington?"

Junkie Dave shook his head and reached down for a dry butt. "No, I mean yes. Not Washington, but yes Washington. They and them are in your eyes when they're driving by, and in your ears when they're telling you what it's all about. And they never fucking stop trying to make you come to them for answers that just don't matter to questions that make no sense."

Quincy laughed again. "Does it pay better than painting? Because, as you know, I'm presently exploring opportunities outside of my previous employers' purview."

Dave straightened the cigarette butt, put it to his lips and lit up, inhaling hard and holding it. The nasty smell of burning filter. "I imagine they print lots of money and pay themselves with it, and as long as you agree that it's worth something, they'll generously shit in your mouth."

"I was thinking something less . . . shitty. That would be nice."

"All they've got is shit. That's the big reveal, man."

Despite the opiate glow, the painless floating, Quincy noticed the absolute still. "Hang on. Where the fuck is everyone?"

He pointed to a trendy bar with a trendy food truck in the lot. Closed, like it hadn't opened that day. "That lot should be completely full, man."

He tried to think back to their walk, but couldn't remember a single detail. Heroin was like that. He paused, about to take a drag. "Did we see anyone since we left my place?"

Dave shook his head. "No."

Quincy's mind tried to wrap itself around a question struggling to form. "That's not normal. That's . . . "

He stepped out of the alcove and looked up and down the street. Not a soul on Pedernales. He found himself about fifty feet away, Dave grinning as he looked up and down 6th Street.

"There's no one there either, Quince."

Cars lined the street; parking here was hard to come by. But no one was around. Quincy walked car to car to car, putting his hand on the hood of each: all cold and wet. The wet was understandable, but this was a busy intersection with people coming and going constantly. These cars hadn't moved in a few hours, at least. None of them had moved.

It was like they'd sat there for days.

He looked at Dave with all the focus he could muster. "Dave, something is going on. Something is very fucking wrong, and it's not just me and the DTs, man."

Dave opened the door of a grey BMW. "C'mon, man, get in. Let's cook a little shit in style, or whatever this is."

Quincy giggled. "Dude, that's fucking crazy. What if they come out? What if the cops come by?"

Dave pointed to an empty cop car across the street. "I walked past that one on the way to your place last night, man. It's still there. No cops here now."

And despite everything he knew about the world, Quincy got in the car with Junkie Dave, closed the door, sank into the luxurious leather seats, and allowed Dave to stick a needle in his arm. They took a little nap, then started walking again. A little higher, and a little less concerned about who they weren't supposed to be anymore.

***

His third shot, and nothing hurt. Not his head, not his stomach. He felt vertigo and nausea every now and then, so he'd puke a bit, but he didn't really care.

And that's the beauty of heroin. You don't feel pain, or loss, or the passing of time, those things that had been his constant companions. Now his companion was Junkie Dave, who turned out to be pretty cool—on an armful of dope.

They whistled as they walked. He had his Walkman, and unplugged the headphones so the songs would come out of the little speaker on the side. "Patience" by Guns N' Roses. Junkie Dave whistled, Quincy sang, and it sounded like music to them. It brought a little tear to his eye, because all he'd ever really wanted was to be a musician. He was pretty damn badass on the bass. He could pull off "Anesthesia" by Metallica and a lot of Geddy Lee's cooler shit, as well as Flea's entire repertoire.

But nobody cared about that anymore. The last gasp of rock was the grunge of the nineties. Now all people wanted was lame hip-hop, which was just Tourette's syndrome with a drum machine. He'd realized that one night in the tank when they'd corralled ten of them into a cell and one of them was a bum who talked shit to people who weren't there.

They whistled, they walked, they sang, but they didn't see a single person. Intersections under water, empty windows, balconies with no one on them. No music but their own.

They saw it at the tire shop at Chicon and 1st.

They hung back at the edge of the parking lot and watched.

An ambulance, lights on, rear doors open. It had clearly been sitting there a while. The engine was off, the lights dimming and slowing their rotations. There was a cop car next to it, engine running, lights on as well.

AMMONIA

A young cop with a buzzcut and jug ears was behind the wheel, staring at the ambulance with a blank, scared look on his face.

His spoke into his radio and slowly shook his head back and forth. He looked mad at whatever he'd heard. He looked all around, his gaze settling on Quincy and Dave for a moment as he continued his scan.

He got out of the cruiser carrying a shotgun, one of those wicked-looking black things with the extended magazine and a flashlight clamped to the barrel. Quincy had only seen cops pull those out on TV.

Impressed, Quincy looked to Dave. "I think we're about to see some actual shit happen."

Dave shrugged. "Nah. Nothing happens in the light."

Quincy wanted to ask what that meant, but the cop was more interesting. He'd flipped on the light on the shotgun and looked under the ambulance, very carefully, obviously scared of what he might find.

When he didn't find whatever it was, he pointed the barrel into the cabin, opening doors and jumping back, never pointing it away from the interior. He clicked the radio on his shoulder, walking to the rear and examining the handles and the hinges holding the doors in place.

Quincy drew closer to see what the cop was intent on. The door handles were nearly twisted off. Something had almost yanked those doors off. It would have taken a truck and chain to do that.

Quincy whispered, "Who the fuck would even bother to do a thing like that?"

The cop whirled around, and Quincy stared down the barrel of the shotgun.

Junkie Dave spoke before Quincy's mind could connect with his mouth. "Hey! Officer! It's all good! No one here but us and the weather!"

The cop stared hard, then lowered the gun and muttered something. He clicked the button on his radio. "Two white males, mid-forties." He glanced at them. "Homeless."

A staticky voice responded. "Proceed with your sweep."

He turned back to his car, opened the door, and threw the shotgun into the passenger seat. At the last second he stopped. "Where are you guys coming from?"

Quincy didn't say anything. Dave answered. "First and Pleasant Valley."

The cop nodded. "Have you seen *anyone* between here and there?"

Quincy shook his head. "No." Then a second later, "Why are you asking that?"

WILLIAM HOLLOWAY

The cop didn't answer. He just shook his head, glanced at them one more time, got in his car and sped off towards the freeway.

Even though Quincy was higher than he'd ever been, and more comfortable in his own skin than he could have ever imagined, this exchange with the cop struck all the wrong chords. "Okay, Dave. Everything that just happened was totally fucking wrong."

"Why? There's nothing wrong; the world's just different now."

Quincy gave him the most confused look he could manage under the circumstances.

Dave put a reassuring hand on his shoulder. "Did you see the look on that pig's face? He's so used to his authority, so used to playing king of the hill, so used to the way it's all supposed to be. And it's all worked out so well for him. I'll bet dear old dad is so very proud. Maybe he was a cop too."

Quincy looked back at Dave. "I guess I shouldn't be surprised that you hate the cops."

Dave laughed. "I don't hate them. Not at all. They're just puppets, like you and me used to be before the Rapture. But now? You and me can see the puppet show, and we can hear the soundtrack. And you of all people know—that soundtrack sucks. And the laugh track? It's been laughing at us since the day we were born. Somebody's got to be the loser on this stage, and you're it. Maybe next time you'll be the knight in shining armor. Maybe you'll get to be that cop."

"What the fuck, man?" Quincy asked.

"Ask yourself why we keep writing such unbearably shitty stories to live out."

"Huh?"

"Maybe it's because we *are* shit."

"What?"

"Think about it, man. If you jumped into a wood chipper, you'd make just as good a fertilizer as shit. So would me and that cop. So would the old man and the baby that momma just squeezed out."

"I have no idea what that fucking means, man."

"It means, dear buddy, that it's time for a nice *big* shot. We've been priming the pump with little shots all day, now it's time to get really, really fucking high."

Quincy was already too high to care. He just laughed.

"So, Quincy, how would you feel about getting tuned up inside an ambulance? I'll bet they've even got Narcan."

44

AMMONIA

Quincy moved around his jaw and his facial muscles, feeling where constant expressions of worry had frozen his face into the shape in the mirror for decades now.

Junkie Dave, good ol' Dave McMaster, sat behind the wheel nodding out, making several attempts to reach the stereo before he managed to get the radio going.

NPR, or something like it. Pretentious-sounding people talking about . . . Quincy wasn't sure, because he kept nodding out.

Dave sighed. "Goddam, dude. Goddam. Poor old Temo should've been the pope. The pope of fucking dope." He laughed. "And I've been scoring down on Rundberg like a chump. I should've stayed over here . . . "

He trailed off, and his head sagged to his chest.

The rain came down in sheets, sliding down the windows, tapping and pelting the roof of the ambulance, blending into a soft sweet static.

Pain free.

All of the regrets so small and distant.

"Since the earthquake that has so altered our world, we've focused much of our reporting on California and the devastation of Los Angeles and San Francisco. Now we turn to the effect the monumental rains have had on our country . . . "

It was unclear what time it was.

Did Junkie Dave find Quincy on his floor yesterday? Or was it this morning?

He wasn't so sure. It was still light out, if you could call the perpetual overcast sky "light."

"Some areas, particularly along the large rivers like the Mississippi, have experienced a constant state of flooding, causing catastrophic absenteeism at businesses and government agencies . . . "

Quincy's head came up, something about the words seeming important.

"Emergency funds have been made available by the federal government for essential city services such as police, fire, EMS and hospital staff, to pay employees to work double and sometimes triple shifts . . . "

Why did these words feel important? He was as close as he could get to being worried in his current state.

"'I've had to work doubles for the last three days because several of the other girls just stopped showing up to work,' said 911 dispatcher Gilberta Gomez of Waco, Texas."

WILLIAM HOLLOWAY

Quincy fumbled over to Dave, shaking his shoulder. "Hey, man, we gotta go. I think something's going on. I think . . ."

The words stopped coming out of his mouth, and his eyelids fluttered. He took a deep, pain-free breath. It felt so good, like an elephant had been standing on his chest for years and now it had finally wandered away, leaving him able to breathe freely again.

No! This is important!

"Dave, hey, man. Dave. We gotta get moving. We gotta call the cops and tell them that everyone is gone. They're gone."

Dave's lids opened, but just a bit, and his eyes rolled lazily over to Quincy. He let out a huge sigh of contentment. "Rapture of the Deep, brother. They're all gone. Like the dinosaurs or some shit. Dodo birds." He laughed and continued. "Extinct. Like woolly mammoths and saber-toothed tigers and . . ."

"No, man, we really gotta call someone. 911. We need to call 911."

Dave shrugged and his head sank back to his chest, but his arm shot up and pointed to a cup holder. There was a clunky-looking cell phone there. "Go ahead, Quince. Tell them the world came and went, that the end already happened. I'm sure they'll understand."

Quincy fumbled for the phone and prayed it wasn't locked with a passcode. It wasn't. Thank God for small miracles. He dialed the numbers 9-1-1 and hit send.

At first there was some mechanical-sounding hold music, then a recorded message to please hold, operators are busy with other callers, but then a very tired and scared voice came on the line. "911, please . . . state your emergency."

Through the heroin fog, an alarm went off in Quincy's head. A very distant alarm, but an alarm nevertheless. "Hi. Hi, um . . . we're on Chicon and 1st Street and . . ."

The voice changed pitch, waking up. "Are you calling from an EMS phone, sir?"

The alarm bells continued in his head. "Yeah, I guess so. I found this phone in this ambulance that's just sitting here . . ."

The voice went up a notch. "Sir, are you okay? Have you seen the crew of that ambulance?"

Dave laughed from the driver's seat. "Pepperoni. Tell her we want pepperoni."

Quincy ignored him. "Yeah, yeah, I'm okay. We're okay. We haven't seen the crew. If they were around, they left a long time ago."

AMMONIA

The voice on the line asked a question that truly scared him. "Have you seen anyone on the streets? Any cars driving? *Anyone?*"

It took him a moment to answer, to get his bearings. "No. No one except the cop that was here when we walked up. But he split."

The voice started, "Okay, do . . ."

Quincy interrupted. "Why did you ask if we've seen anyone?"

And the line went dead.

Dave's voice snapped him out of his fugue. "They hung up on you, didn't they?"

He nodded. "Yeah. Yeah, they did."

He turned to Junkie Dave smiling at him. "I don't think 911 is supposed to be hanging up on the taxpayers. Ain't that a shame. You think maybe they got something else on their minds right about now?"

Quincy thought about it. "Why did she ask if we'd seen anyone? The cop asked that too."

Dave shrugged and leaned forward, put his foot on the brake and turned the key in the ignition. The keychain had been hanging there the whole time. It didn't turn over. Battery was almost completely dead.

He leaned back in his seat and sighed again. "Looks like we're gonna be hoofing it, Quince."

Quincy shook his head. "It's probably illegal to drive off in an ambulance."

"Somehow I don't think the cops are worried about that right now."

"Lemme guess, the Rapture of the Deep? Whatever that means?"

Dave pulled a big black flashlight out from the center console, and handed another one to Quincy. "These things are fucking awesome."

He clicked the light and shined the powerful beam through the windshield. Then he pointed it to his face from below, and did a crappy campfire-tales face. He sang in a goofy baritone. "To walk the night. To feel no love." He stopped and turned off the flashlight. "Cops aren't coming to take us away, so I think I'm going to borrow this here flashlight and see what lies on the other side of the night. Let's go back to your place."

Quincy thought about it a moment. He wasn't scared, even though that distant alarm in his mind was telling him he should be. He grabbed a notepad and a pen from the cupholder. "I'm gonna write down what I see and call 911 when we get back to my place . . ."

"I don't think they care what you see, Quince. I don't think they ever did. Not now, not ever. You understand that, don't you?"

***

He shrugged, and they stumbled into the drizzling rain. At least it wasn't pouring anymore.

Junkie Dave began singing again; Quincy wasn't sure, but it felt like an old punk song, and he picked up the tune. "To walk the night . . . "

They flipped on the flashlights as the night began to fall.

***

And as the night fell, the rain fell from the skies. Quincy leaned his head back, and the water rolled over his face. His eyes closed, he spread his arms and felt free. It was chilly, far chillier than it should have been, and his breath rose as steam. He opened his eyes and watched as the fog of his breath dissipated into the rain.

He looked at Junkie Dave's back, several yards ahead of him, EMS written in large black letters. He was wearing a bright yellow raincoat. Quincy looked down at himself and saw that he was wearing one too. And carrying a big black flashlight, just like his companion.

Junkie Dave called back to him, "We got them in the ambulance, in case you forgot."

Quincy shook his head. This was one of the things he always claimed to hate about heroin, even though he really didn't care right now.

He also claimed to hate junkies. But he'd be at a show, the band blaring, and find himself talking to the junkies. That's the way it always went. They didn't judge him, even though he judged them. He had his problems, but at least he didn't stick himself.

He had more class than that.

Junkie Dave was on to a new song, and Quincy knew it even if he couldn't place the band or the name of the song. "And this room becomes a shrine thinking of you. And the way you are sends the shivers to my head. You're gonna fall, you're gonna fall down dead. As far as I can tell, I'm being dragged from here to hell . . . "

The streetlights shone through the rain, but all the houses were dead black.

Quincy worked his jaw back and forth and his eyelids fluttered, but in the back of his head the questions began again. "Dave, why are there no lights?"

Dave gave him a big gap-toothed grin. He pointed to one of the streetlights. "That ain't good enough for you, amigo?"

Quincy chuckled and shook his head. "I mean the houses, retard."

AMMONIA

Dave shrugged and stopped in his tracks. They were passing the mouth of a pitch-black alley. No streetlights down there. He flipped on the flashlight, pointing it down the black barrel of the alley, the beam crisscrossed in the downpour.

Quincy remembered his flashlight and threw away the soaking cigarette he'd forgotten. He flipped on the flashlight and the powerful beam joined Dave's.

Just then, the night was rent by a very loud siren. He thought he'd heard something like this almost every night for the last week, but he'd been too smashed to question it. But hearing it now, out in the rain and not drunk, was different. The siren joined the chorus of alarms in his head and broke through the opiate fog.

" . . . It's from one of the dams around here, I'm not sure which one. Maybe the one on Pleasant Valley or that one up 6th across Mopac."

"How the fuck did you know I was gonna ask that?"

"Ancient Chinese secret?"

"Really? Seriously?"

Dave regarded him. "Haven't we always been transparent, Quince? I know you have, and me probably to you. But the world's been washed clean and there's no dirt, no rules, no fucking shit to clog the pores in your head. Something like that, man."

Quincy shook his head. "That made zero sense. Are we gonna walk down this black-ass fucking alley?"

"Well, we could stand here, we could go down that alley, or we could do something else. I don't actually give a flying fuck."

"I don't think you ever had a flying fuck."

Junkie Dave walked into the black maw of the alley. "Once more into the breach, dear friends."

Quincy shrugged and followed.

***

Muddy, and mostly a puddle. Old wooden garages given a new lease on life with a thoughtfully hip coat of paint. Gates and overgrown bushes. But no light, no movement, and when the siren abruptly stopped, no sound.

Junkie Dave giggled, whispering in the dark. "Remember when this part of town was a barrio?"

Quincy whispered back. "Yeah. Fucking look at it now." And he shined his light into the black open mouth of a garage and the gleaming red two-door Mercedes, an expensive-looking Mac laptop lying on the concrete beneath the open driver's side door.

Quincy looked to Junkie Dave, waiting for him to dart inside and grab that computer. Laptops left in other people's cars were one of Dave's very favorite things. But he just stood there, barely interested.

"You're not going to grab that?"

Dave shrugged and shook his head. "Whatever for, *mi amigo?*"

"Money for dope? Isn't that and mountain bikes your thing?"

Dave laughed. "I've got a new god."

Quincy squinted, trying to focus his mind. Then he walked into the garage and picked up the laptop. Pieces of glass fell away as he opened it. Someone must have dropped it getting in or out of the car.

He lit up the inside of the car with his flashlight. The keys were still in the ignition.

Dave walked up to the passenger side and tried the handle. It opened, but there were none of the electrical dings you might expect from a new model car. He got in and got busy cooking another shot. "Get in, Quince, it's smack time!"

Quincy shook his head. He was still reeling from the last shot. His head was starting to hurt from the amount of heroin he'd done that day, probably more than he'd done in the entirety of his life.

"I'm gonna hold out for a bit, man. I need to think about some shit, and I can't remember what I was thinking about five minutes before on this shit."

Dave held his lighter to the bottom of his spoon. "Suit yourself. We've got more dope than Jesus."

He sat in the driver's seat and turned the key in the ignition. Nothing. This car had been sitting here a long time, maybe two or three days with the interior lights on because the door was left open. That probably meant the computer was sitting there that long as well. As the dope slowly cleared his system, Quincy's brain gradually engaged. And as it did, the alarms blaring in the back of his mind began to come closer to the foreground.

This was all wrong.

He heard the rafters creak and groan above him, and he glanced in the rearview mirror. He heard a soft splash as something big dropped to the ground behind the car. A shadow, there and then gone, faster than his mind could process. There was a sound of rustling in the bushes outside, then a sound of timbers groaning. Then nothing else.

Quincy blurted out, cracking the silence: "Did you fucking see that?"

Dave nodded. "Yes."

AMMONIA

Quincy was turned around in his seat, shining the light into the alley. The beam played across a puddle behind them, precisely where whatever-it-was landed, then darted away.

Despite the fact that his blood was full of heroin, the hairs stood up on his arms and the back of his neck. Everything about this whole situation was wrong. Only the drug made it so that he wasn't utterly terrified and panicking.

Quincy was in a stranger's car, in the same stranger's garage, while his friend cooked a shot of dope. What the fuck was he thinking?

"Dave . . . where the fuck is everyone? Did this whole part of the goddam city get evacuated while I was passed out? What the fuck was it with that cop and that 911 operator?"

Dave stuck the needle through the skin of his left hand, registered, then pushed the plunger in. He let out a huge exhalation and leaned back, smiling. He turned to Quincy and smiled even bigger. He'd never been this happy in all his life.

"Why don't you mosey on in and ask? Maybe the owner of this fine German automobile can tell you the what for."

He held up his flashlight, and the light fell across the door at the front of the garage. With these small houses in this area, the back door of the house would be just a few paces away.

"Are you fucking kidding me?"

"Do you actually think someone is going to be there? Maybe they just left their garage door open, let the battery on their car die and smashed their laptop for shits and giggles."

Quincy didn't know what to say, so he sat there like a fool with his mouth hanging open.

Dave sighed, then got out of the car and walked to the door. "Come on, man, let's see how the other half lives."

***

She'd thrown up her IHOP breakfast, even though she'd had a kind of ravenous hunger she'd never experienced before. Erwin tried not to stare, but she caught him.

He sat across from her, drinking his coffee black, the only thing on the menu suitable for a man of his stature, and because he spent several hours a day doing Pilates and wasn't about to ruin it for a fucking Rooty Tooty Fresh 'N Fruity from the most plebian establishment on Earth.

She caught him staring when the nausea hit her.

I am disgusting and pathetic.

WILLIAM HOLLOWAY

I am a failure.

I am nothing.

The entire contents of her stomach fountained into the piss-stained bowl and stared back at her, its bright red candy foam declaring her guilt. Her slutty whore guilt. Her dirty, craven, gold-digging whore guilt.

That's right, slut, bulimia is the ticket, your way in. Gotta keep up that figure if Erwin is gonna get that Pulitzer. If that happens, you'll get your own byline, your own column in the Post. *Not whatever that podunk rag was called back in Austin. The fucking* Post!

But this isn't bulimia, is it? This is something different. Something with a specific name, and a specific connotation.

You're pregnant.

Erwin ran a hand through his immaculate hair, took off his glasses, and wiped them with his tie. He held them up to the light and squinted, rubbing and buffing at the lenses. He didn't know, but this action was his tell. Natalie was familiar with this. He did this when the subject was going to become uncomfortable.

I swear, if they don't give you a raise next year, I'm gonna go right over management's head and straight to the owners!

I think that dress is nice, but it looks . . . inexpensive.

She looked at his apprehensive eyes and his fidgeting hands and knew which track he wanted her to take.

And she knew which track she was going to take, too.

She was going to go back to Austin and take care of it.

She caught his glance and nodded. "I'm going to be gone for a few days, back to Austin. Take a breather. When I get back . . . "

She trailed off. Did he want her to come back?

He put his glasses back on and nodded. He understood. "Yes, yes. Of course. Take your time."

"And when I come back?"

He nodded and looked down at his coffee.

***

If anything, he looked sweatier and more scared than the last time she'd seen him. She had a gift for remembering people, but with everything going on, she was scrambling to name him. He had a plain, fat face and an unassuming demeanor that made him invisible to most people, no more noteworthy than a potted plant or . . .

"My name's Chester Slayton."

AMMONIA

She turned towards him, and he smiled. She caught herself gaping stupidly, something that movers and shakers simply don't do. They are poised, always. They are cool, always. And she'd let her guard down.

He was still smiling at her, fully aware that her mental calculus had zero to do with him as a human being.

He offered, "We met here before."

She processed it. Yes, they had. That same motionless Marine and that same secretary ignoring them for her crossword puzzle.

"NOAA, right? You were going to brief the big man and we were talking to the Speaker, I believe."

He smiled again, wiped his hand on his cheap tan jacket, and offered her a shake. She took it. Still sweaty. Nothing would ever make this guy a player in this town.

She cocked an eyebrow and gave him her best facial angle. "More info on the auroras, or some new theories about what caused the whole thing?"

The smile fell from his face and he looked sheepishly at his shoes. His voice was barely a whisper. "I don't even know why I'm here. Nobody listens to me, because nothing I have to say helps anyone politically."

She put on a caring and sympathetic face and put a hand on his shoulder. "Chester, I know how you feel, but you've got to tell your truth, no matter if it feels like people aren't listening."

He nodded his head like a schoolboy getting picked last for kickball.

She smiled, putting on the megawatt charm. "Hey, they're gonna be a while, believe me. I know this. So we can sit around here sulking or we can get things done."

He looked confused, lost. "What can we do? We're nobodies."

She turned it up a notch. "You're nobody until you get the pitch down. That's what it all comes down to in this town. The pitch, the big sell."

"What do you mean?"

"I mean we go for a walk and I show you how to do the elevator pitch. That means you say what you've got to say in the least amount of words possible, and focus it for who is listening. You've got an idea, and you need to sell it. You tell it to me, and I tell you how to deliver it to these stiffs. Whaddaya say, Chester?"

His surprised fat-guy face went one step further down the road. "Why . . . why would you help me?"

She laughed and leaned in. "Chester, I'm a glorified intern. I sit in waiting rooms and get coffee for other people. If I'm lucky I get to pick up dry cleaning. Helping you work on your delivery will be the most interesting, non-demeaning thing that's happened to me in weeks."

As they stood and left, Natalie glanced at the secretary and the Marine. The secretary smirked; she saw the con. The Marine was expressionless.

***

"Wait, hold on a second . . . there's a trail of radiation particles leading from Jupiter back to Earth, to where the iceberg broke off?"

Natalie wanted to be smug, wanted to say something pithy, but she didn't. She still didn't know exactly what her status would be when she returned from Austin, returned from . . . taking care of it.

She nodded. "There is a trail of radiation, a 'rad signature' that exactly matches the burst of radiation that was detected when whatever-it-was happened in the South Pacific."

"The event."

"Yes, the event."

Erwin sank back into the seat of his crass BMW, confused. "The fuck does that have to do with climate change?"

She shrugged. "Well, you could definitely say it changed the climate."

He gesticulated, pantomiming, working it out. "So you're saying that egghead from NASA just told you that this has fuck all to do with climate change?"

"Yep. Indeed."

He gave himself a perplexed look in the rearview mirror. "And you believe him? He's telling the truth?"

She smiled and laughed, trying to show her boss just the right amount of attitude. "That guy couldn't lie his way out of a wet paper bag. He's just reporting his findings. And it's NOAA, not NASA, even though the Europa info came from NASA."

"Europa?"

"One of Jupiter's moons. One of the places in the solar system where there could be life. The whole thing is a liquid water ocean, covered with a thick layer of ice."

He didn't look at her, just at himself in the rearview, his eyes wide and scared-looking. "What do they think it was?"

She shook her head slowly, back and forth. "They have no idea, only that it caused a big crack in the ice on Europa, left a trail of radiation, and hit the Ross Ice Shelf with, and I quote, 'Much more force than Tunguska.'"

"What the fuck is a Tunguska?"

AMMONIA

***

The hinges squealed as the old door opened to the little back yard. The door, like everything else, had been given a fresh coat of thoughtfully hip-toned paint. The little back yard was an urbane hipster's playground, albeit semi-submerged now. A trail of granite pavers led to the back door, also old, but revitalized for the new breed of East Side inhabitants.

It sat ajar, and the blackness within was total.

Junkie Dave put his flashlight under his chin and crooned, "Yoo-hoo, is there anybody home?" He put a theatrical hand to his ear to listen for a response that wasn't going to come.

Quincy sighed and rubbed his face, his breath steaming in the damp and cold. "There's not going to be anyone in there."

Dave looked him in the eye. "Let's go take a look. I've never actually taken the time to admire the inside of these kinda folks' homes."

Quincy shrank back into the garage. He'd broken the law before, a lot, but he'd never broken into anyone's home.

"Technically it's not breaking and entering if the door is sitting open."

Quincy's expression went to total incredulity. "How the fuck would you know I was thinking that?"

"Like I said, baby, we're all open books. All you gotta do is start reading."

"Maybe I should have taken you up on that last shot."

"We've got the Narcan, thanks to our friends from the ambulance, but I always hated that scene. Angry recriminations. It's always the most senior junkie's fault. It's probably best for you to hold off for a bit."

In spite of himself, Quincy chuckled. "That's big of you, Junkie Dave!"

"I'm here to serve our New Gods. And for whatever reason, they want you alive."

Quincy chuckled again, and shouldered past his friend up the little path to the door. He turned to say something pithy, but stopped when he spotted the tree. There were things in the big green juniper, and he shined his light to get a better look.

It was baby clothes. Diapers. Baby shoes and stuffed animals. The tree seemed to be decorated like a Christmas tree, but with baby stuff.

The hairs stood on end on every part of his body.

"What the fuck is this shit?"

Junkie Dave shrugged. "Creativity? Abstract reasoning? Entertainment and philosophy?"

The alarms going off in his mind came as close to the foreground as the heroin would allow.

"Dave?"

"Yeah, Quince?"

He didn't know what to say to his own question. Then he heard a groaning of old timbers as whatever-it-was moved around on the roof of the garage again.

It was back.

He reflexively shined his light towards the roof of the garage and saw something. Something shapeless that seemed to disappear, kind of, when his light fell on it. The groaning of the timbers became a squealing as whatever-it-was seemed to launch itself over their heads and onto the roof of the house. There was a shuffling, thumping, and dragging sound all at once, and then a big splash from the front yard of the house.

"Dave! What the hell was that?"

Dave laughed. "Perhaps a raccoon? I don't think they're into cave painting or whatever's going on with this here tree. But . . . I also don't care."

"Dave, something was on that roof and it jumped thirty fucking feet right over our fucking heads!"

Dave shrugged again. "I dunno. There's nothing I can do about it. The state of man is perpetual fear. Maybe that's just being washed away."

"Did you not see what I just saw? Did you not hear that?"

"I did."

"And that doesn't fucking bother you?"

"Like I said, there's nothing I can do about it. What's to be done anyways?"

Quincy stared at Dave, hard. He was starting to hate him again. *What the fuck am I doing? Why am I out here wandering the streets like a homeless person with Junkie fucking Dave?*

He sighed. He shook his head. Dave had always been obtuse and full of stream-of-consciousness nonsense.

Dave put a hand on his shoulder. "Let's go inside and have a chill on the couch."

They walked in and Quincy called out in a loud whisper, "Is there anybody here?"

Quincy looked to Dave, but didn't say anything. He knew all he'd get back was nonsense, but the smell was here, too. Faint, but still undeniable.

AMMONIA

Dave whispered, "Guess what, Quincy."

Then he flipped on the lights.

Quincy felt like he could cry, and would have if it wasn't for the dope.

"How the fuck did you know those lights were gonna work?"

"The streetlights are working, so these would be working too."

"Then why the fuck has every light in every goddam motherfucking house and apartment we've passed been off?"

"I'm guessing someone turned them off."

Quincy shook his head again. He was going to need another shot to continue tolerating Junkie Dave.

He opened his eyes and involuntarily sighed. This house was beautiful. It was everything he could never have, because the owners were everything he could never be.

They stood in a kitchen full of gleaming new appliances, shining with chrome and mid-century modern tones. He'd learned that term working construction. This was the look favored by the kinds that had gentrified the East Side. He'd always claimed to hate it, because it was out of reach for him. Everything in here was.

These people were simply better at being people than he was.

He walked to the living room and dropped onto the tasteful black leather couch and turned on the little lamp at its side, an old-fashioned rotary phone next to it. *Lucite. That's what that material is called.*

An enormous framed poster of John Coltrane looked down at him.

Junkie Dave mangled the French words adorning it.

"Blah, blah, blah, Paris, France, 1965."

Quincy whispered, "That poster costs more than my rent."

Dave nodded. "Probably about three months of your rent." He turned and winked. "My line of work has led to an ability to assess the worth of certain *objets d'art*."

Quincy lit up. "Why do I get the feeling that these people are never coming back?"

"Probably because they *are* never coming back."

Quincy sighed and stood. "I need to take a look around, then I think I'm gonna take you up on another shot. A little one."

Dave was looking through the selection of Blu-ray discs. "Hey! *Finding Nemo*, I love this one!"

Quincy ignored him and walked down the little hall to the bedrooms, passing a nursery and into the master bedroom.

Like the rest of the house, it was scrupulously tasteful, but there were suitcases thrown on the bed, drawers yanked open and left on the floor. The owners had been packing to leave.

In the bathroom he saw that they'd ransacked the medicine cabinet, throwing everything into a big purse on the floor. On the counter were two modern-looking pistols with laser scopes. There was a pile of magazines with nasty-looking hollow-point bullets. His and hers pistols.

The tub was full too. He ran his hand through the water, and the smell of ammonia got stronger. The water was cold and cloudy. It had been sitting here a while. For some reason, this struck him as significant, but he couldn't say why.

Quincy walked back to the nursery and flipped the light on. Two empty cribs.

These people had been frantically packing to get the fuck out of Dodge. So why were their cars still in the garage?

"Maybe they got a ride from a friend?"

Quincy looked to Junkie Dave. "I think something terrible has happened."

"I'm pretty sure terrible things happening are the reason we humans exist."

Quincy shook his head. "I want to take a look at the next door neighbor's house."

Dave giggled. "A voyeur of the apocalypse."

"Leave the lights on here."

"Whatever you say, boss."

So they walked the short distance to the next house. As with the last house, the lights were off, but turned on just as easily. The front door was closed, but unlocked. One of the little glass panes in the door was broken. It was the same story here: a faint smell of ammonia, and signs that the owner had been packing to leave.

In the bedroom, Dave paged through a photo album of picture-perfect people. A happy couple, this time in Thailand, the next time in London. Perfect smiles and perfect lives.

"I think the cops must've come by and evacuated. Everyone is fucking gone!"

"Nope."

"And you know this how?"

Dave was rifling through a dresser and held up his find. "Oh my, but it appears the Smiths were indeed keeping up with the Joneses!"

AMMONIA

It was a fair-sized baggie of cocaine.

Dave took a large mirror off the wall and set it on the bed, about to lay out some rails.

"Stop, I can't be doing that now."

"Why?" Dave asked.

"Because if I start, I won't be able to stop, and . . . "

The bathtub in the attached bathroom was full, the water a bit cloudy, exactly like in the last house. Quincy ran a hand through the water, and just like in the last house, the smell of ammonia grew stronger.

"You don't want to do a fat fucking line of blow? What on earth is the matter with your priorities?"

Quincy shook his head slowly, back and forth. He barely whispered, "Just save it man, we'll get tuned up back at my place."

Dave exhaled, disappointed, then shrugged. "A shot of dope and line of blow is heaven on earth. Let's get to your place."

They left through the front door. Quincy didn't say, but he had no desire to walk back down that black alley. As he closed the door, he glanced to the first house they'd visited. It took a moment on all that dope, but he realized what was missing.

The lights were off again.

***

Quincy flexed his jaw. In and out and left and right as his eyelids fluttered, his eyes alternating between staring and drifting closed. His head nodded to his chest and bounced slowly back, over and over.

Was he awake or asleep? He didn't know. He'd reached a place chemically that he'd never been before. Sure, he'd done lots of dope in his day, but alcohol was his thing. Not wanting to be a pathetic junkie kept him from doing little more than social experimentation with heroin in the nineties, and a first-hand understanding of the physical draw of cocaine had kept him a safe distance from that vice. The occasional bump at a bar was it, and it was a long time since anyone had wanted his company enough to be that generous.

Suzy. Yeah, Suzy was the last one, and only a few times, at the very beginning of their relationship. Having to buy a useless drunk his drinks was one thing; having to pay for blow was another.

His face was numb and buzzing, and his apartment swam in a constellation of dingy yellow light that had never been gold until now. Junkie Dave smiled a mile wide, and his words spun through the air towards Quincy like jeweled birds.

WILLIAM HOLLOWAY

His thoughts bent and curved into purple and green glowing bubbles and he felt himself drifting, sinking into a deep abyss. Music played from somewhere. It had been Black Sabbath, but sounded more like Beethoven's Emperor Concerto now.

Quincy smiled, unsure if his lips moved, then laughed, unaware if it had made any sound, but he'd never cared less if the world heard his voice. Junkie Dave wouldn't care how clever it was that his mind turned Black Sabbath into Beethoven, and neither would the world or anyone in it. No one would ever appreciate how clever, how genius his hallucination was, but he didn't care. This wasn't a tragedy; this was the joy of melting.

The burden of knowing the world hated him, condemned him, was nothing in this place. The world was fallen and broken and just didn't get it the way he did, just didn't get him in the way they should.

There was no weight, no pain, no crushing hope.

There was only light . . .

Lights in the deep. Black lights. Green and purple. Gold and crimson, moving and waving and flowing around him, hot and cold.

And he didn't care.

It was beautiful. Terrible and comic, and tragedy and farce, a joke on him and the entire universe. And he had never cared less.

And he knew, he knew as his body fell into the deepest abyss, to the very bottom of the world. He showed the world and it showed him, and then he knew.

He was the world. He was the universe and the universe was him. Everything that could be and everything that couldn't, broken and perfect, and mattering not if it existed, because nothing mattered. Not here, definitely not here, and definitely not anywhere else.

The curtain rose before him and the play began. The question came to him how he got here. Wasn't he in his apartment? Why was he in this outdoor theater? Where was Junkie Dave?

Quincy smiled and the words, "Just let go," flowed through the deep waters of this abyss, and he was back in his apartment, but that was just a part of the theater as the lights came up and the actors floated in from stage left and right.

The forms were human, but nothing lived behind their eyes. They billowed and flapped as if they were nothing but human skins motivated by another form of locomotion. This was a play, performed by puppets that had given up on being people.

60

AMMONIA

A mother and father holding their adored infants. They jerked and twitched their joy at their creation, but the world had its evil way. He was afflicted and died, she knew nothing but poverty and pain, and the child was deformed.

It shrieked, and its screams fled out into the night, falling upon the deaf ears of a God that existed only to torment the mother and father with His deafness, His blindness, His unconcern.

More fathers and mothers followed, more children followed them to bear their own children, and soon the land was covered with their lives and their deaths. And they never understood why their instinct to live drew them on, mile after mile. On to nothing, on to nowhere.

Quincy saw these puppets build empires and cathedrals, only to see them burn and plagues claim their best and brightest, snatching defeat from victory at every turn.

And Quincy didn't care. He breathed in and out, slowly, ever more slowly until he saw the giant black eyes, the many arms of the puppeteers. They showed him, yes, they showed him that even futility did not exist.

Only pain.

And that it all ends in death.

That it is better to never have existed.

That it has always been this way.

That it would always be this way.

The sun would rise tomorrow, and set the same day, overlooking nothing.

And it would happen again and again and it would never mean anything.

Giant black eyes; many, many arms.

Blood and screaming and terror and agony.

It had happened before, the harvest, and it would happen again when the stars were right.

And right now, the stars were right.

***

For the first time in several years, Quincy awoke without a hangover, but this was worse in its own way. He remembered that girl, Gretchen was her name, who spoke in group therapy during one of his stints in rehab. She said she'd picked up the needle to quit drinking, that being strung out worked better than being a drunk.

At least it had worked better initially.

61

WILLIAM HOLLOWAY

This wasn't better.

Not at all.

Not even a little.

He was dope sick from doing too much smack, but needed more to get over the dope sickness. And the withdrawal from alcohol was the worst he'd ever experienced. Every time was worse than the last, but this time would be the last time. And he was sure that he would lose this fight.

The light through the shades was a blinding thing, even as the sun hid behind the ever-present clouds. Everything was wreathed in a razor-sharp nimbus of light, jagged shards to pierce his eyes and stab into his brain.

He rolled off his mattress and crashed to the floor, feeling like his bones were bruised and bleeding. He crawled and writhed to the toilet and heaved until he was sure his guts would erupt from his mouth. But nothing came out. He hadn't eaten since . . . since that fat bitch Luz Marie had insulted him so gravely.

His stomach groaned and flopped, unsure if it wished for sustenance or to eject anything he put in there.

But despite all of this pain, there was a feeling like a hand pushing him from behind, and a voice in his mind screaming to get out.

Get away.

Far away.

The mountains, the desert, anywhere but here.

Somewhere very high, somewhere very dry. Somewhere not touched by the event . . .

And what exactly had happened to the last day? Or was it days?

His eyes fell across Junkie Dave's backpack and darted over to the puncture marks on his arm. A new wave of nausea crashed over him. He'd been shooting dope with Junkie Dave and wasn't sure how long. And just like alcohol, heroin left everything a blur, with some places left completely blank.

Dave was gone, but his backpack was still here.

There would be dope in his bag.

Quincy felt cold slimy sweat begin to prickle his scalp and forehead. His hands shook so badly it would be difficult to even light a cigarette. He needed to level out to where his hands didn't shake and he could get some food to stay down.

He braced himself against the wall for the walk over to the bag, and his eyes settled on the little table. Somebody wrote in big black magic marker,

AMMONIA

"For You," with an arrow pointing to a black tarry ball atop a bit of weed in a small pipe.

Dave had loaded a bowl for him, complete with some black tar, before he left.

He picked up the pipe and smoked, and within seconds the world stopped spinning. The soundtrack of the entire world vomiting stopped its ceaseless torment.

He breathed. In. Out.

Air filled his lungs. It felt as if he hadn't breathed for decades.

Quincy looked at his hands. They were no longer shaking.

He heard a sound above him, a groaning of timbers and a dragging, shuffling, sliding sound. Something was up there in the crawl space, something very big and very heavy. Something that didn't move right, or something that moved very, very differently.

This was an old apartment building. It had been here before he'd moved to Austin in the early nineties. He'd lived in innumerable buildings just like it ever since. He knew the sounds they made: the pops, the cracks in wind and rain and heat and cold.

This was unlike any of those sounds.

The alarms in his head, although dulled by the dope, kept screaming for him to get out, get away, far away.

His hands were shaking again, and the breath hitched in his chest. The last days were a blur, but flashes of memory came to him. Empty houses with perfectly functional lights, but all turned off. All with the same lingering smell of ammonia. Empty streets, cars that hadn't been moved in days. An abandoned ambulance and a call to 911.

There was a bright yellow raincoat in the corner with EMS in bold, and a serious looking flashlight next to it, and an official-looking cell phone protruding from the pocket.

They'd seen a terrified cop examining that ambulance. He'd asked if they'd seen anyone. They'd said no, and he took off.

They'd called 911 from that phone, and they'd asked if they'd seen anyone. They'd said no, and they hung up on them.

Something had yanked the rear doors of that ambulance almost completely off. Something had leapt from the roof of that garage to the roof of the house, further than he could imagine anything leaping. Something that seemed to fade into the shadows themselves.

And last night . . . he'd dreamed.

Oh my God.

It was the story of us all, it was his story, it was the story of a pointless, terrified and painful existence rightfully extinguished.

He could no longer pretend; either he or this city had lost its mind. His brain was begging him, pleading with him to leave, just leave.

His mind returned to Junkie Dave's backpack. For all of his anarchic rants and indifference to the material, Quincy recalled something from the opiate blur of the night before.

Junkie Dave had tens of thousands of dollars in his backpack.

***

Natalie had heard other journalists describe airports around the country shutting down because too many employees had simply ceased coming to work. Like many unconfirmed stories, it smelled like bullshit, but right now she saw the truth of it. Why Austin Bergstrom International Airport was still open was anybody's guess.

Apparently only a few guys were unloading luggage, and they'd been pulling doubles for a few days now. Baggage claim was a scene from the fall of the Tower of Babel. Hundreds of people waiting for hours for baggage that came with no rhyme or reason.

She thought she'd bide the time by getting her rental car, only to discover that the rental agency closed, even though she'd pre-booked her car before leaving DC. Every single one of the other agencies was closed as well. She'd intercepted a hapless TSA agent only to discover that the story was the same; they were closed because there were simply not enough employees to run them.

He gave her a harried look and recommended the half-mile hike to the nearest hotel, to try the car rental agency tomorrow. And, so sorry, the shuttle to the hotel wasn't running because there was no one to drive the van.

Austin hadn't been hit with an earthquake or a tsunami, only flooding. Granted, the flooding was worse than had ever happened during Natalie's life, but none of this added up.

She saw a line of people queued up for taxis that weren't coming. She saw another line headed out into the rain, luggage in tow, for the hotel that would have been visible if not for the rain.

She wracked her brain, trying to remember her last flight into Austin. Yes, there was a big Hilton hotel that should have been visible from here, even in the rain. Were those people headed to a hotel with no power? Had people been stuck here that long? Were things really that bad?

AMMONIA

She watched the line fading out into the darkness, and a nameless chill crept up her spine.

There wasn't a chance in hell she was going to follow them. She looked at the hundreds lying on the floor, trying to sleep through to the next day when things would allegedly get better. Something told her this was a vain hope. Something else told her not to stick around to find out.

You've got to get out of here.

Natalie hadn't been to Austin in several years, hadn't spoken to anyone from Austin either. Sure, she kept in touch, wished happy birthdays and made all the right comments on social media, but that was about it.

She took a deep breath and started looking through the contacts on her cell phone. She tried one after another. No one answered. After she'd tried eight different numbers, leaving apologetic, pleading messages, involuntary tears flowed down her cheeks.

She was pregnant. She was here for an abortion because a man she was sleeping with (for all the wrong reasons) didn't give a shit about her.

And she didn't give a shit about him.

And now she was going to get on a table and let someone stick a tube inside her to kill her baby.

And she couldn't do that either, because she was stuck in this fucking airport.

Should she call Erwin?

He doesn't give a fuck about you.

Could she call her *abuela*, could she tell her what she was up against, could she tell her what she had done and why she had done it and what she was here to do?

She felt her forehead against cold concrete and realized she had buried her face in her elbow and was sobbing into a wall.

No one on earth had ever managed to fuck up to the degree that she had. No one . . .

"Natalie?"

She looked up and groaned, probably out loud. No one, with the possible exception of a very temporary boyfriend, Quincy.

***

"It's, ummm . . . right down this way." Quincy looked back to see if Natalie was still following, to find her shaking her head and glaring radioactively.

They walked the decline of the parking lot to where he hoped he'd parked the car. He was a bit hazy on that point. He hadn't taken a mental note of where he'd left the car, but it felt like he was going in the right direction.

"Slow the fuck down, I'm wearing heels." Natalie was frantically checking her cell phone again, going through the contacts, calling each number.

"Hey, uhhh . . . no problem, Nat, we're . . . " He paused to look around, the parking lot full of bright and new cars. He scanned up and down the rows, looking for Suzy's dilapidated Camry.

She stared down at her phone, muttering beneath her breath. "Okay, what kind of car is it? What are we looking for?"

He cleared his throat. "It's a, uhhh, yellow Camry. Yeah, yellow and . . . "

"Please tell me you know what kind of car you drive."

"Sure, sure, of course, it's a yellow Camry or Corolla."

She stopped, worry pasted across her face. "So you really don't know what kind of car you drive?"

A cold sweat of confusion began to form on his brow. "It's not actually my car, it's my girlfriend's, I mean ex-girlfriend's. I'm not actually sure where her and I stand right now."

"But you drove her car to the airport?"

He started walking, motioning for her to follow. "It's cool. We're cool. It's just a thing, you know?"

She started walking again. "I don't care. Just get me to that hotel over there. We'll talk about it some other time."

They both knew they wouldn't talk about it another time. They hadn't spoken in more than a decade, and her last words to him hadn't been kind or forgiving.

He looked down and nodded. "Yeah, cool."

He started walking, and she looked at his back. A momentary twinge of sympathy crossed her mind. He was helping, after all.

She followed, and he slowed so they could walk next to each other, a study in contrast: her a polished DC professional, he as disheveled and dirty as a person could be without being homeless. "So, explain this to me again. You drove up here to buy a ticket and get a flight somewhere? You didn't pre-book it?"

He nodded and kept walking, still scanning for Suzy's car. "Yeah, and not a single one of the airlines had a single person there to sell tickets."

"You know there are kiosks to just buy a ticket, right?"

He nodded again. "They don't take cash."

AMMONIA

She couldn't look more incredulous. "Who drives to the airport in the middle of the night to buy a ticket in cash and then wait for the flight? You're not selling drugs, are you?"

He laughed and shook his head. "No. Bad things happen to people who sell drugs."

Quincy stopped and sighed in relief, pointing to Suzy's beat up old yellow Camry. "There it is, finally!"

Her expression was the opposite of impressed.

She'd been so busy searching her phone for any alternative to going anywhere with Quincy, that she hadn't taken in the details of their surroundings. About every tenth car had its trunk open, some with luggage sitting right next to them, as if the owner just forgot about it. She'd never seen anything like it. "Quincy, did you not notice all of these open cars just sitting here like this?"

He paused, and she caught a glimpse of the confusion and fear behind his eyes.

"Quincy, are you running from something? Is it drugs?"

He didn't say anything; he just seemed to stare off into the distance.

"Look, Quincy, you know that I know you've had some drinking problems, but before I get into a car with you, I need to know if you're fucked up or what. Just tell me. I'll understand. But I need you to be honest with me."

His eyes grew wider and became focused. He opened the door, reached over and yelled, "Get in, get in now!"

He never stopped looking at that point off in the distance of the parking lot.

Natalie wrinkled her nose at the smell of the car, or maybe his smell. But she followed the line of his vision to that distant point in the garage.

And in that moment, a light went out in that far corner, and she heard a muffled shout echoing through the parking lot. And then another light was extinguished, and then another.

A bolt of fear shot up her spine, a kind of twisting fear she'd never experienced. She whispered, "Please go, Quincy. I want you to go, I want you to get me out of this parking lot. I don't want to be here anymore."

As they pulled out of the parking lot, they passed the attendant's booth, the glass shattered, the attendant missing.

***

It was less than a mile to the big round Hilton hotel, but no way to tell from inside Quincy's borrowed little yellow Camry. The rain came in sheets, cutting visibility down to a matter of feet. As they neared the hotel, they could see the comforting glow of the lights inside.

Natalie let go of the grip she only now realized she had on Quincy's arm. He let out a frightened little laugh. She let out a strained little laugh too as they pulled underneath the overhang and into the grand entrance area.

The pounding rain ceased, and she looked to him with a constellation of emotions crossing her face. She'd treated him dreadfully for being who he was, all the while doing nothing but trying to help her.

She looked into the sedate golden light of the lobby, wanting to flee Quincy and wrap herself in comfort and normalcy. But she needed to at least give him some kind of acknowledgement.

She smiled and put her hand on his forearm. "Thank you . . . thank you so much, Quincy. I know you didn't have to help me, and I've been a total fucking bitch. It's just that things have gotten so . . . "

"Fucked?"

She nodded. "Yeah. That pretty much sums it up."

He didn't say anything, he just looked down and nodded. "Yeah. Lemme pop the trunk."

They got her bags to the curb, and she smiled awkwardly. She didn't want to walk into that lobby with him. He looked like a homeless person or a junkie, or both, and he probably was.

She shook her head. *Who the fuck have I become?*

He spoke first. "Just hear me out. Some things around town have been more than a little off. I'm gonna walk in there with you, even though I know you'd rather I didn't."

Natalie began to shake her head, denying the obvious, but he put up a hand to continue.

"I get it. I look like stir-fried shit and I sound . . . fucking crazy. But just indulge me this one thing."

She nodded, obviously not feeling it. "Okay, Quincy, that's very chivalrous and all that."

He grabbed her bags and wheeled them in. The sliding doors hissed smoothly, and they were hit by a wall of stately air conditioning. Quincy stopped dead in his tracks.

Natalie's own internal radar went off, and a cold bolt of fear gripped her guts. In spite of herself, she whispered, "What is it, Quincy?"

AMMONIA

His voice shook. "Do you smell that?"

She nodded, unclear on what had frightened him, and involuntarily frightened her too. "Yeah, that's bad. It's like they just mopped the entire lobby with ammonia."

He took a tentative step, then another, and she followed. The lobby was beautiful, wreathed in a golden light, with soaring staircases and gleaming silver elevators. Tasteful and understated jazz wafted through the air.

But there was no one there. Not behind the counter, not on the sumptuous couches, not at the adjacent bar. Several large potted plants were knocked over; one of the couches was on its side.

Natalie stepped over to the check-in counter. Her breath hitched in her chest.

No one.

She rang the little silver bell, and its sound filled the air, so much that they looked up to see the balconies of expensive rooms and suites looking down on them.

But no people.

Empty. Completely empty.

This hotel should be packed, especially given what they'd seen at the airport. Where the hell were all those people they'd seen hiking from the terminal through the rain? They should be here. This lobby should be full of people.

Then they heard it. A single long scream from far above them, cut off.

Then the lights went out.

The ambient jazz music stopped.

Even the background hum of the air conditioning ceased its relentless drone, and they stood in complete silence and darkness.

They ran.

They strained at the sliding doors, then fumbled with the car doors, their hands shaking from a primordial, airless fear.

The drive took them back past the terminal. The lights were off there too, and the backup lights had come on. The rain was too heavy to see what was happening inside, but they saw the tiny, feeble backup lights extinguishing one at a time. In seconds, it was completely black, save for their headlights.

They drove past the passenger drop-off, completely vacant as well, where it had been crowded with hundreds of people just a short time before.

The only thing left was a handful of cars idling at the curb, their doors open to the rain, no one inside.

***

Juanita Castellanos lived on Holly Street, and had since Natalie could remember. She'd played in the little front yard and in the street with all the neighbor kids. She'd gone to the little elementary school right around the corner. Over the years the area had gradually changed complexion from a Hispanic family neighborhood to one exclusively populated by vulgar white trust funders.

Her *abuela*'s house now stood out like a sore thumb. She was a tight-fisted woman and wasn't ever going to waste money on an expensive car or, even worse, on the faux-legit trappings of the new urban bourgeoisie. Her twenty-year-old Dodge Ram sat in the tiny driveway, still in the drizzling rain.

Natalie's grip on Quincy's arm hadn't loosened since they turned down Riverside onto Pleasant Valley. He'd told her that the last few days had been off, that people were missing, but she hadn't been prepared for this.

Even after the sanity reducing experience at the airport, she hadn't been prepared for this. At the airport they hadn't actually seen anything, just an absence of people where there should have been crowds, but what she felt down to her bones here was no mere absence. This was a presence. Of what, she didn't know. But she could feel it, and even more so, she could *smell* it.

She could look up to the lights of the buildings on the west side of Interstate 35, but on this side of the freeway, every light inside every house was off. The only lights were the streetlights, and lights outside of houses.

She wondered for a moment what those people in those tall buildings thought when they looked down and saw only darkness.

Her *abuela*'s house was pitch black.

She stared straight ahead and cleared her throat. "Quincy, what am I going to see when I go in there?"

He nodded, paused, and nodded again. "The lights will turn on. It will smell like ammonia. For some reason the tub will be full, but your grandma will be gone."

She cleared her throat again. "Where is she?"

He shook his head.

She turned to look at him. "What does that mean, Quincy? What the fuck does that mean?"

A tear formed in the corner of his eye. "I thought I was losing it, I thought it was all some kind of alcoholic . . . breakdown. But you're real, you're not like Junkie Dave. You're seeing this too."

She stared for a moment and blurted, "You're fucking nuts . . . " But the invective trailed off. Her eyes stared into his and registered the ugly truth. What she'd seen was no hallucination, unless she was sharing a mind with a guy she hadn't seen in years.

Something was happening. Something enormous. Something apart from the earthquakes and tsunamis. Something apart from the event.

Natalie sat staring straight forward, but didn't reach for the door handle.

After a few moments Quincy whispered, "Do you want me to go knock on the door?"

Tears fell down her face and a stifled sob escaped her throat. She nodded, ever so slightly.

Quincy took a deep breath, grabbed the big flashlight they'd stolen from the ambulance, and walked up the little path to Natalie's childhood home. He steeled himself, then knocked on the front door.

Natalie watched the door swing open and saw the black chasm inside. The tears fell freely now as she watched him cover his nose with his shirt and walk inside. She saw the beam flitting through the windows, then fade away as he walked towards the back of the house. A few moments later he came back out, the constant drizzle pasting his hair to his forehead.

He got in the car, but didn't look at her.

He didn't need to.

They drove away.

***

"We've got one cook, and I'm apparently the waitress tonight." She looked terrible. But no one in Austin had seen the sun in days, so it was understandable. She turned and pointed to a table about halfway to the back of the restaurant.

"That one is clean. I'm . . . sorry about the mess but we're really, really short-staffed. Go sit. I gotta run." And she was off to the kitchen.

Quincy and Natalie walked to their appointed table. Every other table on the way there was piled with dirty dishes. Apparently there was no bus boy or dishwasher, either.

There were a few tables with people at them, but nothing of the boisterous crowds that should fill Stars Café. They sat in ones and twos and only looked up from their food to cast around furtive glances. They looked every bit as terrible as the hostess-turned-waitress: hair soaked and disheveled, clothes damp and sticking to grey pasty skin. They looked like refugees.

That was the term that came back over and over as Natalie cast her gaze around the restaurant. *These people are refugees, and I became one of them the second I stepped off that plane.*

She looked over to Quincy. He was holding a hand up, watching it shake, forgetting that she was seated across from him. When he looked up, an expression of shame crossed his face, then a moment of frustrated anger. He exhaled loudly, looked around, took out a cigarette and lit up.

Natalie gasped. It wasn't the 80s or the 90s anymore, and Austin had zero tolerance for cigarette smoke.

"Quincy . . . what the fuck are you thinking?" But then she looked around. A few other diners were lighting up, expressions of relief at the first big exhale of smoke.

The hostess/waitress made a beeline for their table. "Gimme one. No one rides free."

Natalie scoffed, and the waitress rolled her eyes. "This place is ordinarily a cop hangout. At least one table full of cops. I haven't seen a single one in fucking days."

She shrugged and exhaled, then looked out the window to the empty interstate highway, at the single car at the stoplight in front of the restaurant. "I don't know if cops are a thing anymore."

Quincy nodded. "I saw one the other day. He looked . . . bad. Asked us if we'd seen anyone else since we left my place. We said no and he took off."

The waitress shook her head. "Migas. We got migas and that's it. You guys want migas?"

They both nodded and she walked away.

Natalie closed her eyes and shook her head. "This whole thing has done a big number on my head." She nodded, eyes closed, and continued. "I'm gonna take care of business and get the fuck out of this city. Go back to my life. Go back to normalcy. Go back to sanity. Get away from this . . . whatever this is."

Quincy nodded. "Yeah."

She scowled at him. "Yeah? That's all you've got to say?"

He looked apprehensive, even cowed, but he spoke up anyways. "We drove up Pleasant Valley. Took Manor up to Dean Keeton. I don't think I saw a single house with a light on inside till we crossed MLK."

AMMONIA

She grabbed the pack of smokes and lit up, loathing printed on her face. "They evacuated. The cops must've told them to turn off the lights on the way out."

He shrugged, and the waitress brought them their plates. At least migas were fast. He asked her, "Were the people south of here evacuated because of the flooding?"

She stopped and stared off into space. "No. There were some evacuations in New Braunfels, but there's no more place to put evacuees in Dallas, so they told people to stay put and . . . *go about their lives*. Brave new world, eh?"

She looked back out the window at the car still sitting at the stoplight in front of the restaurant. "That light changes every three minutes. I timed it one night. That car has been sitting at that light and hasn't moved at all in about twenty minutes. And the passenger side door is sitting open in the rain. I don't think there's anyone in that car."

Natalie rolled her eyes and continued shoveling food. "Fascinating."

The waitress gave her a look, then gave one to Quincy. He shrugged. She walked away.

Quincy tried not to regard Natalie like she was a complete bitch, but wasn't hiding it well. She put down her fork, took a drag and looked at him. "I'm going to stay at the hotel here behind the restaurant. Thanks for everything you've done. But after we eat I need to . . . I need to be alone."

He nodded. They might be sitting together at a restaurant in Austin, but they were worlds apart.

***

"Yes, ma'am, I understand, and we can take you in tomorrow. Due to all of the flooding, we're really short-staffed, so the doctor won't be in till 4 PM. We can take you in at that time and the procedure can be done at 6."

Natalie nodded, taking a drag from the smokes she'd swiped from Quincy at the restaurant. He hadn't seemed to care, so lost in his head that he'd barely acknowledged when she stood up to leave.

She left a twenty on the table and walked out, stopping by his car and lugging her shit across the parking lot to the hotel.

She looked in the mirror and wondered if he was still at that table staring at his half-eaten dinner. She didn't want to feel sorry for him, but she did. She'd treated him like shit. She'd treated him like he'd caused her problems, rather than helping her when no one else was around to do so.

The face in the mirror wasn't smiling back. It judged her. It judged who she'd become. It judged why she was here in the first place. It judged . . .

Her brow furrowed at the part that still made the least sense. Why on earth was Quincy there in the middle of the night to fly somewhere, apparently anywhere? Why didn't he have any luggage? Why was he wanting to pay in cash?

She closed her eyes and shook her head. Why should she care what a person like Quincy did? He was a barely functional alcoholic. Even when she'd known him years ago, he was hanging on by a thread.

After she'd told him she was leaving, he became practically catatonic, then asked the waitress for a pen and wrote down his phone number on a napkin. She'd politely muttered some kind of thanks, but he knew she would just throw it away.

Had that loser somehow managed to fall in love with her? Were freaky phenomena and mass flooding somehow a romantic cue for him?

She whispered to the mirror, "Fucking idiot . . . "

She looked at the clock. 1 AM.

She walked to the little sink and ran water over the stinking cigarette. She hadn't smoked in years. This was a non-smoking hotel, but she didn't give a fuck. This city had bigger problems than one uppity cigarette smoker.

Her eyes closed as her head hit the pillow, and another tear squeezed from the corner of her eye. Was Quincy really such a garbage person that she could judge him and throw him away? What made her worth preserving and him so disposable?

Maybe a pretty face?

For all of her accomplishments, what had brought her here? Had she betrayed herself? Or was that just window dressing to hide the truth, that she was only a pretty face and nothing more? Maybe there was nothing there to betray. Maybe she'd gone through the motions, said the magic words, and this was her great reward, to slog through a flooded waste of a city to abort her baby.

Maybe it was a mercy.

***

Natalie sprang from the hotel bed and landed on the floor. Whatever that sound was, her sleeping mind categorized it as *wrong*, and ejected her from a black dream of writhing sweat and nauseous sight. It had been a world where everything was a dripping, bleeding, shitting orifice that birthed more of the same.

Then she heard it again. A thump against her door, and then another.

Fists. Someone was pounding on her door.

AMMONIA

A man's voice cried out in hysteria. "You! You are so beautiful! You alone amongst the stars! You alone in the deep and the dark! You alone amongst the stars!"

A deranged man was beating on her door, and unless her ears were failing her, he was fucking chanting.

"You alone amongst the stars! You alone in the deep and the dark! You alone amongst the stars! You alone amongst the stars! You alone in the deep and the dark! You alone amongst the stars!"

Natalie crept on all fours to the door and slid up against it, extending her legs to brace against the bed frame. She risked a quick peak through the peephole and slid the chain lock in place.

It was a soaking, filthy homeless man. Bearded, bleary.

From down in the parking lot she heard a police siren whoop once, twice, then a mechanical and staticky-sounding voice: "Step away from the . . . "

Then she heard a loud car-crashing sound and some sort of screeching, hissing *thing*.

And then it got much worse.

She'd heard this sound before, when she went to Iraq. Fully automatic gun fire. Not an AK. Definitely not an AK. An M4. She'd learned the distinct difference between the sounds. One was the good guys, one was the bad guys.

This was the good guys. But this good guy wasn't firing the short, controlled bursts associated with disciplined American soldiers. This sounded like a panicked Iraqi guerilla. They just pulled the trigger and held it until the magazine was empty.

This wasn't the practiced, efficient aspect of a trained American cop.

This was a person firing out of terror.

He emptied the magazine in seconds.

He slapped in another one and emptied that magazine too.

Then there was the squeal of tires, and then silence.

After several minutes, Natalie peeked through the blinds. Her homeless man wandered the parking lot. There was no movement beyond that. And that cop was gone.

***

Erwin had taught her about taking risks for the big story, but Natalie was pretty sure he'd be screaming if he could see her now. She nodded her head. *Yeah, you're crazy.* But then she shook her head. *I'm not half as crazy as what I'm looking at right now. And it's that fucking smell again too.*

Ammonia. Overpowering ammonia. Like she'd opened a bottle of that nasty shit and stuck her nose right in it.

The rain had come and gone, just like it always did now, and the lights reflected off the glistening blacktop of the parking lot, but that rain hadn't been enough to clear out the smell of ammonia.

And the rain couldn't do anything to conceal the obviousness of what she was viewing.

The cop had pulled into the parking lot, probably to chase off the homeless guy, but then something went completely off the rails. She squatted down and picked up the brass and held it up to the lights.

.223 full metal jacket. Standard issue for police and military in the Western world.

She turned around to the empty feeder of I-35 and heard the sporadic traffic up on I-35 itself. She visualized the cop pulling in, saw him in her mind's eye talking on the loudspeaker, but couldn't fill in the blanks for the rest, even though several cars in the parking lot were thoroughly ventilated with automatic weapons fire.

The homeless guy obviously wasn't the target, because he was still wandering door to door, pounding away. "You alone amongst the stars! You alone in the deep and the dark!"

Apart from him, she was completely alone in this parking lot. Sixty-odd rounds capped off not ten minutes ago, and she was completely alone. There should be a hundred cop cars and helicopters with searchlights. The SWAT team should be here. But apart from an occasional car whizzing by on the interstate, it was just her and the homeless guy. No looky-loos from the other hotel rooms, no furtive eyes behind the blinds.

She stood beneath the skyline of Austin, lights on in the big buildings, and she wondered again what it would look like from up there. What would they see? Quincy had mumbled something earlier about not seeing a single light in any house until they got north of MLK.

She walked across the parking lot to the little reception area for the hotel. Earlier there was a snotty hipster girl with a tacky chest tattoo above her tits to give her the keys. Now, nothing but knocked over plants and touristy magazines on the floor.

And that fucking smell.

Exactly like they'd smelled at the bigger and much nicer hotel at the airport.

AMMONIA

Exactly like they'd smelled before an animal terror sent them running out past the vacant terminal, where lights winked out one at a time . . .

She walked back to the hotel. She walked door to door and knocked, but no one answered. A few just swung open to reveal empty rooms, but no people.

Natalie swallowed hard. She'd been in actual terrifying situations before. She'd seen war up close as a journalist. The same sort of perspiration that had clung to her brow then had formed now.

She walked out of the little hotel lobby and back to the restaurant. There was no one there either. No one in front, no one in the kitchen. The grills were still hot, and the only reason the smell of ammonia wasn't overpowering back there was the food burning on them.

She turned them off one at a time, then fished through her pocket for the number Quincy gave her.

"Natalie." He didn't sound surprised, only frightened.

"How long did you stay at the restaurant after I left?"

"Couple minutes. That's about it."

"Did you go home?"

"Yeah, I'm at my place now. Do you need me to come get you?"

She paused, inhaled and exhaled. "Yeah. Please. And please hurry." She looked around; never had an empty restaurant seemed so utterly alien or terrifying. "I don't think it's safe. I think . . . I know it's not safe."

She heard him breathing, and a jangle of keys. "Okay, I'm heading there. What room are you in?"

"I'm not waiting in that fucking room. I'll be in the hotel lobby. I'm locking the doors."

She could see him nodding his head in her mind. "Probably fifteen minutes."

She screwed up her face into a fury and shook her head angrily. Relying on a moron like Quincy was maddening. Him being right in some way was worse. "Aren't you even going to ask why?"

He paused. "No. I think I know, but I'd be a crazy person if I spoke it out loud."

She laughed, but she didn't smile while she did it. "What do you think I'm looking at right now?"

She heard him stop in his tracks. "You're looking at nothing. You're looking at nothing but empty space."

"I've never seen nothing before."

"I don't think it's ever existed before."

Natalie heard his door and the shuffle of feet descending apartment stairs, then a car door, then the engine wheeze and turn over. She sighed loudly in relief. She hadn't even considered what would happen if his piece of shit car wouldn't start. Probably call a cab, but something told her there weren't any more cabs.

"Can you hear me, Quincy?"

"Yeah, I'm going as fast as I can in the rain with this car, which just isn't very fast."

"That's not your car." Not a question, but not really a statement either.

"Yeah, Suzy. It's her car. I don't think . . . " He stopped mid-thought.

"You don't think what, Quincy?"

He cleared his throat, and over the cell phone she could hear the car cutting though puddles, and the slap of the wipers. "Okay, I'll ask, and I want you to try to be straight with me, Nat. What got you spooked?"

He could hear her anger on the other side, anger that came from not knowing, and not knowing what she didn't know.

He nodded, held the wheel and lit a cigarette while holding the phone in the crook of his neck. "You don't have to answer that, Nat. I'd have a really hard time answering that too." He paused, then finished his thought. "I just lit a cigarette that I didn't pay for. I was just about to hit my third beer from a case I didn't pay for, either."

He let that hang in the air between them for a moment.

She let out an angry, nervy little laugh. Her voice quivered. "I don't know why you're telling me that."

"I'm just about to cross 12th Street, just so you know. Still no lights in a single one of these fucking houses. Streetlights, but nothing else. In my neck of the woods, all of the streetlights are broken now, too."

"So?"

"No people, not a fucking one, but someone broke every single goddam streetlight. No cats, no dogs, no lights."

Natalie didn't say anything. Something about the enormity of the absence of was squeezing her chest. "That's because the cats and dogs are all inside."

"Could be. Maybe so. I've gone to the little Habeeb store on my street every day now for three days straight. I've grabbed smokes and beer and left an IOU on the counter for my friend Raj."

Her voice shook even more. "Okay, why are you telling me this, Quincy?"

AMMONIA

"I turned up 12th to Chicon. There should be a hundred crackheads here, even in the fucking rain. I'm almost up on the feeder now."

She breathed another, louder, sigh of relief. He could feel her tension and shapeless fear. "I keep asking you why you're telling me this and you never say why, Quincy." There was a noticeable lack of anger to her voice as it took on a pleading tone.

He took a drag on his cigarette and blew out, hard. "I'm telling *you* this so you don't have to tell *me* this. You're smart and you got your shit together. You'd never be able to say it out loud without talking yourself out of it on the way."

She didn't say anything.

"I'm just going to blow right through this light here at Dean Keaton. Tell me why I'm totally okay doing that, Natalie."

Her voice fell to a whisper. "There's no cops that far south."

He cleared his throat. "Yeah, that's why. But the real thing is to ask why that's why. I'm just a few blocks away now."

"I don't think there's going to be any cops as far south as I am now anymore, either."

"Why do you say that?"

"Where are you?" she asked.

"Pulling up right now."

***

Blackness. Complete and utter blackness.

Natalie had never seen the world so dark before. Her mind raced for a point of reference and took her to the time she toured the caves near New Braunfels during a school field trip. She didn't recall much, but did remember that the tour guide told them all to stand very still, and he turned out the lights.

Blackness, complete and utter blackness.

That's what this felt like, even if she could turn to look to the skyline of Austin. Modern, gleaming glass buildings, a veritable citadel of light.

She could see it, but it did nothing to illuminate what lay around her.

And Quincy was right. Sometime since they'd gone to her *abuela*'s house, someone had broken every single streetlight. Every light in every house was off, and now there wasn't even the cold comfort of streetlights.

The breath in her chest shook, and left with a quaver in her throat.

She had run to his car and jumped in the passenger seat, gasping, "Go, go, just go . . ."

Quincy hadn't needed any more motivation. He hit the gas and they were out of that hotel parking lot, that terrible empty restaurant in the rearview mirror. Terrible, empty and silent, save for the alien reek of ammonia.

He floored it up the feeder to 38 1/2 Street and ran the red light, heading west. The contrast was instant and immediate. Practically every house had lights on inside. They even passed a man in a raincoat trying to walk a dog that stymied his every step by facing east and howling.

They turned south on Red River. "We need to go downtown." Natalie pointed to the black glassy block of the Omni hotel.

In the parking lot of the LBJ Library, they saw the first column of armored vehicles. Quincy had seen these things in news reports about the Middle East wars, but didn't know what they were called. Eight giant wheels and a confident-looking soldier manning a giant machine gun.

Nothing about these soldiers had the first thing to do with flood relief. Quincy and Natalie glanced at one another, but neither said a word. Everything in their lives had flown off the rails. This was just one more point in the alien constellation.

As they continued down Red River, the contrast between the east and west sides of the freeway couldn't have been plainer. Here was a living city, albeit flooded, albeit in the middle of the night, but still very much alive. They drove past bars and nightclubs that appeared to be mostly empty, but were open nonetheless. Life had returned to something like normalcy on the West Side.

They were pulling into the Omni hotel when Natalie breathed through gritted teeth, "Goddam it. Fuck."

Quincy looked to her, the concern on his face notching upwards.

She shook her head. "I don't have my wallet. No credit cards. Nothing. It's all back at that fucked-up hotel behind the restaurant."

He nodded and swallowed hard. "Everything is back at my apartment. I've got cash, I'll just need to go get it."

She looked at him. Uncertainty.

He nodded and put up his hands. "It's not like that." He let out a scared little laugh. "After this day, it definitely isn't like that."

She was still uncertain.

He nodded. "If you want . . . you can wait here, in the lobby. I'll bring money, you can get a room and call me tomorrow."

She laughed and shook her head. "Stress, man, stress. I'm scared. I don't even know what I'm scared of. I haven't seen a thing. I don't think you've seen a thing either. Just a fucked-up situation and lots of people not where they're supposed to be."

He shook his head ever so slightly. "Go on, I'll be back in a bit."

She flipped down the little visor and looked at herself. No makeup. Hair gone wild from sleep and rain, random t-shirt and flip-flops. Her pajama ensemble.

Suddenly she felt absolutely absurd.

"No, I'm going to go with you to your apartment and make myself presentable. You get your wallet and your cash. Then we'll come back here. And I *will* be paying you back for this."

Natalie laughed. "And you're still sleeping on the couch, buddy."

***

As they drove south down the feeder of I-35, the rain began again in earnest, and as they crossed the freeway going down Cesar Chavez, the world became a black tunnel lit only by feeble headlights.

Natalie's confidence went back to zero. Laughing at nightmares was easy in the light. She pressed back into her seat and reached for the pack of smokes on the dashboard. A prayer from her childhood came whispering. "Hail Mary, full of grace, the Lord is with thee . . . "

Not a single streetlight. Not a single light in any house.

At 1st and Chicon, Quincy slowed. The ambulance was still there.

He muttered, "That's been sitting there for at least two days now."

Natalie continued her silent prayer.

***

As they approached Caney Street, he angled to the left. A familiar shape sat in the middle of the street, door open in the rain, no lights inside. It said *Luz Marie's Tacos* in bold festive print on the side.

***

Natalie looked to him.

Quincy sat staring straight ahead, slowing to a stop next to the little white truck. He reached for the door handle, and Natalie grabbed his arm. "It's pouring out there, Quincy."

He exhaled hard. "I know her. She's a . . . friend of mine."

He turned to her, and she looked skeptical. "A friend?"

He didn't answer; he just opened the door into the driving rain. He looked back to Suzy's little yellow car and Natalie's scared face through the window, then flipped on the powerful flashlight. The truck was empty, the inside completely soaked. It had been sitting open to the elements for a long time now. He put his hand on the hood. Ice cold. This hadn't happened recently.

Even in the roaring rain he heard the rumble, and turned to face north to see the blaring lights a few street corners to the north. Something was heading down 5th Street, parallel to Cesar Chavez.

He ran to the car and jumped in, soaking wet.

Natalie saw it too; she was already pointing in that direction. He reached down and turned off the light, then cut the engine.

It was another group of those gigantic armored vehicles. Natalie breathed, "They're called Strykers. Armored personnel carriers."

Two men were atop each one, running powerful searchlights over everything. They counted three, then a fourth turned down Caney. Natalie grabbed his shoulders and pulled him down, hiding them from the soldier's line of sight.

He hadn't been expecting that. "What? What are you doing, Natalie?"

She hissed, "They shoot looters."

Quincy started to protest. "But I'm not a . . . " He didn't finish that thought. If they shot first and asked questions later, it wouldn't matter.

The metal behemoth slowly trundled past them as they held their breath, the beam of the searchlight stabbing through the car. Nat grabbed his hand, and they both instinctively squeezed their eyes shut until the sound of the armored giant safely receded. They peeked over the seats to watch it crossing Cesar Chavez, pressing southward.

Quincy's hands shook, and he whispered, "We'll take the alleys."

He started the car and felt Nat's hand on his. He looked over to her confused face.

"Quincy . . . why would they bring out those things to deal with looters? That thing's for fighting World War Three, not whatever this . . . *thing* is."

He winced. He hadn't thought about it that way, but he was a looter. The flashlight, cell phone, and raincoat were all stolen from that derelict ambulance. Avoiding getting shot for looting became the single focus of his mind as they splashed through the waterlogged alleys.

Then they both saw it.

A form darted in front of them. It didn't run, but rather seemed to extend across the alley, then snap across, too fast to even approximate its shape.

AMMONIA

If it had one.

Too fast to register, and blurred to the point of being practically invisible. The only sense they got was that of size. Bigger around than their car, and thirty feet long.

Natalie screamed.

Quincy tried to scream, but only a wheezing came. His foot slammed on the brakes and the car jolted to a halt.

Nothing in front, but Quincy threw it into reverse as the wheels squealed in the mud and they lurched backwards. Right towards another formless blur snapping across the alley to their rear.

He slammed the brakes again, and they lurched back in the direction they'd been heading.

Natalie faced to the rear. "There's another one! And another!"

Quincy saw one, then two, then more passing in front, illuminated for a split second, then gone. To the rear was the same story. Something, *some things* they couldn't visually grasp were heading north en masse.

He slammed on the brakes yet again, but this migration of shadows was over before it had begun. They were alone again, hyperventilating. Natalie's nails dug into his arm in a primitive grasp for security.

They saw strobing flashes, then the unreal grinding of automatic cannon fire. A river of tracer rounds flew over the houses, turning one ahead of them to a cloud of splinters.

Dirt, fragments, mud, and steam rained down on them.

More flashes, then a series of booms, and more debris splashed down around them.

And then it was completely silent.

Quincy didn't wait. He floored it and the wheels spun a trench into the mud, finally catching and sending the little yellow car lurching forward, until they passed the place where a house had been before cannon fire turned it into so much confetti.

Their eyes registered this for seconds as they bounced into the next cross street. They saw two Strykers stock-still in the rain, and in the other direction saw the Stryker that passed them earlier retreating, in reverse, westward. The hatches closed, the big lights—and big gun—on top missing, seemingly *torn* away.

The smell of ammonia was so thick their eyes watered.

They skidded into another cross street, the battle—or whatever they'd witnessed—behind them now. No words, just terrified breath and shaking hands as they plunged through the silence and darkness of rushing water and lashing rain.

***

"Are you sure the power's on over here?"

Quincy nodded, his pulse still racing. "Yeah, but like I said, someone or . . . Someone took out the streetlights last night."

Their whispers were a foreign thing in this place. They sat in Suzy's little yellow Camry, in the same spot it had occupied before. Here he was again, and none of the other cars in the parking lot had moved. Nothing had moved, save the currents of black water swirling through the streets.

"I'll bet that gun hasn't moved either."

"You didn't say anything about a gun."

"So much has happened, none of it makes sense."

She sighed, exhaling hard. "And you didn't want to sound crazy."

Quincy squeezed his eyes shut and saw the pounding of his heart behind the lids. "I'm not crazy. This is really happening." A pathetic sob escaped, and he shook his head. "I wish I was crazy. I always wanted it to be the world's fault and not mine, but it was always my fault. "

"Quincy, where's that gun?"

He laughed a little maniacal laugh and sobbed again. "But this time? It's not me, it's not my fault, it's not something I did or didn't do, and it has fuck all to do with the fact that I'm a piece of shit drunk! It's real, and it's really happening."

"Gun, Quincy. Where's the gun?"

He turned and looked at her, his eyes red and tear-swollen. He'd poured out his heart and she hadn't heard a single word. Such was the way of the world when a man confessed in good faith. She was a million miles away, completely uninterested in his truth.

"Quincy. Come back to me, Quincy. Where's the fucking gun?"

He came back, he shook his head. He cleared his throat. "Sorry, it's probably over this way unless the rain washed it away."

He opened the car door into the torrent, and she followed. He pointed the beam into the rushing water and found the pistol just a few feet from where he'd left it.

He hesitated, pointing down. "I didn't want to pick it up. You know, like a crime scene."

He looked at her and she looked at him, two strangers shivering in the rain.

AMMONIA

She grabbed it, sliding out the magazine to check if any rounds remained. There were about four left. Satisfied, she turned back to Quincy. "Let's get that fucking money and get the fuck out of this goddam place."

They walked back and climbed the stairs to his apartment.

As he flipped on the light, they were greeted by a familiar voice.

"Hi, Quincy. And . . . " The voice laughed. "Seriously?   Natalie? Well, this is some bad timing!"

Natalie screamed and nearly emptied Dave's head, but the safety was on.

No one spoke, and their pained breathing filled the ugly void of sound.

Dave broke the silence. "That right there? That was some terrifying shit. Or would have been. Not sure. What do you think, Quince?"

Quincy let out a silly groan of pent-up stress and fear. "You fuck. What the fuck are you doing here?"

Natalie still had the gun pointed at Dave. She hissed, "The fuck is this guy, Quincy?"

He blew out another pained breath. "This . . . this is . . . "

Dave finished for him. "David McMaster. Junkie Dave to the great unwashed, but I guess we're all taking a bath now, right, guys?"

Natalie lowered the gun and slumped against the wall. A terrified sobbing wracked her chest. She squeezed her eyes shut, but tears flowed down her cheeks. "I nearly shot him. I nearly shot him. I nearly shot this guy. Please let's just go. I don't give a fuck about your roommate. Please."

Dave laughed out loud. "I suppose I'm supposed to be hurt! Or dead, I guess, but I digress."

He stood and bowed in an exaggerated way. "I'm Dave McMaster. I think you were my girlfriend for about a week in middle school. I had a pretty impressive kick flip for a guy that age."

She didn't hear his words. "Quincy, we're going. Now. Get the fucking money and get me the fuck out of here!"

Dave flashed a put-upon smile. "This is pretty fuckin' awkward, Quince."

Quincy barely whispered, "The money is . . . Dave's"

Natalie didn't say a word. She just stared out into space, completely checked out.

Quincy cleared his throat and nodded. "Dave. Please. Fucking please. She's terrified. We just witnessed . . . "

He couldn't complete his sentence, so Dave finished for him. "A battle.

Sound and fury, signifying the end of our tenure? An eviction notice? A court summons from a higher power?"

"Dave, please just let me take some of that money and go. I don't know if you understand this, but we're in . . . it's really fucking dangerous. If those soldiers or . . . those . . . whatever those things are . . . "

Dave steepled his fingers, feigning a composed interest. "Go on, this is fascinating. You were speaking of some sort of 'whatever.' Please continue."

Quincy looked to Dave and then to Natalie. "I'll fucking say it. *There's something out there.* Something that took all these goddam people!"

Dave nodded and blew out a big exhale and looked to the ceiling for a moment, then looked back. "Quincy, oh Quincy. This is bad. Now you're seeing things. You switched from booze to smack and now you're hallucinating. We should get you to the bughouse for your own protection."

Natalie, still completely checked out, whispered, "There are no more insane asylums."

Dave beamed. "We've been saved! Hallelujah! Free at last!"

Quincy shook his head. "Dave, you're fucking nuts. You've always been nuts, but now you've completely lost your goddam mind. Half of this fucking city is empty now. There's not a single fucking person between here and 38th Street. They. Are. All. Fucking. Gone!"

Dave took a more serious tone, and nodded. "Yes, I know. I've been a less than sterling example of civic-mindedness, but we need to discuss . . . "

Natalie screamed and raised the gun. "Fuck you, you fucking piece of shit!"

Quincy was paralyzed, Natalie furious, but Dave simply motioned with his hand. "Nat, you're going to have to take the safety off if you want to shoot me."

She stood there agape, but didn't try to figure out the safety.

Dave continued. "All change is difficult, but you guys are adapting so very well! Our god will see this. Birthing pains, so to speak, I guess except in *Natalie's* case."

She reached over with her left hand and began probing for the safety on the gun in her right. He kept speaking. "The Rapture of the Deep, the beginning of a new era for our world. A comeuppance for a species that wasn't supposed to do much but swing through the trees."

There was a click as she found the safety. "But we will be in a better place, a glorious non-existence. And the gift you carry for our gods will . . . "

The sound was deafening.

AMMONIA

She hadn't spoken since they ran out into the blackness and rain. Not a word through flooded streets, nothing as they checked into the hotel and Quincy guided her into the gleaming glass elevator and their sumptuous room, twelve stories above the world.

Quincy looked down into the black void that was the East Side.

He watched as tiny streetlights winked out and the carpet of lightlessness rolled northward, eclipsing everything as far north as 38th.

On one side of the freeway was light and life, on another was darkness and death.

He saw a column of armored vehicles snaking up Red River, all the crossings to the East Side blocked, enormous searchlights probing eastward into the void.

The armored vehicles rolled up just as they crossed the freeway at Cesar Chavez. The ashen-faced soldiers glanced at them, then waved them through. Who they were and what they knew was of no consequence.

Quincy looked north and saw that the soldiers blocked southbound traffic on the freeway, and the last few cars plowed through the rain, leaving the lanes empty. The same thing must have happened far to their south, as the traffic heading north abruptly ceased, leaving I-35 completely empty.

He looked to the southeast, to where the airport lay in the distance. He watched, and he waited, but no planes came and no planes left.

He watched a Chinook helicopter, carrying an enormous chandelier of lights, hover above Town Lake. He watched as a truck tire launched from the north shore and bashed into the side of the helicopter, sending it into a dizzying spin until it dropped the enormous lights and raced away.

He saw a burst of lights—tracer rounds—fly in the direction the truck tire came from, then nothing more.

Natalie, sitting on the bed, was catatonic.

He kneeled in front on her and took her hands, but she didn't move.

He took his hands back and looked at them. They were shaking again.

The mini bar was right there, and money was no object, because he had Dave's backpack. But Dave's backpack held a cure that no amount of money could match.

He got out the gear. The bag of dope, the burnt spoon, a baggie of cotton balls and a pack of syringes, each in a little wrapper labeled: "For diabetic use only."

Time stopped as dope cooked and the cotton and needle scraped across the bowl of the spoon. He looked up and saw Natalie standing above him.

He didn't feel any guilt. And her face betrayed no emotion.

He cleared his throat. "It's this or I have to drink."

She sat and offered her arm. He nodded. He wasn't the only one chased by demons he couldn't explain.

***

The ground shifted beneath her, moving both left and right as a tremor shot up from the soles of her feet. She looked down and saw that she stood upon a nearly featureless stone plain of red and brown. The horizon loomed in the distance, looking down at her, but the horizon wasn't the only inhabitant of that sky.

It was an unbroken curtain of oily black clouds, tossed and torn upon winds that she could see but not feel.

Beneath her feet the ground cracked and split, revealing that it was but a few inches of stone above an abyss of foul mud and black water. This was a place to drown, to disappear down into the cold embrace of nothingness. She reached down to feel the cold and wet, to run her fingers through the slime. She gasped as the chill spread up from her fingers, numbing as it traveled from arm to body. At first it froze, and then it burned, freezing and burning until there was no sensation at all, just a blessed lack thereof.

She looked up to see what remained. Could there still be a world of no sensation, no feeling, no knowledge of who she was or who she had been? Or would there just be a featureless stone plain and black nimbus clouds to close out this brief spark that had been her life?

But it was something else entirely.

She stood at the feet of a colossal Virgin Mary, eyes towards the heavens and heart bared and impaled upon six long, cruel knives. She knew pain, she knew this life, and she knew the death of love. Yet her eyes still cast towards the firmament, a place of sun and stars, a place beyond the black clouds of this place. Her eyes saw faith, her eyes saw love, her eyes saw hope in all things, and in that moment her eyes cast down to see Natalie.

Her eyes did not change; she smiled, and mercy breathed into this world.

But it was not to last.

Lightning wreathed her titanic frame and she fell to her knees, no longer a titan of marble and stone, but a living being of flesh and blood—a

AMMONIA

living being stabbed six times through the heart. She cried out, and her voice flew away upon the wind as more lightning tore the air of this place asunder.

Her eyes were those of terror and confusion as they locked with Natalie's, as the truth of her fall became known. She opened her mouth, and a river of blood poured forth over the empty land.

Natalie reached out to her, and then Natalie saw, and Natalie knew.

This was a river of fetuses.

Her eyes flew open.

She'd awoken in seizing icy terror, barely able to breathe. She saw the little bruise on the inside of her elbow and her stomach buckled and flipped, her heart skipping and stuttering. She collapsed to the floor and gasped for air as the horror of the night before fell over her like an avalanche.

She'd killed a man.

She'd seen the shadow forms of monsters, and a battle that men had lost.

And she'd killed a man.

Her bowels clenched and twisted, and no breath would come.

She was going to die, right on the floor of this hotel. She was going to die of shame and terror and confusion when she had tried her very hardest and done her very best. Yet this would be how she died.

Would her *abuela* die of shame that this was her granddaughter? The girl she raised as her own, dead on the floor of a hotel?

Dead on the floor of a hotel after she'd murdered a junkie.

Dead on the floor of a hotel after fleeing to Austin for an abortion because she'd fucked a man to advance her career.

Was her *abuela* even alive anymore?

Could she call Erwin? Could she ever tell him what had happened in that seedy little apartment? Could she ever tell him what happened after that?

She was naked. She and Quincy had fucked last night. He'd smelled like a dirty toilet full of piss that wouldn't flush. But she hadn't cared. She'd let him shoot her full of dope so she wouldn't feel. And then they'd fucked.

Her breath whistled in her chest, constricting and crushing. She moaned, she gasped, she tried to scream but no words came. Her vision constricted into a black tunnel, the sides squeezing everything to a narrow shaft of light.

Hands around her waist, pulling her up onto the bed. Hands pulling her arm straight. A rough squeezing above her elbow, a little prick as the needle slid beneath her skin.

And then she felt peace. A beautiful thing that breathed into her, opening her heart and freeing her mind from the stabbing icicles.

She could do it. She would be okay. Natalie wasn't afraid anymore. She didn't even feel guilty anymore.

***

Quincy looked down again from his 12th-story hotel room at the scene below. It had rained even harder than was the new norm, and the streets were flooded. The only traffic was giant Army trucks trundling empty streets looking for *something,* but never finding it.

The interstate was still blocked.

The East Side was still blocked off. He shook his head and realized he wasn't going to be headed home anytime soon. He shook his head again at the absurdity of this thought, and a shudder passed over him, thinking of those empty streets and empty houses.

Junkie Dave is dead.

Junkie Dave is dead, brains splattered over the wall in your apartment.

A tremor passed through his arms and legs and squeezed his heart in his chest. A pathetic little sob escaped his lips. When it finally stopped raining and people returned, his body would be found.

And yet another tremor passed through him at the more frightening thought: *It isn't going to stop raining. People aren't going to be coming back. They're gone and this is it. Game over. End of story.*

He looked at his hands, as he always did, to see if they were shaking.

He hadn't drunk in twelve hours, but had maintained with heroin. But his hands were still shaking.

He blew out his breath and turned, Natalie stirring on the bed behind him.

Her eyes were still closed. She cleared her throat and asked, "What time is it?"

He picked up his stolen cellphone and looked at the display. "It's 1:23 PM. You should come take a look at . . . at what's happening out there."

She sat bolt upright, a panicked expression on her face, breasts falling free from the blankets. She looked at herself and back to him and covered up, eyes wide and confused.

He sat down gently on the bed, a careful distance away. "Do you have any big plans for the day?"

AMMONIA

Normal. This is totally normal. You're totally normal.

The floodwaters coming up above the curb and onto the sidewalks?

That's totally normal too.

The fact that there's no one on the streets but soldiers and very strange homeless people chanting?

Totally normal too.

The fact that she'd shot dope three times in the last twenty-four hours?

Totally normal.

She blinked, and little drops fell from the hood of her rain poncho and into her eyes. She moved her jaw around and tried not to let her eyes roll around in her head.

Try to look sober. Ignore that you're wearing clothes (way, way too big) owned by Quincy's girlfriend that you found in the car that smelled so bad you washed them in the tub and dried them with a hairdryer.

Ignore that you're walking through the rain with a guy you haven't talked to in a decade—for very good reasons—to get an abortion, also for very good reasons.

Let's not think about those reasons, let's just get this over with and get back to your real life.

Ignore that everything east of Interstate 35 was blocked off by the military, including access to the airport.

She'd asked at the desk about the airport, and the concierge had cheerily told her she'd need to go to Dallas, that Bergstrom and the airport in San Antonio were now inaccessible. Apparently, San Antonio as a whole was now inaccessible.

The cheery concierge gave her a complimentary rain poncho and recommended their complimentary continental breakfast. And be careful! You wouldn't want to slip and fall on those wet sidewalks.

San Antonio is . . . inaccessible? How is that even possible? Do you have a copy of the *Post*? All internet access seems to be down . . .

We haven't had any out-of-town newspapers in about a week now, but not to worry, the government has it all in hand!

Cash or credit?

She paid with crisp one-hundred-dollar bills from the backpack of a man she'd killed.

Quincy started stupidly whistling. Fucking "Patience" by Guns N' Roses.

She turned to look at his stupid face, his stupid life, his stupid fucking raincoat. Why the fuck did a dipshit like him have an EMS raincoat in the first place?

"Would you please stop whistling that goddam song?"

He stopped and nodded his head. "I think we're here. This is the address, right?"

She stopped and looked up. Yep, she'd been so high that she'd missed pretty much the whole walk here. "How long have we been walking?"

She looked at his vacant, glassy eyes. "About thirty minutes, give or take."

She shook her head back and forth. She wanted to be mad at him for something, for anything. But he really wasn't guilty of anything other than fucking her and shooting her full of dope.

The dope, she'd needed that, even if she'd never even considered sticking a needle in her arm, at least up until last night.

The fucking? The dope had done a perfect job of erasing that.

But it was his slack-jawed, dipshit face that pissed her off most. She wanted to tell him that too, to let him know what a fucking inconsequential piece of shit he really was, how he'd thrown his life down the shitter.

How did an idiot like him even graduate high school?

He looked at her looking at him. "I didn't graduate high school."

She was flabbergasted. "How did . . . ? What the fuck?"

There were the beginnings of tears in his eyes. He shook his head. "I don't know. It doesn't matter. We're here."

The big glass double doors to the office building were right in front of them, along with a knot of homeless people muttering in unison.

Her ears picked up the familiar refrain: "You alone among the stars, you alone in the deep and dark."

She turned to look into his face again, doubly stunned. He nodded, crying gently.

She wanted to ask him how he knew what she'd been thinking. Was she so fucked up that she'd been speaking her thoughts out loud? Was she walking along in the rain muttering like these homeless people?

"No, Natalie. Don't worry about it."

He nodded to the lobby past the double doors.

She didn't know what to say. She wanted to apologize, or something, but smack made it hard to remember what for, and even harder to care.

"Are you sure you're . . . "

AMMONIA

"Yes, I'm fucking certain. I didn't ask you for your input either."

"I was wondering if you're . . . high enough for . . . what you've got to do."

She wanted to scream at him, but screaming wasn't possible now. Still, she wanted to scream. "I don't know. Maybe not."

They walked past the homeless people, and they began shouting: "You! You are so beautiful! You alone among the stars! You alone in the deep and dark!"

Through the big glass double doors and into the crisp, cool, silent and empty lobby. Gleaming elevators and a helpful directory of different doctor's offices on different floors.

They got off on their appointed floor, and checked back and forth. No one.

They slipped into the women's room and cooked a little shot.

***

The office was clean and innocuous, as was the receptionist. She apologized that they were a bit short-staffed, but not to worry. She apologized again that they couldn't process any transactions because all internet access was down, but could write down her information and take care of it after services were restored.

Natalie handed her a stack of one-hundred-dollar bills.

The receptionist looked at her, unsure what to do, and then slid it into a drawer.

A few minutes later she led Natalie to a room. She handed her one of those awful gowns that opened in the front. She told her to lie down on the table. She put in place one of those screens so Natalie wouldn't have to see what was going on down there.

Then she told her the doctor would be in to see her in just a few moments. *Not to worry. It'll be over before you even know it. Just bit of local anesthetic. Make sure to avoid sexual activity for the next seventy-two hours. If you're feeling nauseous you can . . .*

Natalie tuned her out, staring into the big white tiles of the ceiling, lost in the hum and buzz of air conditioner and fluorescent lights. On heroin, everything becomes music.

She heard the crisp click as the receptionist exited the room and closed the door behind her. She closed her eyes and let herself sink back into her mind.

Should she be feeling something? Shame, regret, revulsion?

Thankfully, she felt nothing and began to drift away.

She heard a faint thump and a snap from out in the hallway, but didn't open her eyes.

The door opened and closed, and a cold, clammy, rubbery feeling wrapped around her thighs and pushed them apart. She moved in unison, placing her feet in the stirrups. Thankfully this doctor had no desire to chat.

She felt a pressure down there, but no pain. Just quiet little sounds that she wished she hadn't heard. Her eyes came open, and the tears came too. She shook her head back and forth and whispered to herself, to God, to no one at all, "I'm so sorry."

A cold chill spread up her spine, and the hairs on her body stood on end. Whatever was happening down there was done, and the doctor pulled out and away. And then she was overwhelmed by the strongest smell of ammonia that she had ever known.

She gagged, but nothing came.

***

Natalie waited, and she waited some more. She even fell asleep a few times, but still she lay there and no one came. She pulled her feet from the stirrups and pushed her way off of the operating table. She pushed aside the screen and saw nothing.

Nothing in the room had been moved. None of the surgical tools were touched.

Natalie grabbed her underwear, sliding them on, quickly followed by her jeans and shirt.

Had it been that easy? That quick and sterile? She looked closely at the table and there it was: a single drop of blood.

She pulled up her shirt and covered her face, trying to escape that ammonia smell.

She opened the door and peeked into the hall. No one there.

She whispered, "Hello?"

And louder, "Hello, where is everyone?"

But no one answered.

She walked up the hall and knocked on one door, and then another. She didn't want to open any doors, but finally she did. Just another room, exactly like the one she'd been in.

She tried another, and another, until she came to the last room in the hall. She heard a clatter from inside, and the sound of something snapping into place. She looked up and thought that one of the ceiling tiles fell back

AMMONIA

into place and something pulled up into the space above the ceiling. Then she heard a shuffling and gentle thumping from above.

Then nothing more, apart from another hideous blast of that ammonia smell.

For a few more minutes she searched the office, and found her way to the waiting room, Quincy asleep in a chair.

She kicked at his feet and he stirred, looking up at her with bleary eyes. He sat up, exhaled. "Are you . . . "

Natalie nodded, quickly, up and down. "We need to get out of here, right now."

She took his hand and rushed them out.

She looked around nervously—right, left, up, down—as they rode the elevator down to the lobby, and pulled him into the rain. She pulled her rain poncho on and nodded, frightened, looking into his eyes. Her breath came in short terrified bursts. "We'll drive, we'll drive west."

He slowly nodded, up, down. "Yeah, west. We'll drive west."

A SUNKEN DESERT

by Michelle Garza and Melissa Lason

This story is dedicated to our horror family who exist somewhere between reality and the edge of the void. Your support and friendship is beyond measure.

CHAPTER ONE
A SUNKEN DESERT

MARTA GAZED ACROSS a horizon shimmering beneath the moonlight like black glass. It might have been beautiful if it wasn't natural, the desert sunken beneath the ridge they stood upon, covered in billions of gallons of water and debris stretching for miles. If the flood waters hadn't swallowed her home and everything she owned, it might have been a sight to behold. Instead it twisted her stomach with grief.

Death came for the people of the Sonoran Desert. Something fell from the sky, the news said, and Mother claimed it was the four horsemen come to destroy the earth. After that the rain came, an endless wave that covered everything. People said California was swallowed whole by the ocean, but she didn't know for sure; she only knew that the world would never be the same.

"What's the point of any of this?" she asked the people behind her.

"There's nothing left for us here, but there might be shelter, food, help on the other side," her brother Jose answered.

Marta nodded, knowing his words held truth, yet she still felt something gnawing at the pit of her stomach.

There weren't many who had survived the event, and hidden beneath the water's glistening surface was a mass grave. She shivered, thinking of passing over it in the old inner tubes.

"We've crossed water like this a million times," he said.

"No, we haven't," Marta reminded him. "We crossed the Rio Grande. This *was* the fuckin' deserts of Arizona, it shouldn't be this way."

"It shouldn't be, but it is," Jose said, grabbing her by the arm.

She'd seen this look in his eyes before: begging her to toughen up, to get her shit together.

"This ain't our usual gig. This is something far different," she said.

"Listen, we can do this. We *will* do this. We can't sit on this hill and starve to death."

His words hit home, and Marta's heart filled with pity for the people looking to her with hope in their eyes and their shoes in their hands.

She took a deep breath and nodded. "Okay."

"*Siguenos,*" Jose announced, and the small band obeyed, following close behind the brother-sister team.

Jose collected their worn-out shoes and helped put them away in the backpacks. He steadied them as they stepped into flotation devices. Marta came down the rocky ledge to the black water swirling below. They'd been trapped here for days, riding out the storms, watching the rising water, and receiving static-filled reports before the cell phone batteries died. She felt as if they were stranded on a deserted island, only in the middle of southern Arizona. She managed to call their mother once, and the old woman was certain the end of the world had come. She spoke feverishly in English and Spanish of the gates of Hell flung wide open and death in the form of waves: black, black waves. The phone cut out, and Marta felt as if she was in a nightmare from which she couldn't wake. The water followed them up and up, and finally halted at the edge of a rocky cliff. She knew by the looks of it that it had swept the earth of humanity, submerging all in an invading cold. It reminded her of her first job with Jose, when they brought a group across the border and nearly drowned in the freezing currents of the Rio Grande.

It was an inherited profession, more to help people than make money off them. They'd come to Arizona three years before the catastrophe, and were fairly successful, but there were days when she longed to return to Texas. Watching the black water made Marta wish she was back home with her family again, and able to see her mother face to face. A cold lonesomeness had taken residence in her bones, and refused to leave until she felt the warmth of the old woman's embrace.

"*Adelante,*" Jose coaxed.

Marta pulled the old inner tube over her head and around her waist like a comically large donut. Then she slipped on her backpack and stepped forward. Memories of their truck came rushing through her mind. They were almost washed away in the deluge. They were lucky they kept the tubes in the back, secure in the secret compartment where passengers hid, or they wouldn't be escaping this watery prison. Just remembering the

A SUNKEN DESERT

sound of it, a wall of water chasing them down, overtaking them, trying its best to kill them, was enough to make her hesitate. Marta still hadn't confided to her brother that she'd seen a stroller in the waves, with a pale, lifeless child strapped in. She felt uneasy, as if she couldn't breathe, as if she should just lie down on the rough rocks and wait to die.

"Why don't we wait until morning?" she asked.

"Stop it, sis, you'll scare them. We need to get out of these rocks and find something to eat. Besides, we always work at night, what's the problem now?" Jose asked.

Marta looked to the people ready to follow her: three young men, able-bodied and searching for work before the world came to a watery end. The oldest said his name was Lalo, but his companions didn't offer their names. There were two sisters no older than twenty, Consuelo and Carmen, and their *abuela*. They told her they came from the state of Sonora, seeking a better life. Marta felt she'd failed them when she met their gaze, desperation filling their eyes, stomachs empty from hiding until the rain ended. Guilt prompted her to move.

She put her feet into the black water and felt it crawl up her legs, cold and dark. She shifted back and used her hands to push herself in. It took her breath away—not the frigid temperature, but the fear when her body submerged. The others followed, and her brother took up the rear to be certain they all entered the water safely. He paddled between them, wrapping a piece of rope around each tube to keep them together before signaling to Marta that they could begin the long journey across the sunken desert.

Anxiety constricted her chest, but Marta refused to let the others see her lose control of her emotions. She felt like she couldn't breathe, like her lungs were filling with cold water. *Get it together*, she told herself. She kicked her feet and began across the water.

"There's a mountain in the distance. I remember a town surrounding it," Jose said. "We'll head that way."

Marta could faintly see it, but didn't think it held much more hope than their previous hiding spot. The sky rumbled, and she glanced up to the heavy clouds choking off the moon. Lightning rippled through them. Thunder rumbled and boomed, rattling her ribcage against her stammering heart. Panic rose up from her stomach, threatening to overwhelm her. She didn't want them to get stuck in another storm, adrift over the sunken desert like derelict vessels at sea.

Directly behind her was Lalo, and to each side his companions. Behind them were Consuelo, Carmen, and their grandmother, with Jose tied at the end. Marta heard them praying softly as they began to tread water as a unit. She was certain the grandmother wouldn't help propel them very far, but the strength of the group should be enough to compensate and drag her along. The old woman joined in the prayer, but her voice grew loud and frantic after only minutes in the black water. Marta gritted her teeth and kicked; even without shoes, her feet felt like bricks dragging her down. The water stretched endlessly before her and filled her heart with hopelessness.

The group paddled onward, eyes on the horizon. Hours passed, and exhaustion took its toll. Marta looked back and Jose nodded, aware they were all too tired to continue without a break. Each time she thought they made any headway, it seemed their destination slipped farther and farther from their reach.

Her inner tube jostled and she looked back, shooting an impatient glare at one of the young men behind her.

"Watch it," she warned, not caring to translate her words. The last thing she wanted was to lose her life preserver and be forced to cling to the side of Jose's, like so many times in the Rio Grande, or like the nightmare of their final crossing when the water was filled with corpses.

He shook his head and lifted his hands in confusion. She spun inside her tube when she was bumped again, this time with more force.

Marta froze. She watched confusion replaced by fear in his eyes. Then he screamed as something pulled him underwater. Before she could scream, his arms shot back above the surface, waving wildly as he fought to keep hold of the slippery tube. But whatever had him yanked down again, and he vanished beneath the black flood.

CHAPTER TWO
BLOOD BROTHERS

COLE DROVE HIS fist into the guard's nose. It shattered, and the spray of blood brought a grin to his face. In the darkness, the crimson droplets appeared black, like the water rising up to his knees.

"I'm not sure if you noticed, but the world is fuckin' ending. You really think I give a shit about laws anymore?"

The guard didn't answer; he just fell back with wide eyes, staring up at the ex-con. Cole wasn't worried about going back to the slammer, not with streets filled with black water and soggy corpses. He only wanted to find his brother and get the fuck gone.

"You can't go in there," the guard finally repeated, not putting up the front of an authority figure anymore.

"I've waded through worse than this," Cole answered, staring through a chain-link fence at the prison holding his younger brother, who was serving a twenty-year stretch for armed robbery and kidnapping.

"I'm not going to stop you. I'm just giving you some advice."

Cole glared at the uniformed guard, nose weeping blood onto a badge he knew gave him the right to beat men, shoot them, fuck up their day with bullshit cell searches, and send them off to solitary to rot. "I'm not taking any advice from a pig."

"Then take it man to man," he said, pointing to the name on his badge. It wasn't visible, but Cole got the gist. "My name is Timothy Stern, and believe me when I tell you that prison isn't a place you wanna walk into. It's a death trap."

"Listen, Tim, I'm not a pussy like you and I'd walk through hell for my brother, so kindly shove your man-to-man advice up your ass."

Timothy didn't bother responding. Instead, he rose shakily and held his hands up to prove he didn't want to fight anymore. "Good luck, then."

Cole watched the former guard begin a path through rising water, then turned his attention back to the prison. He hadn't counted how many days the rain had fallen but it was freakishly long by Arizona standards, biblical if you asked his mama. All he knew was, he wasn't going to let his brother drown behind the bars of a cell.

He made his way to the gate, wading through thigh-deep water. Cole halted to rifle through the pockets of a dead guard, and took a good look at him. His face was blue, body bloating, but something made Cole pause. The man had an open wound in his throat and small circular bruises, like bite marks, on the side of his shaved head.

"What the fuck is goin' on here?" Cole asked himself.

He didn't dwell on it. Instead, he took the dead man's keys and gun and unlocked a walk-through gate before heading through rising water towards the prison facility.

***

Anthony floated near the top of his cell, with barely enough room to keep his head out of the black water. There were no lights but for the red blinking of distant emergency back-up bulbs. He felt as if he'd been thrust into a sensory deprivation tank, and it was driving him mad. The water had been slowly rising for days. When the floods initially started, the prison was a clamor of guards and maintenance men trying to get the situation under control. Then, overnight, they vanished and never returned.

Anthony heard the cries for help up and down the cell block. He'd heard them on the floor below him too, before the water rose too high. Then the splashing, thrashing, underwater fight against steel bars that would not give. It lasted just minutes before all was silent again.

He paddled to the door of his cell and gripped the bars, but couldn't see anything more than water and floating corpses. When he was sentenced, he'd accepted it solemnly, as he thought a man in his shoes should. It wasn't his first rodeo, and it wouldn't be his last. But when the flooding began to swallow the prison, he worried that God was finally going to make him pay. He didn't know how much longer he'd be able to hold on.

"Coulda been a lawyer, or a garbage man, or hell, even one of them pigs that used to stand guard over worthless sacks of shit like me . . . "

Anthony had been born and raised in Arizona, and had never seen such rain. It just kept falling outside the tiny barred window near the roof of his

A SUNKEN DESERT

cell. It made him think about the end of days, how his mother promised it'd come one day, and how he needed to get his life back on track before the Lord cast him aside with the rest of the sinners.

"But I chose to put a gun in a bank teller's mouth and take all the money she could give me."

A wet sloshing sound drew his attention for a moment, but he figured it was only another corpse resurfacing after days under water.

"You were right, Mama. The only way to be washed clean of my deeds now is to let myself go into this black water."

"Don't you fuckin' dare," a familiar voice spoke. "This ain't no baptism, it's a breakout."

"Cole?" Anthony said, unashamed to feel tears in his eyes as the silhouette of his brother swam towards him. "How'd you . . . "

"I found the keys!" Cole announced as he doggy-paddled over to his brother's jail cell.

"Get me the fuck outta here!"

Cole held his breath and disappeared under the rising water, red lights reflecting off its surface.

CHAPTER THREE
THE RISEN

"**BRING HER FORTH**," the Seer ordered. "I need to get a feel of her soul. The Old Gods demand it."

She was dragged across the concrete floor by the ones the Seer called the *Hands*. He called most of his subjects that, although there was one that he held in higher esteem, whom he'd named the Heart. Her face bled, unrecognizable after the Hands got hold of her. Too weak to fight after days of torture, she was ready to beg for death. She was propped up on her knees before the Seer as he stood from his throne of garbage to peer into her.

He gripped her by the chin, forcing her to look up at him. Her brown eyes were horrified at the crude depictions of eyes tattooed on his face. His head was shaven clean, and unblinking eyes etched into his flesh, extending around his scalp, down his throat, and beneath his tattered robes. He stared for a long, breathless moment, his eyes seeing right through her.

"Jerry?" she asked through a mouth of broken teeth.

"He is no longer with us," the Seer responded.

"It's me, Nurse Rebecca," she said.

"Hold still while I judge you." His breath was a rancid intrusion into her nostrils.

His gaze intensified as he stared into her soul. She had no idea what he was looking for, but knew in her heart he wouldn't find it. He was a madman leading madmen, but the disaster that had decimated the Sonoran Desert gave them dominion and the chance to run wild.

"I, I tried to help you," she whispered.

"I am much more than you thought, with your clipboards and clinical diagnoses. I received a higher calling."

"It's your addiction, Jerry. Let me go and I can help you," she pleaded.

A SUNKEN DESERT

"She will not comply. The Old Gods won't accept her. Take her to the slop cell," he said, waving her away.

"NO!" she screamed.

Rebecca had been taken days before by the gang of lunatics, and in between beatings she watched them huff silver spray paint on the grimy floor of the old warehouse where the handful of prisoners were held. The slop cell was a bloody holding tank, an un-operational walk-in freezer where they kept humans for slaughter. It wasn't like food was lacking. What could be scavenged in abandoned stores was slowly beginning to rot, but the world wasn't depleted of it yet. The Risen, as the cult called themselves, practiced cannibalism because they could, because it struck terror into the hearts of survivors, and because nothing was taboo under the reign of what they called the Old Gods, who they believed had come to take over the earth.

She tried to fight, but her body was ravaged by hunger and abuse. Her cries echoed, followed by the sound of clubs breaking her bones and the slop cell gaining one more moaning, shattered soul.

The Seer reclined in his seat before an enormous fish tank covered in a black sheet. Inside resided his emissary to the Old Gods. The creature had spared his life, cleansing him of the need for heroin in exchange for servitude. The Seer gladly accepted. He was granted visions of the end of humanity and the beginning of Earth's new kingdom, where the Old Gods ruled. He listened as the storms returned, splitting the night sky in two with lightning. His robes slid open, revealing his nude, tattooed body, a thousand eyes watching as his men came to report.

"Seer, there's cargo being hauled in from the desert sea. My brothers said they'd return by morning."

The Seer grinned. "Good. More of the nonbelievers to fill our guts."

"Maybe this time they'll be live and kickin', like her," the Hand added, pointing to the slop cell, where fresh blood glistened.

"The Old Gods will provide. You'll see," the Seer promised, his voice turning prophetic.

He spun around and placed his hand against the tank, feeling a thrumming much like a pulse. He closed his natural eyes and his skin tingled. The being on the other side was pleased.

**

The barge was once a wealthy family's pontoon boat, but after the rains, it became property of the Risen. It was piloted by the Teeth, a sect of the cult dedicated solely to seeking out food, drugs, and anything else of value to the group. Three men were chosen, wrapped in sheets ornamented with long swirling symbols painted with blood, bile, and feces. Their robes spoke of their station within the Risen, and proclaimed them hunters for the cult. One held a pair of binoculars to his eyes and nodded in satisfaction.

"Food on the horizon, but it looks as if we will have to ask the Children of the Old Gods' permission to take it."

CHAPTER FOUR
OCEAN OF FEAR

JOSE THRUST HIS hand into his backpack and pulled out a knife. Chaos was taking hold as the other men thrashed and beat the surface of the black water. Lalo cried out for his companion. Consuelo screamed as she was pulled through the center of her tube. Marta heard the choked end of her cry as bubbles erupted where she once floated.

"No!" Marta said, frantically trying to pull herself up on top of her tube. But there was no way to get all of her body up without flipping it over.

The old woman's prayers were interrupted by her screams. The water went still, but the grandmother uttered a drawn-out crescendo of building agony ending in a liquid gurgling. The clouds parted unmercifully to reveal blood running from the old woman's mouth. Marta couldn't look away as something long and thin squirmed around the side of the grandmother's face: the tip of a tentacle.

"Jose, *mira!*" she screamed, hoping like hell her brother witnessed the same thing. The last of the travelling women, Carmen, clawed onto her tube, but it sent her head-first into the water. A large bubble breached the surface, but she didn't. The conjoined tubes rose as tentacles wrapped around the grandmother's upper body before a figure emerged to claim her. It dragged its muscular form from the black water, engulfing her head in its multitude of appendages.

Jose gave the knife to Lalo to cut the ropes; it was too dangerous to stay fastened together, it made them an easy target. Lalo quickly sliced the rope, and the tubes belonging to the women from Sonora drifted from the four who remained alive. The thing fed while the nightmare soundtrack of slurping and crunching echoed across the water.

They paddled away, but Lalo's second companion was yanked backwards towards the frenzy. The water was alive with thrashing, and he fought with all he had, but was lost. His screams died as he was pulled downward. The three remaining survivors clawed at the water and swam frantically, but their strength gave out. Their bodies were deprived of nourishment and couldn't continue.

"A squid? Or octopus?" Marta whispered breathlessly. "Impossible."

"The desert is an ocean now. Nothing is impossible," Jose said.

Lalo let out a startled scream as his tube was rammed from beneath. Jose held his knife before him to stab anything that came for him. Lalo cried out in agony as the thing wrapped around his legs, and its sharp, beaked mouth bit into his abdomen.

"*Dame tu cuchillo!*" he screamed.

Jose tossed Lalo the knife, and watched in sickening terror as he stabbed at the tentacles wrapping around him. Lalo accidentally punctured his tube, and the air escaped as blood exited his neck. He sank beneath the surface but kept stabbing his attacker. A smell like ammonia filled the air. It coupled with the essence of fresh blood and choked the cries back into Marta's throat, sick and mortified.

They drifted, letting their burning lungs fill with the night air, when the sound of an engine in the distance filled them with hope. Jose and Marta could see the small vessel approaching, a small beacon against the utter darkness of sky and water. They threw their arms up and cried out for help. They watched the boat as it stopped beside one of the tubes that had once floated men and women looking for the American dream, only to be killed by the brutality of this new world.

"HERE!" Marta screamed.

"HELP US!" Jose cried.

The light turned in their direction, and the minutes for the boat to reach them were an agonizing eternity.

"Please, help us!" Jose pleaded, the light burning his eyes.

"Look what we have here," a voice spoke. "The Old Gods have spared a little meat for us, the believers."

Marta's heart sank, and she knew they would be better off floating across the sunken desert, above the nightmares beneath them.

CHAPTER FIVE
PRISON BREAK

THE CELL DOOR slid open, and Cole grabbed his brother by the wrist.

"I can't believe it," Anthony said.

"I promised Mama I'd always protect you."

The brothers embraced before turning back to traverse what was beyond the barred door. The flotsam and jetsam of the dead bobbed around them—soggy cigarettes, magazines, hand-drawn pictures of scantily-clad women. Blinking emergency lights guided them through the first set of security doors. Between them and freedom was the recreation area; chairs and tables bolted to the floor beneath the water and ruined televisions on the wall. Then two more sets of barred doors, and finally the prison yard.

"Is she out there, waiting for me like she always did?" Anthony asked.

Cole hesitated for a moment before answering. "Yeah, she's out there waiting for us."

He stayed close to his brother after witnessing how Anthony fought to stay above the surface of the water. Cole couldn't imagine the hell Anthony had endured. Days of being slowly swallowed by rising water. Nothing to eat but what floated on the surface, and nothing to drink but the very same filth. They pushed aside bloated corpses of prisoners and guards. It made him remember what his felon father had told him when he felt like white trash in hand-me-down clothes and shoes: "Son, the only equalizer in life is death. We'll all be worm food one day. No one is better than anyone else."

Anthony struggled along, but slid under the water. Cole yanked him back up and wrapped an arm around his shoulder. "Come on, brother!"

"I can't fight it; it's been pulling me under for days. I can't fight it," Anthony said after coughing up a mouthful of black fluid.

"Hang on to me," Cole urged.

"This is a long swim. I don't think . . . "

"Don't you dare give up."

Anthony wheezed in a deep breath. "It feels like it's crushing me."

"Ignore it and hang on."

His brother was having an anxiety attack. The threat of drowning had plagued him for too long, and his strength was giving out. Cole's arms were burning, and so were his lungs. He didn't know how long he could drag Anthony along with him.

They made it to the open recreation room. It was littered with floating corpses, and an idea blossomed in Cole's mind. He grabbed a dead man. The body bobbed, but didn't sink completely with his weight on it. He pulled the morbid flotation device over to Anthony, who peered into the face of the man he remembered as Lavar Stevens, doing time for murdering his girlfriend's father.

"Stay put," Cole instructed, and retrieved a second corpse drifting not far away.

He tethered the two bodies together with his belt. It supported Anthony much better. He gathered a few more and bound them all into a raft. Anthony recognized them all, especially the guard who'd refused to open his cell when the waters reached waist level.

"We'll use this to make it to the other side of the room, rest a little bit, and then swim for freedom," Cole said. "Beyond that hallway is where the water isn't so deep. I'll carry you from there if I have to."

"Mama will never believe this," Anthony said.

Cole kicked and pushed the corpse raft to the opposite end of the recreation room. His brother floated gratefully along, catching his breath and preparing for the last stretch of deep water. The room was dark, but the emergency light at the exit called to them; their salvation awaited.

"We're gonna make it," Cole said.

Anthony opened his mouth to speak, but paused. He turned back in confusion and in an instant was pulled from the corpse raft.

"What the fuck?" Cole hollered.

Something powerful wrapped around his ankle and yanked him back. His nose stung with invading water. He didn't dare scream. He opened his eyes to complete darkness. Cole reached down and gripped the thing wrapped around his ankle. It was firm but smooth, and held him in a grip he couldn't break.

CHAPTER SIX
THE SHIP OF TEETH

MARTA AND JOSE were dragged aboard the pontoon boat. She fought as hands poked and pinched her flesh.

"She's a plump one," a grimy-looking man said with a lascivious grin. He wore a homemade robe. He reeked of shit and unwashed armpits. His companions nodded excitedly.

"Careful with him," the captain instructed as they beat Jose into unconscious silence. "He could be dangerous."

"*Pendejos!*" Marta yelled, frantically crawling across the wet deck to her brother.

"Oh, a little Mexican cuisine. I think the Seer will enjoy that."

"Go fuck yourself!" she screamed.

"Feisty *and* bilingual. We may use her for breeding." He licked his lips and held out his hand to Marta's cheek.

"Don't touch me!" She scrambled and kicked until the three men stood defensively on the other side of the boat.

Marta stood and looked back at the black water and knew she would never survive jumping back in.

"They're hungrier than we are," said the captain. "We could always toss him back in to appease them, if you like," he said, gesturing down to an unconscious Jose.

Her brother lay in a pool of blood, a dark circle seeping out onto the hull. She knelt beside him and placed her hand on his back. She could feel him breathing.

"Stay quiet and still, and maybe you'll both see dry land again," the captain said.

The ghastly crew cackled before returning to their posts, hungry jackals gathering bits of leftover carcasses to calm their rumbling guts.

CHAPTER SEVEN
THE GATHERING OF THE CORPSE

THE SEER DESCENDED his throne to gather his Hands.

"I can hear the winds speaking. The thunder and rain will reveal some great mystery to us. A meeting is in order."

The band of filthy vagrants-turned-cult members howled and beat their chests.

"Bring the Heart."

They fled the abandoned warehouse, seeking the only woman allowed in their tribe, a woman of unholy practice who dwelled among the dead.

***

The city was a waterlogged carcass after the event. The nonstop storms invaded every door and washed away any semblance of civilized living. The streets reeked of dirty, stagnating water, yet the rain kept falling. People died en masse, disease spreading as tides swept across the desert. Sickness of mind eroded many quicker than dysentery, leaving behind survivors raving mad and frothing at the mouth to eat the flesh of anything they could lay hands on. Day in and day out they made sacrifices to what they dubbed the Old Gods, an ancient breed of cephalopods come up from the dark waters, guided by forces from beyond to conquer the drowned Earth. And the Risen were there to assist in the conquest.

***

The Heart was brought before the Seer, the eyes of the Old Gods. He was in an odd mood, even more so than usual. He paced the dirty floor and mumbled to himself, naked but for the tattooed eyes etched into his skin.

"The storms have shown me danger, grave danger. We must put a stop to the strangers. The Old Ones gave me knowledge to read the storms, and I see death." He pointed to the tank, now uncovered.

The golden eyes of the gigantic beast stared out with wisdom far beyond the comprehension of any human. Their lairs at the heart of the sea sang with elder secrets no mortal man could fathom. It pressed its tentacles against the glass, its bulbous eyes speaking to any with the mind to see. They spoke of a new era, one of blood and chaos. The Seer and his people were gripped in sudden mass hysteria by their eight-legged god in its tank of murky water. It lifted the leg bone of its last meal to beat the glass, its drumming entrancing the Risen. Speaking in tongues, they began to profess visions that fractured their already addled minds.

"I, too, have felt it here," the Heart said, her hand to her chest, feeding into the lunacy of the Seer. "My heart, the heart of the Old Gods, beats with fear."

She was toothless, and wore a tattered overcoat soaked in blood. She had been brought from the attic of the local mortuary, where she lived with abandoned corpses and stainless-steel saws.

"I slaughtered the toothin' babe just this mornin', but still the heart beats with warnin'."

The others fell to their knees and began to babble, reciting what sounded to the uninitiated like nonsense. But to them, the gibbering bore grave admonitions.

"The strangers are carrying the corpses of the Old Gods' army. They have tasted the blood of the ancient ones." The Seer was now raving and shouting, spittle hanging from his lips like a mad dog.

The warehouse flew open, frightening the Heart and the Seer.

"We come bearing food!" a voice shouted, and the Seer calmed slightly.

"Bring the meat forth and barricade the door," he ordered, tense and paranoid.

***

Marta clung to Jose. She didn't understand what was happening. Jose put his arm around her as they were forced into the putrid warehouse.

"What the hell are we gonna do?" she whispered.

"Whatever it takes to get out of here."

"I'm scared."

"Remember the Rio Grande," Jose said, and his sister wept.

CHAPTER EIGHT
TO THE DEATH

COLE GRIPPED THE tentacle wrapped around his face and struggled to yank it away. In a matter of seconds, a second tentacle wound around his waist. He opened his eyes, but saw only darkness. His lungs burned, and his body was growing exhausted. It registered that his attacker was some sort of octopus or squid, but it seemed unbelievable. They were in a prison in Arizona, nowhere near the sea, but the water had swept in things the desert had never seen, to usher in the end of humankind. Cole fought the tangled arms dragging him further down. Dead prisoners bumped against him, their staring eyes bearing witness.

A flash of silver in the black caused his attacker to lash out, releasing his waist. Cole pulled his head above the surface as he gagged and vomited. He couldn't talk and didn't have time to question what had even happened. Anthony helped him along until they reached a hallway leading up to the front of the complex. Cole was still hacking and gasping when his brother jammed the key into the lock and slid the barred door open.

"What, what was that?"

"A squid. One took me under, but it was smaller. I was dragged to the bottom while it bit me and tried to choke the life out of me, but thank God one of these dead fuckers was concealing a shank. Good old Lavar."

"A shank." Cole smiled, gripping his chest, thankful his lungs weren't filled with black water.

Anthony pulled a homemade knife from his pocket and grinned. "Used to be a spoon."

The two made their way out of the prison and halted beneath the glow of a streetlight. Splashing and screaming echoed off the brick walls of the building across the street.

A SUNKEN DESERT

"I bet you I know who that is," Cole said, and strode weakly through the water with his brother behind him.

The guard, Timothy, was up to his chin in black water. He was battling a multitude of grappling tentacles. The creature had nearly drained the guard's energy, but he refused to be forced beneath the surface without a fight.

Cole cautiously waded deeper into the water that gathered in a retention ditch in front of the probation office. His brother brandished the shank while he searched for anything heavy enough to beat the squid into submission.

"I'm gonna give you some advice, man to man," Cole said, grabbing a broken tree branch. "Try not to drown while we get this fucker off of you."

The brothers attacked, Anthony's shank fending the beast off long enough for Cole to pull Timothy to safety. The three exited the water as quickly as they could, and looked back at it in disbelief.

"What the fuck was that?" Timothy kept repeating.

"We gotta get out of here. Two of those things nearly killed us in the prison, and there's another guard over there dead, his head covered in wounds from those suction cups on these fuckers' legs . . . there must be more," Cole said.

"Is he coming with us?" Anthony asked.

They looked to Timothy, still in shock. He was breathing heavily, scanning the nearby water for signs of other predators.

"That's a cop, man," Anthony said.

"Like that fuckin' matters anymore," Cole said.

"It doesn't to me, but only weeks ago guys like him were paid to keep me in a cage."

"Listen, this world isn't how we remember it. We want to survive, we gotta change with the times."

Anthony nodded and shrugged his shoulders. "I guess you're right."

"Are you rolling with us, or are you going on your own?" Cole asked Timothy.

The former prison guard stared down into the water. "My gun is down there."

"We're not goin' in after it," Cole said.

"Are you coming or not?" Anthony asked.

"You're welcome to stay here with that thing," Cole added.

"I'm going with you."

The three climbed a steep embankment at the edge of the prison complex that served as an extra deterrent for escapees. In happier times, it was meant to give the guards time to put crosshairs on the back of any man stupid enough to try to break free. It was a bitch to climb, but kept them from the deeper water, where they knew now what was lurking.

"We need to find some weaponry and a safe place to call our own," Cole said.

"I know where we can find the first. The second should come easier once we have firepower," Timothy said.

"Aren't there any more guns inside the prison?" Cole asked.

"No, that's why I came back. I was looking for essentials after I realized this rain ain't stopping and people are disappearing. The cabinet in there has been emptied."

"Where's Mama?" Anthony suddenly asked. "You said she'd be waiting for me out here. We can't leave without her."

Cole shook his head. "I'm sorry."

His brother stopped dead in his tracks. "What do you mean, Cole?"

"You know she had a relapse . . . "

"No," his brother said, his voice breaking.

Cole nodded. "She didn't make it."

Anthony lost it then, and Cole couldn't pretend anymore. He held his brother while they cried, the night swallowing their muffled sobs while the sky opened to weep once again, a never-ending veil of rain that brought the end of mankind.

CHAPTER NINE
SORTING THE MEAT

THE SPEAKING OF tongues and profession of visions faded as the group laid eyes on the new meat from the desert sea. Even the god-spawn in its tank calmed when it cast its gaze upon Marta and Jose, calculating which would taste better.

"I see. She could be useful in many ways," the Seer agreed.

A thump caught the Seer's attention, and he turned to regard the beast with reverence.

"You'll get a feast. I promise you."

"She's got strong legs, and healthy eggs," the Heart said, pointing to Marta. She giggled and motioned to Jose. "He looks like how bacon used to taste. None of him should go to waste."

Marta's anger was kindled by the haggard, toothless old woman's gravelly-voiced rhymes. She kept her arm around her brother to steady him. Jose had taken a heavy blow to his head from the fishermen out on the sunken desert. His blood-matted black hair stained the lucky t-shirt he wore when they helped people cross the border. "Keep your hands off of him."

"There's a fire in this one," the Seer said, and came closer to Marta.

Her stomach turned at the sight of his naked body. The countless eyes in his skin seemed to focus on her.

He smiled and licked his lips. "She smells sweet, too."

Thunder rattled the warehouse, and all in attendance scuttled together, as if Hell had opened up. The Seer's grin faded, and he glared at Marta and Jose. "Could you be the strangers I was warned of?"

Marta looked to Jose, and back to the gang of freaks holding them hostage.

"Danger often comes in sweet packages."

The wind howled through the broken windows of the Risen's hideout.

The Seer took a deep breath as the scent of rain drove in around them. He held his breath and closed his natural eyes, revealing unblinking eyes tattooed to his eyelids as well.

"I can see you both from the inside, and judge you as I have countless others."

The seconds ticked by with the sound of rain battering the warehouse.

"They are not the enemies of which I was warned," he stated. "And yet, you are both a danger to the Risen."

The other cult members sprang forward to hold Marta and Jose in place. The Seer opened his eyes and looked upon them with anger and amusement. "Put them in the cell, and once the meeting with the Heart has ended, I shall decide how they will be used."

Marta and her brother were dragged to a storage room and tossed inside, Jose beaten again until she thought he was dead. When the cult left them, she put her hand on her brother's back and felt it rising and falling weakly. The steel room was a holding cell, but to her it smelled like a mausoleum. There were others, blank and expressionless, who prayed for death. The door closed behind them, leaving them in darkness. The crazed voices on the other side made Marta's limbs shake. Only when they drifted away did she dare to speak.

"Who are you?" she asked.

She was met by silence, and she knew the other captives were as weak as lambs awaiting their slaughter.

"*Recuerde el Rio Grande,*" Jose repeated.

"You won't be that lucky again . . . " Marta said.

He put his finger to her lips to silence her. Blood ran from his head; his face already looked like a corpse's. Her brother didn't just want her to remember the river, but an incident that had happened there. It made her heart pound in her chest.

He was thinking up a suicide mission.

CHAPTER TEN
THE ROAD TO GRACELAND

APACHE WELLS SAT on a slope beside the tip of a small mountain range. It was an old community, built in the fifties. Its streets and buildings followed the rolling terrain amidst lakes where once houses and restaurants had stood, like giant steps at the foot of the mountains. It was nearly a ghost town until a new prison complex created jobs and drew in new residents from other dying communities.

The streets on the southern side of town were nonexistent, hidden beneath the endless flood. The brothers and their companion carried an old extension ladder, using the rooftops to avoid the armed killers hunting the black water. Timothy was still shaken by his encounter, but a burning need built inside of him to kill every last one of the bastards.

"Beneath us used to be a diner, had great donuts," Timothy said.

"Pigs like you would know," Anthony quipped.

"Very funny, Al Capone."

They scurried across the roof to its edge. Anthony and Cole laid the ladder across and held it as Timothy carefully crawled to the other side.

"Where are we gonna get those weapons?" Cole asked as he made his way across and waited for his brother. After crawling across, they picked the ladder back up and followed Timothy, who was giving them a tour of the city. His gallows humor suited them. He was sarcastic, and a team player. If he hadn't been a man of the law, he would have made a great addition to their bank heist team.

"Graceland," Timothy answered.

"I'm not walking to fucking Memphis."

Timothy turned to Cole and grinned, pointing to a tall, cream-colored building. It was directly ahead of them, but they had to pass over four more buildings to get to it. It was visible in the orange glow of lights on its exterior, and in the moonlight peeking out from behind the clouds. "That building over there with all the windows was the sheriff's station. That's where we're going."

"I see it."

"They had a large stockpile of weapons for emergencies. They called it Graceland, like Elvis' mansion, because it had tons of great stuff in it."

"So you don't mind stealing now that the world has ended?" Cole teased.

"It's called survival now," Timothy said with a wink and a grin.

Cole nodded to his brother. Anthony's face still held a haunted, sad expression. He still hadn't come to grips with his mother's death. Cole felt a pain in his heart, an emptiness that nothing would fill.

"You okay?" he asked.

"I will be, in time," Anthony answered.

They crept over walls and across brick fences like spiders, dragging their ladder along with them. The going was slow but safe; it gave them a vantage point from which to scan the surrounding areas. It was Timothy's idea to use the roofs. After his encounter in the water outside of the probation office, he wasn't getting beyond knee-deep again. Rain fell constantly, leaving them soaking wet. They moved like dripping shadows in the darkness.

"Once we get our weapons, we'll find shelter," Cole said.

"A nice secure spot that we can fortify," Timothy added. "Look at me, I'm joining a gang of bandits."

"There will be a harsh initiation, Tim. I'm thinking of making you wrestle one of those stinking squid bastards naked," Cole said.

"I might like that."

"It's funny. I watched so many zombie movies, all claiming the apocalypse would be overrun by walking corpses, but that wasn't true. Our worst enemy is the water and whatever lives in it," Cole said. "Should have paid more attention to *Jaws*."

"Killer octopi," Timothy said, shaking his head. "Was I really almost killed by a squid in Arizona?"

"Un-fuckin-believable, right?"

"Where is everyone?" Anthony asked.

"Many were washed away, some got sick, but mostly they just started disappearing," Timothy answered.

"It was the same around our neck of the woods in Tempe," Cole added.

A SUNKEN DESERT

"Grew up there. Knew everybody in the neighborhood. Then one day they were just gone."

"I have a strong suspicion this shit is national," Timothy said. "If this was only a West Coast emergency, why hasn't the National Guard come, or any other government boys?"

The thought struck Cole and Anthony like a speeding truck.

"We're fucked!" Anthony said.

"Come on, we're getting closer to Graceland. It's on higher ground, so less flooding," Timothy said.

"What's that up there?" Anthony asked, pointing to a gigantic building up on a hillside.

"Some sort of old warehouse," Timothy answered. "The other side of it used to be 'Lover's Leap' because it's a sheer drop with a nice view of the valley bellow. Probably looks like an ocean now."

"Why not make our camp there?"

"It looks like a good option."

"I do have one question, though," Timothy said.

"What?" Cole asked.

"What's our gang name gonna be?"

CHAPTER ELEVEN
A DEBT IS PAID

"**I** MADE A pact with *La Huesuda*, and now she'll collect." His eyelids fluttered, and blood loss left his lips violet. "She spared us then, in the Rio Grande, but I told her she could still have me when she was ready, as long as she left you to live."

"*Calmate*." Marta soothed her brother and laid his head on her shoulder. "Just try to be calm, and we'll think of a way to get out of this."

"I know a way."

Marta's eyes fell on the others in the cell, the living dead. She listened to her brother's breathing and wondered how long he would survive.

"How long have you been here?" she asked the group. She was met with silence.

A woman with dirty blonde hair and bruises on her cheek wept and held a pink teddy bear. An old man fidgeted with a gold wedding band. A girl with dark skin and pigtails defensively held her knees to her chest. She wore an oversized basketball jersey and a scowl. Their minds were lost in memories of their lives, before the floods and before the madness.

"How often do they open the door?"

"Better be quiet," the young girl said. "The last lady who got noisy was dragged outta here and thrown in the slop cell."

"Slop cell?"

"Slop, like pig food, what do you think these assholes eat?" the girl answered before falling silent again. The voices continued on the other side of the wall and Marta breathed easy; the psychos didn't hear their exchange. She would never forgive herself if she got a child killed because she wouldn't be quiet.

The humidity left the cell muggy and rank with the smell of body odor and blood. Thunder boomed, and the wall behind Marta rattled. She

A SUNKEN DESERT

thought of the layout of the warehouse, and a thought registered in her mind. The wall at her back was at the perimeter of the warehouse. She eased Jose over and turned around. She put her ear against the wall and listened. The floor was concrete, and the cannibals probably thought their cell would be impenetrable. But Marta felt a spark of hope in her gut.

Marta stood and sneaked over to the empty shelves bolted to the wall. It was once a storage room, but she couldn't find anything that could be used for escape or self-defense. The cult had been smart enough to remove any useful items. There was also a small boarded-up window near the ceiling. She used the shelves like a ladder, reaching as high as she could. She felt the weathered boards over the windows. They wouldn't hold her back. She gripped the nearest and pulled. It bowed, and determination burned like hot coals in the pit of her stomach.

"These *pendejos* think they can keep us locked up?" Marta yanked another board free. "Not today, bitches."

The window was narrow. She wasn't sure if Jose would fit through, especially in his condition. She looked back to him. He lay on the concrete floor, on the verge of losing consciousness. His face was pale and sweaty, and his lips moved slightly. The wind howled outside and sent a chill up her spine.

"*Estas bien, hermano?*"

Jose didn't answer, but his lips kept moving.

"Sounds like he's praying, to me," the young girl whispered. "That's how my grandma always sounded when she prayed."

Marta turned back to the window and struggled with the last board. The shelves swayed, and she panicked until she realized the girl in the jersey was climbing them.

"I wanna help," she said as she cautiously stood beside Marta. "My name's Sarah."

"You're taller than I thought," Marta said, looking up into the girl's eyes.

"I used to tell people I was going to play for the WNBA, but that all got flushed away in this rain and the end of the world comin'."

Sarah grabbed the last board, then steadied herself before using all of her strength to break the distressed wood.

"Will the window open?" Marta asked.

The girl gripped the latch and it popped open, the window swinging outward. The scent of rain and wind invading the cell signaled freedom.

"Jose," Marta said excitedly, "I'm coming down for you."

"No," he answered.

"I wasn't asking, so get ready."

"No," he said and sat up against the wall, arms trembling.

"Don't . . . "

"I said no. You both are strong enough to go, so get out while you can."

"I won't leave you."

"If you mess around too long trying to take me and you get caught, then you'll doom Sarah to die with you."

Marta looked back to the window. She wasn't sure if they were strong enough to force Jose through the narrow hole, or what kind of drop was on the other side.

Her feet suddenly shifted beneath her as the shelves began to buckle. She felt a hand as Sarah pulled her back. They stood as still as statues, feeling the shelves about to give way.

"I'll pull you up after me," Sarah said before reaching up above her head.

"Go," Jose said.

"*Salir de este infierno!*"

Sarah gripped the window ledge and pulled herself up just as the shelf gave way. She caught Marta by the hand as the metal shelf crashed to the floor.

Marta hung by Sarah's hand, and the commotion echoed. The door swung open, the smell of body odor and death preceding the men who ran inside. Sarah pulled Marta upward and grabbed the window ledge. Marta glanced back as she crawled through the window. Jose got to his feet and screamed in Spanish. He cursed and promised *La Huesuda* that he would repay his debt to her after she took the life of the cult members too.

Sarah dragged Marta through the rain along a steel awning. Shouting erupted inside—the Risen were aware of their escape. The two came to the edge and stopped, seeking any avenue to freedom. Below was flooded, at least waist-deep water in the gray light of dawn.

"We can make it," Sarah said.

"Wait," Marta said, and grabbed the girl by the shoulder.

Her mind went to the sunken desert and the attack from below. She couldn't get rid of the images of the dark, rippling water, of the frantic screams choked off by the mirrored surface.

"We can make it," Sarah repeated. "We have no other choice."

A SUNKEN DESERT

Angry shouting and a droning neurotic voice could be heard over the rain, followed by screaming.

"Come on!" Sarah shouted, and grabbed Marta by the hand.

Marta closed her eyes, praying for her brother and praying they weren't met by tentacles and beaked mouths.

***

The door came open as Jose expected, and two filthy men came in with clubs. Behind them stood the man with eyes tattooed all over his body, and a woman with the voice of a banshee. Jose smiled and opened his arms.

"I'm yours, *La Huesuda*. But remember their faces, the way their fear tastes!"

He concentrated on a silent prayer to Death, and even the sound of his breaking bones could not penetrate the comforting silence he found.

***

The water swallowed them like a cold black maw. Sarah never let go of Marta's hand, even as they plunged to the bottom and hit the concrete below. The air blew from Marta's lungs, and her tailbone stung as her body impacted the sidewalk below. She was yanked up to the surface, and she choked out a mouthful of dirty water as she was dragged along behind Sarah. They waded out through the water. It moved like a river's current, but it wasn't as strong as the liquid serpent she was accustomed to battling. Marta was half blinded by the rain, and memories of the Rio Grande haunted her. Jose, her protector, who had kept her alive along those banks and rambling torrents, was dead, and she refused to let this black flood take her down, if only to honor her brother's sacrifice. She would keep fighting.

"We're fucked," Sarah said.

They were caught behind a tall chain-link fence that was lined with barbed wire across the top.

"Climb," Marta urged Sarah. "Better to get cut than caught again."

Marta unbuttoned her shirt and pulled it off. She threw it over her shoulder and climbed the fence. Sarah followed her lead and took off her jersey, wrapping it around her neck like a scarf. They came to the top and threw their meager protection over the barbed wire. Marta hesitated, knowing it wouldn't do much to save their skin from being pierced, but they had no choice.

"This is going to hurt, but we have to do it," she said to Sarah.

The girl was already ahead of her, throwing her jersey over the wire and preparing to climb over it.

"I'm never goin' back in there again," Sarah said.

CHAPTER TWELVE
TRAPPED

THE TRIO MADE it to the auto shop across from the sheriff's office. It stood out from the black flood waters like an ivory tower: three stories high, its orange security lighting glowing in the early morning hours, a beacon of hope against the gray sky.

"Here we are," Timothy said.

"This is Graceland, huh?" Cole asked.

"Inside it is."

"The lower floor appears flooded," Anthony said.

"What we want is on the second floor, behind a steel door like a bank vault. I know the password to the door," Timothy said. "After we get some weaponry, we'll head up the hill as Anthony suggested."

"How do you know the code? They make a habit of handing those out to prison guards?" Cole asked.

"My ex-girlfriend was a deputy sheriff," Timothy answered, "until I caught her bangin' her boss . . . "

"Ouch."

"In the gun vault."

"That bitch!" Anthony said.

"Guess that makes this heist a little sweeter, huh?"

"You're damn right."

Their plan was clear and easy. They'd snatch whatever weapons and supplies they could find; then they'd make the trek to the side of the hill, overlooking an ocean where miles and miles of open desert used to be.

Cole studied the gap between the auto shop and the sheriff's station. It was too far for the ladder, and too far to jump. "I'm thinking we need to find a boat or something."

Between them and Graceland was a street flooded high enough to cover their heads. Cole wasn't looking forward to getting back in the water after the attack at the prison. The look on his brother's face told him Anthony felt the same way.

"I have to be honest, boys. I'm not terribly excited about getting in that water or even floating on the surface of it," Timothy said, rubbing the side of his face gouged by serrated suction cups.

"We aren't in any danger right now, we have time to think about this," Cole said.

"What are we currently camped out on?" Anthony asked.

"Earl's Auto Shop," said Timothy.

"I'm positive there will be something inside we can use to get across," Cole said.

They leaned over each side of the roof until they located a large window, but it was covered in a roll-down shutter.

"Earl probably kept that open to let the gas fumes out," Timothy said.

"How are we getting it open?"

"You convicts probably know a thing or two about breaking and entering, right?"

"Go fuck yourself," Anthony answered.

"I got it," Cole said. "We'll secure the ladder to that pipe, and you climb down and see if the cover's locked."

Timothy nodded. "Okay, if you two promise to hold on to that ladder and make sure I don't go for a swim."

"You got it."

"And don't shake that ladder."

Cole grinned. "We're thieves, Timothy, not murderers."

***

Cole and Anthony used Timothy's belt to secure the ladder to a rusted pipe that ran down the wall. The brothers held the ladder while Timothy descended. The sun shone through the clouds; more rain was coming.

Anthony and Cole held the ladder as Timothy reached over and shook the shutter on the side of the shop. With a loud crash, the shutter rolled up, and they heard Timothy cheer. He nodded and shouted up to them, "I'm going inside!"

The weight at the end of the ladder eased as Timothy stepped onto the window ledge. The brothers watched him, their arms relieved. He disappeared into the auto shop.

"I'm sick of all this water," Anthony said. "It stinks. Smells like ammonia or some shit."

"It definitely doesn't sit right with me. I mean, sure we're not used to this much rain, but it don't smell right."

Their eyes were fixed on the dark water below when they saw it ripple, and a long, snake-like object shifted beneath its surface.

"What the fuck was that?" Cole asked.

Rain pelted the backs of their necks, but they didn't move, watching the water, waiting for it to move again.

"Did you see that?" Cole asked.

"I saw something under the water," Anthony said.

"Timothy . . . "

A tentacle crept out of the water, long and slick. It snaked up the wall and dragged its body from the dark depths.

***

Timothy found himself standing on top of a row of steel cabinets. In the center of the shop, the roof of a white SUV peeked out from the black water like a deserted island. He glanced around, trying to find anything to use as a flotation device. In ordinary circumstances it wouldn't have been a great distance, but in the current situation, it felt like miles. He knew most shops sold inner tubes to kids to float the river on weekends, but not in a place like Earl's. He would have had better luck with the Smart-Mart, but that was across town. They'd been fine since they'd cleared the prison, but Timothy knew the sense of security couldn't last. He felt an urgency building in him to get to Graceland, and then up the hill as quickly as possible.

A rancid stench filled his nose, like piss and canned tuna. It raised goosebumps on his arm. Having spent his whole life in the desert, it wasn't a natural scent to him, yet it was chillingly familiar. Memories of powerful arms dragging him beneath the water filled his mind. The power of them, that unbreakable grip. If it weren't for Cole and Anthony, he would have been dead. Timothy felt his knees threatening to buckle as anxiety gripped him. He sat down and scooted back until he felt the wall behind him. If he could have receded into it forever, he would have.

Timothy sat there in the flooded garage, listening as a noise below him grew from an occasional faint splash to a full-blown ruckus. It took every ounce of courage left in him to look at the source of the commotion. His heart stuttered, even if he wasn't surprised to see tentacles suctioning to the side of the white SUV, exploring it, testing its challenge to the new predators of Arizona. The car alarm blared suddenly, sending Timothy back to his hiding spot, shaking from the trauma of facing another cephalopod. The siren died as quickly as it began, but his voice rang out in a short scream. He put his hand over his mouth and waited.

CHAPTER THIRTEEN
A CITY OF LAKES

MARTA AND SARAH climbed down the other side of the fence with their flesh weeping blood. The barbed wire had slashed their skin open in too many places to count, leaving them trembling and weak. Their wounds stung in the wind and rain. Their adrenaline hadn't failed them yet, but their bodies wouldn't be able to take much more abuse. Marta knew they needed to find shelter, but they needed to leave the warehouse far behind them first. The water grew deeper as they made their way towards the opposite end of Apache Wells. Her entire being was nothing but nerves, and fear shrouded around her. They bled into the water, and she worried what would taste the trails of crimson drifting along behind them. The revving of motors in the distance filled her with panic. The hunters of the cult refused to let their "slop" leave so easily. Her mind went to Jose. She prayed he didn't suffer, that his spirit was granted the freedom only dead men knew.

"They're coming for us," Sarah said.

"We gotta get out of here, but where?"

"Follow me."

Marta let Sarah guide her over to an old house. It was half-flooded, but its second story was free of water.

"They'll find us here," Marta whispered, listening to the sound of motors growing louder.

"Then we have to kill them," Sarah said matter-of-factly. Sarah was only a teenager, but was taller and stronger than Marta.

Marta hoped it was enough.

They climbed a muddy slope to the boarded-up house. Whoever owned it had abandoned it years before the waters came. On higher ground, it was easier to move. Sarah pulled Marta over to the porch; it creaked as they climbed the steps. The front door was open, and the inside smelled of mold and something acrid. Its walls were decorated with graffiti and fist-sized holes.

"This used to be a place for squatters," Sarah explained.

Marta sneaked to the boarded window and stole a glance through the rotting wooden barriers to see two Jet Skis carrying four of the Risen.

She turned back to warn Sarah, but her feet shot out from under her. The water wasn't deep, but was enough to choke her as she fell. A short cry escaped her before she was wrapped in darkness, a suffocating embrace winding around her. She heard Sarah's terrified, muffled cries from above the water. Marta freed her arms and forced herself upward, managing to get up long enough to pull air back into her lungs. She knew what had her, and the likelihood of surviving the attack. She felt tentacles grappling, binding her hands to keep her from pushing back to the surface. The water around her exploded in frenzy, and a hand grabbed her hair. Her head was tugged up above the water. Sarah was screaming and jabbing at the squid with something, but Marta couldn't see for the dirty water in her eyes.

"Let her go, motherfucker!"

Marta felt a sharp ripping at the flesh near her elbow. The thing was biting chunks from her. Sarah's fingers stayed wrapped in Marta's dark ponytail, and her other arm swung around Marta in quick stabbing motions. Finally she felt the death grip loosen, then free her completely. Marta was dragged to her feet, and as she went limp, she felt herself hoisted over the girl's shoulder. She heard Sarah grunting with exertion, and her vision spun, and she saw Sarah's tennis shoes climbing a set of stairs. The floorboards creaked and moaned beneath them as she gently dropped Marta onto a dusty bed on the floor.

"*Gracias*," Marta wheezed.

"You're welcome."

Marta watched her go to the window and peer through brittle plastic mini-blinds.

"They're still there. Come on, you assholes. Come see Sarah now."

She was only in a sports bra and a pair of basketball shorts, but with her skin drenched in blood, she looked like a warrior.

"How did you save me?" Marta asked.

Sarah spun around and held out a rusty kitchen knife. "I stabbed it in the eye."

Loud voices came from downstairs, and Marta forced herself to stand. She reached down and picked up the broken leg of a wooden chair at the side of the bed, probably for a mother to tend her sick children. At least that was the ghostly vision that flashed across Marta's consciousness for a split second.

"Aim for their eyes, too," Marta said.

***

"We can smell you!" a man's voice hollered.

"Look! They killed a child of the Old Gods!" a second man muttered, his voice a mixture of anger and fear.

"They'll pay for that."

Marta and Sarah stood at each side of the door, waiting for their attackers. Sarah gripped her knife while Marta cocked the broken chair leg back like a baseball bat. The house was two stories but small, with only two rooms on the upstairs floor. It wouldn't take the Teeth of the Risen long to locate their prey. But if they thought it would be easy, Sarah and Marta had other plans.

"Thank you," Sarah whispered as footfalls filled the stairwell.

"For what?"

"Giving me my life back."

The determination in Sarah's eyes was like a wildfire, spreading to consume Marta as well. Her pain fled as her heart pumped pure adrenaline through her veins. The door flew in, and the first hunter followed. Sarah jabbed him in the face, sending him falling into the others behind him. She was fast, moving with the speed of a girl bent on vengeance. She slashed at the man in the lead, opening his throat. He fell, gripping the gash, as if he could hold his blood in by the sheer force of his grip. The second hunter caught splintered wood in the nose. Marta didn't relent; she swung again and hit the third man in line. The first fell forward as a red pool slipped between his fingers. The second and third were injured, but angry.

"Here, piggy, piggy," the second hunter taunted, blood pouring out of his nose.

"Come get it, motherfucker," Sarah said.

He ran, but she side-stepped and spun, leaving her knife planted in the back of his neck. Its rotted wooden handle came loose in Sarah's hand, leaving her weapon in the dying man. The third grabbed Sarah in a bear hug, but Marta swung and connected with the side of his skull, knocking him to the grimy wooden floor. She stood over him and beat his head until he no longer moved.

"That's only three," Sarah said, breathing heavily.

Marta went to the window and tore the blinds away, and the sight of her shocked the last hunter waiting beside the Jet Skis.

A SUNKEN DESERT

"Waiting for your friends?" Marta screamed. She nodded to Sarah as they hoisted the first corpse up to the open window. "Here ya go!"

They dropped the other two dead bodies as the last hunter watched in confusion and anger. He turned and looked back up the hill towards the warehouse before gunning it and heading back to that house of horrors.

"He knew he couldn't take us," Sarah said proudly.

"*Pinche cobarde!*" Marta screamed as he fled.

Sarah pointed out the window. "They left a Jet Ski. Let's get as far from here as we can."

"*Vamonos,*" Marta said.

They headed downstairs, cautious of the many-armed hunters that could be hiding anywhere in the water. They quickly searched and found two filthy sweaters and another rusted kitchen knife. They donned the sweaters, and Marta let Sarah keep their only weapon in her pocket.

***

The city was like a rundown Atlantis, nearly everything ruined. Marta maneuvered the Jet Ski down Main Street, eyes monitoring the water around them and the flooded houses and businesses. She wasn't sure how much fuel the cult had, but she knew their mode of transportation would die eventually. She wanted to be prepared, and to protect the girl behind her. Sarah, though only a teen, seemed accustomed to hard living. Marta wanted to get as far from Apache Wells as possible, but they'd need supplies before making their escape from the territory of the Risen.

"That was the sheriff's office," Sarah pointed out.

"Maybe there are survivors there," Marta said, her voice rising over the Jet Ski motor.

"No, we checked before we got taken by those crazy assholes."

"We?" Marta asked.

"I was with my older brother. My mom didn't make it." The girl paused before continuing. "They killed him too."

"I'm so sorry," Marta said.

"We had no idea what was happening. Everything just turned to shit after the floods. So many people died or just disappeared."

Marta felt Sarah shaking and crying softly.

"We'll make it out of here together," Marta promised.

"I wish we could have killed them all first," Sarah answered, her voice ragged and exhausted.

CHAPTER FOURTEEN
TWO, SEVEN, ONE, NINE

TIMOTHY KNEW IT was coming for him before the smell hit his nose. He recalled television specials showing how intelligent squid could be and how agile they were. It was no surprise when the tip of a tentacle crept over the edge of the cabinet he hid on. Timothy tried to reach the windowsill, hoping to climb the ladder quickly enough to avoid the tangle of suffocating tentacles again. He glanced to his escape route and froze. Two tentacles snaked through the window, followed by the bulbous body of a second creature. Its bulging golden eyes focused on him.

"HELP!" he screamed, knowing his cover was blown.

It came for him, reaching out to the frightened prey before it. Timothy saw the second, larger squid mounting the cabinet top. It all seemed to be the makings of an impossible nightmare—squid hunting flooded deserts—but the pain and fear of his first encounter outside the prison told him it was reality.

The squid crawling through the window spotted its competition and moved in faster, as if reaching him first would cause the other contender to give up. It didn't; it only prompted the larger one to lunge, and its tentacles found Timothy's ankle. The smaller squid reached out, its suction cup-lined tentacle enclosing his wrist in a firm grip.

"NO!"

Timothy lashed out to fight off his attackers, but resistance only made them cling tighter, each end of his body stuck in a living Chinese finger trap. No matter how he struggled, the squid wouldn't release him. He screamed for help until beaks met flesh and turned his words to garbled cries of agony.

***

A SUNKEN DESERT

"Are you sure about this?" Cole asked his brother.

Anthony gripped the ladder and nodded, face determined and every muscle in his body ready. "All I did in the pen was work out. I can hold you."

Cole shuddered at the wailing from inside the auto shop. He descended the ladder as quickly as he could. He came to the last rung on the ladder and peeked inside. Timothy was caught in a tug o' war between two squid. The ladder trembled as he stuck his foot out and stood on the window ledge. He glanced up at his brother and shook his head. He could see Anthony's face fall into an angry frown.

Cole stepped inside, repeating to himself that he wouldn't let Timothy die beneath those tentacles and snapping beaks. He stood on the top of the large steel cabinets; the smell of blood and the unrelenting screams of his companion shook him. The smaller squid had nearly torn Timothy's arm off, while the larger one claimed his abdomen, its beak slick with blood as it tore into his soft flesh. Its tentacle had already plunged into a deep wound, and Cole couldn't tell it from Timothy's innards.

"Two, seven, one, nine!" Timothy hollered.

Cole was confused, but his anger was building. He took one step forward and Timothy screamed, "No! Two, seven, one, nine!"

Cole halted; Timothy was shaking his head weakly.

"Two, seven, one, nine."

Cole realized he was relaying the code to Graceland. Timothy knew he wasn't going to survive.

"Go!" Timothy screamed as blood flowed from his mouth.

Cole retreated back out the window and looked up to Anthony. "It's too late."

He held the ladder, and gave Anthony a second to get a good grip on it before ascending. Timothy's cries silenced, and it felt like a knife in Cole's gut. He'd never have believed it, but he'd begun to like the prison guard. A screech of metal took him by surprise, and he felt himself falling.

***

Anthony held the ladder in place for Cole. His arms burned, but he was used to pushing himself to his limits. He was laid out on the graveled roof of the auto shop, the top rung of the ladder in his hands. He was far stronger than his older brother or the prison guard, and he was confident he could hold their weight long enough for them to climb back up, but the look on Cole's face at the window told Anthony to expect the worst. He'd seen that look before, and it was always a bad sign. His brother re-emerged without Timothy, and Anthony knew he was dead. He watched Cole climb back up, when suddenly the sound of screeching metal filled his ears. The old extension ladder broke, sending Cole into the black water below.

"No!"

Anthony watched, and time slowed to a crawl. The only family he had left disappeared in the dangerous flood. Anthony leapt from the roof, hell-bent on rescuing Cole or dying beside him.

***

Marta and Sarah heard the commotion coming from the side of the auto shop.

"What the hell is that?" Sarah asked.

"Sounds like trouble to me," Marta answered.

They inched closer to find two men in the flood water, bound in tentacles and fighting to the death.

"Should we help?" Marta asked.

"I don't want to risk it."

"We can't just let them die."

"How do we know they aren't some of those assholes in the warehouse?"

"If they are, then we'll toss them back in. But I don't think these things go after them anyway."

"Okay."

Marta nodded and sped forward on the Jet Ski. They came within feet as the men struggled; one appeared to be dressed in the bright orange jumpsuit of a prisoner.

Cole's head popped up out of the water, gulping before being dragged back down. His cheek had circular red marks from tearing a tentacle from his skin.

"They're both tangled up with a smaller one," Marta said.

Sarah pulled the old kitchen knife out of her pocket. "How should we do this?"

Anthony surfaced, coughing out a mouthful of dirty water. "Help!" he pleaded.

Sarah leaned out to hand him the knife. He took it and returned to battle, slashing and cutting until the squid gave up and released them. Cole surfaced and wheezed in deep lungfuls of air. Anthony handed the knife back to Sarah, who was holding her hand out anxiously.

A SUNKEN DESERT

"Hold on," Marta ordered, and towed them to a submerged truck where they could climb up onto its roof. "Who are you?" she asked, wary that they could be the lunatic cult members who wanted to eat her.

"We're just passin' through," Cole said.

"We're leaving town," Anthony added, holding his hands up calmly.

"How do we know you're not dangerous?" Marta asked, eyeing Anthony's prison garb.

"I guess in this kind of situation you don't, but I can assure you we aren't going to try any shit. We just want to get as far from this place as we can," Anthony said.

"Same here."

"It's safer in groups," Cole said.

"We're not interested," said Sarah.

"Would you mind givin' us a lift to the sheriff's station, then?" Cole asked.

"That's where we were headed," Sarah said, and looked to Marta, who nodded. "But I'm going to warn you, if you try to hurt us, I'll kill both of you." She held the knife out before her, its blade stained with black blood.

"We're not going to hurt you; in fact, we might be able to help you, repay you for saving us," Cole said.

"How so?" Marta asked, shooting a glance over her shoulder at Sarah, who tensed up.

"There should be plenty of weapons in that station, and if you give us a lift, we'll share them."

"Why not leave you here and claim them for our own?" Sarah asked.

Cole grinned. "Because they're locked up, and I'm the only man who knows the code."

CHAPTER FIFTEEN
HUNT

THE SEER'S MINIONS had rarely seen him so angry. He paced the warehouse with the Heart on his trail. She babbled and spat prophesies of blood and dead gods.

"I have seen this, it was shown to me," he raged. "The others, like maggots, will devour us all unless we skin them alive."

The Heart fell silent and nodded. Her eyes went to the corpse hanging from the ceiling. It was the brother of the troublemaker, the woman who'd escaped with the dark-skinned girl. The Heart's hands were bloody from stealing Jose's heart. It was the only way to stop the power in him. When he cursed the Risen with the name of his death god, *La Huesuda*, she felt a wind so cold it took her breath away. He died after their clubs broke every bone in his body, but the Heart still felt his spirit stalking them. So she'd suggested removing his skin and heart. The Seer agreed, and his orders were fulfilled.

"We must find them," he said, his voice drawing the Heart's attention back to him.

"And bleed them dry, make them rain like the sky," she agreed.

The Seer stood before the tank to ask the beast for its knowledge. Its eyes glowed a yellow gold, and he felt his resolve growing. He could feel a second pulse within him. The Old Ones wouldn't let the girl escape so easily, but the Risen had to do their part as well. He placed his hand on the tank and felt its power, calling out to its brethren to kill the women who had escaped.

"Gather the hunters and send them out for her again. I should not have underestimated them before. I should have sent more men, but who would have thought a woman and a girl could be so vicious . . ."

The men came forward, slapping their chests and howling, ready to avenge their brothers.

A SUNKEN DESERT

"Bring the leftovers. I want to question them," the Seer ordered.

An old man and a blonde woman were thrown at his feet. The blonde held a pink teddy bear and kept her eyes on the floor. The old man gazed up at the Seer, his face an angry snarl.

"Where did they go?" the Seer asked.

"We don't know," the blonde answered in fearful obedience. "They didn't say anything about where they were going."

He looked to the old man. "I was asking you too."

"They didn't say anything about their plans . . . but I hope they come back and tear your head off," the old man answered. His hands came together, and he fingered his wedding ring again. It gave him the strength to defy the Seer, to initiate his death sentence.

"You have gotten brave," the Seer sneered.

"The woman made me remember my wife. She was strong like that girl, but you killed her!"

"Oh, your wife," the Seer scoffed. "She tasted fine but was far too bony."

The old man rose faster than the Seer expected and landed a swift punch to the cult leader's nose. He was dragged away and beaten until blood ran from his nose and eyes. He was flung in the slop cell, far closer to death than life. Three in all, their meat wouldn't sustain the cult's hunger—or that of the one in the massive tank.

"It's time to hunt."

The blonde captive remained still and quiet, clutching her teddy bear. The haggard woman stood before her and put her filthy hand out to the child's toy.

"Your babe sleeps well, but your babe sleeps in hell," the Heart sang.

The blonde began to weep, and it drew the Seer's attention.

"Keep quiet or you'll join the old man. If you're a good girl, then perhaps I'll grant you a new child," he whispered, placing his hand on her stomach.

"Wives, you need wives, perhaps spare the traitors' lives," the Heart sang.

"The youngest may stay for breeding, but the woman, I shall feed her piece by piece to the child of the Old Gods."

***

They poured from the warehouse and made their way to a makeshift dock. They climbed onto Jet Skis and into small two-man boats. Their fishing vessel was too large to traverse the city, but the smaller craft could hunt its many alleys and yards. They made their way into Apache Wells, searching for the treacherous woman and the girl.

They were sinewy and gaunt from their diet of human flesh, the only food the Old Gods approved of. Meat was harder to find since they'd hunted the survivors of the floods into near-extinction. The weeks and months of behaving like gluttonous worms would haunt them soon, when there wasn't anything left but old bones to chew upon. They needed the flesh and marrow of the escapees to hold them over until they brought more captives back to the warehouse.

Those in the lead were drawn to the distant sound of a Jet Ski engine. It signaled that they hadn't lost their prey yet, and soon they would reclaim it to lay at the Seer's feet.

CHAPTER SIXTEEN
CUBICLE MAUSOLEUM

THEY PEERED THROUGH the broken doors of the sheriff's station, the water high enough to submerge the front desk, deep enough to reach Marta's chest.

"You two stay on the Jet Ski and ride in as far as you can. We'll wade through and try to find a way upstairs," Cole said.

Marta nodded. They ducked through the doorway. Cole and Anthony followed, senses on full alert. The stagnant water stank of ammonia.

"Watch the water."

"You're not the only one who's nearly been killed by those things," Marta said. "Just hurry up. We've got more to worry about than what's below the water."

Anthony and Cole exchanged a glance. They had no idea what she was talking about, but it didn't sound promising. They rushed toward an open stairwell at the opposite end of the room.

Cole hardly breathed. Every time he bumped against something beneath the water, he felt tentacles twining around his ankles. His nose and lungs burned from nearly being drowned by a smaller one. He wasn't sure he could survive one any larger.

He looked over to his brother. Anthony looked so much like their mother, his heart ached. But he knew he was being selfish. She was one of the lucky ones, and he was glad she'd passed on before she was forced to fight for her life against armies of invading cephalopods.

They reached the stairwell and breathed a sigh of relief as they started climbing. The stairs were lit by faint fluorescent lights. A low hum from a back-up generator chased away the suffocating silence of the main lobby.

Cole was tired of water, tired of being wet, tired of the smell of flooded streets and houses. His journey to rescue his brother had taken him through nightmare zones, survivors escaping the ruins of their lives. He hadn't helped. He was focused only on Anthony. Now flashes of their suffering came back; it haunted him that those hollow-eyed people were probably dead now. He paused as the horror threatened to take him over.

"Is the whole world this way?" he asked Anthony.

"This has to be big. Timothy was right when he asked where the government boys are. This is serious shit, and no one came to help . . . "

Cole came to the steel door leading into the second floor. Anthony stood behind him, ready to fight. "Ready?"

"Open it up," Anthony whispered.

Cole turned the doorknob. On the other side was an ordinary office: desks separated by low cubicles, paintings of the desert alongside framed awards for bravery in the face of grave danger. There were filing cabinets, and an L-shaped desk with butterfly stationary and a cat calendar on top. It looked as if nothing had happened.

"Kinda eerie to look at," Anthony said.

"I wonder where she is now?"

Cole picked up a coffee mug and turned it over in his hands. It, too, was painted with butterflies.

"She sure liked butterflies."

"She sure did," Cole said, and the finality hit him.

"Leave it as we found it."

Cole made sure to place it exactly where it was before everything went to hell. "Over there, in that office."

"I don't remember Timothy giving us the code."

"It was the last thing he said to me before he was killed," Cole said.

"I wish things were different. I actually liked him."

"Me too, brother."

They tried the door, but it was locked. Anthony picked up a rolling chair and tossed it through the window. The blinds hung cockeyed, but Anthony yanked them down before climbing through. Cole followed.

They'd made it to Graceland.

Timothy's frantic last words replayed in Cole's mind as he typed two, seven, one, nine. A red light on the keypad turned green, and Cole pulled it open. The heavy door swung open like a bank vault and the brothers stepped inside. Excitement changed quickly to disappointment.

"It's already been pilfered," Anthony said.

The walls were lined in shelves, but most were already empty.

A SUNKEN DESERT

But not completely.

"There's still stuff left. Grab what we can and let's get outta here."

"I remember how this goes. Just like the good ol' days, eh, brother?"

Cole laughed while Anthony ducked back into the office and returned with an old laptop case to use as a bag for carrying bullets.

"I wish Timothy could have seen it," Cole said.

They collected three pistols and two shotguns. As Cole pulled the slide back on the pistol and felt it lock into place, he suddenly felt not quite so helpless. Once they had everything they could carry, they jogged back the way they came.

As they opened the door to the stairwell, they were met by screams and the sound of splashing. Cole readied his pistol and entered the waist-high water as silently as he could.

***

"Could you teach me Spanish?" Sarah asked Marta.

"Of course."

"I always wanted to learn, but I never stayed in one school long enough. It sounds really cool when you talk like that."

"Thank you."

"Are you from Mexico?" Sarah asked.

"I was born there, but moved to Texas when I was little, so I learned to speak both English and Spanish."

"I only know the bad words," Sarah said, and it made Marta laugh.

"Everyone says that."

She liked having Sarah around. It helped, being without Jose. Her eyes watered just thinking about her brother.

"I'll teach you everything you want to know," Marta promised. She felt Sarah relax a bit against her back. "Are you tired?"

"I could sleep for days."

"Once we get out of here, we'll find a place where we can rest."

"I'm starving, too."

"You're a growing girl. You need some food after all the fighting we've done," Marta said softly.

She felt Sarah's arms tighten around her stomach, then heard the girl scream as she was tugged away.

"No!"

Marta spun around, and a bubble the size of her head breached the surface, along with a strangled cry. Marta dove from the Jet Ski. The flood consumed her in darkness and a strong grip wrapped around her throat. She clawed at the tentacle as it tightened around her neck. The beast drew her near, its bulging yellow eyes staring with hungry anticipation. Her lungs burned, but the sight of Sarah in its grip sent her adrenaline into high gear. Marta raked her nails across one bulbous eye. The creature loosened its grip and scuttled away with its first prize. Marta grabbed the squid by the tentacle, and it dragged her along for a few feet, but got spooked by her ferocity and released Sarah.

Marta grabbed the limp girl and forced Sarah's head above water, screaming for help. The Jet Ski was only feet away, but in her terror the distance looked wider than the Rio Grande. She struggled to carry the larger girl back and laid her head on the footrest of the Jet Ski. She wasn't breathing, so Marta did as Jose had showed her when she was still only a teenager. She tilted Sarah's head to open her airways and breathed air into her lungs.

Gunshots rang out. She saw the brothers coming for her, unleashing at the squid. It had climbed atop a sunken desk to challenge them for the prey Marta had stolen from it. Cole blasted a hole through it. Black blood and chunks rained down, and the air reeked of ammonia.

"Help!" Marta called, her voice breaking as she began to cry.

Cole struggled to her side. He gripped Sarah's jaw, tilted her head back, and began administering CPR. The girl coughed and gagged. He jerked back as black water and vomit spewed from her mouth. She was breathing again. Marta gripped his shoulder and wept.

"Thank you," she repeated over and over. Her relief was shattered by the sound of approaching motors. She lifted her head in the direction of the sound. "It's them."

Sarah was exhausted and confused, but at the noise covered her ears in a vain attempt to block out the truth.

The cult had found them, and the warehouse awaited them. The slop cell was emptying quickly, and required fresh meat.

Anthony looked to his brother and nodded grimly. "She warned us about the dangers above the surface."

***

"Do something!" the Seer shouted at the winds battering the warehouse. "These strangers can't be allowed to test your power!" His frustration had brought his rage to its peak. "Show me your power!"

A pounding on the glass brought the Seer to the tank. He fell to his

A SUNKEN DESERT

knees reverently and placed his palms against it. The glowing yellow eyes in the murky water began to pulse, and his heart thundered in his chest.

"Yes, yes, I beseech you. We must end the strangers."

The Seer closed his eyes as a wave of power swept through him. His flesh began to itch and burn. Every tattoo felt as if it had been doused in gasoline and lit with a match. He breathed deeply to control the pain setting his nerve endings on fire. The cloud of agony began to dissipate, and a picture formed in his mind: a vision of hundreds of tentacles, writhing and reaching, golden unblinking eyes: an army of the Children of the Old Gods descending upon Apache Wells. The Seer understood the pain pulsing through his human body was a battle cry. The Old One released him, and he fell to the warehouse floor, each tattooed eye raised into bleeding welts.

Feed me.

The Seer rose shakily to his feet. He had been in its thrall for months and hadn't questioned it even once, not after the first time it claimed his mind. When it showed him the god it spoke for, it had left him in terrified awe. He stumbled to the corpse of Jose and cut off a chunk of exposed meat from the dead man's leg.

"I should never have challenged the Ancient Ones, or you," he said as he brought the meat to the tank.

He watched it sink into the dark water, leaving a wavering crimson cloud. A massive tentacle shot out and the child of the Old Gods ate, its eyes fixed on the Seer, a silent warning that he would be the next meal if he chose to question again.

***

The sounds of revving engines were followed by the voices of the Risen, whipped into a frenzy by the thought of spilling Marta's blood. The Seer demanded her back, and they meant to oblige. Food ran low and the Risen only had a few females for breeding.

The sound of gunfire drew them to the old sheriff's station. Their leader was the man who piloted the boat that fished the desert sea. He held a hand up to silence the rest.

"They're here, but we must be sly. They must have found the last of the officers' guns inside." He turned to a man with three teeth left in his mouth. "You said there were no more guns in the city."

"Those who fled took the last of them."

Another shot sounded in the distance. "Obviously not."

"We searched everywhere and didn't find anything left," the toothless one explained.

A shock of worry ran through his insides. The Seer had sent out groups in search of guns, and they'd found very little. The survivors of Apache Wells had fled to larger cities, seeking refuge after the flooding and sickness. Those stubborn enough to stay became prey to the lunatics of the Risen.

"There was a safe within the second floor, one we were never able to open," the toothless man admitted.

"And how did they?" the leader asked.

The toothless one lowered his eyes.

They floated for a moment, watching, waiting, when the dark water around them began to ripple and bubble as sets of golden orbs breached the surface. The leader was caught off-guard by the sheer numbers of the Children amassing.

"The Old Gods smile upon us," he proclaimed, and a cheer went up from his men.

"They don't have enough weaponry to stop us now," the toothless old man said.

"I know you demand payment for coming to us in our time of need," the leader said, speaking down to the water.

He grabbed the toothless hunter by the hair, dragged a knife through the flesh above the man's Adam's apple, and dropped him into the water with a choked gurgling cry. The Children tangled around the sacrifice and pulled him under. A massive bubble came to the surface, signaling their acceptance of the flesh of this man who had failed.

The leader looked to his men. "Ready yourselves. And mark his example."

***

"They're waiting for us," Anthony whispered as he looked out the window of the flooded sheriff's office.

"What are they packin'?" Cole asked.

"I was held hostage by them for, I don't know how long, weeks, months," Sarah said. "I never saw them with any guns."

"They're in for a surprise, then," Cole said.

"We don't have much either," his brother reminded him.

"I know you're accustomed to old Ralph's warehouse filled with street sweepers, but these pistols and shotguns are better than nothing."

A SUNKEN DESERT

"You got that right. What's your plan?" Anthony asked.

"Five guns is better than zero, and these bastards are about to find out why."

Cole gripped his brother's shoulder and laid out his plan and a way to achieve vengeance for the horrors the women had suffered at the hands of the men outside.

CHAPTER SEVENTEEN
AN ARMY OF HUNGRY CHILDREN

MARTA SLID DOWN from the Jet Ski. Anthony handed her a gun, and Sarah the bag of ammunition. He helped them through the deeper water to the stairwell with the shotguns. He and Cole armed themselves with handguns. They hoped it was enough to end the threat beyond the station doors.

"Just stay here," Anthony said.

"Be careful, those pieces of shit are crazy," Marta warned.

"I've dealt with some awful people in my time. I've found that most only respond to broken bones and bullet holes."

She watched him wade back to his brother waiting on the Jet Ski.

"Do you think they'll make it?" Sarah asked.

"We gotta have faith that they will."

The women ascended a few steps and sat down. Sarah held Marta's hand, and Marta wondered how long it had been since the girl had felt the presence of a motherly figure. She had no idea if God had turned His back on the human race, or if He was behind the brutal cleansing of the earth, but still she prayed silently to herself. Tears stung her eyes when her mind turned to her brother. She knew he couldn't have survived his wounds. He knew that, too, and had died to save her, and yet she really didn't want to believe she would never see him again. Marta wondered how her mother fared in Texas. If it was anything like Arizona, she doubted the old woman would be alive. She squeezed Sarah's hand at the thought of her mother trapped in the same hell she was. Sarah laid her head on Marta's shoulder and whispered, "We can make it through this."

Marta wiped the tears from her eyes and pushed aside the crushing thoughts of the future. Anger replaced sadness. Thoughts of revenge filled her mind. The need to shed blood would sustain her.

A SUNKEN DESERT

Gunshots echoed nearby, and sudden booms filled the stairwell. Sarah tensed and got to her feet. Marta rose beside her.

"They found us," Sarah whispered.

Marta imagined the memories running through the young girl's mind, the horrors faced at the hands of the cult. She put her hand on Sarah's shoulder to calm her.

"We will make it through this," she said to Sarah. "And I'm going to make those bastards pay for all they did to us and all they took from us."

***

Anthony and Cole emerged with guns blazing. Anthony popped up behind Cole, while Cole drove one-handed, firing a pistol. The group awaiting them wasn't as large as they expected.

The Risen fell back into retreat.

Cole and Anthony didn't hesitate, nailing bullets into their backs. The Risen fell into the black water, never to emerge.

"This is like shooting fish in a barrel!" Anthony laughed, blasting a hole through the chest of a scumbag trying to escape.

They meant to chase all the Risen down and fill them with holes, but an unseen obstruction was forming, a hungry one with snapping beaks and reaching arms.

"What the fuck?" Cole cried, and whipped the Jet Ski away from the remaining men.

"What?"

"The water!"

The flooded streets were rippling and writhing, teeming with squid. They came, tentacles snaking to grip the ankles of Anthony and Cole. The stench of ammonia and stagnant water filled the air around them. The sound of outboard motors signaled the retreat of the Risen. They were leaving the brothers to the hunters in the flood waters.

"Keep shooting!"

They needed to warn Marta and Sarah of the growing danger. Cole hit the gas, powering towards the station, but felt the engine sputter.

"Fuck!" Cole cried.

The Jet Ski coasted to a slow halt within feet of the sheriff's office.

"Let's go!"

Cole and Anthony climbed down, fearing at any moment they'd be pulled under the surface. They'd passed through the wide doorway when they heard splashing. Cole spun around as hulking tentacles grabbed the

Jet Ski, searching for prey. It slunk back down into the black water, and he lost sight of it.

"Fuck, they're comin'."

"Up the stairs!" Anthony shouted.

The water came to life with scrambling limbs and bulbous heads through the open doorway. Cole turned and fired, leaving a few mortally wounded. He pulled the trigger until the gun was empty as he waded backwards towards the stairwell.

"Go!" Anthony screamed, and fired while his brother headed to the stairs.

Cole ran up the steps to find Marta and Sarah frightened and confused.

"The men?" Marta asked.

"Fuckin' squid!" Cole answered.

Marta handed him a shotgun. He pointed up to the next floor. "Get through that door up there and lock it. I'll knock when we need in."

She nodded and grabbed the last of their weapons. Sarah watched him running back downstairs while the echoes of Anthony's gunfire rang in her ears.

***

Anthony pulled the trigger until the gun emptied. The eyes of the hungry horde focused on him and the useless weapon in his shaking hand. He hurried backward as they came for him. They hung from the walls and perched atop submerged office equipment and swiveling office chairs. He heard his brother's feet pounding the steps behind him when his legs were dragged out from under him.

Black water invaded his nostrils as he was pulled below. He slammed into a hard object and came to a stop, the tentacle around his ankle yanking, trying to dislodge him. He felt around, and the shape of the object registered as a desk. His left arm was yanked to the side, a painful wrenching of his shoulder that caused him to scream, expelling the last of his air. He reached up with his free hand, dragging the desk drawer open.

He choked as water worked its way up his nose. His fingers ran over pencils, pens, and a stapler. He felt an oval-shaped hole, and a spark of hope flared in his mind—scissors. He brought them down into the rubbery tentacle yanking his arm back. It released him. He stabbed at the tentacles wrapped around his ankles and feet. The arms retreated, and Anthony got out from under the desk, getting air into his lungs.

***

A SUNKEN DESERT

Cole lost all control when he saw the bubble of air where his brother had been. It breached the surface, and all he could think of was never seeing Anthony alive again. He pumped the shotgun and unloaded into the gelatinous creatures crawling up the walls and swimming his way. He wanted to put the barrel in his mouth and pull the trigger. Without his brother, he no longer wanted to live, and he would have splattered his brains against the sheriff's station wall if it wasn't for Sarah and Marta. Black blood and the stink of death surrounded him. He didn't have many rounds left in the shotgun, and he'd be forced to leave his brother's body somewhere in the filthy flood. He remembered his mother's voice, begging him to keep his brother safe once she was gone. Cole had failed her.

Water flew as a mass burst from beneath it, choking and wheezing, wielding a pair of scissors stained with black blood.

"Anthony!" Cole screamed.

He waded through the water, emptying the shotgun as he pulled his brother behind him. Anthony was hacking and vomit flew from his mouth, thick mucus laden with noisome water. Cole killed three more squid before the gun was useless. He flipped it around to wield as a club while he guided his brother back to the stairwell.

"Go! Back to Graceland!"

Anthony stumbled up the steps with Cole behind him.

"Fuck!" Cole cursed.

Behind them followed the Children of the Old Gods. They climbed up the walls and fought amongst themselves to be the first to tear the flesh from their human prey.

***

Marta waited on the other side of the door, her ear pressed against it. Each gunshot twisted her heart with fear. They were going to be cornered in the office, and she wondered if it would be their tomb. A pounding startled her, followed by Cole's frantic voice, and she fumbled to open the door. Anthony was pushed inside and Cole followed, slamming the door. Anthony fell to the floor, gasping.

"What are we going to do?" Sarah asked.

"Kill everything in our way," Cole answered.

CHAPTER EIGHTEEN
BLOOD FOR BLOOD

MARTA FELT HIS words light a fire in her heart. She could envision her brother's face, and she knew she wouldn't rest until she killed more than the squid beating the office door. "I wanna kill those men, too."

"I said *everything* in our way."

"Give me a gun," Sarah said.

Cole looked to her and then to Marta. In ordinary circumstances, he would have been wary of handing a girl a deadly weapon. But these weren't ordinary circumstances.

"I don't want to feel scared anymore."

Marta nodded to him and said, "I'll teach her."

"Okay."

***

The Seer knelt before the tank and pressed his palms against it.

"Only a few returned. Your Children should be destroying the nonbelievers as we speak."

The glass between him and the Child of the Old Gods thrummed with energy. He could feel the internal fires threatening to consume him again.

"I know if they survive, they will come for us. We need you to protect us," the Seer said through gritted teeth, his pain growing beneath the gaze of the ancient one.

It showed him the price he would pay for asking another favor.

"I . . . I . . . yes, master."

The stench of burning hair and flesh filled his nostrils as his lungs struggled to draw breath. It brought to his mind the day he was given the title *Seer*. The touch of the beast passed through him, his heart stuttered, and he lost consciousness. He was shown the Old Ones and their Children

A SUNKEN DESERT

making way for their return. The Children were innumerable, a legion of demigods to turn the earth into a mass grave. The hideous, looming presence of the Old Gods waiting to claim the world of man; he'd rather be their servant than their prey.

He was released, and slumped to the floor. In his mind he saw its demands increasing each time he convened with it, and knew it was tiring of the human it had chosen. The Heart came to gather him, and felt his skin burning with fever. He babbled softly to himself with his eyes half shut. She fanned with him a grubby hand until he came back around.

"Feed it," he whispered.

"Right away, right away, we must keep the Child at bay."

The old hag went to the hanging corpse of Jose and sliced a jagged chunk of flesh from the dead man's thigh. She cautiously tossed it in. The tentacled creature inside lashed out and snatched it up before it ever sank to the bottom.

"More," the Seer urged her.

She removed another thick cut of meat. The thing beat the side of the tank furiously.

"We must appease it!" the Seer said frantically.

"Come, help me!" she begged the remaining hunters from the shootout at the sheriff's station.

They helped, but watched the tank warily as the Child of the Old Gods went into a frenzy.

"Feed it the whole thing!" she cried, pointing to Jose's body.

The men hurriedly did as they were told, and the beast ravenously wrapped itself around its meal, tearing it to pieces with its tentacles and beak.

"We must keep it happy. We cannot fail the Child," the Seer kept repeating.

***

The ruckus on the other side of the door ceased, and the silence left behind was more frightening than the sounds of the creatures trying to get into the office.

"Why did they stop?" Anthony asked, his voice hoarse.

"Maybe they're waiting for us to come out," Cole said.

He walked to the door and pressed his ear against it, hearing nothing but a wet sliding and sloshing from the first floor. He put his hand gently on the handle and turned it as silently as he could.

"Don't," Marta whispered.

He held his finger up to his lips before gently opening the door wide enough to get a quick look. The stairwell was empty; there wasn't a squid to be seen. He was struck with confusion. "They're gone."

"Why would they leave?"

"Maybe they're just waiting for us," Anthony said.

"No. He can *speak* to them," Sarah said.

"Who?" But as Marta asked, the answer came. Her mind conjured the lunatic in the warehouse, the man with eyes tattooed all over his body.

"The Seer. I saw him talking to one of them he kept in a big tank. He calls these smaller ones the Children of the Old Gods."

"And it spoke back?" Cole asked.

"No, no, it only stared at him, but he said it showed him things. It gave me the creeps . . . He fed it pieces of people."

Marta felt her stomach rise into the back of her throat. The thoughts of her brother being fed to a monster in a tank left her sick with rage and sadness. Sarah's face only fueled her need for vengeance. She knew the girl had seen and experienced too many horrid things to ever speak out loud. She wanted closure for Sarah and for Jose's spirit, lost inside the lair of the Seer and his men.

Marta said, "We can't sit here and wait to see if they come back. I want out of this town."

Cole helped Anthony to his feet, and they prepared to go back downstairs.

*****

The water filling the lobby was motionless and dark, like a mirror in the night.

"Be careful," Cole said as they crossed the space to the door. They halted there while Cole took a look outside. He cursed and shook his head. "They're all going up the hill."

The others joined him and watched the writhing masses of squid heading upward. Some swam; others climbed over cars and along the storefronts. But they all moved in the same direction, as if following a call.

"They're going to *him*," Sarah said.

"I don't think we can take them all on," Anthony said.

"You don't have to, but I will. I can't leave, not without burying my brother," Marta said.

"You won't be alone. I have to see them die," Sarah said.

"Count us in too, then," Cole said.

A SUNKEN DESERT

***

The streets were a slow-moving river, the four of them moving against its flow. The black mass far ahead told them the squid were heeding the silent call to the warehouse on the hill.

They left the deepest of the flooding and crept up the hill. They used houses and businesses to keep from being seen by sentries, even though something about their enemies' retreat told them that the Seer was fully aware of their approach. He knew they would come for him and his bloodthirsty people. They stopped in the back yard of a house, the water resting around their knees.

"Take a look inside that house. I have a plan," Anthony said.

"What are we looking for?" Marta asked.

"Anything flammable."

"I like the sound of that," Sarah said with a grin, following Marta through the open back door of the single-story home.

***

The Seer felt them before they arrived, smelled them coming to their master. *His* master. He looked to the hunters he had left: a meager group, and all terrified.

"Do you not believe in the Old Gods?" he asked them.

The men who once proclaimed their loyalty to the Risen looked among each other, uncertainty twisting their faces.

"We will be victorious!" the Seer proclaimed.

They would have normally howled and beat their chests, but they remained silent, listening to the army gathering outside, slapping the side of the warehouse, snapping their beaked mouths hungrily. They had never seen such a massive group of the Children gathered in a single place. It had to be a hundred of them in varying sizes, ready to kill for the Ancient One in the tank, the voice of the Old Gods.

"It doesn't matter if they have firearms, we have them out-armed!" the Seer joked, his gallows humor falling on deaf ears.

The Heart was unusually quiet. Ordinarily she would dance about and spout morbid rhymes, but her mouth was shut, eyes fixed on the tank where the Ancient One was stripping the flesh from the dead man's bones. She felt a pain in her chest, a dire warning. She backed away slowly while the Seer spoke to his men. She faintly heard weeping from the slop cell. It was the blonde girl who gripped a teddy bear. The Heart went to the door of the slop cell to listen. She slid the lock open and shot a glance over her shoulder. The Seer was busy. The Heart stepped inside, where the girl sat crying among corpses and blood.

"Child, my heart has belonged to the wrong side for a long time. Death is outside. I can feel it in my bones."

"Help me!" the blonde cried.

"Come this way," the Heart said.

***

The writhing army waited outside the great warehouse door, their stench nearly unbearable in the breeze of an approaching storm.

"We gotta light this shit before the rain starts," Anthony said.

Cole smiled. "Well then, what are we waiting on?" He nodded to Sarah and Marta, each armed with a shotgun and pistols tucked in the backs of their pants. "Wait until we signal you."

"We know the plan," Marta said, her face grim.

The brothers left them hiding behind a van sitting on deflated tires. They watched as Cole and Anthony split up to opposite ends of a parking lot in front of the warehouse. They sneaked as close as they could before getting down to the business of killing. They stood and tossed propane tanks out amidst the gathering of squid, praying they weren't empty as they bounced and came to rest among the grappling and groping arms.

The brothers drew pistols and fired, causing two booming explosions. Black blood and chunks of flesh were sent flying. Cole kept firing, drawing the creatures to him. The move gave his brother time to pull a grocery bag off his shoulder and remove four Molotov cocktails. He only had three matches. He lit the first and tossed it in the middle of the creatures heading for his brother. The flaming bottle exploded, sending a fire sweeping outward. The Children of the Old Gods hissed and tried to flee, but were engulfed in hungry flames. He ducked back down to light the second bottle, but knew he'd been spotted. He noticed the creatures moved slower on flat land, but that was a small comfort with them bearing down on him. He lit one and held a second up to light the rag tucked in the neck of the bottle and save his last match. He rose again with the two flaming liquor bottles, and a handful of squid slid towards him.

"Eat this!"

He tossed the bottles one after the other as the squid recoiled, their tentacles slapping helplessly at the fire consuming them. He knelt down and lit the final bottle, while his brother continued to blast them as they tried to escape or fight. The brothers were steadily evening out the odds.

A SUNKEN DESERT

Anthony stood and tossed his final explosive, and it incinerated a group of squid escaping back towards the warehouse door. Cole slapped another clip into his gun, and then shouted back to Marta and Sarah. It was time for reinforcements.

***

The explosions rattled the warehouse windows. The sounds of screeching, and an acrid stench of burning cephalopod, wafted in on storm winds too late in bringing any rain. The Seer's men panicked and scrambled for weapons and places to hide from those who sought vengeance.

"Rise and fight!" the Seer ordered, but only a few obeyed.

He went to the warehouse door and listened to the dying Children of the Old Gods. He spun around, his gaze going directly to the tank and the massive squid going mad within. He'd never placed anything over the open top of the tank. That was what the creature had ordered of him. It pulled its massive body free and slunk down the outside of the great tank.

The Seer no longer felt the voice of the Old Gods. He had failed the beast, and he knew the consequences. It came directly at him, and the feeling of his insides on fire drove him to pull the door open.

He was met by a handful of charred but living squid. He took off running, naked but for his tattoos, through the middle of the fray. Behind him came the creature, seeking blood and flesh in payment from the human who drew the Children of the Old Gods to their ends.

***

The Heart dragged the young woman along behind her. She watched the Seer flee into the approaching storm with the monster close behind him. It was her chance to escape back to the old mortuary, where no one spoke but ghosts.

"Hurry!" the old hag cried.

She tugged the girl along, around the side of the warehouse to avoid the war raging between the nonbelievers and the Children of the Old Gods. They rounded the corner, but were met by a half-burned creature. It was angry and on the verge of death, a deadly combination.

"Take her!" the Heart urged, and pushed the bloody blonde out before her in offering to the beast.

"No!" she screamed.

"Why do you think I brought you along?"

A stray bullet split the air, and the squid's head burst in two. It writhed and died. The young woman turned and eyed the Heart holding hands up before her.

"Now, now, I helped free you."

"You don't think I remember . . . do you?" the young woman asked.

"Remember?"

"I heard a woman's voice singing the day my child was taken away," she said.

The hag's face fell as she recounted the day when the Seer handed her a child no older than nine months. She cooed and sang it a song. Then she cut its head off.

"You just sang me that little song about my baby being in hell . . . "

The old woman turned to run, but the blonde was already on her. She grabbed the Heart by her hair and rammed her face into the warehouse wall. Her nose broke with a crunch and blood poured down into her mouth.

"I'm going to send *you* to hell, bitch!"

She slammed her face into the warehouse wall again. The Heart went limp in her hands.

***

Bullets flew like lead bees, buzzing the promise of death. The Seer didn't attempt to placate the monster, because words would be useless. Instead, he ran for his life. He felt a pulse run through his body and he fell to his knees. The creature was calling to the other Children. The remaining squid turned from the gun-wielding humans to gather around the Seer.

Silence filled the evening air, and grey storm clouds gathered to watch the fall of the lunatic. They descended with powerful tentacles, gripping his arms and legs. The master of the horde fell upon the Seer and ate through his tattooed abdomen. His blood sent them into a frenzy, and flesh pulled from his bones in long, dripping strips.

***

Sarah and Marta held each other and watched the gruesome display.

"It's over," Marta whispered to the girl.

Anthony and Cole opened fire on the last of the squid, even the giant beast slaying the one who failed, killing them all one by one. Then their guns fell silent, the ground littered with chunks of burning flesh and black blood.

"What do we do now?" Marta asked Cole.

"I say we hijack that boat they got docked over there in the flood water and become pirates."

"I like that idea."

"Me too," Sarah said softly.

A SUNKEN DESERT

A blonde stumbled in their direction, and Anthony raised his gun. She was covered in blood and crying hysterically.

"She wasn't one of them," Sarah said.

"Does that make her one of us?" he asked.

"Yes," Marta answered.

THE RISE AND THE FALL

by Brett J. Talley

For my little girl—always dream big.

CHAPTER ONE

SEXTON WASN'T A soldier. He knelt behind the broken stone wall, clutching his AR-15, and wished he were one. He wished a lot of things. He wished he was anywhere but here, that the Rising had never happened, that it would stop raining.

Water poured from the barrel, making it slick in his hand. He wondered if the rain was bad for it. He didn't know. All they told him was which end was dangerous when he pulled the trigger.

They got a kick out of that. But they weren't laughing now.

This was supposed to be an easy crash and grab. They'd seen the abandoned farmhouse a few days earlier, on a recon mission. If anyone was alive beyond the wall, they hadn't found them. They were supposed to scavenge what they could and be back before lunch. So easy that they broke Rule #1—never go anywhere alone. They took one jeep instead of the standard two.

At first, things went well. There was grain in the barn, and the lady of the house had been handy with preserves. They'd even found jugs of homemade moonshine. The jeep was packed by noon, and there was enough left to justify return trips. It was the kind of find that gave Sexton hope that they'd make it through this after all.

Then the jeep wouldn't start.

It was like something out of a horror movie. No matter how many times they tried, the engine wouldn't turn over. Peters knew a little bit about cars, at least enough to tell them what was wrong.

"Fuel pump," he said with his hands on his waist.

"What do we do now?" asked a squat little man named Arnold. Sexton didn't know what Arnold had done before it all went down, but it was clear he wasn't a soldier either.

Vasquez was in charge. He was the only one with any real training in the field, but that was all of two years in the Air National Guard.

They had a battery-powered two-way radio in the back. Vasquez keyed the mic. "This is Ranger One, we've got a problem, over."

Static answered at first, and then Rachel's voice. "Roger, Ranger One. What's the problem, over."

"Busted fuel pump on the jeep. We can't fix it here. We'll need evac, over."

"Negative, Ranger One. Both Ranger Two and Ranger Three are in the field. ETA one hour before sunset, over." She said it matter-of-factly, but Sexton felt like she'd just read his death warrant.

"Fuck, Rachel, what are you trying to tell me?" Vasquez said, dropping all pretext. Silence and static followed.

Finally, "I'm sorry, Vas. If you can't get out yourself, you'll just have to hunker down and wait. We'll be out to get you at first light. Over."

Vasquez threw the mic back in the jeep. No one said a word. His hands went to his head as he paced back and forth.

"What's the plan, boss?" Peters asked.

"You heard the woman," he said. "We hunker down and they pick us up in the morning."

"You can't be serious," Arnold said. "We can't stay out here. Not at night."

"We don't have a choice. Besides, there haven't been any reports of them this far north. Probably nothing to worry about. Check your weapons."

They all did. They checked and re-checked, because it took their mind off what might be coming. When he couldn't check any more, Peters spent a couple of hours messing with a fuel pump he didn't know how to fix. Noon came and went, and with every minute that passed, the sun sank and the clouds grew thicker and darker.

Arnold rocked back and forth, clutching his rifle to his chest. If Vasquez noticed, he didn't say. Instead he stood, staring into the forest beyond.

"Like I said, probably nothing to worry about. But if they come," he said finally, "it will be from the south. Through those trees." He pointed to the forest beyond a broken-down stone wall behind the barn. "We'll set up behind the wall. Remember, aim for the funnel, right between the eyes. That's the way to kill them."

He said it like it was easy. Like more than a handful of people had done it before.

THE RISE AND THE FALL

Vasquez took his knife in his left hand and sliced it open. He didn't flinch. "Bring me your guns." He dipped his finger in his blood, then drew upon each weapon. A single main line, then three lines branching off to the left, two to the right. He did it on each, and on his own. "Maybe that will help," he said.

The rain started, like clockwork, just as the sun sank below the horizon. The four men crouched behind the broken wall, staring into the darkness. Their eyes adjusted, and Sexton watched the trees. Rain poured from the end of his barrel, mixed with the oil from the gun and Vasquez's blood, the sigil he had drawn fading with every drop.

Hours passed. Sexton began to think maybe they'd be okay. He watched the trees sway in the breeze. He was so tired, their hypnotic motion almost put him to sleep.

The chill down his spine woke him up right quick. The trees swayed in the breeze, but there was no breeze.

Then the adrenaline hit. Everything sharpened; every sense was on edge. He glanced down the line and knew they'd seen it too. They were as ready as they could be, other than Arnold, who was nearest him. He shook so badly Sexton doubted he could get a shot off, much less hit his mark.

The trees shook and swayed as if caught in a gale. Sexton had seen tornados as a kid, seen storms come down and destroy everything they touched. The storm was truly upon them now. He gripped his weapon, stared down the barrel, looking for something to shoot. The trees bent and cracked, and then . . . it all stopped. The forest went still, and the only sound was the patter of rain.

Sexton's eyes began to play tricks on him. He'd see movement and swing his rifle to the spot, and see nothing at all. Nothing but the never-ending rain.

When it happened, the smell came first, a blast of ammonia so strong Sexton could vomit. But it was the sound that made Arnold break, a sound like a swarm of locusts, if locusts could speak.

Arnold uttered a muffled cry, dropped his rifle, and stumbled to his feet. He didn't make it a yard. Sexton didn't want to watch but couldn't turn away. Arnold simply floated into the air, as if gravity no longer applied to him. It was only when Sexton's eyes adjusted that he saw the thing, a beast that never should have left the sea. Tentacles wrapped Arnold's chest and legs. He didn't have time to scream. One movement and the thing had ripped Arnold in half, bathing Sexton in blood.

Rifle fire crashed around him. Bullets pinged inches from Sexton's head. Peters was firing wildly, each blast drowning out his cries. Sexton fell onto his back, firing as fast as he could pull the trigger, wishing for an automatic. A tentacle whipped out and wrapped around Peters' throat, plucking off his head like an apple from a tree. Peters' body took a moment to catch up to the facts, firing three times before collapsing to the earth.

Sexton ran, with every step expecting the cable-like arm of the beast around him, to feel himself torn to pieces before he died in agony. From behind him, Vasquez's rifle echoed in the night. He hadn't run. If he had, they'd both be dead.

He ran until he reached the barn, and he would have run through it until he couldn't run anymore. But one moment his foot fell on wooden boards and the next, nothing but empty air. He was too shocked to scream. Down he went, banging his head on a beam as he fell. As darkness covered him, he heard a final rifle shot, followed by Vasquez's scream.

***

When Sexton woke, the rain had stopped, and a rare beam of sunlight cut through the roof of the barn, falling on his face. He blinked twice, then stumbled backward when he remembered where he was.

"Whoa, soldier," a voice said. "You're all right now."

She knelt beside him, rifle in hand: one of the M-16s they gave to real soldiers. Fully automatic, unlike the ARs civilians like him were lucky to carry. The bars on her collar said she was a lieutenant. Her voice was kind, but her cold eyes had seen too much to pretend. He looked down and realized he'd landed in a pile of manure.

"You're lucky," she said, gesturing. "Stuff probably saved you. Covered up your scent."

"Vasquez?" he said. He knew the answer, but it seemed the thing to do, to ask. She shook her head and held out her hand.

"Come on, let's get you home."

He took her hand, and she pulled him up. Beyond the barn, soldiers huddled together, weapons at the ready. Sexton's head ached, but even through the haze of a concussion, he thought their tension strange. It was daylight, and the things only came at night, yet he could sense the soldiers' unease in the air.

"Don't look," she said as they stepped out into the daylight.

"What?"

But he did look, past where the soldiers stood, to what had set them on edge.

THE RISE AND THE FALL

"Oh my God," he murmured. "Oh my God."

It was Vasquez. And Peters. And Arnold. Their heads, at least, mounted in a grisly sculpture that defied all that was holy, a sculpture made of the men who had been his friends. He couldn't say whose torso or arms or legs made up the base of this abomination, but he knew one thing for sure—whatever made it was the Devil incarnate. And by all rights, he should be part of it.

CHAPTER TWO

THE CONVOY ROLLED back toward Fort Resistance. They'd loaded the trucks with the rest of the stuff at the farm. Sexton leaned out the open window, glad that at least he wouldn't have to go back. They'd burned the bodies, what was left of them, and as they crossed the bridges over the Alabama River, Sexton averted his gaze. He knew he wouldn't see them in the water, but he didn't want to take the chance.

In the distance lay the ruins of Montgomery, where'd he'd grown up, where he'd lived before the Rising. He'd been one of the lucky ones, reaching the old Air Force base just before they closed the gates. They'd put him to work, and in a daze he'd helped build the walls, mount UV lights along their tops, paint the sigils he didn't understand but was told would keep out the enemy. Then they'd trained him. He didn't have any other skills that would be missed if he didn't return from a mission. He became a soldier. After a dozen uneventful trips, he'd seen action, and he'd run. He wondered if they would shoot him as an example.

The convoy reached Fort Resistance. The walls loomed above them, giant crosses and what Dr. Sayre called the "Elder Sign"—the same sign Vasquez had scrawled on their guns—in black paint along their sides. Men stood on the wall, manning machine guns. The squid hadn't hit the fort yet, and they'd never come during the day, but there were other things to worry about. Roving groups of bandits, for one. Not that they'd seen any, but they had to exist; it stood to reason. There had to be something beyond Fort Resistance, someone else left. Someone other than the cultists who worshiped the things beneath the waters.

There'd been rumors, spread by soldiers back from patrols. They'd found things in the forests, things unconnected to the squid. Abandoned camps, mysterious figures drawn in dirt and carved into stone. Writing no one could understand. And bodies, bound and gagged and bled out. The squid did terrible things; Sexton had seen it with his own eyes. But this was the work of men.

The gates swung open and the convoy entered, the gates closing behind. When the truck rolled to a stop, Sexton didn't wait to open the passenger side door and jump out.

"Not so fast, soldier," the woman who'd found him said. "We've got to get you to medical."

"I'm fine," he said.

She glared at him. "You're not, and I didn't ask."

The infirmary was on the other side of the interior fence that had been the boundary of the old Air Force base. They walked through the tent city between the two barriers. The grass had turned to mud and the people stared at them, dead-eyed. It reminded Sexton of refugee camps in warzones on the other side of the world. Those reports had come home. He didn't have a family, just himself, and one of the benefits of serving in the Guard was a spot in the barracks. He avoided the camps unless he was on patrol. He didn't like to think about what they'd become.

In the midst of the camp was a parade ground where assemblies were held. Reverend Acker stood on a raised platform preaching, a crowd gathered around him. The woman escorting Sexton—he'd forgotten her name and felt strange asking now—stopped to listen.

Acker had that way with people, and the crowds were larger by the day. Sexton was a Christian, too. His mother had taken him to the Dexter Avenue Memorial Church, where Dr. King had preached during the days of Jim Crow. The reverend there, Dr. Stanley, was a kind old man who talked of love and Jesus and coming together. Reverend Acker had a different message.

"You all know," he said, "that we have been punished. Punished for the sins of our society. Punished for our pride, for our hubris. Punished for losing our faith in God, for putting our faith in ourselves. In science."

The crowd murmured and nodded in approval. A woman in the back shouted an "amen."

"The Lord is not slack concerning his promises. He promised that this world would end. That the sinful would be punished, lo, that even the righteous would suffer for their sins. Well, they are punished now, and we with them."

The amens came from across the crowd, and there was anger, too. It was hard to argue that the Rising wasn't an act of God. Harder, though, to find someone more tangible to blame. But the reverend was trying.

"Can you deny it?" he asked. "The scripture tells us, 'And the fifth angel sounded, and I saw a star fall from heaven unto the earth, and to him was given the key to the bottomless pit.' We know, my children, what came out of that pit. Some have seen them." As he spoke, he turned and looked at Sexton, locking on him with his eyes, hate burning within. "To them was given power, as the scorpions of the earth have power. To punish. Their teeth were like lions' and their arms like cables, tentacles to rip and destroy, and their king was the Emperor of the Deep, the master of the bottomless sea. He will not be defeated with guns. He will not be held back by pagan scrawlings. Only the cross will stand against him.

"Put not your faith in guns and soldiers," he said, pointing in their direction. "Or the blasphemies painted on the wall. Only God will save you. Only God, and his servants," he said as he clasped his hands before him and strode down the wooden steps into the crowd. They surrounded him, reaching out to touch him.

"Maybe he's right," the woman said to Sexton, her eyes still following Reverend Acker. "We can't stop them. It'll take a miracle. Come on."

They moved on through the crowds, past the hovels, to the interior base guarded by two heavily-armed men. They both saluted. The woman threw up a response, automatic and without feeling. The infirmary was just beyond the gate.

"I'm really fine," Sexton said as he sat on a cot.

"Then this shouldn't take very long," said the woman, standing at ease beside him.

"What's your name, anyway?" he said, finally getting around to it.

"Anna. Lieutenant Anna Blackwood."

"Sexton Davis," he said, extending his hand. "Pleasure to meet you." She stared at his hand for a moment, then shook it.

"And thanks," he said. "For everything."

She nodded. "Just my job."

"Right."

Doors opened and closed, doctors and nurses came in and out, but none of them noticed Sexton. Even at the end of the world, some things didn't change. Outside the doors was the murmur of an agitated crowd. The doors burst open. Anna snapped to attention as Colonel Stryker strode in, flanked by two armed men. Stryker returned the salute, turning to Sexton sitting on the bed, staring at him, dumbfounded. It was only after an awkward moment that Sexton realized who he was.

THE RISE AND THE FALL

If there was a man who gave hope to the people behind the walls, it was Stryker. If there was a man making them think that survival was possible, it was him. He had organized the camp, brought in the refugees, and built the wall. But he had done something so much more important than that—he was the only man they knew of who had ever killed a squid.

"How are you feeling, son?" the colonel asked, with genuine concern on his face.

"Fine, sir. Just a bump on the head."

"You're lucky. Not too many people see them and live to talk about it."

Sexton nodded, but he couldn't meet the colonel's eyes. The only reason he was alive was that he'd run while others stood their ground.

"How do you figure it happened? Why are you so lucky?"

The colonel knew, so there was no point in lying. Sexton wondered if there was a firing squad in his future: his back against the wall, and men better than him standing on the line, rifles at the ready, his death riding on the end of a bullet.

"I ran, sir," he said. "Then I fell into some manure and knocked myself out. They missed me somehow."

For a second, the colonel was silent. Then he burst into laughter. "Saved by shit. I'll be damned. Yes, sir, Dr. Sayre seems to think that it screws with their ability to track you. Since we don't actually know how they track you, we aren't sure why, but what you're telling me confirms some other reports we've heard. Tell me this: you ashamed?"

Sexton hesitated. "I am, sir, but it would be a lie if I told you I would do it different if it happened to me again. I've never seen anything like that. Never been so scared."

The colonel nodded, then sighed. "Well, you should be ashamed. Good men died and you lived, and you should feel bad about it. But I'll tell you something else—you did what you had to do. You poor bastards were fucked six ways to Sunday. The four of you? A recon crew, not even real soldiers? Hell, could have been forty of you and the only difference would be more of you dead. So take that shame and use it. You're special now. You've seen those bastards up close and personal. I've seen 'em too. You're off recon duty. Rest up, cause now you're with me."

CHAPTER THREE

SEXTON WAITED LONGER than he liked, but the doctor said he didn't have a concussion, and there was no reason to keep him. Lieutenant Blackwood told him he should spend the night anyway, just to be sure, but that was the last thing he wanted. She eyed him as he left, the same indifference on her face she'd worn ever since he met her.

They fired up the great lights along the wall as Sexton left the infirmary. The gloom lifted as each bank came on, artificial day supplanting the setting sun. It was never night in Fort Resistance. If you'd asked him before it all started, Sexton wouldn't have believed he could miss the darkness. In the light was hope and safety, but he was losing his mind in the never-ending day.

Long shadows stretched across the yard. Fires burned in metal barrels, and figures huddled around for warmth or to cook bits of scavenged meat. The evening meal line formed near the commissary. Sexton had already eaten dinner, one of the varieties of gruel that differed only in color. He cut through the crowds to the east side of the camp, where families were stationed.

There was life there, real life that knew no fear. The children, at least, hadn't changed. They ran in circles, chasing each other through the false light. They didn't live in terror, buried under ceaseless stress. They didn't know, couldn't know, that the squid wanted them the most.

Jenn's tent was on the far side, in the shadow of the eastern wall. Sexton rapped against the wooden pole, and the flap flew open. A little girl ran to Sexton's arms.

"Oh, you are getting heavy," he said as he lifted her up into the air.

"Nu-uh!" she squealed.

A petite woman, with golden-colored hair and a very pregnant belly, followed her into the night. "Now, Sadie, don't you go bothering Mr. Davis."

THE RISE AND THE FALL

"Oh, she's no bother," he said, lowering the girl to the ground.

Sadie looked up at him with shining eyes. "I saw you last night."

Sexton laughed. "No, honey. I wasn't around last night."

"But I saw you. In the stinky place. I'm glad they didn't find you."

Sexton's mouth hung open, part in confusion and part in fear. "I'm glad too, honey."

She smiled and giggled, and ran off into the night, to join the other children.

The woman still smiled, and Sexton figured she hadn't heard what he had. She stood, hand absently rubbing her stomach, her eyes following the little girl until she vanished in the gloom.

"How's she doing?"

"She's better today. Her headaches . . . I don't know. They seem like they're getting worse, but the doctors don't know why. She never had them before."

"Before?"

"Before," she said, waving her hand nonchalantly. "Before all this. And sometimes, when I look in her eyes, I don't know. It's weird. I can't explain it. It's like, oh, I don't know, like she's looking though me. That sounds crazy, doesn't it?" She laughed, the nervous tension riding along the sound. "But yeah, the headaches are killing her, poor thing. Must be stress or something. The head doctor, Dr. Sayre, he even took a look at her, which freaked me out, if I'm being honest. Made me think something might really be wrong with her if even he was concerned."

"Did he have any ideas?"

"Not really," she said, furrowing her brow. "He just said she was a 'very special little girl' and that he'd like to see her again. That freaked me out, too."

Sexton laughed. "Maybe you shouldn't be so paranoid."

"In the world we live in? Paranoia is all we have."

"Some truth to that, I guess. And how are you?" he asked, putting his hand on her stomach. He felt a kick. The baby wasn't his, conceived before he'd even met Jenn, but he cared more than he could have imagined before it all started.

"I'm fine. Just fine."

"I brought you something." He reached into his pocket, pulled free an apple. "Found it on my last run."

"Oh wow," she said, taking it. She held it up in the artificial light, grinning. "It's funny, isn't it? A year ago, you could have had as many of these as you'd wanted for a couple bucks. Now, God, they're worth their weight in gold."

"I try not to think about the past too much. Things are different now."

"You can say that again." She looked up at him. Smiled. "Thank you. For everything."

His mind went back to that day, the day people here called "the Fall." It had been evening, the sun long set when the falling star turned night to day, even thousands of miles from where it struck. Then the earthquakes, the chaos that followed. The floods, the storms, the death, as the sky darkened and governments fell to fear and hatred. And that was all before *they* came, before the squid rose from the depths like the advancing army of some alien king.

He'd found her, clutching her child in a burned-out Wal-Mart. He'd planned to go north and west, Nebraska maybe, get away from the sea and take his chances in the plains, or maybe the mountains even further away. But he couldn't leave her and he couldn't take her either, so he'd come here to the camp, where they'd wait it out until things calmed down. But that was months ago, and communications with the outside world had failed only weeks after that. If the colonel or anyone else knew what was going on, he hadn't shared that information.

"Sentry duty today?"

"No," he said, breaking from his thoughts. "I'm off tonight. Back in the field tomorrow, though."

He saw her blanch. She hadn't mentioned what happened to him, how close he'd come to death. But she knew about it, and it had scared her more than she wanted to admit. The thought of him going back out, and so soon, terrified her.

"Really? You can't take some time? Make sure you're okay?"

"You know how it is. Everyone has to pull their weight. Besides, I'd get bored cooped up in here all day."

"You might be surprised."

"I appreciate your concern," he said, reaching out to take her free hand. "But I'll be fine. Can't get much worse than yesterday."

He saw that she wanted to believe that, but they both knew it was a lie.

CHAPTER FOUR

COLONEL STRYKER HAD Sexton up at dawn, just as the massive lights powered down for the day.

"I want to check out that farmhouse again, if you're up for it," he said. "First time anybody's seen the squid this far north. Need to know just how bad the situation is. You good?"

Sexton nodded, pushing the fear down deep. It was daylight, and in daylight they were safe.

They were in a convoy three vehicles deep, which made him feel better. If one broke down, they could make it back before sunset. Sexton's truck was driven by Duane Dickey, a guy he'd known since grade school. He'd called him D.D. then, back in simpler times. When the other man saw him, he gave Sexton the full-on grin that was his trademark. You could always count on Duane for a smile, no matter how bad things were.

"Hey man," Duane said, climbing down from the truck. He clasped Sexton's hand and pulled him in for a hug. "They told me you got in some shit."

"Yeah, you could say that."

"I'm glad you made it out." Duane glanced over his shoulder, his voice dropping to a whisper. "Tell you what else I heard, I heard we're going back out there to that place where it all went down. Colonel's nervous, they say. Little beasties have gotten too close for comfort."

Sexton didn't have anything to add, so he just shrugged his shoulders. "More bad news," he offered.

"No shit. I even heard we might be abandoning Fort Resistance." Sexton's eyes must have shown his surprise, because Duane continued. "Fucked up, ain't it? Can you imagine trying to move that many people north, and at speed? And where we gonna go? The stories out of Birmingham and Atlanta are no joke."

Sexton had heard them too. Riots had burned Birmingham to the ground, and people said Atlanta was completely overrun by the squid, but not everyone had been killed. Refugees from the east told strange stories about hooded and cloaked *things* that moved into the heart of the city, and the nightly rituals they performed with the survivors. Colonel Stryker forbade such rumors, saying they were bad for morale. But after everything they had seen?

"Best go to Nebraska, if you ask me. Somewhere as far away from the ocean as you can get."

Nebraska, Sexton thought. Yeah, he'd considered that. He shook his head. "It's no good, though. They just move up the rivers. Even in Nebraska, they'd find you eventually."

"Well," Duane said, "better than waiting around here. I just don't know how we're going to move everyone." Now his voice dropped even more. "And I'll tell you something else if you swear you won't share it around, and I'm serious. I overheard the LT, and she was saying we might just take the soldiers and go. Leave the civvies to fend for themselves. You know we're in trouble if they're talking like that."

At the sound of crunching gravel, both turned to see an older black man coming toward them. He smiled as he approached, saying, "I believe I'm with you today." He reached out a hand to Sexton. "Dr. Frederick Sayre."

"That's right, Doctor," said Colonel Stryker, suddenly appearing from behind the truck. "You're with us. Let's go."

The convoy roared out onto the main road. Cars, SUVs, and pickups lined the side. One of their first jobs after the fort had been secured was to clear the roads. People tried to flee, and when the roads turned to parking lots, they left the cars behind. That's how scared they were of what came at night.

In those beginning days of chaos and confusion, the first images came from Mobile, on the Gulf of Mexico. Flashes on cell phones, uploaded to social media before the government shut down the Internet. Horrible things that couldn't be explained. Creatures that walked on land when they should swim or crawl.

And the sound.

Sexton couldn't describe it. No one could, really. Something you didn't hear so much with your ears as with your mind. But people stopped asking questions after the clip surfaced of the tentacled monstrosity—what they'd come to call *the squid*, even if it couldn't have come from this world.

It was a cell phone video, somewhere in South America. The video was shaky, grainy, but that made it even more real, more terrifying. The sea at night in a thunderstorm. Roiling madness lit by lightning bolts. It rose from the sea, a pulpy, bulbous head that was too big, just too big. And yet it continued to rise, while thunder exploded and the man filming screamed. He never stopped screaming, not until a tentacle flashed out from the beast. The video had cut out then, thank God.

But that was the end of sanity in the world.

The riots started, and the evacuations. People fled north and inland, away from the sea. The news reports stopped after stories of Central and South American countries overrun, as rumors spread of strange lights off the coast of Europe. Sexton assumed they were everywhere now. He just focused on the day-to-day. To survive till sunrise, to keep his sanity in the never-ending rain. Most of the coastal areas were presumed gone now, sunk beneath the advancing sea. How far it would advance, no one knew.

The trucks pulled off the main road, to the farmhouse. They rolled into a semi-circle in front of the old barn. Sexton shivered as the truck's engine rumbled to silence.

"All right," said the colonel. "Let's go."

"They came from over there, beyond the trees," Sexton said, as he, the colonel, Dr. Sayre, and Duane walked toward the barn. The other men fanned out around them, heavily armed and on alert, even if it was known that the squid only came at night. The human threat of looters, mobs, and maybe even cultists was very real. Sexton's eyes were drawn to the smoldering ashes where the clean teams burned the hideous thing the creatures had left behind.

"Why do you think they do it?" he asked Dr. Sayre, his gaze never leaving what was left of his friends. "Why do you think they make them?"

"Instinct. Primordial memory, perhaps. There are books. Very, very old books," Sayre said, missing the glance from Colonel Stryker that might have silenced him. "They're filled with things that learned men, myself included, long considered to be mere myth." He chuckled to himself. "Professors of folklore aren't supposed to become strategic advisors to military units, and yet here I am. The books speak of certain objects of power that can focus cosmic energies from beyond our own plane of existence. Things we've barely even begun to understand. I've seen diagrams in those books that describe the construction of such blasphemies. It is possible to do so out of stone or wood, but according to those knowledgeable in the old ways, living material is better."

"God," Sexton whispered. "But why?"

"I don't know why they do much of anything, son. Why do they kill and dismember adults, but devour children and the unborn? Who can say? One theory I heard before the blackout concerned stem cells. That they were trying to mutate themselves somehow. Allow themselves to stay out of the water longer. But that was just a theory. I think it's safe to say that now we'll never know."

"Can we stop them, Doctor?"

"All right, that's enough classroom banter for one morning," Colonel Stryker said. "Right now, I need you to tell me exactly where they came from."

They'd reached the low rock wall, and Sexton could see the trees in the distance, still as death. "Right there," he said, pointing to the tallest. "From just beyond there. The trees were moving, but there was no breeze. That's how we knew they were coming."

"Yes," said the doctor. "They move as swiftly through the trees as they do the water. The power of the mutation is incredible."

"Then that's where we're going."

The colonel led them over the wall, into the field beyond. It was quiet, peaceful, and even the gray clouds smothering the world since the Rising seemed lighter. In another time, Sexton might have gone down to the park with a basketball, but not in this time. The shadows of the trees covered him. He wondered if, in those shadows, the things were waiting.

They passed into the forest, unnatural silence falling over them. Sexton knew that where the squid went, life fled. All life. The birds, the animals, they *knew*, just as the people who'd climbed into their cars and left their lives behind knew. The creatures from the sea were the enemies of this world, the enemies of all that was natural and good. They had come to this forest, and now it was dead.

They crept through the trees, their boots like thunder in that unnatural silence. Then the smell hit, the trees broke, and the sight that met Sexton's eyes made him realize that none of them had long to live.

The forest didn't reach the stream. It died before then. The ground was mud, devoid of grass or any other vegetation. The trees had shriveled away, leaving slimy black stumps, like acid had been poured on them.

It was the water that did it: sluggish and sickly green, a flow of toxic sludge. A haze hung over it, and Sexton thought the air itself was poison, the smell of ammonia so strong he gagged.

THE RISE AND THE FALL

"Good God."

"Should we take a sample?"

The doctor shook his head. "I wouldn't have any of our men get that close. It's turned toxic; that's all we need to know for now. The details aren't all that important."

"Davis, Dickey, come here for a minute." The colonel removed a map and handed one end to Sexton, the other to Duane. They held it taut while he moved his finger across it.

"Right here," he said. "That's where we are. And that's the stream. Looks like it curls around for a while and then . . . runs straight into the Alabama." He paused for a moment, then turned to the doctor. "How fast do they move?"

Dr. Sayre shook his head. "We don't know. Can't know, really. Based on where they are now, though, I wouldn't wager we have more than a few days till they reach the Alabama. Even if our defenses hold, the water will be no good. No way we can maintain that kind of population if that happens."

"What are you saying, Doctor?"

Dr. Sayre didn't answer. He didn't have to. Death was coming, and if they didn't run, none of them would survive.

CHAPTER FIVE

THEY RODE BACK to Resistance in silence, the sun hanging low in the west.

Sexton had never let himself accept what had happened to the world. He'd seen men who had. Who sat down with a bottle and waited for darkness to swallow them. Acceptance meant acknowledging what they were up against, that there was nothing they could do to stop it. Better just to struggle on, gathering food, securing weak points, keeping the civilians under control. Ignore the fact that none of it mattered. The ship was sinking, no matter how the deck chairs were arranged.

Resistance loomed in the distance. If Sexton was paying attention, he might have noticed something different. As it happened, none of them noticed anything until the gates opened and a soldier came running.

"Sir!" he heaved, once Colonel Stryker threw open his door.

"What is it, son?"

"Riot, sir. The reverend, he, well, I don't know. I guess he got people riled up. Right after you left, a bunch of them stormed the walls. Covered up those signs that the doctor had us paint on them."

"And you didn't do anything to stop them?"

"We tried to radio you, but the comms have always been spotty. Couldn't get a response, sir. We didn't know what to do."

Stryker nodded, and Sexton wondered how much resolve it took for him to keep his calm. He had to be on edge anyway, in charge of so much he couldn't control. So many lives depending on him, looking to him as a savior. And after what they'd seen today?

Stryker jumped out of the truck. "Your firearm, soldier." The private handed over his M-16 and stepped back. The colonel didn't say a word, just walked toward the gates. The rest of them followed, not bothering to close the doors of the trucks as they did.

The noise hit as they passed beyond the walls. The reverend was preaching. His words were hard to hear over the cheers, but Sexton caught enough to understand that he viewed the doctor's sigils as tools of Satan. Colonel Stryker didn't stop at the edge of the crowd. He muscled through, the rest following behind, no one resisting when they saw the colonel. The gun probably helped. He walked up to the edge of the stage, pointed the gun straight in the air, and fired off five rounds. The crowd shrieked and fell back, while Reverend Acker stopped mid-sentence and turned a hateful glare down onto the colonel.

"Colonel Stryker," he said. "The prodigal son returns."

"Mr. Acker, by your actions you've put every one of the people in this compound in danger. I ought to have you arrested. If you were one of my men, I'd have you shot."

The reverend let the sound of shock ripple through the crowd; then he grinned. "Would you now, Colonel? And on what charge?"

"Treason, to start."

"Treason?" the reverend asked, his voice dripping with mock surprise. "Yes, Colonel. Let us talk treason." The reverend raised a bone-thin finger and pointed it at the colonel. "Let us talk of *your* treason."

"I'm sorry, Reverend. I don't believe I know what you mean."

"Don't you, though?" he boomed to the crowd. "We've heard the whispers, Colonel. We know your plans. To take your men and leave this place. Leave us here to die, with nothing more to protect us than those unholy symbols you and your *scientist*"—this word he spat as if it were a curse—"forced us to paint on the walls."

"Reverend, that's absurd. These men have fought for you. They've laid down their lives for you. When this all started, we opened our gates to everyone who came, even you. Now I need you to stand down. I need you to tell your people to go back to their homes. And then we can forget this ever happened."

Reverend Acker stared. He steepled his hands and took a step down the stairs. "All right, Colonel. My flock and I will stand down." He came face to face with Stryker. "For now."

Duane leaned over to Sexton and whispered, "Shit's about to hit the fan now, I tell you what. People going stir crazy, and the reverend has them right where he wants them."

"What do you think about all that he said, about the colonel wanting to get out?"

"I told you about the rumors, didn't I? Shit, with what we saw today?

I wouldn't put it past him. In fact, I wouldn't be surprised if the plan's already in the works."

***

Dr. Sayre's office was in a building that had been part of the Air Force base. It had been a communications center at one time, and giant flat screens hung on the walls, silent and dead. Sayre's desk was covered in papers, some in languages Sexton didn't recognize. The doctor looked up from a book as Sexton entered, and smiled.

"Mr. Davis, please come in." He closed the book with a thud. "What can I do for you? Please, have a seat."

"Thank you, Doctor." Sexton sat down, rubbing his hands along his pants. He was nervous, and wasn't sure why. Dr. Sayre intimidated him, in the way educated people had always intimidated him. But Sayre wasn't like them. He had a kindness about him. A sadness, too. Sexton wondered if he'd always been that way, or if everything had robbed him of the joy he may once have had.

The doctor looked at him, expectation in his smiling eyes. Sexton realized he needed to say something, to explain himself. He'd just have to ignore that he really wasn't all that sure himself. "Can I ask you a question, sir?"

"Of course, son. What is it?"

"This might seem kinda forward, but is there a way out of this?"

"Well," Dr. Sayre began, his gaze shifting downward, "that's the million-dollar question, isn't it? I hold to the belief that where there's life, there's hope. I realize that's not much of an answer."

"No, no. That makes sense."

The doctor walked over to one of the flat screens. "Do you know how this all began?" he asked as he fumbled with a switch. "I'm sure you don't. The details were really never available to the public." The screen hummed, though the display remained blank. The doctor walked over to a laptop computer and tapped in a few commands. The screen came to life, and Sexton looked at a fuzzy image of a comet.

"Comet 9b-74," Dr. Sayre said. "Doesn't exactly roll off the tongue, does it? One of my British colleagues came to calling it Wormwood as a joke, and the name got around. Doesn't seem all that funny now. When it was first discovered, astronomers assumed it would pass between the Earth and the sun, giving us quite the show in the meantime. Jupiter had other ideas, and instead of the sun, Comet 9b-74 had a rendezvous with the moon

THE RISE AND THE FALL

Europa. You might be asking yourself what this has to do with anything." The doctor looked at Sexton, seeking confirmation that he was, indeed, asking that question. Sexton hadn't been, but he nodded anyway.

"The comet Wormwood is not what hit the Earth to start all this, but it was responsible. When it struck Europa, it melted the ice that covered the moon's primordial sea, plunged deep beneath her waves, and crashed into the ocean floor below. And when it did, something there was awoken. The impact and the explosion were such that parts of Europa's crust were ejected into space, a burst of impossibly strong radiation accompanying it."

Sayre typed some more commands, and the image changed. This was also of something in space, but it wasn't a comet. It didn't look like anything Sexton had seen before. The angles were all wrong.

"There's a story," Dr. Sayre said as he stared, his voice acquiring a dreamlike air, "from long ago, of a king who sleeps beneath the waves in a city not built by human hands. A god, you might say, who ruled the earth and would rule it again. Of course, we mapped the bottom of the ocean floor decades ago and didn't find a city. Or a god, for that matter. But we made an assumption, you see. We assumed the story was talking about *our* waves. How wrong we were. Ironic that this object struck the Pacific Ocean in about the same spot where, legend had held, the city of R'lyeh waited. Ironic, indeed. And when it did, it caused a tectonic event that traveled along the fault line located directly beneath the Ross Ice Shelf. The rest, as they say, is history."

The doctor looked down and sighed. When he turned back to Sexton, he was smiling again. "I wish I had more images to show you. When this all started my colleagues from around the world and I were sharing our data on the cloud. Ha. Foolish faith in the wonders of technology. And about the cloud now? Like mist burned off in the morning sun. I saved a few files, and I'm glad I did, though I'm not sure what good they'll do us in the end. I wish I had some answers for you, Mr. Davis, but I'm afraid all I can tell you is the past. The future belongs to men like Colonel Stryker. If we are to survive, he will show us the way."

CHAPTER SIX

THE SUN HUNG low as Sexton rapped on the loose tent flap of Jenn's front door. She swung it open and smiled.

"Well, hello, Mr. Davis."

"Hello, Mr. Davis!" Sadie squealed from inside. Jenn rolled her eyes. She held back the flap and Sexton followed her inside. On the little plastic folding table sat three plates. Steam still rose from two of them, while Sadie scraped the remains of the food off hers.

"I told her to wait," Jenn said. "She's incorrigible."

"Incorable," the little girl said.

Jenn tousled her hair. "Little monkey. Get out of here and go play with your friends."

Sadie hopped down and ran to the front of the tent, stopping to hug Sexton on the leg. Then she looked up, and Sexton knew what Jenn meant about her eyes. She dropped her head, and said in a voice as serious as a little girl's could be, "The rain, Mr. Davis. You need to stay out of the rain." Then she let go and ran out of the tent.

Jenn's gaze followed her, and Sexton was pained to see a ring of tears around her eyes. Whatever pressure he was under, Jenn was under twice that.

"She's a mess," Jenn said, wiping her eyes as nonchalantly as she could manage. "Just a mess."

"You okay?"

She laughed. "As okay as you can be, right? Come on, we should eat."

"Where'd you get this?"

"I know the guy who runs the food brigade. Known him since grade school, actually. Asked if he'd do me a favor. I can't make you dinner, so it's the least I could do."

"You didn't have to do anything."

"Didn't have to, but I wanted to."

THE RISE AND THE FALL

The unanswered question hung in the air between them. Sexton knew Jenn wanted to hear what they'd found, if he'd learned anything. But moreso, she wanted not to pry, not to bother him. He'd tell her if he wanted to. Honestly, he didn't really want to, but she wanted to hear it, and that mattered to him more than he expected.

"So we went out today," he said, spooning soup from the bowl.

"Yeah, I was worried about you."'

"No need to worry about me. We made it back well before sunset."

"I know. Still." Jenn hesitated. "So, did you find anything?"

They'd found a lot, but nothing he could tell her. Just a creeping dread and the end of the world.

"Not a lot. Went down to the farmhouse. You know, where it all happened."

She reached across the table, covering his hand with hers. "The colonel shouldn't have made you do that."

"It's okay," he said, but let her hand sit where it was. "It had to be done. I owed it to them, to the guys."

Jenn leaned back and looked off into the distance. "This is all so fucked up, you know? God, and I thought my old life was bad. Sadie's dad . . . well, he was a son of a bitch anyway. Left us right after she was born. Then it was just me and her in those projects down Decatur Street, and I thought my life was over. I prayed and I prayed. *Just let something change.*" She shook her head. "What a fool."

"We've all prayed for that, one time or another. Every one of us. I don't think it's anybody's fault. God didn't bring this."

"That's not what the reverend says."

Sexton snorted. "The reverend. Now that's one crazy bastard right there."

"It's a crazy world, Sexton. Sometimes I wonder if it's crazy enough that he just might be right." She looked at him, leaned forward and smiled. "But at least we're alive, right? For now? The first month or so I couldn't sleep. All I thought about was Sadie, how I was going to get her out of this, what kind of future we could hope for. We can't stay in this camp forever. Here we're just waiting to die. But at some point, I guess I figured the best thing to do is just enjoy the time we have, help her enjoy it too. All life ends, you know? Maybe we just have a better idea of how and when it's coming."

"When did you start to feel that way?" Sexton said. She took his hand again, but this time wrapped her fingers in his. She stood, pulling him up to meet her. She brought her face close to his.

"That day you almost didn't come home."

Then she kissed him. He'd always wanted this, even if he'd never let himself think it. Wanted it the moment he saw her crouched in the burned-out store, waiting to die. She broke away, brought her mouth close to his ear. "Sadie's with her friends. She won't be back for a while."

His hand brushed her stomach. "What about . . . "

She giggled. "I think we can figure it out."

***

The sun was barely up when Sexton walked into Colonel Stryker's office. He'd received an order to arrive at daybreak. The team was on a special mission, the details of which the colonel was keeping to himself.

The colonel's office was in an enclosed courtyard that had once served as a parade ground. He passed through the small office into the courtyard, saluting the soldiers there. When he stepped out into the cloud-shrouded light, the smell of manure hit him immediately. It was piled in the corner, and Sexton couldn't imagine why. They'd staked out a corner of the old base for growing crops, in case this stay became an extended one. But that was on the other side of the compound.

He stepped inside Colonel Stryker's makeshift command center. Duane was leaning against the doorframe. He gave Sexton a wary look.

"This whole place has gone crazy," he whispered, shaking his head. "Straight insane."

Before Sexton could respond, the colonel noticed him. "Ah, Mr. Davis. Excellent. You know Lt. Blackwood, correct?"

He remembered her immediately, the kind but distant eyes from the infirmary. She nodded to him.

"Yes, sir," he said.

"Good. She'll be helping me to lead this expedition, and I need to make sure we all trust each other."

Sexton looked around. There were two other men in the room. One was tall, lanky, with short blond hair. The other was the opposite: short and stocky, but not fat. Strong, with a thick salt-and-pepper beard to match his long hair.

"Along those lines," the colonel continued, "I want you to meet Chief Petty Officer Matthews and Lt. Day. CPO Matthews has experience in special forces."

THE RISE AND THE FALL

The man with the beard reached out and took Sexton's hand. "Good to meet you."

"And Lt. Day just so happens to have a master's in biology. We're hoping he can help us shed a little light on what we're facing." The tall man gave a wave. Sexton wondered how he'd never noticed these two before. It made him wonder what else he hadn't noticed. "I'll turn it over to the doctor."

Dr. Sayre stepped forward.

"Gentlemen, madam. As you are all aware, our last foray outside these walls raised more questions than answers. We cannot know, of course, what the cephalopods are planning."

"Planning?" Everyone turned and looked at Matthews. "You talk like these things have a mind to think with, Doctor."

"You don't think they do, Mr. Matthews?"

"No," came the simple but emphatic answer.

"Very well, and you may be right. But call it a plan; call it instinct; it seems that they're drawn further up the river. Since the event occurred, we've witnessed a slow but inexorable advance by the creatures into the interior. They are on the march, you might say. And whether driven by conscious planning or something we cannot understand, the motivation won't matter once they get here."

"The point," Colonel Stryker said, interrupting, "is that we don't have the luxury of sitting around and waiting to find out the answer to any of these questions. We'd all hoped that Fort Resistance would be a place where we could regroup and begin the process of rebuilding. But it's become clear to me, and I think it's clear to all of us, that the enemy isn't going to let that happen. They overran the coastal regions, and that was bad enough, but they aren't stopping there. If we're going to stop them, we have to go on the offensive."

"On the offensive, sir?" Lt. Day said, speaking for the first time. "Sir, we wouldn't even know where to start."

"Exactly right, Lieutenant. The kills we've gotten on these things have been mostly dumb luck. Mostly . . . hell, *all* dumb luck, and I count my own in that category, too."

Sexton didn't speak, but he wondered how many kills there had been. The only one he'd heard about was the colonel's, but he didn't let himself hope that maybe they'd had more success against the squid than he'd thought.

"What we need," the colonel continued, "is information. Intelligence. We need to know what we're up against, and if they have any weaknesses. We need to locate their base of operations so that we can launch a counterstrike against them in daylight hours."

"Problem is," Matthews said, "they disappear in daylight. Blend right into the water or wherever else they're hiding. I like the spirit, and I'm damn tired of sitting on my hands, but I don't see what choice we have."

"The problem with your reasoning, Chief Petty Officer, is that you're focused on daylight. When the sun goes down, the Guard goes down with it."

Matthews's eyebrows arched upward. "Sir, surely you're not suggesting we go after them at night. That would be suicide."

Dr. Sayre chimed in. "It would be, Mr. Matthews, if we were to make our attempt without camouflage. But, as I'm sure you know better than anyone, what the enemy cannot see, he cannot kill. Even better if he never even knows you're there."

"Our friend Mr. Davis here," the colonel said, clapping his hand on Sexton's shoulder, "accidently discovered something remarkable. It seems that the squid hunt by smell. If you mask that smell, you can pass by them undetected."

"It's something we always suspected," said Dr. Sayre. "Squid in the wild rely heavily on smell to find their prey. Since these creatures appear to be some sort of mutation, it stands to reason that their sense of smell is particularly acute. But that also makes them particularly susceptible to a pungent olfactory disguise."

"You mean the manure?" Sexton said, interrupting. "You're seriously going to use that?"

"Absolutely."

"You've gotta be kidding," Matthews said, laughing like a man who knew they weren't.

"I know what you're thinking, Matthews," the colonel said, "and I don't necessarily disagree with you. But if we're going to get in close to these things, this might be our only chance."

"And let's say we do get close to them," Matthews said, pushing himself away from the table. "Let's say we get right up on them. Doctor, you think there's any chance, any realistic chance, these things can be stopped?"

"What we need, Mr. Matthews, is information."

THE RISE AND THE FALL

"That's not an answer to my question."

"And I cannot give you an answer without more data."

"We can sit here and debate this all day," the colonel said, "but the fact is, we don't have much of a choice. The world's not going back to the way it was unless we make it. And that's what we'll do."

The debate ended, and the discussion turned to the practical questions of where, when, and how. It was decided to return to the farmhouse and set up operations there. Then they'd go back out to the river till nightfall, see what they could see, learn what they could learn, and head back. Sexton didn't pay attention to most of it. He was still thinking about something the colonel had said.

Sexton knew from the moment this had all started, from the moment another world came screaming down from the sky: there was no going back. This was the world now, and they had to figure out how to live with it. The colonel's talk of reinventing the past didn't give him hope. It worried him. He'd thought the colonel was a practical man. He'd counted on it. What he was hearing now wasn't practicality. It was madness. And he wondered whether it would swallow them all up.

***

The trucks rolled out, Sexton in the lead vehicle with Matthews and Day, and Duane driving the other behind. The manure had been loaded into the last one, and Sexton was glad to be free of the smell, at least for now. They drove past Reverend Acker, already on the platform, preaching about repentance and the shedding of blood for the forgiveness of sins.

"Crazy son of a bitch," Matthews said. "Should have shot him day one." Day laughed. "I guess we're all a little bit crazy at this point. So what's your story, Davis? How the hell you end up here?"

Sexton shrugged. "Got lucky, I guess. Thought about going to Nebraska. Then things got complicated and it was this or take my chances on the outside. Seemed like bad odds."

"Nebraska," Day said. "Fucking promised land. If I could tell you the number of people who've told me they thought about going there. Never was so many people wanting to get into Omaha."

"All the corn you can eat," Matthews said.

"Don't forget the beef. My mom used to get those mail-order steaks. Damn good. What's your story, chief? How'd you end up at Resistance?"

The bigger man pulled a can of tobacco from his back pocket, scooped out a quarter of it, and stuck it in his lower lip. Sexton wondered where he got it, and what he'd do when it ran out. He was pretty sure the tobacco factories had fallen silent, just like everything else.

"Well, after 9/11, I joined up. College wasn't really my style anyway. Found out I was pretty good at killing people. Went special forces. Ended up even better at killing people. Came home. Got a job pushing paper. Fucking hated it. This is the best damn thing that's happened to me. What can I say, this new world is full of surprises."

Day laughed.

These are the ones that will make it, Sexton thought to himself. *These guys and people like them. The only ones left.*

The caravan pulled onto the broken gravel road to the farm. Sexton felt familiarity roll over him. *Like coming home.* Maybe he'd come back here until he met the end he should have met that rainy night. Death had passed over him. Maybe it shouldn't have. Maybe it wasn't meant to. So he'd return, again and again, until a wrong was made right.

"All right, Colonel, how are we going to do this?" Matthews asked after they'd fallen out.

"I'll let the doctor explain."

"Gentlemen," Dr. Sayre said. He nodded to Anna. "Lt. Blackwood. What we do today is of immense importance. We will learn more about these creatures than we've ever known before. With that knowledge will come the power to defeat them and drive them back into the sea."

He spoke like a coach giving a pep talk before the big game. Sexton expected it from the colonel, but not the doctor. He wasn't sure if he should cheer or clap or what. But no one else reacted, so neither did he.

"Now I'll turn it over to Chief Petty Officer Matthews, who will be leading this expedition."

"Plan's pretty simple," said Matthews. "Load up your kit with some of that manure on the back of the truck, as much as you can carry. In any military operation, concealment is important, but none more than what we're doing tonight. The fuckers see for shit. Their sense of smell, on the other hand, is beyond belief. We're going to use that to our advantage. You overload it, say with the smell of manure, and you're invisible. The plan is to head down to the river. Recent intel notes that there's a point just beyond the trees where everything dies, like the water itself has been infected with something. We figure that's the extent of their penetration, and that's where we're going to set up. Right there, where the living meets the dead. Come sundown, you're going to slather as much of that shit on you as you

196

can. No complaints, no excuses. Then, once it gets dark, we'll head downriver, into the dead zone, and see what we can see."

"That pretty much sums it up," said the colonel. "Any questions?"

Duane piped up. "I guess it's too late to ask how I get out of this chickenshit outfit?"

***

At noon the team reached the point they'd visited before. Sexton's heart sank when he realized that the dead zone had advanced a quarter mile in that time. They made their way down till the sickly green water turned a healthier muddy brown and the trees no longer stood like skeletons in a boneyard forest.

They bring death everywhere they go, Sexton thought. *Everywhere they go.*

"They're changing the environment to better suit them," said Dr. Sayre as he stood at the boundary. "Fascinating."

Matthews knelt next to the river, retrieving a sample for Lt. Day, who was setting up his microscope. "It won't be fascinating when they reach the city, when they hit our water supply."

"True, Chief Matthews. But I suspect the colonel brought us out here for just that reason. To put a stop to it." Sayre removed a small scalpel and cut a piece of dead bark from one of the trees. "Have you heard of the Asian carp? I spent some time studying it, back when I was at the university, as it made its way up the Mississippi River toward the Great Lakes. Similar to our squid, in a way. Totally changed the ecosystem. That is, until they figured out a way to kill it."

"I certainly hope you figure out how to do that, Doctor. I'd love to kill a few myself."

Lt. Day peered through his microscope before taking a vial of water and pouring it into a portable machine he'd brought from base. A soft whirring followed, and numbers flashed on a screen.

"Ammonia. Not a surprise, judging from the smell," he said. "High levels. Very toxic."

The colonel peered over his shoulder. "I thought you said they were changing the environment to suit them?"

"They are," the doctor answered. "Remember, they aren't really of this world, not anymore. The event caused a massive burst of radiation in the world's oceans, strong enough to kill most things. But it didn't kill the squid. Instead, it seems to have activated something deep within their genetic makeup. There are people who say that squid are from somewhere beyond our own world, that they didn't evolve here. Instead, they were brought here."

"That's crazy," Matthews grunted.

"Is it, Chief? Look around. Is it?"

Sexton slunk back into the shadow of one of the trees, the one likely to die next. Lieutenant Blackwood sat on a stump, examining her rifle.

"I hate this," she said.

"I don't think any of us are happy to be here."

"It's not that. It's the sitting around, waiting for something to happen. We've been waiting since it all started."

"Where were you, when it went down?" Sexton asked.

"I'm from Montgomery, originally. I was stationed in Korea before this, so I guess I should be used to sitting around, waiting for something to happen. I'd come home on a two-week leave. When everything went to shit, I reported to Maxwell to see if there was anything I could do to help out. I was there maybe two weeks, waiting for somebody to figure out what was going on and what we could do to stop it. But they had no idea. It was too much, you know? We could handle an earthquake or a flood. There were plenty of those going on. But the videos? The rumors about the squid? That broke people. Broke me too, if I'm being honest with you. When shit went down in Montgomery, I went out to try and bring my parents back to base, but they were gone. Left a note that said they were going west and that I should follow them. Nebraska, of course. Instead I went back to the colonel, told him I was with him till the end."

"You think that's what this is? The end?"

She looked up at him, brown eyes flashing. "Hell no," she said. "This isn't the end. This is the beginning. We're finally done sitting around and waiting."

When the sun began to set, the colonel ordered them to spread the manure around.

"This isn't pleasant," he said. "But it will save your life."

Sexton grimaced as he scooped out a handful of manure, rubbing it gingerly on his arms. Anna saw him.

"Here," she said, grabbing a handful. With the other hand, she grabbed his neck. He felt a tingle run down his spine, but only until she rubbed horseshit all over his face. He nearly vomited. "There you go," she said, as she spread it over her cheeks and over her lips. "Worst part is over. Now don't be a pussy."

THE RISE AND THE FALL

When they finished, Sexton looked around at them. What a scene they made. What stark raving madness, like they'd all walked out of an insane asylum, covered in shit like it was the end of the world.

***

Darkness fell as the sun sank below the horizon. The colonel checked his weapon, and the others did the same. "We move upriver," he whispered. "Stay silent and close. No one fires unless I give the word."

They moved into the dead wood. The mud sucked at Sexton's shoes and didn't want to let go. They'd gone half a mile when they heard it. The colonel put up a closed fist, and they all stopped. Stood. Listened.

It was a buzzing sound that Sexton had heard before. It was audible, carried on the wind, but Sexton had a feeling that it was something else too, inside his mind as much as it was outside. He thought he heard words. A name. Something calling. Asking him to do something. But what?

Sexton's gaze went to the river, moving in silence, sickly green water seeming to glow in the darkness. The water rippled, then churned. The surface erupted with writhing tentacles, thick cables against the surface of the water. Sexton wanted to scream. To run in terror. But the first beast burst from the water, rising up on its eight great arms. Its two tentacles flashed out, searching. One crashed against a dead tree, the giant hooks on the end ripping rotten wood to rain down upon them, so small, so insignificant, so defeated. The colonel motioned to back away, and they did, guns pointed helplessly at the beast before them.

The creature moved forward against the current. It stepped from the brackish green water to the fresh, and Sexton watched as the river seemed to die around it.

"Its very flesh is poison," the doctor whispered. "Amazing."

The colonel glared at Dr. Sayre, telling him with his eyes to be quiet. But then lightning flashed and thunder rolled. The wind whipped up, and down came the rain.

It fell in sheets, and Sexton thought back to that night at the farmhouse and wondered if these creatures could change the weather, too. He caught the colonel's eye, and it was no longer anger he saw.

It was fear.

Sexton looked down, saw the rain splash against his arm, saw the congealed excrement thin and slide off. He cursed, looked around and saw that the rest of them knew it too. How could they have been so stupid? Their camouflage was washing away.

The colonel reached out, grabbed Sexton, pulled him forward. He put Day beside him, then Dickie, then the chief. He took his place beside Matthews, and Anna took up the other flank, just to Sexton's left.

"Look for the eyes," he shouted, his voice masked by the thundering rain. "Aim for the funnel."

Oh God, Sexton thought. *We're going to try to kill it.*

"Hold."

Sexton gripped his gun tight, so tight he thought it might snap.

"Hold!"

The creature lurched forward, water splashing around its bulk.

"Something's not right," the doctor whispered, crouching behind them. "Something's off."

Sexton wished he'd shut up.

"Fire!"

Their guns erupted as one, cutting through rain and lightning and thunder. Bullets ripped into the rubbery flesh of the creature. It stumbled backwards, lifted itself up on its back four legs, and roared. It was a sound no creature of the sea should be able to make. Tentacles flashed out, slammed against the trees. One trunk exploded, and half crashed down just beyond where Anna stood.

A tentacle lashed out. Duane Dickey stood not ten feet from Sexton. One moment he was there, his friend since childhood, firing on full auto. Then the tentacle launched him through the air. Even as he flew, the gun never stopped, arcing bullets into the distance. Duane crashed down into the green sludge of the river, the last Sexton ever saw of him.

"Keep firing!"

No one had to tell Sexton. He fired until his rifle wouldn't fire anymore. He released the magazine, slamming in another. From the corner of his eye he saw a tentacle swinging towards his head like a steel whip. At the last second, he ducked. The cable passed over his head so close that the wind almost knocked him off his feet. In horror, he saw hooks at the end flash out and connect with Lieutenant Anna Blackwood's face.

For a moment, it stuck to her cheek like putty. In the next, the hooks took hold, and the side of her face and the jaw beneath were gone, torn away like tissue paper.

She screamed, and Sexton knew that whether he lived to ninety or another ninety seconds, he would never forget the sound. That scream came from the depths of her, erupting from her throat to where her mouth should

THE RISE AND THE FALL

be to mold it, to shape it into a sound he could know. Instead it spilled into the world, raw and gurgling and coughing on blood that poured down her throat.

To his right, the colonel fired again at the beast. His left hand pulled a pistol from its holster, and without taking his eyes off the squid, he leveled it and fired. The bullet caught Anna in her right temple, and her scream ended. The colonel re-holstered his pistol, trained his gun on the beast, and unloaded. When the metallic click signaled that he was empty, the squid seemed to sway in the wind before crashing down into the water.

The rain fell, their guns sizzling with each drop. They'd killed a squid, but no one celebrated.

"Shit." The colonel spat on the ground and jammed a magazine into his gun. Matthews stepped beside him casually, and Sexton wondered what he must have seen in war that gave him nerves like that.

"What now, boss?"

The colonel cast a glance to Anna in the mud.

"I think it's time we left. Day, gather your stuff. We're getting out of here."

"But, Colonel, we can't leave yet!" Sexton turned to Dr. Sayre, and in Sayre's eyes he saw something he didn't like. The doctor pushed past him. "There's more we can learn."

"Doctor Sayre, it's raining, and that means our camouflage, such that it is, is useless. And I don't know if you noticed, but we barely made it out of that last encounter," Stryker said, pointing to Anna's body, "and I don't intend to lose more men."

"But Colonel, we came here for a reason. To learn. If you leave now, she will have died in vain. It will only add to the tragedy of . . . "

A roar in the darkness cut off the doctor's words. It was answered by another. Chief Matthews craned his neck to hear. Another roar, this one closer than the last.

"Well, fuck."

"Gather your gear!" the colonel shouted. Matthews turned back towards him, slamming a full magazine into his gun.

"Too late, boss. They'll be on us before we make it fifty feet. Gentlemen," he said, looking at the others, "it's been an honor."

The colonel turned and pointed at Day. "You got that tarp?"

Day hesitated.

"The tarp, the clear one."

"Yeah?"

"Get it."

Day dropped his pack, digging around inside until he pulled out a folded piece of clear plastic. The colonel ran to the packs that carried the manure, checked them, and nodded.

"I think we have enough. All of you, get down on the ground. On your backs. It's our only chance."

They didn't ask why, dropping to the ground in a line. The doctor lay beside Sexton, mumbling about missed opportunities. The colonel grabbed the tarp, spreading it over them. He then dumped the manure on top, spreading it quickly and covering them as best he could. Then he lay down, slipping under the edge of the tarp.

Sexton lay there, staring up through a gap in the manure, the dead trees looming over him. Another roar echoed through the dead wood, closer this time. Then it happened.

He couldn't see it, but he could hear it. The sound of the river rent in two as something split it in half, as walls of water rose and crashed on the shore, almost to where they were lying. Sexton began to shake, fear coursing through him. *What could have done that?* he thought.

Then the earth shook with him. It shook like thunder, shook like bombs were falling. It shook every time what had come from the water took a step.

With it came the storm.

The rain came in torrents, lightning so often and so close that thunder boomed on thunder, and still the sound of the beast drowned it all. Beside him, Dr. Sayre's eyes went wide, and he turned them on Sexton.

"The other," he said, mania creeping into the edges of his voice. "I knew there was something wrong. I knew it."

The falling footsteps grew closer.

"It was an adolescent," Sayre said, and then laughed. "Just a child. A child!" The laugh turned into a cackle, and then into one long scream.

Above them, in the next flash, Sexton saw the titan, the Kraken, a tower that walked: dwarfing them, dwarfing the thing they had killed, dwarfing the world. Dr. Sayre continued to scream, screamed till his vocal cords were shredded and blood poured from his throat.

CHAPTER SEVEN

THEY LAY THERE all night as the mud turned to mire in the endless rain. They watched as nightmares passed in an endless march: one after another, beyond all counting, an endless army. They didn't stir until the sun crested the trees.

As bad as it was, part of Sexton didn't want to climb out from underneath that tarp. For once they did, it would be time to face the world, to face the reality of what it had become. Even the colonel sensed it too, for he waited a good fifteen minutes after sunup to stir.

"All right," he said finally. "All right. Let's . . . let's go."

He pulled himself from underneath the tarp. The rest followed, except for the doctor, who had mercifully passed out in the night. They dragged the tarp off him, and Day knelt down to check his vitals. Even as he lay unconscious, his body shook, and Sexton heard his fevered mumblings.

Anna was gone. No one had seen them take her. All that was left was a pool of blood swarmed with black beetles, the only living thing Sexton had seen in the forest. What was left of the forest. The dead wood ran as far as he could see, the river green with sludge. He didn't want to know how far it had spread, but he knew that last night they had moved farther than ever before, enraged over the murder of one of their own, if things like that felt rage. But of course they could, he thought. There was no doubt of that now, just like there was no doubt about a lot of things.

"We should get back," Matthews said. "We need to organize things."

Organize things. Sexton wondered just what that meant. Organize a withdrawal, or organize a last stand? And did it really matter? Where could they go? Nebraska? Sexton laughed to himself, and Matthews shot him a glance. He didn't care. Life itself had become absurd.

They carried the doctor back to the trucks. They propped him up in the passenger seat of the colonel's. Day slid in beside him, checked his pulse, shook his head.

"Straight back to the base," the colonel said. He eyed Matthews and Sexton as if they might do something else. Maybe strike off on their own. Head north and west and leave this shitshow. Sexton had no interest in that. He figured it wouldn't make any difference. The trucks rumbled to life, and they pulled onto the road.

They'd ridden for a while before Matthews spoke. "I first went to Afghanistan when I was 19 years old," he said. "Ended up liking it more than I thought I would. Lot of guys didn't, of course. Gotta have a little bit of crazy in you to enjoy it, I think. Surviving something like that isn't as hard as some people like to make it seem. And getting killed, well, more often than not that's just bad luck. But sometimes it's more than that. It's failing to understand when things have gone totally against you, and thinking you can be a hero. Do you understand what I'm saying?"

Sexton didn't, not really, but since Matthews had started talking, he'd felt a sense of unease drift over him.

"Anyway, I've never seen anything like what we saw last night. I'm telling you all this because you seem like a solid, honorable guy. I've never seen anything like it. Nothing even close. Understand me when I say this: we can't stop something like that. No way. Each one of us is going to have to make our own call on how this ends. I can't make the call for you, but time is running short, my friend. Pretty damn short already."

Matthews fell silent. The only sound was the road rumbling beneath them. Sexton said nothing. He'd made up his mind already.

***

The trucks rolled through Fort Resistance with two fewer people than the day before. No one would know, Sexton figured. Anna had no family, at least none there. He couldn't be so sure about Duane. Maybe he had a wife and kids. They'd lost touch years ago, and it was this . . . *thing* that brought them together. But he'd never found out what had happened in the intervening years. Something told him, though, that there was no one.

And that meant no one would miss them or mourn them. The colonel would keep it under wraps. Morale was bad enough already. Then he'd figure out how to save these people; or, maybe, how to leave them behind. Sexton didn't plan on sticking around to find out.

They dropped the doctor off at the infirmary. He was babbling, but his words were blessedly incoherent, so that was good. Sexton attempted to slip out unnoticed, but the colonel was waiting at the door.

THE RISE AND THE FALL

"Mr. Davis," he said. "Obviously the details of the expedition are classified."

Sexton thought that he should just nod and go on. But he didn't. "Classified? Classified by who?"

"By me. That should be good enough for you."

"Because your run this place, right?"

"That's right. Because I run this place."

Sexton felt the anger well up inside of him. "I hope you know you have a hell of a problem on your hands, then, fearless leader. You saw the same thing I did. The same thing we all did. It's not going to get better. We aren't going to build some kind of new society out here. They're coming."

"You don't think I know that? Don't ever imagine that you've thought more about what we're facing than I have. At the end of the day, we'll just have to think about our priorities, won't we?" The colonel's voice remained calm, under control. But even Sexton, who had never been good at reading people, could see that it was only barely so. The colonel's control was slipping. Sexton wondered what happened when a man like that finally lost it.

"In any event, you'll keep what happened to yourself, or I'll have you arrested. Is that clear?"

The colonel's cold blue eyes locked on him, but Sexton didn't blink. He just held that gaze, then walked off.

The sun was setting, and the great lights on the walls fired up one after another. There was a calm that was palpable, and Sexton was surprised that he didn't hear Reverend Acker echoing across the courtyard. The dinner line had formed outside the commissary, and quiet conversations filled the still air.

All Sexton could think was that these people were doomed. He knew that he should warn them, that he should try to save them. But he also knew that he wouldn't, and he didn't feel all that bad about it, not as bad as he might have in a life before this one. But he'd seen what walked beyond these walls. He knew what moved, even at that moment, closer and closer. He made his way to Jenn's tent.

She stood outside staring at the sky, one hand on her hip and the other rubbing her swollen belly. She smiled when she saw him coming. "Hey, you."

"You should gather your things."

Confusion spread over her face. "What? Why?"

"We're leaving tomorrow."

Confusion turned to fear. "Sexton, what are you talking about? Did something happen?"

"It's hard to explain," he said, taking her hand, "but whatever this is, it's not safe here anymore. We need to go inland. Away from the sea. Do you understand?"

"No, I really don't."

"Then I'll need you to trust me on this one. Can you do that?"

"Of course I trust you." Lightning flashed across the darkened sky. "You should come in. Looks like it might rain."

Sexton glanced up into the night sky. Thunder rolled in from the west. "Rain . . ."

That's when the lights went out.

***

It happened in an instant. One moment, the camp was bathed in light so bright an artificial sun might have been shining down on them. Then, darkness. Complete darkness. Like the breath before the fall, darkness was followed by silence. Like everyone, Sexton was so shocked that he didn't know what to do.

Then the screaming started. It came from all over the camp, blooming up in random bursts of recognition.

"Oh my God," Jenn whimpered. "Oh my God."

The reality still hadn't hit Sexton. He stood there, bathed in night, trying to understand where the lights went.

"Sexton!" Jenn shouted, pulling him out of his stupor.

"Go inside," he said. "Don't come out until I get back."

"But Sadie . . ."

Sexton's stomach turned to ice. He'd assumed Sadie was in the tent the whole time. "Where is she?"

Jenn shook her head, and with his eyes adjusted to the darkness he could see the terror in her eyes. "With her friends. I don't . . . I'm not . . ."

She was panicking, and he had to make a decision. Try and get the lights back on, or go find Sadie. He was about to go for the girl when he heard the first gunshot. Someone else screamed. Then another shot.

He turned back to Jenn, grabbed her by the arms and pulled her toward him. "Something's very wrong. I have to go help get the situation under control. Get the lights back on. Once the lights are on, we'll be safe, even if we haven't found her yet."

THE RISE AND THE FALL

"I can't just stay here."

"Jenn, it's pitch black. You won't be able to find her."

"I have to try."

Another gunshot. He had to go. He couldn't argue any more.

"Okay. Go find her. I'll be back as soon as I can." He pulled her in close, kissed her quickly, and ran into the darkness.

***

He heard shots all over the east side of the camp now. He ran towards the gunfire, wondering what had happened. He assumed that one of the roving gangs had sneaked someone in to cut the power and had attacked. It was something they'd worried about, trained for, prepared for. If everything went according to training, it should be over quickly. But Sexton understood enough to know that things rarely went according to training.

A woman ran out of the darkness, nearly colliding with him. She tried to keep going, but he grabbed her and pulled her in to face him. "What's going on?"

"I don't know," she said. "The lights went out and they started shooting. I don't know anything else." She yanked away from him and rushed off. He didn't follow.

Sexton continued on, the gunfire intensifying. He slowed, fearing that he might run straight into a bullet. A building emerged from the darkness. He sprinted to it, throwing himself against a wall. He inched along its length. The firing intensified. It suddenly occurred to him that he had a problem. He wouldn't know the good guys from the bad guys. He was just as likely to shoot his own people as the enemy.

"Shit," he muttered to himself. He didn't notice someone coming out of the darkness until he slammed into the wall beside him.

"Relax, Davis," the man said when Sexton nearly jumped out of his skin. It was Matthews.

"What's going on?"

"Don't know. I was up on the wall when it started."

"Someone break in?"

Matthews shook his head. "Couldn't have. We had the place locked up tight."

"But that means . . ."

"Yep, someone from the inside. Killed one of them already. Dude I think I'd seen skulking around the place. He was wearing this."

Matthews held out a chain. A pendent slid down its length, twirling in the darkness. To Sexton's eyes, it seemed to glow. It was green, a circle around a tentacled creature with a human body, an alien head, and evil eyes. Sexton had heard about the cults, of course, but until now, he'd never believed the stories.

"Oh shit."

"Oh shit is right." Gunfire echoed from around the corner.

"But how do we know their guys from ours?" Sexton asked.

Matthews cocked his head at him. He reached into his pocket and pulled out a glow stick. "Don't you remember?"

Like a fool, Sexton had forgotten. The glow sticks marked them to prevent friendly fire.

"Just recall," Matthews said as he cracked one and tied it to Sexton's right arm, "they make for a hell of a target to shoot at."

"Thanks." Sexton noticed that Matthews wasn't wearing one. "What about you?"

Matthews shrugged. "I prefer to arrive unnoticed. Besides, our guys are lousy shots." More gunfire. Matthews gave Sexton a wink, then charged around the corner. Sexton took a breath and followed him.

The building sat at the edge of the parade ground. At one end was the generator station. Rifle flashes burst from rough barricades in front of it. Matthews fired off a few rounds in that general direction and made for the opposite side, where the pale glow of green lit the faces of scared men. Sexton followed as Matthews leapt the wall of old steel barrels. More gunfire kicked up dirt and rocks, and Sexton felt one bullet come so close that it singed his hair. Then he was behind the wall next to Matthews.

"Report!" Matthews barked. In the green glow, Sexton recognized Day's face.

"Thirty of them, we think. Took the generator station sometime after dark and cut the power. But we've got them pinned and surrounded. They won't be able to break out."

Matthews shook his head and glanced at Sexton. "They're not trying to break out. They're right where they want to be."

"What do you mean?"

It was Sexton who answered. "They didn't cut the power to take over the camp, or even to escape from it. They're trying to let something else in." Lightning flashed, and Sexton saw Day blanch, the visual made all the worse by the sickly green glow.

"All right," said Matthews. "Here's the plan. Day, take your team

208

around to the left. Make a lot of noise, break operational cover, all that jazz." Matthews grabbed the green light from Sexton's shoulder, throwing it to the ground. "Sexton and me, we'll take the right side. Come up on them silent and slow. When they're fully engaged with you, we'll hit them from the back. Understood?"

"Understood."

"Godspeed."

Day shouted orders to the men around him. Only a handful had served in anything more than the Guard; most had never served at all. Sexton wondered how much time they had.

"Give them a moment," Matthews said, checking his weapon. "Then we head out."

"They're coming, aren't they?"

"Hell yeah, they are. No point dwelling on it now." From the left side, gunfire erupted.

"That's our cue. Let's go."

Matthews ran into the darkness, and Sexton followed.

***

In the dead forest, the darkness coalesced. Rising from the waters, things walked that should have crawled.

***

Sexton stuck close behind Matthews as he dodged from one building to another. The fighting had intensified on the left. Day brought more guns to bear on the defenders, who pulled more men to meet the ferocious assault. Sexton worried that Day was almost too convincing. If they had a commander worth his salt, he'd know something was up. He and Matthews might be walking into a trap, not that he had any choice. They had to do something, and it had to happen fast. In his bones, he could feel the squid approach.

Matthews reached the last barracks on the parade ground. This was as close as they'd get. Sexton fell in behind him. Thunder cracked, and the rain began.

"Great," Matthews spat. "Just great. Whatever. Better to cover our approach."

A crackling filled the air, like electricity set free from its wires, but it wasn't lightning. Then came the voice, one that Sexton knew too well.

"People of Resistance, the time has come for you to bow your knee to the new gods."

"Well, I'll be damned," Matthews said, spitting almost reflexively. "Sounds like the reverend has found a new vocation."

"The end is here. The end of all things. You have heard of the new heaven and the new earth. But before the new can come, the old must burn away. A cleansing tide rises from the depths. Their teeth are the teeth of lions and their sting is like that of a scorpion. They come to make the way for those who were and who will be again."

"Never did like that guy," Matthews said. "Didn't peg him for a crazy, though. Well, not that kind of crazy."

The reverend's voice droned over the thunder and the pouring rain. Then the roar came and covered all.

Sexton felt his gaze drawn to the sky, as if the thing that birthed the sound would be there, staring down at him with hate-filled eyes.

"Shit. Shit, shit, shit. New plan, Davis. I'll take care of this. You get to the wall."

"Wait, what?"

"They're here, man. If we don't get the lights back on, we all die. And if we don't hold them off until we get the lights back on, we all die. Go. I got this."

Matthews was around the corner and gone. Sexton stood rooted in place, listening to machine-gun fire and unsure of what he should do. Then he heard the roar again, and he was sprinting past the barracks to the outer wall.

The camp was a madhouse. People rushed about, screaming, crying, shouting. But none knew where they were going or what to do. Panic was all they had, short of death, and Sexton was sure that in some of the tents, men and women were taking their lives. Over it all, Reverend Acker droned, citing prophecies long forgotten, calling for the end times, welcoming what he called the Old Ones. When the voice stopped in mid-sentence, Sexton thanked whatever gods that they'd cut the power. Hopefully that meant they were retaking the facility.

Sexton reached the wall and sprinted up to the walkway around its perimeter. He nearly ran into a soldier, his rifle shaking in his hand so violently that Sexton was afraid he might drop it. He was hunched over, sight to his eye, scanning downrange. Sexton looked out into the darkness, but there was nothing. Not yet.

"Gentlemen! The time has come to put your training to the test." Sexton turned to see the colonel walking swiftly down the line. He had his rifle, and he looked sure of himself, truly sure, for the first time in a long time. As he passed Sexton, he clasped his hand on his shoulder, looked him in the eye, and nodded. Then he kept moving.

"Whatever comes out of those trees, we have to stop, or at least slow down. Men are working even as we speak to restore the power and turn the lights back on. We need to buy them time."

Another roar, closer this time, and Sexton heard other things too. Voices in his head, in tongues no man had heard in millennia, if they ever had.

"All right, men. Here they come."

The sounds of rifles clanking against the wall echoed up and down the camp. Sexton bent over, staring downrange. Every shot needed to count.

He didn't see them emerge from the forest, didn't see them step from between the trees. They were simply there, a few hundred yards away, as if they'd always been there. As if that was where they belonged.

They towered, monsters from a nightmare. Their great arms rose and fell, propelling them forward as if born for the land. Tentacles swung freely, lashing out—to grasp, to rend, to destroy.

For a long moment, no one fired. Then the boy beside Sexton placed his rifle gently against the wall, unholstered his sidearm, and shot himself in the head. That was the signal everyone else needed, and machine-gun fire lit up the night.

Sexton heard the voice in his head, the one urging him to surrender, to accept the new way. The voice promising him wonders he couldn't imagine. He drowned it out with the sound of his rifle firing.

"Target the one in the middle of the line! The one closest to the wall!"

Sexton adjusted his aim, firing at the beast taller than a skyscraper. The other men did the same. From somewhere to the far left, someone fired a rocket launcher, and Sexton followed the RPG across the sky before it slammed into the beast with an explosion that split the night like thunder. The squid roared like something from a time before time, and with a great crash fell to the earth, never to rise again.

A cry went up from the soldiers, so filled with wild abandon that for a moment Sexton thought maybe, just maybe, they could pull this off. But where one beast had stood, two took its place. And the inexorable tide rolled on.

A scream erupted to Sexton's left. The beasts before him jerked in that direction, and he saw why—the wall had been reached. Colonel Stryker ran down the platform, shouting orders as he went. Men fell in behind him, and Sexton with them. An explosion lit up the night, and men went flying. Someone had panicked and fired an RPG too close to the wall, and had paid the price. More men converged on the left flank, firing up at squid thirty feet tall, smashing tentacles like bridge cables down on the wall. But they were holding them back, maybe even forcing them to retreat, if only a bit. It was good they hit there, Sexton thought, as the buildings in that corner were abandoned. If they'd hit the right, then the civilian barracks would be in immediate danger.

And then Sexton thought of the power plant, of the feint by Matthews and his men, of their strategy. And then he knew.

He ran towards the right side of the base. If he passed a man, he'd yell at him to follow, but he didn't stop to see if he did. There was no time. He leapt down the first ladder and sprinted towards the barracks.

He heard the screams before he saw the carnage. The squid had slipped over the wall. Stealthily, silently. They'd hatched a plan, put it into action, executed it flawlessly. It was the kind of thing that, if the doctor had still been sane, might have driven him mad.

To his left was gunfire, and Sexton zigged that way between buildings. He slowed down, as he was no good to anyone if the squid caught him out in the open. He stopped at the edge of one of the barracks, peered around the corner. He saw a soldier, brave or just out of his mind, firing his weapon full-auto at two squid above him, tentacles swinging in lazy arcs, studying him like a specimen in a Petri dish. He fired until his magazine ran dry. Then one of the squid took off his head, as casual as could be.

One of the fort's walls was a hundred yards to Sexton's left. There was an exit there, locked but easily forced open. From there, it was a short jog to the highway. Grab an abandoned vehicle and start driving, and he'd be away before the squid had a thought about him. Then the sun would be up, and he'd have a head start to Nebraska.

Sexton made a decision. If they couldn't get the lights back on, everyone was dead. There was no stopping the squid, no pushing them back, no killing them all. Like Colonel Stryker said, sometimes you had to focus on priorities.

A group of soldiers stumbled into the courtyard. They started firing at the squid. Sexton gave one last glance in their direction and then turned, running to Jenn's tent.

***

THE RISE AND THE FALL

He cut through some warehouses, around the large parade ground. He dodged into the shadow of the commissary, then north toward Jenn's tent. He'd expected panicked people running in all directions, but found nothing but silence. The hairs on the back of his neck prickled, and he hoped that they cowered inside the flimsy tents, hoping the angel of death would pass them by.

He was on the edge of Jenn's sector when he found the first body. It was a child, a girl of no more than six. *Not Sadie, thank God,* he told himself without guilt, not that it would be easy to tell if it had been her. The child lay on its stomach, and whatever had killed her had scooped out her back up to the skull, pulling out the brain and spinal column. Sexton thought back to what the doctor said about stem cells and how the creatures used them to evolve. They hunted children, he thought. Children and pregnant women especially. He spared one more look at the dead child and kept moving.

He ran into an abattoir.

The tents were awash in carnage. Bodies ripped apart, blood spattering canvas. Sexton didn't check if anyone was alive. He kept moving, his humanity slipping with each step.

He came to Jenn's tent and skidded to a stop. He'd risked everything to get here, but now hesitated. He knew if he found them dead, that would be the end for him. He might as well eat a gun. His hand shook as he grabbed the tie holding the flap closed. He pulled it loose, and the tent fell open.

Inside, there was nothing.

She'd gone for Sadie, and hadn't made it back. His heart sank; she could be anywhere. Into his mind came a voice, but not the voice of the creatures, not that horror. A voice, familiar yet not. The voice of a child. He started running. The voice guided him, even if he couldn't make out the words. He ran past empty tents and dead bodies, past offal that had been human beings. He slipped past giant beasts and the screaming men and women fleeing them. Then he skidded to a halt. In an opening between two banks of tents, one of the things towered. Standing before it, a flaming log in her outstretched hands, Sadie clinging to her legs, was Jenn.

The squid stared down with giant black eyes. There was no hate there, no anger. There was nothing, and it struck Sexton that there never would be. These things would never love, never build. And when they killed, they did so without passion, like machines. Their eyes were black for a reason; these were the eyes of death.

"Jenn!"

She turned and screamed his name. Jenn's gaze went from him to her daughter. She shouted, told her to run. Sexton could barely hear her over the voice of the beast raging in his mind.

The girl ran, and the squid noticed. A tentacle flashed out like a whip crack. It would have gotten her, but Jenn brought down the torch like a hammer. The creature didn't like the fire. It recoiled mid-strike, howling in pain. Another tentacle wrapped around Jenn's legs and lifted her just as Sadie slammed into Sexton. He stumbled backwards, every fiber of his being screaming to charge forward in helpless rage. But there was Sadie, and he knew what he had to do. He picked her up. Then he ran.

He looked back over his shoulder. The thing held Jenn up to eye level, studied her. For an instant she stopped screaming, stared at it as it stared at her. Then the thing wrapped a tentacle around her stomach and ripped her open like a piece of overripe fruit, scooping out the unborn child in one movement.

CHAPTER EIGHT

SEXTON RAN BLINDLY for five minutes, clutching a sobbing Sadie to his chest, when the lights flashed on. The roar of a thousand horrible voices echoed through the camp and through his mind, so overpowering that Sexton collapsed and screamed in pain. When the screaming stopped, the creatures were gone, up and over the walls and into the night. Sexton hoped the light hurt them. Hoped it might have killed some of them. But he doubted it. By the time he laid Sadie down in her bed, the sun was rising.

"Get some sleep," he said. "I'll be right back."

"No!" She grabbed him, her tired eyes wide. "You can't leave."

"I've gotta go make sure it's safe, honey." But he saw in her eyes that she'd have none of that. "You sure you don't want to sleep?" She shook her head. "All right, then you need to come with me."

They emerged into a sunlit warzone. Crews of soldiers and conscripted civilians gathered bodies—and parts of them—into wagons for disposal. Fires burned, fueled by blood-spattered tents and human remains. Sexton glanced down at Sadie, regretting bringing her, but he saw no emotion, no fear. She'd seen enough that sights like these would never pierce her conscience again. She was no longer a child, no longer innocent. She was battle-scarred and broken, probably the best thing in this new world.

A tired-looking sergeant met him in front of Colonel Stryker's headquarters. "He's at the parade ground," he said. "With the reverend."

Sexton half-expected the man to spit at the mention of Acker. Sexton thanked him and headed to the parade grounds.

Matthews was headed there too, his rifle slung low across his chest. He nodded to Sexton as he approached. "Going to see the show?"

"Something like that."

"Might want to leave the kid."

"She's staying with me."

"Can't say I blame you. Met up with Day earlier. Says they've been counting who all we lost. Squid seemed to have taken a very targeted approach. Seems they mostly went after the little ones."

Sexton shivered. Of course they had.

A crowd had gathered around the platform, and Acker stood upon it, spitting vitriol and hatred, just like any other day. But today, Stryker stood beside him, Acker's hands tied behind his back. But he wasn't gagged, and his madness raged.

Some curses Sexton understood. Others were in a language Sexton had never heard, a language of too many consonants and not enough vowels. A language Sexton knew wasn't made for the tongues of men.

"You fools," he said between incoherencies, then laughed. "Do you believe you can stand against them? Do you believe you can survive? No one will survive. No one but those who serve the gods that were and that will be again."

Colonel Stryker struck him across the mouth, spraying blood on the stage. He looked down at the man, then stood there, arms behind his back, at perfect parade rest. "I don't think we need a trial."

He unholstered his pistol. In the distance, Sexton heard thunder. The reverend looked up at the colonel and grinned, blood dripping from his lips. "Death comes for us all, Colonel. Death comes for the world."

Stryker raised his weapon and fired. The reverend crumbled. Sexton watched without emotion as the blood pooled beneath him, pouring down to the dirt below the stage. The colonel slipped his pistol back into its holster. Somewhere on the wall, a machine gun opened fire and someone screamed.

The crowd turned as one. The colonel spat out a curse, but there was doubt in his voice. Another heavy machine gun opened up. Sexton glanced at Matthews and caught his eye. Sexton couldn't read what he saw there.

"Sexton," the colonel said, "come with me."

Sexton looked from him to Matthews. With a movement almost imperceptible, Matthews shook his head. Then the roar came, and Sexton knew.

The squid had returned, and they had come in daylight.

Stryker broke into a run, heading for the wall. For a moment, Sexton didn't move. When he looked back, Matthews was gone. Chaos bloomed as the crowd dissolved into panic. More machine guns opened up. What foolish courage was that, he wondered, to try and beat back a tide that

THE RISE AND THE FALL

would never recede? He thought back to what he'd learned from Dr. Sayre before his mind broke. He thought of the children they took and what they used them for. And he thought about how powerful evolution could be, if a creature could control it to eliminate weaknesses. Then he looked down at Sadie, clinging to his leg. She didn't cry. Didn't even seem scared. Sexton picked her up. And then he ran.

He ran through screaming crowds, past soldiers running to the wall. He ran to escape, not sure where he was going, only that it was away from them. He heard a roar and turned to see a massive squid, bigger than anything he'd seen before, lift itself up in the air before crashing down out of sight. It had scaled the wall in one movement. Others would follow. Anyone who stayed here would die.

But where to go? To try the gates was death. They would be there, legion, to devour anything that came through. Especially Sadie. They would scoop out her insides, devour them and become stronger in the process. So he ran, blindly. Then the wooden structure beside him exploded.

He fell to the ground, shards of wood showering down around him. He lost his grip on Sadie, and she landed with a cry. He looked up, and where the building had stood was a squid. Not the largest of the monsters, but big enough. His gun lay five feet away, but it might as well have been a mile. The creature roared, and Sexton said a silent apology to Sadie, to Jenn, and everyone else he had failed.

Machine-gun fire erupted behind him, precise, targeted. The creature stumbled backwards and then fell, never to rise again. Matthews grasped Sexton's hand, pulling him to his feet.

"Well, this has been a shitty day."

"Yeah," Sexton said, gathering up Sadie, "something like that."

"Assume you're checking out of the facilities?"

Sexton nodded. "Yeah, yeah we are."

"Well, the front door seems like a bad idea. But there's a way out the back most people don't know about." Matthews jerked a thumb over his shoulder and grinned. "And it just so happens I keep a jeep fueled up and ready to go for just such an occasion. How 'bout I give you a ride?"

"Sounds like a plan."

"Ain't got no booster seat."

"I think we'll manage."

They ran, Matthews leading the way. They cut through the maze of barracks and support buildings. Sexton shut out the screams, ignored the rifle fire that diminished with every passing second. The clouds seemed to close in, the shadows upon them thickened, and rain began to fall. They were splashing through puddles by the time they emerged into an open area. A jeep was parked across the field, and the back wall was in sight. Sexton could see the gate and the exit, unguarded.

But it wasn't the gate that made them skid to a stop. It was the giant beast looming over all.

It was the biggest one yet. Massive, something from another age, if things that overwhelming had ever existed before. Sexton was nothing before it. Not a man, not a creature worthy of notice. Nothing. But the thing did notice. It fixed its great alien eyes upon them, and then it saw Sadie.

It took a step forward, and the earth shook. Matthews shifted left and opened fire. Bullets slammed into the creature, but if it felt them, it gave no sign. Sexton dropped Sadie, putting himself between her and the beast. Then he moved to the right, firing, hoping to confuse it, hoping they would get lucky.

But their weapons had no effect, and the creature knew what it wanted. A great tentacle lashed out at Sexton. He leapt in the air to avoid being crushed as it swept the ground. But he landed wrong, slipping and falling. His gun clattered away. The beast took another great step forward. And so did Sadie.

It happened so fast Sexton didn't have a chance to scream, to tell her to run. She stepped forward into the shadow of the monster that had come to take her life. She raised both hands. If she was afraid, she didn't show it, and in her face Sexton saw something far older than the handful of years she had on this earth.

The creature stopped in its tracks. It looked down at her, confusion in the soulless black pits that were its eyes. The earth trembled, and from where Sadie stood, something came. Something that tore the ground in a widening arc, speeding toward where the creature stood. That something slammed into the creature with enough force to knock it back. Down it went, felled like a mighty oak split by a woodsman's ax. It didn't stay down, but when it rose, it fled, possessed by an emotion Sexton hadn't thought possible.

Fear.

Sadie stood for another moment, arms out. Then she swayed, falling to the ground. Sexton got to his feet and ran to her.

THE RISE AND THE FALL

"She all right?" Matthews called.

Sexton leaned over her, peering at her face, peaceful as if in a deep sleep. Then her eyes fluttered and opened.

"Yeah," he said. "I think she just fainted."

"Now that that's out of the way . . . what the hell did I just see?"

"What is it you told me once? This new world is full of surprises? I guess you were right after all."

Sexton picked up Sadie, and she clung to his neck, a little girl again. Matthews ran to the jeep and jumped into the driver's side. The engine fired on the first try.

"Something finally goes right for once."

He threw it into reverse, skidding to a stop as he came to Sexton. Sexton dropped Sadie into the back and climbed into the passenger seat. Matthews gunned the engine, and they shot out onto the road, leaving Fort Resistance behind.

"You think any of them will make it out?" Sexton asked.

Matthews shrugged his shoulders. "Don't know. Maybe what that little girl did will scare them off. But with the squid in this area able to walk during the day, they'll all have to find a new place. As good a time as any to strike out on our own. Which brings me to my next question," he said, as he swerved onto the main highway. "Where we going?"

In the passenger seat, Sexton grinned.

"I don't know," he said. "You ever been to Omaha?"

THE GREAT BEAST

by Rich Hawkins

"Who knows the end? What has risen may sink, and what has sunk may rise. Loathsomeness waits and dreams in the deep, and decay spreads over the tottering cities of men."

—H.P. Lovecraft

To Willow and William, my star-spawn.

PROLOGUE

WITH ITS DOORS locked and barricaded, the church was the last refuge for the villagers. The congregation numbered almost three dozen, buzzing with murmuring voices and whispered prayers and pleas to holy saviours: a gathering of desperate people united in supplication and fear.

Screams and shrill cries rose from the village. The monsters were closing in. Families huddling in the pews took paltry comfort in Reverend Linwood's words from the pulpit. Old married couples held hands and muttered shared entreaties to their God. A baby cried, and a little girl sobbed with her head buried against her mother's side. A slouching man clasped his hands together and stared at the cavernous ceiling high above.

Josiah sat alongside his father, helping the old man remain upright on the wooden pew, which was creaking from the shifting and shuffling of the people alongside them. Father sat with his head lowered, mouth moving silently, spindly legs splayed. Josiah could do no more for him. There was nothing more to be done. Despite being a believer, Josiah took no solace in this place of worship and consecrated ground, because it wasn't enough to stop the monsters. He knew this with the certainty of lunar cycles and tides.

But the illusion of hope had to be maintained by Linwood until the doors came down. The reverend told his people to be righteous in such dark times. In the quivering light of a candle upon the rim of the pulpit, Linwood's face seemed sunken and malign, like a waxen mask left to dwindle for years. And his eyes gleamed with fervour, mixed with euphoria, fear, and apprehension. His hunched, thin shoulders shuddered as he quoted holy verses written by long-dead and forgotten men.

The congregation nodded, sniffled and simpered. A woman called out to God. Linwood said salvation was approaching. Their souls would be saved. The Lord would not forsake His children.

"God loves you all," Linwood said with the assurance of a man sliding towards zealotry, moments before the large stained-glass windows overlooking the congregation exploded inward and tentacles, tendrils, and horrid beaks fell upon the terrified people.

***

Perhaps some massive evolutionary leap or mutation had brought the squid out of the oceans, to be a plague upon the earth.

They ranged in size, the largest over four metres tall and wide—though there were whispers of even larger ones glimpsed in the wild—while the smallest were no bigger than a large dog. The stink of ammonia steamed from their slime-coated forms. They moved upon the tips of their tendrils, or hung from walls or beams in the high places. They swooped down upon their victims, moving with effortless grace and agility, grasping and snatching in the flickering light of the candles.

The screams of the congregation were followed by the chattering and clamouring of the squid as they swarmed and began to feed on their stricken prey. Flailing tendrils plucked people from the floor towards snapping beaks and dripping maws. Some tried to flee, but they were picked off by tentacles that coiled around their bodies and stripped away skin and flesh with serrated, ringed suckers of chitin. Blood sprayed, dousing the flagstone floor and the old walls, as limbs were ripped asunder and faces shredded.

Josiah was on his hands and knees, bleeding from a gash beneath his left eye. He tasted blood. Time moved in fragments since the windows had shattered inward and sent glass shards flying. He'd fallen from the wooden bench, pulling his crying father with him, knocking his head on the pew in front. Sweat stung his eyes and blurred his vision. He called for his father, but there was no answer. He jerked around, glancing around the chaos of the feeding. Looking up, he saw a large squid hanging from a stone pillar, using its busy tendrils to cram a man head-first into its gaping mouth. The creature's eyes were the size of footballs, swimming in weeping fluid, and its awful beak bit into the man's head and gulped at the contents of his skull. And once it was finished with that, it tore open his chest cavity and snaffled up internal organs like so much soggy pudding.

Blood gushed and splattered upon Josiah. He choked on a scream. People were being eaten alive around him.

He saw Reverend Linwood cornered by two squid that came at him from across the walls to either side. The reverend clutched one side of his face where the exposed cheekbone glistened, the eye drooping and useless. He babbled wordlessly, clutching a Bible, with nowhere to go.

THE GREAT BEAST

Josiah watched in horror as the two squid pounced upon Linwood, lifting him screaming from the floor and pulling him apart as they each took a share of him. Then they skittered away, leaving only sopping scraps of Linwood on the floor.

Josiah crawled through ropey viscera and puddles of red, and found his father cowering between pews on the other side of the aisle. He looked at Josiah as if he didn't recognise him. His face was covered in blood that wasn't his own, and he trembled, hands drawn to his chest.

As dark shapes writhed overhead and scraps fell from above, Josiah grabbed his father and helped him to his feet. He took the old man's hand and led him through the swarm of bodies and killing tendrils.

They didn't get far.

A monstrous specimen swooped down and took Josiah's father, limbs coiling around his thin torso and squeezing tight. Josiah gripped his father's hand with both of his own. He tried to pull him free, but he wasn't strong enough. His eyes met his father's in a moment of understanding before the old man was hauled into the shadows above. The sounds of wet dismantling followed.

Josiah turned away, his heart breaking, and fled to the barricaded door at the side of the church. While the squid worked to consume the last of the congregation, he tried to push the piled furniture from the door. But he was beyond terror, strength gone, tears rolling down his face.

He glanced back at the slaughter, but looked away when he saw one of the children embraced by coiling tendrils. Little bones cracked and shattered. He staggered away from the barricade and made for the door to the bell tower, all the while waiting to be snatched and brought to the terrible mouths awaiting him.

He reached the door on numb legs, whimpering in his throat, blinking sweat from his eyes. His hands slipped on the door handle as he twisted and pulled, and he thought it a small miracle that it wasn't locked.

"I'm sorry, Dad," he murmured. "I'm so sorry."

The sounds of snapping bones and ripping meat were left behind as he closed the door in the sudden darkness, breathing hard and trying not to vomit. He waited for the squid, but nothing came, and he pulled his cigarette lighter from his jacket pocket and made a flame in the dark as he climbed the stone steps. Past the door to the belfry, the steps growing steeper, and he was at the top of the tower, the death and carnage far below.

He opened the hatch above and climbed into the soft rain and darkness.

He closed the hatch, which would offer little resistance to any squid that climbed the stairs after him. He realised he wasn't overly bothered by that fact, because he'd take care of himself before they arrived.

Josiah climbed the slippery, lichen-dotted parapet and gazed down at the churchyard and the village beyond.

"Oh God, oh God," he whispered, extinguishing the lighter's paltry flame. "God help us. Please help us."

Fires burned in the village, smoke streaming, joining the low cloud cover in the darkened sky, becoming both and neither. Screams echoed from nearby streets, fading away until the only sounds were his heartbeat and the faint hiss of the rain.

Then he saw the monsters.

Droves of squid swarmed through the tall trees at the roadsides, using the high boughs for cover and ambush, flitting from branch to branch, glimpsed as a flurry of graceful motion in the weak glimmer of streetlights. They moved in silence, only the scraping of a branch or the rustling of leaves giving them away.

It was beautiful and awful and terrible.

The squid entered houses through windows and doorways, and once inside there were only the screams of their victims. Those screams never lasted for long. Josiah couldn't watch, and looked away, down at the gravestones far below.

"Oh God, help us," he said, but there was no answer. He remained on the parapet, shivering in the downpour, looking out at the end of the world.

CHAPTER ONE

IN THE DEAD silence of deserted streets, Josiah turned his face to the grey slate sky, grimacing within the hood of his coat. He hadn't seen the sun in months. He'd forgotten what a sunny day and blue sky looked like. The image was like a distant memory slowly fading.

He wiped his bearded face, looked around the high street from his watching place in the doorway of the carpet shop. Nothing moved. Abandoned cars scattered along the road. Rusting shapes in the rain, slumped and useless. Everything awash in ashen light.

He gripped the crowbar to his shivering body. His legs ached from crouching in one place. He rose, pulling tight his holdall over one shoulder, wincing as his stiff joints pained him. He edged onto the pavement, through dark puddles and drifts of dead leaves, past a burnt-out Indian restaurant and a clothing shop with a smashed storefront displaying pale mannequins draped in rotting rags.

He quickened his pace, watching the creeping shadows. His boots kicked up water as he crossed the street, a shade amidst left-behind cars, keeping his distance from the open manhole in the road. Its cover was nowhere to be seen. He cast a quick look back before he reached the double doors of the pub.

His heartbeat was rapid. The metal sign over the doorway creaked in the wind. He peered through the frosted glass to see inside, but could only discern dark, ambiguous shapes in the main bar area. A trembling chill ran through him when he imagined the pub full of spindly figures seated at their tables, slouching over their drinks, waiting for him to arrive. A surprise for a lost wanderer. A welcoming party of grinning shadows.

Josiah pulled back from the window, swallowing down his itchy throat. He took out the LED head torch from his coat, pulled the strap tight around his head, and switched it on. The narrow beam gave him some comfort as he stepped over the threshold, clutching his crowbar. He halted as the doors swung shut behind him, smothering the daylight. Motionless and rigid, he sucked in a breath and only released it when he heard no sounds inside the pub. There was no immediate smell of ammonia, just the ghost fumes of spilt alcohol and stale bar snacks. His stomach creased with hunger, and saliva pooled at the back of his mouth.

Entering the main bar area, he stepped over glittering shards of smashed glasses and bottles on the hardwood floor. Knocked-over tables and chairs impeded his way. He crouched to check the pockets of scattered jackets and handbags, but found nothing except for a cigarette lighter and a few sticks of spearmint chewing gum.

He stood and looked around. There were no bodies, no tell-tale stench of rotting human flesh and innards. His torchlight revealed speckles of black mould on the walls. Decaying food on plates upon tables, infested with insect larvae. Chicken bones and mouldering lamb chops. Dirty cutlery. Continents of grime stained the carpet. A woman's red high-heeled shoe lay on its side next to a mobile phone with a cracked screen, the remains of a night out interrupted by something terrible. He thought about the church on that final night. He thought about the screams and the sounds of death, and then shut his eyes and inhaled a shuddering breath. The image of his father, snatched away and slaughtered, came to him and forced him to lean on the nearest table to steady his weakened legs. He opened his eyes and spat, letting out a sob for the memory of the lost world.

The bar itself was wrecked, the optics pulled from their brackets. Shattered bottles of wine and spirits. Such a waste.

Josiah went behind the bar and tried the draught pumps, but they were dry. Then he picked amongst the wreckage, muttering, gritting his teeth, and scavenged two packets of ready-salted crisps and a bottle of rum with the seal intact. He gulped down several mouthfuls of rum, the rich alcohol spreading warmth down his throat and chest. His head spun for a moment.

Josiah burped, wiped his mouth, and screwed the cap back on the bottle, resisting the temptation to drink again.

**

His torchlight cleaved the darkness. The cellar was looted clean. Empty metal kegs on the walls fed the pumps in the bar. He stood amongst torn boxes and packets of pork scratchings. A smell of urine wafted from one corner. He noticed a child's Mickey Mouse watch on the floor and went to pick it up, but faltered and stepped away.

He sat down on a keg and drank more rum.

THE GREAT BEAST

***

Back in the street, ash fell with the rain and made grey slurry on the pavements, blocking the drains and gutters. He hurried beneath the overhang at a looted charity shop and sheltered with his arms around his chest.

He wondered about the ash. Radioactive fallout had been a fear since the first days of the apocalypse, and each time the ash fell, Josiah became certain his time had come and a slow painful death was all that remained. Radiation sickness terrified him as much as the squid stalking the flooded ruin of Great Britain.

But at least death at the awful thrashing of a squid's beak would be relatively fast.

As quickly as it started falling, the ash stopped, leaving only turgid slurry in the street. Josiah watched the rain dissipate the ash-fall and wash it away. Within minutes, the ash was gone, maybe just a momentary illusion manifested from his tired mind.

CHAPTER TWO

JOSIAH TRUDGED ALONG, watching the street around him, breathing low and anxious. He felt like a scavenger, one step above a carrion eater in the food chain. He imagined himself as a gangly vulture-thing shambling the streets in clothes stolen from the dead.

The rain formed grey veils in the air, blurring the outlines of buildings. Desolation and dreaded silence, the streetlights broken and smashed by the squid.

A plastic bag drifted on the wind, skittering across the road like a hollow ghost. It came to rest on some iron railings, deflated and raggedy.

He passed the charred supermarket with its collapsed roof. Its blackened innards, flooded with rainwater, couldn't offer shelter. The supermarkets and food shops, the obvious places to search, had been looted or burnt in the chaos. There was nothing to find, and he didn't like the look of the houses along the street, their doors open or hanging off their hinges. When he neared, the stench of ammonia drifted from shattered windows. The reek of it was in the gardens.

He winced, inhaled and spat, then kept moving. Each scavenging trip took him farther from his hideout and increased the danger. He hadn't encountered another survivor in months; the town was completely abandoned. If slim pickings continued in Pendlebury, he'd have to leave town to search for supplies, and that formed a frisson of panic in his gut. For all he knew, the rest of the country was just as lifeless and barren.

There was an hour or two of light left in the sky. He had to hurry. The squid came when the day darkened. Maybe they were already emerging from the black water to hunt for prey.

Yes, he had to hurry.

He stopped at a building site. It looked deserted, lifeless: unfinished houses opposite a portacabin on the far side of the property. The metal gates, chained and padlocked, shivered in the wind. Too high to climb over.

THE GREAT BEAST

He walked the perimeter until he found a gap between the bottom of the fence and the ground. He took off his holdall and pushed it through before he rose to a crouch and slung it over his shoulder again. His clothes were smeared with mud. He wiped his dirty hands until his pallid skin was revealed. His fingernails remained black.

Sighing with weariness, he looked around. The rain had lessened. Faint pattering fell upon plastic sheeting and metal. The ground was mud and grit, turgid puddles the colour of oil. Josiah stood, hefting his crowbar, wincing at his joints as he moved deeper between the skeletal houses and limbs of scaffolding. Windows without glass. Tarpaulin sheets flapped in cold gusts, flailing like persistent signallers seeking his attention.

He peered through doorways without doors. Hollow interiors and bare plaster. Exposed walls. A mound of bricks next to a plastic yellow bucket encrusted with dried cement. Stacked lengths of timber, all neat and tidy.

He went through all six houses, finding nothing, but his luck changed in the portacabin, where he discovered Ritz cheese crackers and beef jerky in a cupboard. Fighting back tears, he wiped his eyes, unable to look away in case it was an illusion of food cravings and delirium. There was still treasure in the dead places.

"Better than nothing," he whispered, looking towards a poster of some buxom bikini model on the wall. "Better than nothing at all."

Despite the maddening temptation to start eating, he stuffed the entire cache into his holdall. He crawled back under the fence and started back, pulling his coat tighter around his shoulders. The holdall swung against his hip as he moved. It was time to go home.

He was feeling hopeful for the first time in a while, when a pack of feral dogs emerged from the shadows between two houses.

They saw him. Mangy, half-starved creatures. Livid eyes and spittle-flecked mouths. Pink gums pulled back to show killing teeth. Josiah halted, raised the crowbar, sudden fear turning his limbs to water. His breath caught in his chest.

The dogs sniffed the air, inhaling his scent in the rain, then began towards him, snarling and growling.

They, too, were hungry.

CHAPTER THREE

JOSIAH SHOUTED AT the dogs, but it didn't deter them. They kept coming, spreading out to flank him as he backed away. Hunting behaviour. The alpha was a large Alsatian, leading eight dogs. There was a Labrador, a border collie, a boxer, a few mongrels. Emaciated things with dripping mouths and filthy hides. Crazed hunger in their eyes. Quivering flanks and painfully-defined ribcages. Their sharp claws scraped the road as they stalked forward.

"Good doggies," he said, his voice wavering. He was surprised they hadn't already been taken by the squid. The squid were indiscriminate now. When they moved through an area, they wiped it clean of life, taking their victims back to the water.

Josiah waved the crowbar, trying to hide his terror, to assert dominance, but the animals had lost whatever bond they'd had with people. They saw him only as warm meat to be torn into pieces.

He ran down a side street, and the dogs chased, yipping and snarling like demons on his heels.

***

Josiah stumbled through stinking water, tipping wheelie bins as he passed to impede the dogs.

Scrabbling claws in pursuit. He didn't look back. He kicked his legs harder. His heartbeat was a constant crashing, almost drowning the shrill barks and rabid growls behind him. The sounds of the hunt echoed through the dead streets, over flooded roads and the wrecks of vehicles.

Josiah's chest tightened around his innards. He breathed wheezing gasps, his mouth gulping air. When he risked a glance, he saw through blurred vision that the dogs were closing in.

He emerged into a wider street, weaving between abandoned cars. His feet trailed as his strength faded. He braced himself for biting teeth and jaws around his legs. The pain would be immense. They would rip through his clothes and eat him alive. He whimpered in his throat. His legs failed, his lungs deflated, and he cried out, his voice trembling with terror and exhaustion.

Ahead of him, a church spire appeared, and then the black iron gates of the graveyard. The hope of salvation in more ways than one. He barged through, flailing and tripping onto the flagstone pathway. His momentum took him into the masses of gravestones, clipping his shoulder as he faltered and tumbled to the sodden ground. He scrambled and staggered away, limping on one leg, gritting his teeth and crying.

He'd gotten twenty yards when he realised the holdall was gone. He skidded to a halt, slipping in the mud, barely staying upright. Then he looked back.

The dogs had ceased their pursuit, distracted by his holdall where he'd dropped it. The beef jerky was inside. The alpha sniffed while the other dogs gathered behind it, panting with lolling tongues, waiting.

The alpha pounced upon the holdall and the others followed, ripping with claws and teeth, pulling at it with their jaws. They snarled and yipped and growled, like hyenas over a carcass.

Josiah despaired as he watched them rip apart the packets of cheese crackers and beef jerky. They especially liked the jerky, snapping at each other for a decent share, scattering food and shredded plastic and cardboard.

His hand tightened on the crowbar. All that lovely food, gone to the bellies of feral dogs.

At least the rum bottle and packets of crisps in his coat were some consolation. And he was still alive.

He fled from the graveyard before the dogs finished their stolen meal.

CHAPTER FOUR

THE DOWNPOUR HALF-BLINDED Josiah as he
hurried down streets of tall shadows. He was exhausted and
dripping rainwater, the world of broken despair slowly wearing
him down.

The industrial estate was on the east side of town, where the urban
sprawl faded into undeveloped land and waterlogged fields. Factory
buildings stood against the sky, adjacent to car dealerships, garages, tool
shops, and garden centres. Office blocks like tributes to Soviet architecture.
He'd scavenged everything useful from the area, hence his trip deeper into
the town.

With the rain falling about him, Josiah cut through a stretch of weed-
ridden brownfield. He glanced around as he entered the car park, eyes
straining with fatigue, hands slowly going numb in the wet cold. The
warehouse was directly ahead of him. The car park was empty, the workers
long gone, their obligations and tiresome shifts meaningless when the
world ended. He passed a skip loaded with scrap metal and plastic. A lone
crow, bedraggled and lean, flapped away as he approached the main
warehouse. He took keys from his pocket and unlocked the side door, then
looked back as the rain shrouded the grey lands.

***

As the beam pierced the darkness, he walked down aisles of metal shelves
piled with engine components.

His boots treading a well-worn trail on the dusty concrete floor, he left
the main storage area, entering silent, lightless corridors. No windows. It
reminded him of a tomb composed of narrow walkways. He passed the
shuttered canteen, then the toilets, on his way to the storeroom where he
laid his head each night. His footsteps echoed ahead of him.

The storeroom was his nest, his refuge from the rain. He locked the
door behind him. He'd cleared the room of equipment months ago to make

the space a little more comfortable. In the glow of the Coleman lantern, he took off his wet clothes and hung them on the cord attached between two standing shelves. The air smelled of old sweat, bad breath, and stale food. His body stank, unwashed for a long while. Infantile graffiti and nonsensical scribblings covered the walls. Shivering in his boxer shorts, he added the crisp packets to his supplies in the cardboard box. The four large bottles of water did little to lift his spirits. His mouth watered at the thought of the beef jerky he'd lost to the dogs. He needed more protein. The muscles in his limbs felt withered and soft.

Josiah changed into dry clothes, then sat swaddled in blankets and rolled a cigarette. Next to the bed was a leaning pile of porn magazines amidst the trash, and he eyed them for a moment, but masturbation was losing its appeal in a post-apocalyptic world. It had become a mechanical, thoughtless action, closer to a bodily function than pleasure. All the naked women with their inviting eyes were dead or insane by now.

Everyone he'd ever known was dead.

And in that moment, when loneliness and the faces of lost loved ones weighed upon his mind and weakened his heart, he drank the rum and stared at the door, wondering if the squid would finally arrive that night.

CHAPTER FIVE

JOSIAH DREAMED THE dreams of hunted men. He saw the terrible glory of alien oceans and heard the cries of tortured voices from abyssal waters. The drowning screams of billions.

And, beyond it all, the immense form of Cthulhu, the dreamer in the deep, the bringer of madness and death, rising from green slimy vaults to conquer the world.

***

Another day awaited him. He rose from the camp bed, his head whirling, mouth dry with a bad taste on his teeth and tongue. The empty rum bottle stood next to the bed. He exhaled, rubbed his brow to relieve the throbbing beneath his skull. When he cleared his throat, it sounded guttural and phlegmy. Then he sat, his head in his hands, recalling last night's dreams.

Splintered images flooded his mind: of the first days, when the Pacific Rim was devastated by earthquakes and tsunamis. Coastal communities wiped away. Cities destroyed and millions dead. But it had just been the start of it all.

Josiah opened his eyes and took his hands from his face. The images faded, replaced by a deep sense of grief for all the dead, trembling in his hands like a form of palsy, a depression hanging over him like black clouds.

He gulped water and downed paracetamol, then rose to start the day.

Another day.

***

As the rain fell, a constant in this broken world, he huddled under the smoking shelter with a cigarette and watched the dim sky. It was a grey morning, just like all the mornings since the end of the world. The rain quickened, then slowed, then became heavier again. The fall was never-ending, a punishment upon the remaining scraps of mankind.

Josiah took a drag and held it. The smoke was harsh in his lungs, but not unpleasant, and reminded him he was alive. He checked the packet and found only three cigarettes left. Another trip into town was due, to scavenge shadow-filled buildings and lifeless rooms.

***

He pulled on his waterproof coat and rucksack, then left the warehouse. He carried the crowbar in both hands and headed deeper into town, nerves fluttering in his chest and stomach, mixed with cold dread and creeping anxiety.

Crows flapped overhead, weaving through the rain.

He stepped through the broken doorway of a newsagent's and looked around; but it had been looted of anything useful, and the floor was flooded with a few inches of water. A rotting body face-down in the filthy broth, the rags of its clothes trailing like tendrils. The horrendous stench sent Josiah falling back to the street. He spat and muttered, then moved on to a row of houses down the road.

The first house appeared intact, and he thought his luck might be changing. When he tried the door, it swung inwards, and he raised his crowbar and entered in silence. He crept through the downstairs, checking for company and ignoring the accumulated memories and mementos of the family that once lived there. There was no smell of ammonia, and for that he was grateful. Cobwebs draped the walls and high corners. No sign of spiders.

Josiah searched upstairs, and scavenged a jar of vitamins and some antiseptic cream from the bathroom. The master bedroom was an artefact of the old world, revealed in the light from the window. He stood motionless, like a shadow hoping to join the other shadows, lost in reverie. He'd seen the photos of the people who'd once lived there, and grew maudlin and tearful at the probability of their deaths. A happy family like so many others, wiped from existence in the drowned world.

Dabbing his eyes, he turned from the immaculately-made bed to leave, when voices rose outside. He moved to the window and peered down at the street, careful not to make any sudden movements.

Several men stood on the road, dressed in tarpaulin cowls that sheltered them from the rain. Over a dozen men, shabby and dripping. They were armed with knives in dirty hands, or tucked into rope belts around their waists. Eyes within faces smeared with dirt glanced about the street, a visible hunger in their subtle movements and mannerisms.

They were searching for someone.

Josiah stepped back from the window. Were they looking for *him*? His shock at seeing other people mixed with the fear of being hunted. When he chanced another look down, the group was splitting in different directions. One of the men—a spindly, nasty-looking specimen clutching a butcher's knife—started towards the house. Josiah remembered he'd left the front door open. He stiffened. The man was already downstairs, prowling the dusty rooms. The air pressure changed, stifling Josiah's breathing and edging him close to panic. His heart toiled in his chest, beating stronger, soaked in adrenaline. When he imagined the blade pushing into his stomach, his insides loosened and bubbled.

He heard footsteps on the stairs, climbing, getting closer.

Fighting the panic rising in his chest, Josiah moved quietly away from the window and hid behind the large wardrobe to the left of the doorway, out of sight.

Footsteps thudded on the landing. Silence followed.

Josiah gritted his teeth, tightened his hands around the crowbar, praying he wouldn't have to use it. The thought of the crowbar against flesh and bone—to stave in someone's skull—made him ill and hopeless. He had survived by running and hiding, not fighting. He wasn't an apocalyptic warrior, just a scared and desperate wretch cowering in a drowned world. A hunted animal whose days were numbered.

The footsteps trampled through the other rooms. There was a harsh cough, clotted with phlegm and mucus. The plastic crackle of tarpaulin grazing against the walls. Knocks and scrapes.

The unmistakeable stench of human shit tainted the air. He was in the doorway, wheezing through a damp mouth. The floorboards creaked as he entered just on the opposite side of the wardrobe. Josiah pulled himself against the wall and bit his lip to stifle a cry. Tears dampened his eyes. Tremors wracked his body as he held the small silver cross around his neck.

The man sniffed at the air, inhaled deeply, and breathed out. A muttered word was muffled by saliva-drenched gums.

Soft footfalls drew closer, almost upon him, when loud voices rose outside the house. Whooping and hollering. The man halted, murmuring, then left the room, his footsteps receding down the stairs and outside.

Josiah was only aware he'd been holding his breath when his chest tightened, and he exhaled with wild relief and peered around the wardrobe to make sure the man was gone. He wiped his face with unsteady hands, adrenaline rushing in his system. The horrid stink of the man remained, thick and grainy in the air.

THE GREAT BEAST

From outside came more raised voices and whooping calls. He went to the window on the landing and looked out over the sodden garden and the undeveloped land beyond, where a man in a green waterproof coat ran for his life.

The men in tarpaulin were in pursuit, and gaining on him. Two of them sprinted to close the distance. The fleeing man turned back and swung his hatchet, but it was an exhausted action, easily dodged by his pursuers, who felled him with knives to the small of his back.

The man stumbled and tripped, then fell, crying out in pain as the two men stood over him, their shoulders heaving from exertion. He tried to crawl away, but one of the men delivered a kick to his ribs and he collapsed in the mud. He was all used up. The men snatched the hatchet from his hand. The back of his coat was darkened with blood. The hunt was over.

The other men caught up. They gathered around him with their knives. One of the men stepped forward and crouched next to the man's head and spoke to him. The wounded man looked up, nodding slowly, as though in acceptance.

Josiah watched, fascinated and horrified.

The crouching man spoke a little longer, his filthy mouth moving, then stood and backed away. He gestured to the others, and they grabbed the wounded man and rolled him onto his back. They unzipped his coat and exposed the pale skin of his stomach.

Josiah turned away before they went to work with their knives.

CHAPTER SIX

FROM THE DOORWAY of the house, Josiah checked up and down the street before he stepped outside. The rain fell in thick droplets, with the feel of grease and the smell of ash and rotting vegetation. It dripped from his waterproof coat. He crouched in the garden, watching for the men. It wasn't far to the warehouse and his refuge.

He staggered across the road and through an alleyway dotted with sodden trash and tipped-over bins. He moved quickly, gaze darting around, through silent streets and flooded avenues, past traffic jams of rusting cars and toppled streetlights. One junction was a traffic accident frozen in time, the drivers long gone. The sagging buildings surrounded him and seemed to rise into the grey sky, the charcoal clouds like the ceiling of a tomb.

Thunder crackled in the distance.

Whilst trudging behind a bank, Josiah heard voices rise from the adjacent street. He edged towards the mouth of the alleyway, his back against the stone wall, and peered around the corner towards the voices. A gust of wind spat rain at his face.

Out on the street, one of the filthy men in tarpaulin was struggling to apprehend a teenage boy and a little girl. He was dragging them with one arm each, but the children were resisting, pulling back and hitting him. The girl was screeching.

The boy kicked the man, but he overbalanced and lost his footing. He fell, hitting his head on the road. The girl cried out and crouched beside the boy, on his back, dazed and spluttering.

The man's shoulders juddered with anger. He wiped his mouth, then took the knife from his rope belt. Rain dripped from his long, matted beard, and he grimaced, flexing fingers around the knife handle.

The children looked up, faces taut with fear and defiance. The boy held the back of his head. The girl's lower lip trembled, whimpering as the man stepped forward with the knife raised. He sneered. She began to sob.

THE GREAT BEAST

"If you little pricks don't get moving," he said, "I'm gonna cut your fucking bits off." His voice was nasal, without accent. He pointed the knife at the girl. "I'll cut out your little cunt, then castrate the boy. My brothers aren't fussy about missing parts."

The children didn't move. They said nothing.

The man took another step forward. His face creased in anger. "Come on, let's go." Spittle flew from his mouth. "The others will be pleased with me. I might even get a reward." He let out a burst of laughter, jackal-like in the thick air.

Thunder boomed high in the sky above. The heavens wailed.

The man didn't notice Josiah behind him until the crowbar was arcing towards his head. And when it slammed against his skull, the expression of shock and disbelief was almost comedic. He collapsed to his knees, then his back, out for the count. He sprawled in the water sluicing over the road. A trickle of blood reddened the puddles. His eyes fluttered. He was still breathing.

Josiah stepped away, speechless and wincing at the stench of smeared shit from the man's face. He couldn't even recall walking up behind him. When he'd swung the crowbar, it felt like someone else controlled him. It was all vague, like a memory viewed through mist.

The children stared at him.

He offered a frail smile, entirely inappropriate in the circumstances, and it faded quickly.

"My name is Josiah. Let me help you."

CHAPTER SEVEN

RAINWATER FROTHED IN blocked drains. Dark puddles spread, as though with intent. The downpour did not abate. Thunder filled the sky.

They were safe, for now. The men hadn't reappeared.

Josiah led the children towards the warehouse. They eyed him warily, the boy limping with a twisted ankle, the girl helping him along, both exhausted, malnourished and faltering. Josiah offered to help, but the boy shook his head and glared, holding the knife he'd taken from the unconscious man.

They reached the awnings, sheltered from the rain at last. The children shivered amongst stacks of cardboard boxes. He sensed them watching as he fiddled with the lock. Their lack of trust wasn't surprising.

He opened the door, then strapped on his head torch. Then he pulled out a penlight torch, tossing it to the girl. She frowned, confused by the kind act, then switched it on.

"It'll be dark soon," Josiah said. "Best to get inside."

"The squid," the girl muttered.

Josiah nodded and led them into the dark.

***

The children followed to the storeroom. They didn't ask about the warehouse. They didn't ask about anything.

Josiah lit both Coleman lanterns. "It's safe from the squid. I don't think they come around here."

The children noticed the porn magazines, and exchanged apprehensive looks before Josiah threw a musty blanket over the magazines, acting as though nothing had happened. He offered a meek smile, which he realized looked more like a grimace, so he stopped smiling. His face flushed uncomfortably, and he glanced away.

"I have food and water," he said. "Plenty to share."

THE GREAT BEAST

The children looked at him with unease. Nervous expressions. Rainwater dripped from their waterproof clothing. The knife blade gleamed in the lantern light.

"I'm not going to hurt you, I promise. I haven't seen anyone in months, let alone children. I'm sorry if I seem a bit weird—been on my own too long. I must look in a right state." His voice trailed off and he looked at the floor, unable to meet their eyes.

There was a long silence, then the boy said, "Thank you for helping us."

"You're welcome."

"You're not from the cult?"

"I'm not with those men. I'm not with anyone. I'm just a survivor."

***

Josiah cooked two cans of baked beans and pork sausages while the children settled down on the opposite side of the room. They hung their coats and took off their shoes and socks to dry near the stove with Josiah's wet gear. He'd given them his spare blankets and a bottle of water. They'd been hesitant to drink the water at first, but he'd reassured them, and they seemed to believe him. They'd already drunk half of the two-litre bottle.

The girl helped the boy sit with his back against the wall. She rolled up the leg of his trousers to expose his injured ankle. The boy complained, but was compliant as she lifted his foot and laid it atop a box of bleach bottles. Then she placed a blanket over his legs. The boy thanked her, said she would make a good nurse one day. She gave a tired laugh, possibly the most joyous sound Josiah had heard since the world ended.

He couldn't help but admire them.

"Food's ready," he said. "Hope you're both hungry." He immediately regretted saying that, and silently admonished himself. He ladled beans into paper bowls and grabbed plastic spoons from his supplies. It was all clean, and there was plenty left.

The children received their meals with undisguised hunger. The girl sat next to the boy. Josiah sat on his side of the room and blew wisps of steam from his food.

They ate in silence, only the faint crashing of thunder beyond the walls.

CHAPTER EIGHT

AN HOUR LATER the girl was asleep, wrapped in blankets on the floor, her jumper for a pillow, her breathing low and steady. It was reassuring. The boy sat close, keeping an eye on her, swaddled in his layers. He winced whenever he moved his ankle. Occasionally he glanced at Josiah to check that the bedraggled stranger kept his distance.

The room smelled of baked beans and damp clothes.

Josiah sat across his bed, back against the wall. He sipped water while craving some decent alcohol. There was vodka somewhere in one of the cardboard boxes, but he thought it best not to drink tonight. Best to keep a clear head and not seem like a pathetic drunk. He also thought it stupid and ludicrous that, with most of the human race dead, he cared what these children thought of him.

"My name's David," the boy said. "She's Primrose."

"Pleased to meet you," replied Josiah. "What happened to you out there? Who was that man?" He chose not to mention what he'd seen that day. Not yet, anyway.

The boy wiped his eyes. "He's part of the Chorus of the Void."

"Who?"

"They're a group of crazies. There are loads of them. They worship the thing that rose from the ocean. They like to sing about it. You know what *thing* I'm talking about."

Josiah's insides went cold. "Yeah, I know."

"They're insane."

"Sounds like a cult."

"That's the right word," David said, nodding. "A cult. Me and Primrose escaped from their commune. They think I'm special. They want to keep me captive."

"Why do they think you're special?"

THE GREAT BEAST

"I don't know."

"What about Primrose? Why do they want her?" Josiah asked.

"They were grooming her to be a breeder."

"How did you escape?"

"One of the men, Nash, helped us. He wanted to leave too. He had a change of heart. We arrived at the town this morning, but the Chorus was close behind us. Nash told us to run and hide while he distracted them. So we ran. I hurt my ankle, and then one of the cultists caught us. We tried to fight him off, but . . . " David paused. "Then you arrived, Josiah."

"It was pure luck that I found you."

"I don't know what happened to Nash." David's face creased with sadness and pain. "Did you see him at all?"

The boy stared at Josiah, desperation trembling in his lower lip.

Josiah had to look away. He sniffled, wiped at his face.

"Do you know what happened to him, Josiah? I can see it in your eyes. Please tell me."

Josiah swallowed a mouthful of water. He turned back to David. Such exhaustion and suffering in the boy's face. Josiah felt guilty to add to the boy's anguish, but telling the truth was the right thing to do.

"Was he wearing a green coat?" Josiah asked.

David gave a slight nod of his head. "Yes."

"He didn't make it. The men caught him. They used their knives on him."

"Did he suffer?"

"Not for long," Josiah lied.

After that, nothing else was said.

***

David fell asleep later, snoring gently beside Primrose. They looked at peace. Josiah hoped their dreams were a refuge from reality. He left one of the lanterns on, in case either woke up during the night.

After a few swigs of vodka, Josiah lay on his bed, listening to the storm as it raged outside. The squid would be out, picking through the leavings of previous hunts. Searching for survivors.

His body ached, pulsing with a low pain in his muscles. His head hurt. Flashbacks of the past day played out with visceral clarity. His heartbeat spiked. Adrenaline flushed as he recalled the cracking of the man's skull as the crowbar swung down. The memory of blood in water.

He didn't sleep for a long while.

CHAPTER NINE

IN DREAMS OF black skies, Josiah stood gazing at the withered effigy of Christ nailed to the cross. Thunder and tortured voices echoed in the wind. Sunken cityscapes dwelled on the horizon like blackened tumours. Red puddles pooled around Josiah's bare feet.

The effigy was clad in soiled rags. Eyes closed. Blood trickled from the crown of thorns, down that gaunt face.

Josiah spoke through a mouthful of stagnant water. "Lamb of God. Nazarene. Hear me."

The effigy's head turned to Josiah, to stare down with pleading and pain. The mouth opened to reveal smashed and broken teeth.

Seconds later, the change began.

The thin form began to thrash, as though suffering some kind of seizure. Josiah stepped back as the skin of Christ's face split vertically in an inward collapse. Squid tendrils, long and gnarled, emerged as the maw peeled back to reveal a fleshy cephalopodic head.

The appalling creature, a corrupted vision of something pure, opened its jagged beak and shrieked in the pouring rain to herald a new age.

***

Josiah woke gasping for breath. A tight feeling remained in his chest, like a leftover dream of the abomination upon the cross had descended to embrace him with its squirming limbs in appreciation for his worship.

The children were awake and watching him from their side of the room, with their backs against the wall.

Flustered and sweaty, Josiah sat up. His mouth tasted like ashes and chemicals. In his mind, the Christ-abomination continued to shriek.

"Are you okay, Josiah?" It was the boy who spoke.

Josiah attempted a reassuring smile, but it felt like a bad joke playing across his face. "I'm fine."

"You had bad dreams," Primrose said. Not a question.

THE GREAT BEAST

"Yeah, I did."

"Don't worry," she replied. "We all have bad dreams now."

***

They shared a breakfast of Ritz crackers and tinned fruit. Josiah was tempted to gulp down some vodka, but settled for coffee on the stove. He'd run out of powdered milk, so he took it black and bitter. It woke him up, cleaned the cobwebs from his mind.

"We can't stay here," David said.

Josiah looked up from his mug of coffee. "What do you mean? Where else will you go?"

"A place called Fool's End. Nash told me about it. It's farther north. Higher ground, away from the rising floods and the Chorus."

"They'll find us here," Primrose said. "They're very good at finding things."

Josiah put down his mug and shook his head. "I can't let you go back out there alone."

"Then come with us," David said.

"But this place is safe. There's no reason to leave."

"Nothing is safe. There are no safe spaces. They'll eventually track us down and take us. They'll kill you, Josiah—and it won't be a quick death. You said that Nash didn't suffer, but I know you lied to protect my feelings, because the Chorus doesn't believe in mercy for its enemies. I know what they did to him with their knives."

Josiah looked away from the children. The thought of travelling beyond the town, into the unknown wastelands, terrified him.

"If we stay," David said, "we die."

CHAPTER TEN

JOSIAH SMOKED A cigarette in the doorway, watching rainwater drip from the awning above. Beyond that, the downpour continued. The car park was lost to the rising floods. He imagined the British Isles were underwater, save for a few mountains and hilltops. There would be no escape for any survivors then.

A flicker in the dark water on the far side caught his eye. He stared at where the movement had been. Something thin and glistening had emerged for a split second, only to disappear. But there was nothing there now, no ripples on the water's surface. Just the rain.

He watched long after finishing his cigarette. Maybe his eyes were failing him, or his mind. It wouldn't be a surprise if that were the case.

Casting one last look around, he shut the door and made sure it was locked. Not that a simple locking mechanism could do much good against the things in the water.

He was walking back to the storeroom, guided by his head torch, when a scream echoed and he quickened his pace.

***

Josiah arrived at the storeroom to find David in the throes of a seizure. The boy was wracked by convulsions, rigid arms crossed over his chest, eyes shut tight. Primrose knelt and turned him onto one side, placing a pillow under his head. She looked up at Josiah standing in the doorway.

"This isn't his first seizure."

Spittle flecked the boy's lips and mouth. He made a low whimpering, and his movements slowed. Then his eyes snapped open and he glanced around, as though seeking something hostile in the room.

Primrose placed her hand on his shoulder. David regarded her with damp, bloodshot eyes. He wiped his mouth.

"What did you see?" she asked him.

David sat up and let out a rattling breath. Sweat dripped from his face.

THE GREAT BEAST

"I can't say. I won't say. I just want to forget." Then he looked up at Josiah, hands shaking in his lap. "We don't have long left."

***

Josiah made three mugs of tea and added plenty of sweetener from his dwindling supply. They sat on the storeroom floor, cradling their drinks. Josiah savoured the steam rising at his face.

"How are you feeling?" he asked David.

The boy took a sip and pursed his lips. "I'm fine. I'm used to the seizures by now."

"How long have you been having them?"

David hesitated, glanced at Primrose before looking at Josiah. "They started after that thing rose from the ocean."

"Do you see that thing when you have a seizure?"

David said nothing, biting his lip as he looked down at his drink. He gave a barely noticeable shrug of his shoulders.

"Why can't you tell us?" Josiah said.

"Because it scares me."

"It's okay. Nothing wrong with being scared, David."

"I can't tell you," the boy said. "I'm worried that if I tell you, it'll come true."

"That won't happen."

"How do you know that? You *can't* know that. You don't understand, Josiah."

"I want to understand, David."

The boy smiled a sad smile and shook his head softly. "I can't. I just can't. I'm sorry."

"It's okay," Josiah said. He finished his tea. "You should get some rest."

David muttered, "We need to leave."

"You can't leave now," said Josiah, shuffling across to place his mug by his bed. "It'll be getting dark soon." He didn't mention what he'd seen outside earlier.

David downed the rest of his drink and handed the mug to Josiah. "Thank you for the tea. We'll stay tonight, but leave at first light in the morning. You can come with us or stay here, but whatever you choose, we're going."

Josiah looked from David to Primrose and back again. "Maybe you'll feel different in the morning."

"No."

"Doesn't Primrose get a say?"

The girl sniffled, glanced at Josiah.

"She agrees with me," David said.

"Is that right, Primrose?"

"I'm protecting her."

Josiah considered this. The girl was shaking. He took one of the spare blankets and put it over her shoulders. David watched him.

"Fair enough, you've made your decision," Josiah said. "In the morning I'll give you some food and water for the journey."

"Thank you," said David.

"No problem. Get some rest."

CHAPTER ELEVEN

AFTER AN AWKWARD farewell, the children left, and Josiah watched them disappear into the rain. A pang of regret troubled him as he shut the door. He returned to his den and brooded for hours, drinking straight vodka and lamenting the end of all things.

At some point in the afternoon, he passed out, and dreamed of lost children in a drowned world.

***

Josiah woke to a loud ringing inside his head, a leftover from his dreams of maniac gods. He pushed away the empty vodka bottle, grimacing at the fetid taste in his mouth. The storeroom swayed. His stomach roiled and gurgled. He checked his watch, saw it was almost midnight. Fuck, he'd been unconscious for hours, like some degenerate drunk. All because he felt guilty for letting the children go. It was pathetic.

He struggled to his feet and placed one hand against the wall, stifling the urge to release the bile at the back of his mouth.

After grabbing his crowbar and head torch, he went into the warehouse and took a walk.

***

The torchlight speared the darkness as he checked the doors to make sure they were secure. He just wanted to sleep, regardless of the bad dreams awaiting him. The sound of rain was a constant reminder of the cataclysm. It always seemed to rain harder at night.

He'd found one of the side doors ajar and swaying in the wind, which had blown rain inside on the warehouse floor. He looked out at the dark beyond the doorway, his body rigid with sudden dread. The sight of the open door sobered him, and his fear was vivid and impossible to control. He stepped forward, hands shaking, head aching, and stood in the doorway. The wind spat rain at his face. A glimmer of movement out in the dark night caught his eye, but there was nothing. It had been an elegant motion, like a shape of water in the downpour. Then he turned away, and his torchlight revealed a trail of wet shoe prints on the floor, leading deeper into the warehouse.

Someone had come in from the rain.

He raised the crowbar, and a strangled gasp stuck in his throat.

A low cry of anguish rose from inside the building. Josiah's heart floundered, and the realisation that he wasn't alone tightened his chest and turned his guts to water. The cold air prickled on his skin.

He shut and locked the door. It took all his nerve to follow the trail into the darkness.

***

Another anguished cry drifted towards him as he searched the dark. Thick pillars and tall racks of shelving loomed in the snatches of light. He paused, adjusted the strap around his skull, then moved on again, listening for approaching footfalls or signs of an ambush.

The next cry rose into shrill laughter that told of madness and hysteria, spinning around in the air, disorientating him until he flailed at imagined figures and forms in the darkness.

The laughter faded into silence, and Josiah wasn't sure which he preferred. He walked on, following the trail of watery smears, and his torchlight found a crouching shape twenty yards away on the bare concrete floor.

He halted as the shape turned towards him to show ruined eyes within a bloodied face. It was the man he'd hit with the crowbar. The cultist who'd tried to abduct David and Primrose.

The skin around his useless eyes was raw and bleeding. He grinned with a severe mouth, the bandage around his head stained with filth. The unmistakeable stench of shit and piss rose from his tarpaulin cowl and the raggedy clothes beneath. He looked like something dragged up from a waterlogged grave.

"You shouldn't leave your doors unlocked," he muttered, barely restraining his mirth. "Any old weirdo could wander in." He tittered with his hands at his scabbed lips, then stood, wavering on unsteady feet.

Josiah said nothing, unable to work his throat.

"My brothers took my eyes," the man said. "This is my punishment for letting the children escape. But now time is up for you. You're in some trouble now."

THE GREAT BEAST

When the loud banging began on the outer sides of the warehouse's doors, the man raised his arms in elation and laughed as though privy to a joke between himself and the dark. The banging was deafening, blunt weapons and fists against metal, hammering to get into the building.

The blind man lowered his arms, one hand tightening on the knife grip. "My brothers are here. They're not happy that you interfered, and they'll punish you for it."

Josiah put his hands over his ears. The impacts echoed around the warehouse, like the sounds of devils trying to break through from hell.

The blind man lunged forward, baring his teeth in a mad grimace, the blade sweeping inches from Josiah's face.

Josiah reeled away with his crowbar raised, leading the man to trip on his own feet. The man fell in a pathetic heap and lay on his back, laughing with the conviction of the deranged as the banging continued. The knife slipped from his hand, but he didn't notice in his fit of mad merriment.

Josiah stood over him, readying himself to swing his crowbar, when the warehouse doors burst open. The man's laughter grew with babbling and spluttering, until he began convulsing, arms seized with palsy. And just before Josiah fled deeper into the warehouse, the man smiled a loathing smile in the pale light of the torch.

Josiah switched off his head torch and groped through the darkness, barely quicker than walking pace. The banging stopped, and in the following silence, his panicked breaths echoed around him. He glanced back to see torchlight at the far end, and heard doors opening. Slapping footfalls followed as the cultists entered with knives and torches. Grunted voices mixed and thickened. A burst of laughter, damp with sickness.

In the blinding dark, Josiah tripped and stumbled forward, foot pulsing with pain, before clipping his right shoulder on the metal shelving. He stifled his cry as he tumbled to his knees, but the scuffle of his boots had already alerted the cultists, now pointing their torchlights in his direction. He was out of their range, but not for long.

Josiah did the only thing he could do. He hid.

CHAPTER TWELVE

AS THE RAIN battered the roof and walls, Josiah prayed to the God he loved in unrepentant desperation and terror. Gripping his crowbar in bloodless hands, he crouched amongst pallets and boxes, waiting for the cultists to head his way. If he stayed in one place, they would eventually find him. They would find him and make him sorry for helping the children.

Voices echoed through the warehouse, fading and rising again. Torchlights flashed and glared in the dark. Josiah gritted his teeth, bowed his head as though it would hide him amidst the abandoned things. The cultists had already found his den, and now it was beyond his reach, along with his supplies. The situation was near-hopeless; there was nothing left but escape. The thought of fleeing blindly through the night, at the mercy of the squid, brought him close to tears, but it was the only option left.

Gathering his nerves, he hunched over and crept out from the cardboard boxes and wooden pallets. He tried to move in silence, but his body felt weak and full of water, like a make-believe man lost in the dark.

When torchlights approached, he hid and waited for the footsteps to pass. More footfalls moved around the darkness, accompanied by sweeping torchlight.

He darted from his hiding place for one of the side doors, fifty yards away. The smell of rain served as a motivation to escape, and he prayed he'd soon feel the downpour on his face.

He was within touching distance of the doorway when a flare of torchlight caught him, and he halted, frozen in place. He turned towards the light, mouth dropping open, hands dangling, a prey animal trapped in a hunter's sights.

Voices rose from tarpaulin cowls and hoods. Threatening movements in shadows. Torchlight flashed upon the blades of knives.

"Little lamb!" one of the cultists said. "We've found you!"

THE GREAT BEAST

"There he is," said another, giggling lowly. "My knife is ready for him."

"Can we cut him?"

"Of course."

"We'll watch him bleed!"

Josiah ran for the door.

***

Into the downpour, rain stinging his eyes as the cultists chased him. The beams of torches danced on his heels. Josiah gasped and groaned, struggling through puddles, his boots scraping on the tarmac. Witless with fear, he fled with no plan in his head. All he could do was run.

At the edge of the car park he climbed the fence, his feet slipping and barely gaining purchase on the metal links. With a cry of exertion, he tumbled over to the sodden ground on the other side. The cultists were close; by the time he'd started running again, they were climbing the fence.

The rain fell harder, kicked by the wind, slowing him as he flailed and stumbled. He was already soaked to the skin. There was little difference between the ground and the sky, everything shrouded in darkness.

He whimpered between each gasp as he fought to stay ahead of his pursuers. He stared straight ahead. Time became fluid and his mind slipped away for sporadic moments.

At some point in the lightless night he collapsed and cried out. But when he looked back, expecting the approach of torchlights and sneering faces, there was only dark and rain, and nothing else.

He was alone.

CHAPTER THIRTEEN

JOSIAH FOUND A house and took shelter in its living room. He huddled within scavenged blankets behind a sofa, shivering with terror and cold. The rain worsened outside. The constant fear of being found wore him down, and as the night went on, he sobbed and cried into his hands.

Sleep came and went, with vivid dreams, bad memories, regrets and guilt. At one point in the dark hours, he went to the window and glimpsed spectres of hunting squid streaming past. A swarm of ghosts in the night, almost beautiful in their movements. They spat sounds that could have been words, mimicking their victims. Hungry monsters full of cunning, completely amoral, a force of nature that scoured life from the planet.

Josiah returned to his place behind the sofa and closed his eyes.

***

In the morning he returned to the warehouse and found it deserted. He'd expected an ambush by the cultists, but there was nothing. His supplies were gone. They'd used pages from his Bible to smear shit across the walls of his den. His camp bed was in bits, and soaked with urine. The cultists had ripped his clothes into pieces. The fuckers had even stolen his porn magazines. Nothing was salvageable.

He clenched his hands into fists. All he had was the clothes he wore and what was in his pockets, which amounted to little. Such despair fell over him that he contemplated ending it all by jumping off the warehouse roof.

He left the ruin of his den and knew he'd never return.

***

An awful smell of offal led him to the corpse of the blind man. Josiah stood over the man's remains and fought back an aching groan at the sight. "Dear God. Dear God in Heaven."

The blind man, face set in a toothy grimace, had suffered terribly before death. He was naked and lying on one side, hands tied behind his back with barbed wire. His throat was cut to the bone. He'd been sodomised, and his genitals had been severed. Judging by the dried blood around him, he'd been dead for several hours. It had been a torturous end.

Josiah left him and walked away.

***

His torchlight revealed a scrawl of large spidery writing on the back wall inside the warehouse: *You alone amongst the stars; you alone amongst the deep and dark.*

He had no idea of its meaning, and just thinking about it made his head hurt. It was a manifestation of madness, the scribbling of disturbed deviants who raped and murdered their own. But part of it was correct, for he was, indeed, alone.

***

Josiah left the warehouse a while later, shivering in the cold and rain, to search for supplies. He moved with care and watched for the Chorus, in case they had returned for him. He picked through deserted houses and domestic tombs, ignoring mouldering remains in armchairs or beneath dusty bedsheets. The lulls in the rain offered the sombre silence of a dead world. The country was a graveyard, reduced to ruins by unearthly powers. The untold dead gnawed at his mind, along with the possibility that he was the last of his religion, a thought that scared him beyond measure.

After three hours, he found enough food and water to last a few days, if he rationed. It wasn't much. Two tins of baked beans, a packet of ready-salted crisps, a cereal bar, and a Snickers. The 750ml bottle of water would only sustain him for so long. All of it, along with a blanket, a change of clothes, and a new Bible, went into a rucksack. Using a map from a car's glove compartment, he located Fool's End and marked it in red pen. Miles upon miles to travel northwards. It would take several days even if he wasn't waylaid by hostiles. The axe he'd recovered from a garage still retained a keen edge, despite the speckled rust of the blade.

He would need to find more supplies if he intended to follow the children to their destination.

CHAPTER FOURTEEN

JOSIAH HEADED NORTH, aiming for the uplands, avoiding the worst flooding while he hunched over in the rain and clutched the axe. He was little more than a vagrant creature in the downpour. His body ached, and blood ran slowly through his veins. Dull cramps needled his legs. The world softened to greyness and black water, the sky full of thunder as he trudged the dim of midday. Abandoned cars littered the tarmac, reminders of the chaos in the days after the cataclysm, rusting shapes with deflated tyres and the occasional skeleton inside.

The sign posts at the roadsides remained, tilted and rusted from the severe weather of the last months, but they kept him pointed in the right direction.

He passed houses on the outskirts of villages and checked for survivors. Spoiled food in kitchen cupboards. The bones and scattered feathers of a parrot in a cage. Smashed windows. Black mould on walls. The stench of ammonia in back rooms and hallways.

He looked for signs of David and Primrose, if they'd left any markers for him, but there was nothing.

The rain continued to fall.

***

The cloying mist drew in around him and obscured the way ahead. He blinked rain from his eyes and glanced around as figures and shapes seemed to materialise in the mist, phantoms come to visit him. And beyond them, impossibly, cyclopean structures arose into the sky. Black cathedrals and alien monoliths, like he was crossing through other worlds, and other dimensions were revealing themselves through a grey veil, to confess their existence at the end of it all.

He walked on, staring straight ahead, ignoring the voices that called in siren song and lullaby.

***

THE GREAT BEAST

Farther on, Josiah arrived at an isolated church sagging in the downpour, blackened and deteriorated. It was a pathetic sight that offered melancholy, and memories of the night the squid attacked his church. The building gave no comfort, only reminded him that his faith was wiped from this world.

He went inside, through the dripping doorway after the waterlogged graveyard. He switched on his head torch at the foot of the aisle, breathing slowly in the darkness. His light repelled the shadows it created. Rainwater dripped from the hole in the roof, forming little streams amongst the scattered bones on the stone floor. Human bones.

God is dead.

The air was ripe with smells from the pews. Fungal blossoms on damp wood and stone pillars. Spores and miniscule grains roamed in the torchlight. Josiah cleared his throat and spat, imagining blackening fungi within his lungs.

The altar had been desecrated with shit and blood, encrusted and festering. Insects skittered and crawled. Josiah fought back tears at such an unholy act. This violation and sacrilege. This degeneracy. It spat in the face of God.

God is dead.

He shook his head and stepped away, unsteady on his feet. And when he paused to lean against a stone column, his torchlight swept ahead of him to reveal the most terrible of all tableaus.

He let out a gasping sob and put one hand to his face. The air rushed from his chest. The world seemed to fall away before it returned with horrific certainty. Nausea loosened the back of his throat, and his heart ached. His gaze never moved from the monochrome painting of dread Cthulhu and a swarm of ravenous squid filling the wall from floor to ceiling. The swarm surrounded the towering figure as it rose from the sea, its head great against the sky, its tentacled face awe-inspiring in the dark of the church. Its squalid skin glistened with slime. Deep eyes of disdain for this world.

Josiah whimpered as the beast's head turned towards him and its eyes fell over his shaking form. It regarded him with sheer apathy and the cunning of untold eons as the squid writhed and thrashed and shrieked with their mock-human voices.

Cthulhu reached for him with dripping claws.

God is dead.

He screamed.

The next moment he was staring at the tableau, merely a depiction again, and he collapsed onto a rotting pew and put his head in his hands and cried.

God is dead.

CHAPTER FIFTEEN

The church was corrupted, defiled, but it was the only shelter as the day dimmed outside. Josiah settled in a back room, away from the horror and defilement, and lay on a tattered couch staring at the ceiling. He listened to the rainstorm break upon the earth. Concussions of thunder filled the sky.

He wanted to die and go to Heaven. He wanted to be with the people he had lost. He wanted to rest in peace.

These were his last thoughts before he fell asleep.

***

Terrible dreams of saints with rotting faces and black tendrils, corrupted by dread Cthulhu as the beast created its acolytes. Nuns wailed as their bodies contorted into piscine-like forms. Holy men kneeled and worshipped in orgy of violence and sexual depravity. And when their lusts were sated, they clutched their hearts and severed tongues and muttered alien words before the beast consumed them.

***

Josiah woke on his knees before the depiction of Cthulhu. He gasped, drool trickling over his lips and chin. Delirium broiled like a sickness. Hysteria forced a choking burst of laughter into his throat.

His hands formed into a gesture of prayer towards the terrible things upon the wall. He unclasped them, palms slick with sweat, as the air trembled around him and blurred the horrific visage. Then nihilism filled him like black water and drowned the hope he had nurtured. He broke down, pressing knuckles to his mouth, biting at the skin until he tasted blood.

On feet he could barely feel, he stumbled outside, collapsed to his knees, and cried to the squid in the night. They would be hunting. They would be roaming the land. They would hear him if he spoke the correct words and honoured their strength and hunger.

He called again, raising his arms, and begged them to kill him. Begged them to rip him asunder. He waited for them out in the inky darkness, but they never came. He was alone, a lost soul in the rain.

***

Josiah left the church at first light and continued through the flooded wreckage of the country. Sunken houses and villages marked the way. Roads vanished into the water.

It drove him to despair, even as a sliver of hope kept him placing one foot in front of the other.

***

From out of the mist-wreathed floods, a skiff had come to rest upon the "shore," merely the broad slope of a hill. Josiah went to the boat, keeping an eye on the black water as he hefted his axe.

The skiff was abandoned, with nothing to scavenge and no sign of whoever had piloted it. He looked around, disappointed and tired, dabbing the rain from his face.

"Where did you go?" he said. "What happened to you?"

He turned away and lowered his axe, and was walking back to the road when something moving in the water froze him in place. His hands trembled and stiffened, and it took all of his nerve to turn back towards the shore.

A squid rose with all the grace of a lithe dancer. It was ten feet tall and twice as wide, due to the length of its tentacles. Its disc-like eyes centred upon Josiah. The terrible beak at the centre of its squirming limbs snapped open at the anticipation of succulent prey.

Josiah raised his axe as the squid skittered towards him. He screamed and waited for the end.

The monster was almost upon him when it reared up and shrieked in pain.

CHAPTER SIXTEEN

JOSIAH TRIPPED OVER his onto his back, dropping his axe in the mud, breath forced from his lungs. The squid thrashed, as though stung by electrical shock. It shrieked again, caught in spasms, then fell away from him, its limbs scraping the boggy ground, spraying rainwater and mud. Its eyes bulged with agony, and then, in a frenzy, it fled and submerged, leaving ripples as it dove.

Within moments the water was still and flat. Only the smell of ammonia remained.

Josiah slumped in the mud, gasping, heart lodged in his throat. He was trembling violently. His hands dug into the ground. He should be dead now.

Footfalls drifted in the mist to Josiah's left, and David emerged from the greyish veil like a wraith. Josiah watched the boy approach, struck dumb, his mouth dropping open as he struggled to regain his breath.

David stood over Josiah, his eyes bloodshot, face wan with exertion. His hands shook as they hung by his sides. Rainwater dripped from his chin. He glanced at the flood beyond before offering a soft smile from within the hood of his waterproof coat.

"I knew you'd come after us. I knew you'd find us."

Josiah coughed until his chest hurt. His voice came out in a rasp. "What happened to the squid? It was going to kill me . . . "

"It won't return. Not for a while, anyway. And by then we'll be gone."

"Why didn't it kill me?"

David offered his hand down to Josiah. "I'll tell you when we reach the hiding place."

**

The boy led Josiah through the mist and rain until they arrived at an abandoned lorry. The livery on the sides had faded, and its tyres were sagging. Josiah and David passed the darkened cab to the end of the trailer, where the boy knocked three times.

A few seconds passed before one of the doors opened and Primrose's pale face appeared. Her eyes widened when she noticed Josiah, and her mouth formed a nervous smile. She seemed tense and anxious within the bundled layers, like a little bird wary of circling predators.

"Anything happen while I was away?" David asked her.

She shook her head as she helped him up into the trailer. Then David crouched down and pulled Josiah up with him.

Primrose closed the doors.

***

The candlelight formed phantom shapes inside the trailer. Rain pattered the roof. The sweeping wind sounded like pain. Cold draughts entered through minute cracks and troubled Josiah's ageing bones.

They sat on the floor, eating junk food from a village several miles away. David stared at the candle's dancing flame.

"What happened back there?" Josiah asked the boy. "Why didn't the squid kill me?"

"I told the squid to go away," David said.

"How?"

"I'm changing."

"What do you mean?"

"I'm becoming something else."

"Becoming what?" Josiah asked.

"I'm not sure." David stared at his hands, held before his face. "Something that's not quite human. It's why we're heading to Fool's End. Nash said they can help us."

"Why didn't you tell me before?"

"I was scared. But once you saw me drive the squid away, I didn't have much choice but to tell you, did I?"

Josiah looked at Primrose, morose as she scratched the floor with a damp stick. Then he turned back to David. "Does it have something to do with the squid? Are you linked to them somehow?"

"I don't know. But I was able to scare away that squid just by thinking about it. I'm connected to them. All of them."

Josiah shook his head, but found himself believing the boy. It was merely another symptom of an insane world of death and monsters.

CHAPTER SEVENTEEN

JOSIAH WAS THE last to fall asleep.

His dreams echoed with screams. Voices whispered in the crimson dark of a sunken world. And beyond it all, the Nazarene hung upon the cross, crying as his face drooped and writhed before assuming the form of slack feelers.

Once more, Josiah stood trembling and powerless when the Nazarene tore free from the cross a in a distressingly puppet-like motion and fell upon him. The Nazarene lowered its awful face onto Josiah's to kiss him with busy, dripping tendrils that burrowed with a terrible insistence.

Josiah's muffled screams joined with the others into the sky.

***

He woke as the doors burst open and harsh light flooded the trailer. Primrose called out to David before she was hauled outside. Josiah reached for his axe, but cold hands gripped him and stinking bodies clamoured around him. He tried to break free, but a fist struck him across his face and knocked the fight out of him. He slumped, groaning, light stinging his eyes, the stench of shit all around. Some of the cultists were laughing.

David struggled as two men held him. He cried and grimaced, his face a mask of fear as a burlap sack was pulled over his head. The cultists tied his hands behind his back. He slackened, trembling and whimpering, when one placed a knife against his ribs.

"Leave them alone," Josiah shouted.

"Silence, heathen," one muttered in his ear, spitting rank breath. "Speak again and I'll end you."

"Fuck off."

"Your choice, heathen."

It was the last thing he heard before something harder than a fist hit his head and all went to darkness.

***

Josiah came to on his stomach. His face and his head ached and throbbed, and when he put his hand to those places, the skin felt tender and bruised. He glanced around the windowless room, its dour walls and ceiling, then sat up and rubbed his eyes. The bare room spun, the floor tilting before righting itself again. The low smell of decay permeated the air, reminding him of his father's shed back in the old days.

He stood on weak legs, tottered to the door on the opposite side, and tried the handle, but it only rattled. Then he put his ear to the door to listen beyond the room. There was just silence. He swore under his breath. When he thought of what the cult might be doing to David and Primrose, he clenched his jaw with anger. He kicked the door until his feet hurt.

Eventually he inspected the walls for any possible ways out of the room, but they were solid and intact. He spat and stared at the door while holding the cross around his neck between finger and thumb.

He waited.

***

Hours passed in the silent dark, a cold terror at the possibility that he'd been left to die in the room. He prayed for salvation.

And then his prayers were answered.

The door clicked open, and two cultists entered with knives held for him to see. Their grimy faces stretched with wolfish grins. Josiah looked up, contemplating attack, but his nerve abandoned him and they grabbed his arms and hauled him to his feet. They brought faces close to him, yeasty breath spilling from their mouths. The man to Josiah's left let out a series of hacking coughs, hinting at degrading health. He wiped his mouth and chuckled.

"We're going to see the bishop," the other man said, his voice a throaty rasp.

"Who?" Josiah asked.

"You'll find out. You'll find out about lots of things, my little lamb."

CHAPTER EIGHTEEN

THE MEN SAID nothing as they dragged Josiah through darkened corridors of dust and grime. They passed doors where chanting and muttering arose. Echoes of laughter drifted along, mixed with pained screams fading into silence.

They climbed stairs to higher floors. Josiah glimpsed grey daylight through windows, relieved he wasn't in some underground bunker. But what kind of house was it? It had the feeling of a stately home fallen to ruin. The higher they went, the more lavishly decorated the walls became.

Eventually they halted before double doors painted in red and gold. One opened, while the other cultist pushed Josiah into a grand room of antique furniture, thick rugs, and walls of oak hanging with medieval weapons, oil paintings of aristocrats, and mounted heads of exotic animals. A lion, a tiger, a buffalo, a gazelle, a tusked boar with gleaming eyes. Silk curtains on windows looking out at pouring rain and stately grounds. The sound of the downpour mixed with the creaking of the walls. The room smelled of old things slowly degrading. A corruption.

"Sit down," one told Josiah as they gestured to a plain wooden chair opposite an ornate armchair. He sat, staying silent for his own good, seething with dull pain inside his skull. Beyond the armchair were grand double doors reaching to the ceiling.

"Stay here," one of the men said. "Don't fucking move." They stood on either side of him, breathing lowly.

Moments later the double doors opened, and a heavily-overweight man clad in a cloth gown shuffled into the room. He wheezed through a damp mouth as he sucked on a cigarette. His skin was jaundiced and sallow.

The sight of him unsettled Josiah. There seemed something fundamentally *wrong* with him. Something inside him. He offered a kindly smile and sat down. His eyes never left Josiah as he spoke to his subordinates.

"Thank you for bringing our friend here, gentlemen. You may leave us now."

"Yes, Bishop." They departed and closed the door behind them. Now it was just Josiah and the strange man, staring at each other.

Josiah was the first to look away. He wrung his hands together. The air seemed thin as he took deep breaths.

"Welcome to Avalon House, Josiah," the man said. "I am Bishop Fife. Would you like some food? Maybe a drink of water?"

Josiah looked back. He ignored the thirst burning his throat. "How do you know my name?"

"The children told us. They've been very helpful since their return." Bishop Fife's smile thinned into a bloodless curve in the doughy skin of his face. He wiped at the gingery bristles on his chins and flabby throat. "I must say, you've caused us some trouble in regards to David and Primrose."

"Good," said Josiah, glancing at the dead eyes of the animal trophies around him.

"Although you were very kind to lead us to them."

"What do you mean?"

"My men followed you from Pendlebury. You were our only hope of finding the children. We really couldn't have found them without you."

Josiah blinked back tears and bit his tongue to stifle a cry of anger. He'd been so foolish and stupid. He glared at Fife. "Why haven't you killed me? I've seen what your men do to their enemies."

"We are not above mercy."

"David said you're called the Chorus of the Void. Bit of a crap name for a cult."

Bishop Fife ignored the jibe. "Oh, we're called many things in many places." His damp eyes flicked towards Josiah's cross necklace. "You're a Christian, I gather?"

Josiah tucked his cross back under his shirt. He nodded, said nothing.

Bishop Fife simply smiled. "I used to be, before all this happened. Before I was awakened."

"That's hard to believe," Josiah said.

"Not at all. I was a true believer. I was a dutiful member of the flock. And despite my sins, I was a good Christian."

"What were your sins?"

"Lust, greed, gluttony. The usual. But now I see that I was wrong to

THE GREAT BEAST

think of them as sins or vices. Those urges were part of me. At least now I can indulge them without fear of being punished."

"You don't think you'll be punished?"

"By whom? You, Josiah? God? I don't think so. In the reign of the Great Beast, we are free to be ourselves and discard all the false piety and self-righteous bullshit."

"You're delusional," said Josiah. "You're mad."

"We're all mad." Fife wiped his mouth as his smile broadened, exposing his blackened teeth. "Tell me, do you still believe in your god? I mean, *really* believe."

Josiah exhaled, dug his fingernails into his palms. "Yes, I still believe."

Bishop Fife shrugged. "Even now, when dread Cthulhu has claimed the world as his own?"

"Yes."

"Why?"

"Because I do. I don't have a choice."

"Your god is dead, Josiah. Your religion is dead. Your faith is nothing but ashes in the ruin of this world."

"It's all I have."

Fife shook his head. "No, it's not. You have so much more to give."

"What do you mean?"

"I admire you, Josiah."

"What?"

"I admire you for surviving for so long, for keeping going. That takes strength and character and adaptability. Those are the sort of qualities I like to see in the Chorus."

"You want me to join your cult?" Josiah asked.

"Yes, I would like that very much."

"I'd rather die."

"That's disappointing. Are you sure? Would you like some time to think about it?"

"Just kill me. I've had enough. I'm finished."

Fife leaned forward, his eyes gleaming with malice. "We've only just begun, little lamb."

***

That night, several of the men arrived at Josiah's room and set to him with fists and feet. By the time they finished, he lay in a bloodied heap on the cold floor. They left him unconscious, and halfway between worlds.

RICH HAWKINS

In his nightmares, he witnessed the Great Beast—that was what Fife called Cthulhu, wasn't it?—rise into the mist from a sea littered with the corpses of marine life and wrecked hulks of battleships and submarines. The bodies of men floated in the water, faces frozen in madness and terror. There had been a confrontation, a brief engagement of ordnance and heavy weaponry, but it had been in vain. It had barely been a battle.

The Great Beast roared, a sound to end worlds.

CHAPTER NINETEEN

DAYS PASSED. The cult enslaved him. Josiah thought of David and Primrose, but held little hope he would see them again. There was no sign of them, nor were they ever mentioned. Hope was beyond him.

His waking hours were spent emptying primitive latrines and other menial tasks in the service of the Chorus. He stank of shit and piss, mostly his own. Most days they beat and abused him, and on special days he was tortured both physically and mentally, worn by the cult's fists and words. He survived on stale crackers and brackish water. They treated him as less than human. He would only be human once he joined the cult.

Some nights, Bishop Fife visited Josiah and spoke in soft tones, trying to lure him into sordid arrangements, but he refused, even as he cried with agony.

Time lost meaning in the constant rain beyond Avalon House. Time became pain, and pain was life.

***

Bishop Fife visited him late one night, but for different reasons.

A guard opened the door, and Fife stepped inside with a small LED lantern that pushed the darkness from the room.

Josiah sat up, pushing back against the wall, shivering beneath his stinking blanket. His hands balled into aching fists at Bishop Fife, who sat down and placed the lantern on the floor.

Fife smiled with a note of sadness and folded his legs. He placed his hands together. "This is your last chance, Josiah. We've been more than reasonable to you. We've been patient while waiting for you to convert, but your time has run out. Join us, and cast away your frail religion for a new one. Come and worship with us in this new world."

"This is a dead world," said Josiah, not looking away from Bishop Fife. "Your pathetic cult will go the same way. So fuck off."

Fife glowered as he shifted his bulk upon the chair. He raised one hand to scratch at the twitch under his left eye. "Okay, you've made your choice. Tomorrow you'll be crucified upon a wooden cross, just like your beloved Messiah." He rose and wheezed through his smacking lips. "We'll see you in the morning. Sleep well, little lamb."

Josiah watched Fife leave, then bowed his head as the door shut and the lock clicked. His body was wracked with pain. Exhaustion pulled at his limbs. His belief that he would go to a better place soothed him against the agony waiting on the cross.

He passed out and dreamed of monsters rising from the deep.

CHAPTER TWENTY

JOSIAH WAS TAKEN from his cell, led through Avalon House, and brought into the first light of the misty morning. He held on to his silver crucifix.

The rain fell slow and thick.

They took him from the house to the very edge of the sweeping grounds, where the rest of the cult waited, gathered in ranks around the wooden cross upon the ground. There were well over fifty men; amidst them Josiah noticed Primrose, with slumped shoulders and a sorrowful expression. She was bruised and wan, little more than a shade of a girl.

Bishop Fife emerged from the crowd, playing the role of a reluctant executioner, arms spread wide to welcome Josiah. He watched as Josiah was stripped to his stained underwear and left to shiver in the rain.

Josiah wrapped his arms around his chest and lowered his gaze to the ground. All eyes were upon him, weighing him down, a last burden to be carried before death.

"Take him to the cross," Fife said.

They forced him upon the cross and held his arms along the horizontal beam. The wood was cold and slick. Grinning faces closed around him. Muttering and giggling rose from the crowd. He stared at the grey sky, rain in his eyes and mouth, beading on his face. There was no fear in his heart, and he felt the acceptance of the inevitable. He was numb to it all.

The men wrapped rope around his legs and pulled it tight, securing him to the vertical beam. He gave no sign of pain as the rope bit his skin. The men spat at him. He closed his eyes and whispered a prayer. Then there was just the pattering of rain and the hushed anticipation of the crowd.

"To all gathered here today, we witness the punishment of Josiah, who rejected us despite the love and guidance we gave to him. But we shall not hate him, for there is nothing but pity on this solemn day. And he shall be held aloft upon the cross of his dead religion, like the old ways of this world.

This will be his end. He will either perish slowly or be taken by the squid in the night. But he will die, and we will move on to pursue our glory in this, our *new world*. We are chosen. We are strong. And we will thrive in the new age of the Great Beast."

"*Hail the Great Beast*," the crowd muttered as one. "*Hail Cthulhu*."

Josiah opened his eyes to Fife standing over him. The man held his hands together and shook his head at Josiah, who found the strength to mouth a silent *fuck you* before Fife kicked him in the ribs. The pain was excruciating, and his insides rattled. He gritted his teeth and waited for the pain to fade. Then Fife crouched beside him and stroked his face, his hand colder than the rain.

Moments later, more men came to hold his arms and spread his palms upon the cross. One held a large hammer and a handful of long nails.

"Hurry up and get it done," Josiah whispered. "You fucking cowards." He tensed as the tip of a nail was placed upon the centre of his left palm. His muscles trembled. He breathed hard through gritted teeth as his nerve crumbled and tears filled his eyes. Fife was watching, smiling like a kindly grandfather.

Josiah prepared and kept his eyes upon the sky.

The hammer rose, and when it fell and connected with the head of the nail, the agony that followed blinded him and almost stopped his heart. He screamed, mouth gaping, body rigid and shuddering. It felt as though his left hand had been torn in half. He bucked and thrashed, tried to break free, but the cultists held him and laughed. He blacked out for several seconds before one spat in his face and pinched his nose to rouse him. Awed mutterings rose from the crowd. Someone chanted nonsense words.

The men turned to Josiah's right hand. The buzz of excitement made their movements hurried and shaky, and their faces stretched with grins and lunatic grimaces. One licked his lips and stared at his trembling hands. Josiah saw it all through tear-blurred vision. The world passed through light and darkness, his nerve endings on fire, his limbs useless. Chemicals in his blood tried to numb the pain. His mind tried to find a memory where he could hide from this torture.

But he did not beg for mercy.

And when they impaled his right hand, the agony was even greater than the left. They laughed as he cried out with all the pain and hysteria in his heart. He was hyperventilating. They used ropes to pull the cross up to a vertical position and then secured it within the ground.

THE GREAT BEAST

It was unbearable. His mind began to fray. All was agony and torture, as though he was coming apart.

The cult left him and returned to Avalon House.

He screamed for a long time, hours into the night, until oblivion took him.

CHAPTER TWENTY-ONE

TIME PASSED IN darkness and daylight, torment and woe. Dehydration and hunger weakened him. He tried to drink the rain. In moments of lucidity, he vomited pale gruel down his chest and stomach. The constant pain reduced him. His insides felt hollowed out, and every muscle and tendon in his limbs burned.

Josiah saw visions of people he knew in the old world. Hallucinations visited him, familiar faces. He called to them, but they merely looked at him.

He prayed for salvation. He prayed for death.

Moments before he passed out, an inhuman shriek echoed around him, and he hoped something had finally come to end his suffering.

To save him from purgatory.

***

Josiah woke to a strange mewling below him, but when he tried to look down, all he glimpsed was a vague shape near the foot of the cross. Moments later, the cross started shaking as the thing below pushed and slapped upon the vertical beam, its mewling rising to a pained shriek. The movement of the cross exacerbated the pain of his nailed hands. He cried out, his voice rasping, as the cross gave way with a wrenching crack and toppled backwards. The impact rattled his bones and took him to new levels of agony. He screamed until his lungs gave out.

When he could scream no more, he passed out again.

***

He opened his encrusted eyes and assumed that Primrose standing over him was merely his imagination—until she touched his face, wiping away raindrops with her hand.

"It's okay," she said. "It's okay." She crouched down to cut the ropes around his legs. He gasped as the pressure of the ropes dropped away. He couldn't feel his legs.

THE GREAT BEAST

Primrose took out a pair of pliers, oversized and ridiculous in her small hands, and told Josiah to brace himself. She struggled for minutes, as Josiah cried and whimpered, but eventually ripped the nails out and tossed them into the floodwater.

"Thank you," he said. His voice was a pathetic croak.

Primrose took a roll of bandages and bound his hands. She helped him up. He could barely move without shuddering in pain. His muscles felt as though they had atrophied. His breath came in trembling gasps.

"What's happening?" he asked her. "The cult will hurt you for this, Primrose. They'll kill you."

"No they won't," she said. "Everything's changed now. You have to see, Josiah. David saved us."

CHAPTER TWENTY-TWO

PRIMROSE TOOK JOSIAH back to Avalon House, struggling to keep him upright as he hobbled with his wrecked hands drawn close to his chest. He shivered and sobbed, and when he took a breath, it felt like glass shards down his throat.

He glanced around, confused and disorientated at the dead silence all around. It permeated the air and surrounded the darkened house.

They walked through the open doorway into the entrance hall. They halted. Josiah gave a breathless gasp at the crumpled cultist at the foot of the grand staircase. The man had been disembowelled; both legs were torn away and dumped nearby. His throat was gaping and still wet. He had died with his eyes bulging in shock and pain.

"There are more," Primrose said quietly, as though not to disturb the dead man. "You have to see."

***

The corridors, hallways, and rooms were littered with the Chorus. Ravaged, mutilated corpses sprawling on the floors. Some had been partially eaten.

Josiah and Primrose stood over Bishop Fife, whose stomach and chest had been ripped open by insistent hands. Splayed ribs dripping red. Exposed organs. Most of his face was gone.

"Who did this?" said Josiah, surveying the carnage.

Primrose's voice was low. "It was David. He did all of it."

"How?"

"He transformed. The cult kept him in a holding cell, but he became too strong and he escaped. He killed everyone. He was so angry."

"Why didn't he kill you?"

"He spared me. He spoke to me, inside my head, told me that it was just the beginning."

"He pushed over the cross," Josiah said.

"Yes."

THE GREAT BEAST

"Where is he?"

"Out in the rain, somewhere."

A shrill cry rose from outside and echoed throughout the chambers of Avalon House.

***

Josiah lay on a makeshift bed of padded blankets as Primrose tended to his pierced hands and the rope burns on his legs. He winced and groaned as she cleaned his wounds with wet wipes, then applied antiseptic cream and fresh bandages from the cult's supply stores.

Once she was finished, she gave him water and painkillers, then fed him a chocolate bar. After that, Josiah slept, in and out of fever dreams.

More days passed as his wrecked body began to recover from the trauma of the cross. His nightmares were of black water filling Avalon House, flowing down corridors and hallways, pouring from the walls of silent rooms. He saw Bishop Fife, wearing that malevolent grin. He saw silhouettes of squid swarming outside his window, calling out in the stolen voices of their victims. Their mimicry had been honed to perfection. One spoke in the voice of his father and told Josiah he was loved.

Each time he woke to find Primrose beside his sickbed, her face pensive and forlorn as she stared out the window.

The days went on, bleeding into a timeless fugue, punctuated by David's shrieks beyond the walls.

CHAPTER TWENTY-THREE

O N ANOTHER RAINY day of grey light, Josiah, lucid for
the first time since the cross, managed sit on the edge of the bed.
The tremors in his limbs had receded to something he could
tolerate. He wore a t-shirt and pyjama bottoms. His vision swam when he
looked around the room. Wincing, he grabbed the water bottle and drank
until he was out of breath. He emptied the bottle, groaning as his guts
cramped, then stood against the wall to stay upright, gritting his teeth
against the spinning inside his head.

He shrugged on the fleece jacket nearby, then stepped into his boots,
the shrunken muscles in his legs trembling and stiff. Stabbing pain down
his spine brought him to tears. Aches and needling twinges tormented him.
He took the blanket over his shoulders. Nausea swam at the back of his
mouth as he took his first steps. He swallowed sour saliva and placed one
foot in front of the other until he was at the door.

Fumbling the door open with his wrists, he stepped into the darkened
corridor. He held his bandaged hands close to his chest and followed
Primrose's voice deeper into the house. He wasn't sure, but she seemed to
be singing a lullaby. And as he neared, he thought he recognised the tune,
although he couldn't remember what it was called.

Through corridors and stately rooms, past alcoves, ornate mirrors, and
grandiose portraits of dead lords. Chandeliers and dried blood stains. The
bodies of the cultists were gone. He walked until he arrived at an oak door,
behind which Primrose's voice was loud and clear.

The singing stopped when Josiah opened the door. He entered and
found Primrose at the end of an antique couch. A crumpled form in filthy
clothes lay beside her, face obscured within a deep hood. The dim
daylight from the wide windows gave them the appearance of lethargic
wraiths.

Primrose looked up at Josiah, her eyes damp with tears. He sat nearby

THE GREAT BEAST

in an Elizabethan-style armchair that smelled of dust. He eyed the sleeping thing beside the girl.

"It's David," she said in a hopeful voice. "He likes it when I sing to him. It helps him sleep."

Josiah didn't know what to say. David made a faint mewling noise within the shell of his filth-encrusted clothes. He smelled of brine and blood.

"I need to see his face," Josiah said to Primrose. "Pull back his hood."

The girl seemed hesitant. She blinked, wiped her eyes, and then gazed down at David. "He's dreaming. He's dreaming of going home."

"Show me his face."

Primrose reached down, and with care pulled back David's hood to reveal a wretched creature, the lower half of its face covered with pale tendrils, each approximately eight inches long. Wispy hair remained on David's scalp. His ears had receded into fleshy nubs. His skin was threaded with black veins. When his face-tendrils shifted, they showed a glimpse of his severe bloodstained mouth, crammed with carnivore teeth.

"Mother of God," said Josiah.

"Part of him is still David," Primrose whispered. "He's not fully gone. It's a gift from his ancestors, activated by the Great Beast's presence."

Josiah opened his mouth, but said nothing.

David opened his eyes and stared at Josiah. His eyes were still those of a little boy.

***

Glancing at Josiah, David retreated to a corner of the room and crouched, raising clawed hands as if to protect his face.

Josiah pulled his blanket tighter around his shoulders. His chest rattled. The soreness of his body felt like little mouths gnawing him.

"David wants to leave this place," said Primrose, "because the squid will eventually come, and he can't hold them all back. Not a whole swarm."

"And where will we go?" Josiah asked.

"Fool's End."

"I can't make it there, Primrose. I can barely walk."

Primrose looked at David, then back to Josiah. "We won't be walking."

CHAPTER TWENTY-FOUR

THE NEXT DAY they travelled the deep floodwater in a small wooden sailboat. It was old and dusted with cobwebs, but its hull was intact, and held enough room for the three of them and some supplies.

David crouched at the bow, hunched and silent, watching the water. Josiah and Primrose sat at the stern, huddled under blankets and a tarpaulin to shelter from the rain. Josiah worked the tiller to steer the boat where David pointed with one gnarled hand.

Cold drizzle pattered the frayed sails in the wind.

"He doesn't want to be alone," said Primrose. "Not until he's fully transformed."

"And what happens when he is fully transformed?"

Primrose didn't answer.

Josiah looked over the black water, checking for signs of the squid or any other aquatic dangers. They passed the tops of houses—chimneys, sloped roofs, attic windows, and satellite dishes. The lowlands and valleys had been consumed by the floods.

"The water should take us all the way to Fool's End," Primrose said. "That's what David told me."

"How does it work?" asked Josiah.

"How does what work?"

"This link you have with him."

"I don't know. But I hear his voice—his old voice—in my head." She went to say something else, but then closed her mouth and looked away.

"What is it? You can tell me."

Primrose regarded him beneath the tarpaulin cover. Her eyes were bloodshot and tired. "When he speaks inside my head, I can hear other things with him, like the screams of monsters, like someone's being tortured."

THE GREAT BEAST

"It's okay, Primrose."

"Do you think David hears those screams in his head? Do you think he hears them all the time?"

Josiah looked towards the boy-creature. Then he held his silver cross between two fingers, comforted by its touch. "I hope not. I think that would be awful."

***

The boat sliced through the water, past a church spire poking the oily surface. Trash and detritus drifted in eddies and currents. Josiah thought of the world beneath them: the streets, fields, and houses in the silty gloom, the drowned landscape lost forever. He wondered if anything dwelled in the submerged houses, nesting amidst the wreckage of domestic scenes. He imagined fish darting through a living room, weaving between furniture and doorways; an octopus' reflection in a dead television screen; crustaceans skittering through a child's bedroom.

He worried that the boat might scrape the roofs of taller buildings, or even run aground. How deep was the floodwater? He peered over the side of the boat and tried to discern any recognisable shapes beneath the water, but it gave no secrets to him.

They passed the top of a tall tree above the water level and saw a skeletal corpse embracing the dripping trunk, arms and legs wrapped around it even in death.

Primrose turned from the sight and lowered her head, preferring to look at the floor of the boat.

***

Soon afterwards they skirted the wreck of a yacht, its bow protruding from the dark water. No sign of movement on board. Josiah wasn't surprised.

David made clicking noises in his throat. Josiah looked at Primrose, but she only shrugged. There was nothing to be said.

CHAPTER TWENTY-FIVE

HOURS LATER THEY passed a drowned village, steering around roofs and chimneys. The wind had weakened to a frail breeze, slowing the boat while increasing Josiah's anxiety about the dangers in the water.

Primrose was the first to see a squid emerge from the half-sunken building to their right. She called out. Josiah stifled a cry and stared in shock.

It was an immense thing, the biggest specimen Josiah had ever seen, its thick tentacles swaying as its great head rose from behind a crumbling wall. A staring eye regarded them with interest.

David made a gurgling sound at the creature.

The squid pushed away from the wrecked building and glided towards them, its massive bulk cutting through the water and forming waves. It loomed over them, dwarfing the boat, keeping pace with no effort. The leviathan's vicious beak opened to emit a shrill cry.

"Oh Christ," Josiah muttered. "We're fucked."

Primrose stared at David. "No we're not."

The boy stood and looked up at the squid, his face-tendrils flailing.

"They're talking to each other," said Primrose.

"This is madness."

The girl's mouth made something like a smile. "Yes, it's madness. All of it. The world is madness, Josiah."

In one swift movement the squid dove and vanished from sight, the power of its submergence rocking the boat. David sat down again and exchanged a brief look with Primrose.

"The squid have eaten their fill," she said, "and now they're returning to the deep."

"Did David say anything else?" Josiah asked.

"Yes. He said we're nearly at Fool's End."

THE GREAT BEAST

***

Ahead of them, the dark shore appeared out of the mist and rain. Josiah steered into the shallows. David jumped out and pulled the boat onto the mud. With some difficulty, Josiah disembarked, his arm hooked around Primrose's elbow. He had to stop and gather himself, waiting for the pain to lessen so he could climb the slope before them.

David watched the mist, his awful face hidden within his hood. His limbs twitched. He wheezed.

Primrose held on to Josiah. "David knows where to go."

***

David led the way into the uplands. They walked, struggling through surface water and mud.

Josiah winced and groaned with each step. "How much further?"

"Not far," said Primrose.

They cut through a road littered with rusting cars. Rain tapped on metal and glass. The daylight was fading, the air growing colder, the mist thickening until it was on their heels and in their faces.

David collapsed to his hands and knees and began shuddering violently. Primrose rushed over and crouched beside him, placing her hand on his back. She whispered in his ear as he whimpered and whined. He slapped his clawed hands in the mud and puddles, his whining lowering to a deep growl that resonated in the air and turned Josiah's legs to water.

But then David quieted and fell onto his side, wheezing through his nightmare of a mouth, and closed his little boy's eyes before he slowly sat up with his limbs twitching. A few seconds later he was motionless except for the swaying of his face-tendrils.

Josiah stepped back, looked at Primrose. "Is he okay?"

"He hasn't got long left," she said.

CHAPTER TWENTY-SIX

THEY ARRIVED AT Fool's End just before dusk. It was a hamlet of no more than eight houses, a small community hall, and a church, bisected by a single main road. The streetlights were dead but still standing. Josiah took that as a good sign, for all it was worth, but the deserted street and silent houses left him unsettled. It was a familiar sight to him.

"It's just a dead place," he said as he sat on the kerb and dropped two painkillers into his mouth. He gulped from his bottle, sagging into his wet clothes. The dim houses were like mausoleums. Distant thunder echoed.

David was staring towards the community hall at the end of the street.

"He wants us to follow him," Primrose said.

"To where . . . ?"

"Something is at the community hall."

Josiah exhaled through clenched teeth and shook his head. Primrose helped him up and they followed David, glancing at the windows of the dead houses, watching for eyes watching them.

They reached the community hall minutes later. The front doors were closed, the windows dark. David skittered up the stone steps and opened the doors, disappearing inside.

"Come on," said Primrose, pulling on Josiah's arm. "We should go with him."

***

Josiah and Primrose stood in the doorway, fighting the urge to vomit at the stench of rotting meat.

Human remains covered the floor. Scattered bones and body parts. Flesh and skin torn by unknown assailants. There was barely anything recognisable amongst the viscera, which had been there over a week, judging by the decomposition.

David stood staring at the carnage, his awful hands clenching and flexing. His head swayed as he sniffed at the air, and he made a low keening sound of anticipation and hunger.

"Who were they?" asked Josiah. "Who did this?"

Primrose looked at David. She frowned. "He knows who did it, but he won't tell me. These were the survivors; they'd been hiding here, safe from the squid, but something else happened."

David crouched to touch a severed arm on the floor when pattering feet nearby startled him, and he growled as he turned to the far corner of the room, where some small form stood in the thick shadows. It had been watching them. Josiah and Primrose followed David's gaze. The thing in the corner was the size of a child, but with limbs that drooped distressingly. It bobbed its head, made a clicking sound, and loped forward to reveal itself.

Josiah and Primrose stepped back.

David whined at the creature just like him. Another transformed child of this drowned world, with tendrils that hung from its face and dripped a gelatinous fluid. Its eyes were human, unlike the rest of its horrid form, in wet clothes little more than rags.

"The cosmic spawn," said Primrose. "That's what David calls them."

"*Them?*" Josiah replied. "You mean there are more . . . ?"

Primrose looked at him. "David said we should run."

The creature released a horrid shriek and bolted forwards, its claws bared. David met it halfway and tackled it, and they flailed amongst the mutilated flesh and splintered bones, snarling and screaming as they struggled.

Primrose pulled Josiah through the doorway, into the heavy rain. They struggled down the street, aware of the movements at their flanks. Shrill calls echoed around the abandoned houses.

More of the cosmic spawn were emerging, to get a taste of the new arrivals.

CHAPTER TWENTY-SEVEN

THEY STUMBLED INTO the church and shut the main door, then crouched amidst the pews, shivering as rainwater dripped from their clothes. Lowing calls and hoots echoed beyond the church walls.

After a few minutes of waiting for the cosmic spawn to enter the church, Josiah rose and slumped upon one of the wooden benches. Moments later Primrose sat beside him, staring at the floor.

"David is with them," she said. "He's with the cosmic spawn. They're out there."

Josiah found it an effort to speak. His slurred voice sounded like someone else's. "What are they doing?"

"I don't know."

"Okay."

He lowered his head and rubbed his eyes. It hurt the muscles in his neck when he yawned. He was beyond exhaustion, his body ruined and sore, and he felt like he was crumbling into dust. This was the end of the line for him.

He looked ahead at the chancel at the top of the aisle, and the font and the pulpit. The statuette of the Virgin Mary. Saint George slaying the serpentine dragon at his feet. They gave him some comfort.

The rain was incessant upon the roof of the church. Thunder growled high above. Winds swept against the walls. Josiah and Primrose sat in silence for a while, but as time passed without incident, they fell into a stupor and Josiah waned from exhaustion and trauma.

"You believe in God, don't you?" Primrose said.

"Yeah."

"I don't know if I do. I never thought about it much."

"That's fine."

"Do you think I'll go to Heaven when I die?"

THE GREAT BEAST

Josiah considered his answer. He sighed out a rattling breath. "I think you will, Primrose. I think you'll be okay."

"It scares me a bit."

He looked at her and tried to smile. "You've got nothing to be scared of. You're a good person. Good people go to Heaven."

"Okay. Do you think you'll go to Heaven, Josiah?"

He managed a muffled laugh that descended into a coughing fit, and then passed out with his head bowed to his chest.

***

Josiah dreamed of broiling black seas covering the Earth. It was peace at the end of the world. No more pain.

***

Primrose shook him awake. He flinched, throwing up his hands before she calmed him and he heard the distant booming.

"What is that?" he asked her. But he already knew, at the back of his mind. The dread coiling in his gut told him.

"The cosmic spawn are happy, because the Great Beast is coming for them."

Josiah put his hands to his face and gritted his teeth against the palpitations in his chest. His heartbeat filled the inside of his skull.

"You have to leave, Primrose," he said, his voice low and weak.

The girl's eyes dampened with tears. Her mouth trembled. "Where would I go?"

"Anywhere but here. You have to go on and survive. You could be all that's left."

She began to cry. "What about you?"

"I can't go any further. I have to face this thing. It's all I can do."

The girl looked at him. She said nothing.

CHAPTER TWENTY-EIGHT

JOSIAH GAVE PRIMROSE the remaining supplies, and she went off into the mist and rain beyond the village, vanishing like a frail memory. He wished the girl well and said a prayer for her before stepping outside with his shivering arms across his chest. He looked around, preparing to meet the cosmic spawn, and went out to the street, but found it deserted. Then he saw them gathering at the end of the road, excited and yipping. There had to be several dozen. He noticed David amongst them, recognising the remains of the boy's clothes.

The inhuman booming grew louder.

The cosmic spawn vanished into the rain.

Josiah followed.

***

He went down to where the land met the deep floods, as the cosmic spawn dove and swam towards the horizon. The terrible sounds of booming and crashing scraped inside his head and almost deafened him.

A distant, towering figure emerged from the mist. The Great Beast. It was an immense thing, a primordial form, alien and obscene. Frothing waves rose and fell as it waded through the water. The ground shook.

Cthulhu.

As the creature neared, the cosmic spawn climbed onto it and burrowed into its rugose skin.

Fighting the fading of his mind, Josiah took off his silver cross necklace and wrapped it around one hand, collapsing to his knees in the stinking mud. He made sure the cross was facing the Great Beast.

Screams flailed inside his head. Flashbulb images of old friends, his father, the Jesus-thing from his dreams, and finally Primrose walking through the rain, all alone, into an uncertain future.

He clenched his jaw until several teeth cracked. Enamel shards stabbed his tongue. He bled from his eyes, ears, nose, and mouth, then fell onto his side, holding the cross above him in his final resistance towards an unstoppable force.

The Great Beast barely noticed Josiah, and it did not care for him. Its eyes fell upon him only once, enough to bring such exquisite agony terrible glory. He was a wretched mammal, a witless ape, unable to comprehend the end of all things made by Man.

Thunder filled the black sky. The water began to rise.

Josiah muttered the Lord's Prayer as the vast, unknowable shadow of Cthulhu consumed him, the last worshipper from a dead world of fallen gods.

ABOUT THE AUTHORS

William Holloway is a horror novelist from the great state of Texas. He is known for his dark and uncompromising interpretation of Cosmic Horror. He has three novels published with Horrific Tales, entitled *Lucky's Girl*, *The Immortal Body*, and *Song of the Death God*.

Michelle Garza and Melissa Lason have been dubbed the Sisters of Slaughter for their work in the horror and dark fantasy genres. Their work has been published by Thunderstorm Books, Sinister Grin Press, Bloodshot Books, and Death's Head Press. Their debut novel, *Mayan Blue*, was nominated for a Bram Stoker award.

Brett J. Talley is the author of several best-selling novels and anthologies, including *That Which Should Not Be*, *He Who Walks in Shadows*, and *The Fiddle is the Devil's Instrument*. He has been twice nominated for the Bram Stoker Award, the highest honor in horror fiction. He lives in Alabama with his wife, Annie, and their dog, Nyarlathotep, the barking chaos (Nyla for short).

Rich Hawkins hails from the depths of Somerset, England, where a childhood of science fiction and horror films set him on the path to writing his own stories. He credits his love of horror and all things weird to his first viewing of John Carpenter's *The Thing* back in the early Nineties. His debut novel *The Last Plague* was nominated for a British Fantasy Award for Best Horror Novel in 2015. His latest book is *The Cold* from Horrific Tales Publishing.

Printed in the USA
CPSIA information can be obtained
at www.ICGtesting.com
LVHW091325151023
761014LV00004B/51